BUCKHORN:
BLOODTHIRSTY

BUCKHORN:
BLOODTHIRSTY

WILLIAM W. JOHNSTONE

with J. A. Johnstone

PINNACLE BOOKS
Kensington Publishing Corp.
www.kensingtonbooks.com

PINNACLE BOOKS are published by

Kensington Publishing Corp.
119 West 40th Street
New York, NY 10018

PUBLISHER'S NOTE
Following the death of William W. Johnstone, the Johnstone family is
working with a carefully selected writer to organize and complete Mr.
Johnstone's outlines and many unfinished manuscripts to create additional
novels in all of his series like The Last Gunfighter, Mountain Man, and
Eagles, among others. This novel was inspired by Mr. Johnstone's superb
storytelling.

All Kensington titles, imprints, and distributed lines are available at special
quantity discounts for bulk purchases for sales promotions, premiums,
fund-raising, educational, or institutional use. Special book excerpts or
customized printings can also be created to fit specific needs. For details,
write or phone the office of the Kensington sales manager: Kensington
Publishing Corp., 119 West 40th Street, New York, NY 10018, attn: Sales
Department; phone 1-800-221-2647.

PINNACLE BOOKS, the Pinnacle logo, and the WWJ steer head logo are
Reg. U.S. Pat. & TM Off.

ISBN-13: 978-0-7860-4488-7
ISBN-10: 0-7860-4488-8

First printing: December 2016

10 9 8 7 6 5 4 3 2

Printed in the United States of America

Electronic edition available:

ISBN-13: 978-0-7860-3806-0 (e-book)
ISBN-10: 0-7860-3806-3 (e-book)

CHAPTER 1

For the most part, Joe Buckhorn was a somber man seldom given to outward displays of emotion or flights of fancy. When folks tried to kill you fairly often, it helped to be cool-nerved and levelheaded. However, when the telegram from Andrew Haydon reached him, inviting him to New Orleans for the sake of discussing a "lucrative" job proposal and including an offer to provide advance payment for traveling expenses, Buckhorn's reaction was to not only be interested but actually quite excited by the prospect.

New Orleans. The Crescent City. The Queen Port of the South.

Buckhorn had heard many tales of the place, the exotic melting pot of so many different cultures and influences. Beauty and artistry and rich heritage to be found in its finer sections, mystery and menace lying within its darker recesses.

Menace was hardly a stranger to him. He'd encountered plenty of that—and a smattering of mystery, too—in his dealings throughout the Southwest territories and along the Mexican border. Hell, it wouldn't be hard to find those who'd claim he was pretty handy at dishing out his own brand of menace. Even though he'd grown more selective in recent years, that aspect was still generally what those who sought his services were looking to pay for.

If the particulars of Haydon's job proved to be outside the boundaries of what Buckhorn was willing to hire out his gun for these days, he'd have to turn it down. Regardless, he meant to seize the opportunity to finally respond to the lure of New Orleans that had so long tugged at him yet he'd never gotten around to answering.

As he leaned on the railing of the *Hannibal Belle*'s observation deck, Buckhorn reflected on those things and more. Many would have found him quite interesting to observe. Tall, trim, broad shouldered, and clad in a matching suit jacket and vest over a boiled white shirt with bold red string tie, he could have been taken for anything from a businessman or plantation owner to a riverboat gambler.

Had anyone guessed the truth, of course—that he hailed from the Western frontier and made his way with a gun—their intrigue would have been even greater.

One thing was evident in any case. The grim lines of his face and set of his jaw, the deeply burned ruddy complexion, the dark, ever-alert eyes that seemed to penetrate whatever they locked on, and the crow's-wing-black hair spilling from under a precisely cocked bowler hat marked him as someone not to be trifled with.

For Buckhorn's part, a trip on a Mississippi River paddle wheeler was something else he'd always wanted to experience. So, while his course from northern Texas where Haydon's telegram had reached him could have angled all the way down on a more direct land route, he'd opted to make a slight out-of-the-way jog to the east and catch a New Orleans–bound steamboat in Natchez.

After all, what better way to arrive in the fabled city than by means of the equally fabled river providing so much of the commerce that supported and helped spread the word of her bountiful charms?

As Buckhorn was thinking of New Orleans' bountiful charms, coincidentally—or maybe, it remained to be seen, *not* so coincidentally—a young woman possessing features equally befitting such a description appeared suddenly at the rail beside him.

She looked to be in her early twenties, with glossy black hair piled high above an exquisitely lovely face and a fetchingly shapely form. Her skin, immodestly displayed by an off-the-shoulder gown and a long, elegant neck, was as smooth and milky white as porcelain. Her eyes, almond-shaped and nearly as dark as her hair, met his gaze with a directness that was borderline disconcerting.

When she spoke, it was with the faintest of Southern drawls. "I'm glad to find someone besides me seeking a reprieve from the cigar smoke and bluster of the lounge. When I saw you take your leave, I was hoping you weren't headed directly to your room."

"Not hardly," Buckhorn replied. "This is my first time on the river and I want to savor as much of it as I can."

"I understand that perfectly. I was practically born on the river, but I still savor every moment around it on the occasions when I return. I especially love the evening air on the water, but aboard a boat like this, I never feel completely comfortable or safe out on deck alone."

"I'd think a pretty gal like you," Buckhorn replied,

"would hardly have trouble finding somebody to keep her company wherever she went."

"Very gallantly spoken. But surely you understand there is 'company' and then there is *company*. A young woman must always be careful about attracting the wrong kind."

"Not being a pretty young gal, I guess I never looked at it that way," Buckhorn conceded.

"And why would you?" The question was clearly rhetorical and the girl quickly moved on from it. "A big, rugged-looking individual like you . . . I suspect you feel quite safe wherever you go. Any unwanted company that comes around most likely you shoo away like annoying mosquitoes."

Buckhorn grinned. "Big and rugged-looking, eh? In other words, rough around the edges and kinda on the homely side."

"Oh no!" the girl was quick to protest. "I neither said nor meant such a thing. Not at all. Anyone who knows me can tell you I am someone who speaks her mind and always says what she means."

"Those who know you," Buckhorn said. "What is it they call you?"

The girl smiled coyly. "Why, by my name, of course. Angelique."

"Angelique. Very pretty, which makes it very fitting."

"Ah, more gallantry. And your name, my fellow connoisseur of fresh evening air on the river?"

"Joe. Joe Buckhorn."

"Joe. Yes. Straightforward and basic. It suits you." Angelique gave a faint nod of approval. "If you don't mind my saying, however, the Buckhorn part is rather unusual."

"I'm mixed blood. My father was Cheyenne Indian, my mother a white woman," he explained.

"How fascinating."

His mouth twisted wryly. "Fascinating maybe. But not a particularly pleasant thing to be born to. Out West, a half-breed is never really welcomed by either side. Seems like I've been fighting against one or the other most of my life."

"I'm sorry I brought it up then. I had no idea—"

"Forget about it." Buckhorn held up a hand, stopping her. "Let's just move on to something else. Like, say, you telling me about yourself."

A soft breeze lifted up off the water, carrying the smell of the river along with shoreline aromas that were foreign and intriguing to his nostrils. More captivating than any of those, however, was the subtle, musky scent of Angelique's perfume, also freshly stirred by the breeze.

Gazing into those eyes, intoxicated by the rush of her perfume, he found it very tempting to let down his guard and simply lose himself in the illusion that he had this rare beauty all to himself. While he knew, despite his earlier self-deprecating remark, that some women were drawn to his powerful build and grim, hawklike facial features, he also remained aware he was far from classically handsome and therefore a hell of a lot more apt to cause members of the fairer sex to steer wide rather than throw themselves at him.

When one did, more or less, his habit was to automatically raise his guard and hold it fast until he had a chance to determine, one way or another, what was afoot. Especially in this instance when, only a short time ago at one of the gaming tables in the lounge—where Angelique had admittedly taken note of him—he'd walked away with considerable winnings. That made it easy to suspect her interest might be more for what was contained in the money belt around his waist than anything else about him.

Still, Buckhorn told himself, there were worse ways to kill some time than allowing a beautiful young woman to fawn over him, no matter her motives . . . as long as he kept a sharp eye peeled in case her scheme included an accomplice showing up to put a knife to his throat or bounce a club off the back of his head.

In addition to the alertness that was second nature to him, Buckhorn was hardly unarmed. In deference to the setting, he did not have his usual .45 caliber Colt Peacemaker holstered on his right hip, but he was carrying a smaller, lighter Colt Lightning tucked behind his belt at the small of his back and under the fall of his suit coat. Sheathed inside his right boot was a bowie knife with a ten-inch blade.

In response to his query, Angelique was saying, "I fear there's not very much interesting to tell about little ol' me. You *are* easy to talk to, though. I feel very comfortable around you so I'm sure we could find lots else to converse about . . . together." She wrapped her arms around her bare shoulders and gave a little shiver. "On second thought, I don't know that out here in the evening air is the best place after all. It's growing chilly and I don't even have a shawl."

Buckhorn began unbuttoning his suit jacket. "By all means, let me—"

"That's not necessary." She put a hand on his arm, stopping him. "Really. I think a far more sensible thing for us to do would be to simply retire to my cabin. It's one level down, almost directly below where we happen to be standing. We could continue our talk there and, if you need further persuasion, let me say that I have a fine vintage of wine on hand. In the lounge, I noticed that your preferred drink was wine."

The lady was very observant, Buckhorn told himself. If his suspicions weren't so fully aroused, he would find that quite flattering. He tried amending his thoughts to consider the possibility his suspicions might not be warranted after all, but fell short of successfully buying it. All of this felt too much like a setup.

In the event it wasn't, he'd just have to make sure such a discovery didn't diminish the pleasure of spending time with the lovely Angelique under more desirable circumstances.

"I have to admit, a glass of good wine always makes a tempting offer," Buckhorn said. "Not that spending time in your company really needs any added incentive. But from your standpoint, are you sure that having me in your cabin is really a good idea?"

"Whatever do you mean?"

He cleared his throat. "Well, not being sure of your station or status, ma'am, I can't help but wonder if an unescorted young woman keeping company with a fella like me might not be looked on by other folks as—"

"Oh, hang other folks and their dirty minds if it comes to that. We're two adults who have paid the asking fare for transport on this vessel and have conducted ourselves quite properly ever since coming aboard. A lot more properly than some of the lecherous old goats down in the lounge, I assure you! If we choose to spend some time together—whenever and wherever we please, I might add—then it's nobody else's damn business!"

It was quite a speech and Buckhorn couldn't find a thing about the words that he didn't agree with. Damn, he wanted to like this gal and wanted her to *not* be what he suspected her of being, but her ploy of so boldly attempting to lure him down to her cabin was yet another sign that she almost certainly was up to no good.

He could actually see the scene in his mind's eye. She would usher him into the room ahead of her, where there was sure to be no interruptions by someone unexpected happening by and where the shadows would be nice and deep. Before she got the lamps turned up, Mr. Accomplice would step out of the shadows and take care of Buckhorn before he realized he'd been suckered. As soon as he'd been relieved of his winnings and everything else of value, over the side he'd go—maybe already dead, maybe just close enough it would be easy for the river to finish the job—and then Angelique and her partner would move on to start trolling for their next victim . . .

"Well, Mr. Buckhorn," Angelique said, with a trace of tartness in her voice that hadn't been there before, "are you interested in joining me for a glass of that wine? Or are *you* perhaps the one who finds it too forward of me to be extending such an invitation?"

He smiled down at her. "Lady, if you're being too forward, that only means there are way too many other women in this ol' world who are too damn backwards."

She returned his smile, though hers was far more dazzling. Moving closer to him, she said, "I was hoping that's how you'd feel."

CHAPTER 2

Buckhorn was so convinced the actual physical attack on him wouldn't come until after they'd reached Angelique's room, he damn near missed the attempt to brain him right where he stood.

The split-second warning came from a flickering reflection on the glass housing around a lantern fastened to a deck post rising just above Angelique's pile of hair. It revealed a burly gent looming directly behind him with one arm raised and a bulging sap gripped in his fist.

It was all that saved him from getting his skull busted open like a peanut shell.

He reacted by thrusting Angelique away and letting his knees buckle in unison so he dropped suddenly, squatting down as low as he could. The sap slashed through the air above him at the exact level his head had been only a moment earlier.

The empty swing made a great *whoosh* and the man behind it grunted with the vicious effort he put into it. Swinging so fiercely and not connecting with anything pulled the would-be head crusher off balance and caused him to stagger as he attempted to regain it.

Buckhorn was determined to have a say about that. Staying in his squat long enough to twist around toward the man, he straightened his legs with a hard thrust, exploding upward faster than he'd dropped down.

As he shot to his full height, Buckhorn slammed the top of his head up and under the sapper's chin. The man's teeth clacked together loudly and he emitted a desperate gagging sound as his head snapped back. Adding to that, Buckhorn drilled an in-close right hook hard to the sapper's unprotected ribs. The victim howled in added pain. Buckhorn liked the sound and feel of what he'd done so much that he immediately repeated it.

The man lurched away, trying to separate himself from Buckhorn. He staggered sideways, blood streaming from his smashed mouth as he hunched over to protect his battered ribs. Taking advantage of the opening, Buckhorn threw a high left cross to the side of the sapper's throat. The punch knocked the man back, slamming him hard against the deck railing. His knees sagged.

Buckhorn overestimated the damage he'd done. He stayed close, cocking his right fist, meaning to bring it up from knee level and deliver another smashing uppercut, but when his fist started to rise, the man on the rail pushed forward to meet him. At the same time, he chopped down savagely with the sap. The weapon scored only a glancing blow on Buckhorn's forearm. It didn't break bone, yet landed solidly enough to stop the momentum of the intended punch and sent streaks of fiery hot numbness all the way up to Buckhorn's shoulder.

Buckhorn backpedaled, grabbing the injured arm with his left hand. He clamped it tight, rubbing frantically, trying to get some feeling to return as his opponent took a moment to recover.

"You've got him now, Henri," Angelique shouted, encouraging the sapper. "Hurry up and finish him. But be careful. He's quick and dangerous!"

"Not to mention a great conversationalist," Buckhorn muttered through clenched teeth. "Did you forget that part, darling?"

The gleaming blade of a short but wickedly pointed punch dagger appeared in Angelique's delicate hand. Her luscious lips peeled back in an ugly way. "Come near enough for the embrace you were so hungry for, you pathetic fool, and the bite of my fang will sever your vocal cords so no one has to be subjected to your dull babbling ever again!"

"Tempting as the offer is," Buckhorn replied, "your pet ape Henri got in the request for this dance first. Be plumb rude of me to all of a sudden give him the cold shoulder in favor of you."

"The thing that will very soon be cold," growled Henri in a faint French accent coming through puffs of labored breathing, "will be your dead flesh once I have broken you in two."

"That's gonna be mighty hard to do after I split you from Adam's apple to belly button and your hands are busy trying to keep your guts from boiling out all over the deck." As he said this, Buckhorn crouched ever so slightly, just long enough for his hand to streak down and pull the bowie knife from its boot sheath under the cuff of his trousers. He could have gone for the gun under his coat but, since no other guns were in play, the bowie seemed adequate and more appropriate.

He held the weapon out in front of him in a practiced knife fighter's pose, gripping it in his still-tingling right hand. His eyes gleamed almost as bright as the reflections playing up and down the ten-inch blade and the harder he squeezed the handle, the more the tingling abated, as if his hand and arm were drawing recuperative strength from the bowie.

Henri's eyes grew wide with alarm as he watched the knife.

"Do not hesitate. We can still take him, Henri!" Angelique urged her man. "Engage him but for a second and I will strike from my side, opening his carotid artery with a lightning thrust of my own blade."

"She talks a good story, big boy," Buckhorn said, taunting. "You willing to bet your life on her doing what she says she can do? Because I guarantee you, *I* can do what I say."

Buckhorn's taunting and the urging of the girl propelled Henri into reckless action. He lunged forward, wielding the sap skillfully, slashing down at Buckhorn's knife hand, aiming to break his wrist and disarm him.

The attack came so fast Buckhorn scarcely had time to jerk his hand out of the way.

Instead of letting the empty swing unbalance him, Henri was prepared and held his momentum in check. Not only that, he instantly course corrected and brought the sap upward in a follow-up sweep, a wide-reaching backhand aimed at Buckhorn's head.

Buckhorn pulled his head and shoulders away, again at the last second, in order to avoid getting his skull caved in. Though Henri had once again maintained his balance, the extended swing of his arm had—just for an instant—left the whole front of him totally exposed.

An instant was all Buckhorn needed. He snapped forward and hurled himself straight into Henri's bulky body. As their chests thudded momentarily together and then bounced apart, Buckhorn sank his bowie deep into Henri's gut, just above his belt buckle, and began ripping the razor-edged blade upward.

Buckhorn silenced Henri's scream with another head butt. Continuing to drive forward, he rammed Henri once more to the rail. Pulling his knife free at the last moment and giving a final shove with his free hand, he sent the carved-open sapper up and over! And down into the black nighttime water of the Mississippi.

But that wasn't the end of it.

True to her word, Angelique proved willing to play a more direct part in the attack. With a screech of "You murderous bastard!" she launched herself at Buckhorn like a she-devil. Leaping full onto his back, she wrapped her shapely legs about his middle and hooked one surprisingly strong arm under his chin. With the hand clutching the punch dagger, she began fiercely slashing and stabbing.

Caught off guard though he was, Buckhorn managed to thrash and jerk his upper body from side to side even as he staggered somewhat under her slight weight. Once, twice the dagger sank into flesh, but his frantic gyrations were enough to throw off her aim, causing the glittering blade to bite into his shoulder rather than the side of his throat.

Finally, with a desperate shrug, he dislodged the wildcat from his back and sent her sprawling onto the deck. She sprang instantly back to her feet. With her once beautiful face distorted with rage, she rushed him again with undiminished fury.

Buckhorn blocked her dagger thrust, his forearm slamming upward and outward against hers, knocking it wide. Then he swung his arm in a left-to-right backhand that crashed the side of the fist holding the bowie against her jaw.

The powerful blow spun her around and pitched her facedown to the deck. An odd bleating sound came from her. Buckhorn took a step toward her but stopped short as she pushed herself to her feet and turned toward him.

The dagger she had been holding was buried in her throat.

Her eyes bugged wide with disbelief and pain. In the space of a single blink, the luster was suddenly gone from her eyes, replaced by a flat dullness. She was dead even as her body started to crumple.

Buckhorn grabbed her before she could collapse all the way. He held her upright for a long moment but was unable to meet her dull, unseeing gaze. She had brought her death on herself, but it still bothered him.

For most of his life, such a turn of events wouldn't have caused him to blink. He would have figured she had it coming for trying to rob and murder him.

In recent months he had changed, trying to live more like a normal human being instead of a cold-blooded hired gun. That meant having some sympathy for other folks, even when they were to blame for their own problems.

On the other hand, since he'd killed Henri in self-defense and Angelique's death had been an accident . . . and since he had a potentially lucrative job offer waiting for him and didn't want to get tied up with the law . . . he lifted her higher, whirled her in a half turn, and flung her corpse out beyond the railing and listened to it splash into a watery grave.

No point in going overboard—so to speak—with the business of being a decent human being.

* * *

In his cabin, Buckhorn stripped off his blood-spattered clothes, scrubbed his hands like he was trying to rub the skin off, then refilled the washbasin with cold, fresh water and scooped repeated handfuls to his face.

He dried off, donned some clean pants, and sat on the edge of the bed to tend to the dagger punctures to his shoulder. Inasmuch as it was the shoulder to his gun arm, he had more than a little concern for the degree of injury done.

Far more important than the minimal bleeding was whether serious damage had been done. He quickly cleaned off the blood, bandaged the shoulder, and donned a clean shirt. As far as he could tell there was no serious muscle or joint damage. He'd no doubt have some stiffness of movement for a while, but as long as it didn't last more than a few days he should be all right.

The whole incident troubled him some, yet given the same set of circumstances all over again, he couldn't see himself doing any different. A hardness, a savageness, had been deeply ingrained in him a long time ago. When somebody harmed or threatened him, he retaliated with a fierce finality that put the matter forever to rest. It was a way of survival and it meant not having to look over his shoulder for ghosts of unresolved conflicts seeking retribution.

Angelique and Henri had meant to kill him so he'd needed to stop them. It was really as simple as that. The fact that Angelique was a lovely female was unfortunate, but that was all.

His decision to quickly distance himself from the

bloodied scene when he heard fast-approaching footsteps and rumbling voices of those who'd been drawn by the sounds of the fatal scuffle and its accompanying curses, howls, and shrieks hadn't been a hard one to make. Luck had been with him. By ducking and dodging any encounters with other passengers or crew members who surely would have balked at his gore-streaked attire, he'd made it safely back to his cabin.

A contingent of men led by the *Hannibal Belle*'s first mate came knocking on his door a while later, inquiring, as they were of all passengers, if he'd heard or seen anything that might be related to signs of violence found up on the observation deck. He put on a shocked and apologetic act of having nothing to offer.

After they were gone, Buckhorn's thoughts returned to the woman's death. In his early years as a hired gun, he'd taken on jobs strictly for money. The often harsh duties he was required to perform were of little consequence to him. Growing up a half-breed, the abuse he'd endured from both sides of his bloodline had made him bitter and dispassionate, devoid of feelings for the misfortune of anyone placed in his path.

But then he experienced a failed, tragic love affair and a brush with his own mortality. He'd emerged from those with a new perspective on things, most especially on the kind of man he was. He didn't like what he saw. While he figured it was probably too late for redemption, he made up his mind to nevertheless try. Since gun work was the only trade he knew, he continued to pursue it but with a vow that he would not kill indiscriminately and would only hire out his gun to those who were on the right side of a situation.

That brought him back to his conviction that Angelique and Henri had certainly been on the wrong side of the situation. He had no compunction at all about

killing Henri. And while his head told him there was
no difference between the sap artist and the beautiful
young woman and her dagger, a knot somewhere deep
in his gut wasn't quite ready to unclench over that part.

As he wrestled with those feelings, he worked his
arm from side to side, now and then rolling the shoulder, testing the tightness already starting to form
there. It wasn't a big worry, not yet. It was to be expected. He made up his mind that the shoulder would
loosen back up just fine . . .

And so would the knot in his gut.

CHAPTER 3

When the *Hannibal Belle* docked in New Orleans, Buckhorn was ready to have his riverboat experience over with. For starters, it felt mighty good to leave the cramped confines of the craft and set his feet on solid, dry land again. Secondly, he welcomed leaving behind the tension and lingering sense of suspicion that seemed to hover after the signs of violence were found on the observation deck and two passengers were discovered to have disappeared. And last but not least, it was just plain fine to at last be in New Orleans, the place he'd had a hankering to visit for such a very long time.

Except for the smell of the river, the crowded, noisy activity around the dock wasn't that much different from the trading hubs of other large cities where he'd been. Some of the goods being handled—huge bundles of cotton, tobacco, and the like—weren't common to the frontier he hailed from. They held his interest for a time, but not all that long. Mostly, he wanted to get to the historic and colorful heart of the city.

"Mr. Buckhorn? Joseph Buckhorn?" a voice at his elbow said.

When Buckhorn looked around, he at first didn't see anybody. When he dropped his line of sight, he found a short, scrawny Negro youth of about fourteen standing beside him. The lad was dressed in a faded blue work shirt, tan pants with yellow suspenders, and lace-up work shoes that, if they fit properly, meant the rest of him had quite a ways to go before he grew into his feet. The hair on his head was cropped to mere bristles and perched atop the resulting dome was a somewhat battered bowler hat similar in style to Buckhorn's own.

Buckhorn nodded. "That's right. I'm Joe Buckhorn."

The boy held out a thin white envelope sealed with a dab of melted wax.

"My name's Lucien. Mr. Haydon sent me. He said for me to give you that envelope and then to take you and your things to the Hotel Laffite. He said the message inside would explain the rest." Lucien pointed. "My carriage is right over there."

His eyes following the line of the pointing finger, Buckhorn saw a nicely dressed-out carriage hitched to a sleek black horse. The latter was tied to a post with an iron ring in it. He cut his gaze back to Lucien. "You handle that rig through these busy streets all by yourself, do you?"

"Sure enough. Have been for quite a spell now."

"That's mighty impressive," Buckhorn complimented him.

The corners of Lucien's mouth lifted in a brief smile, demonstrating that he liked the praise but didn't want to show it too much. "You got luggage and such? I can get it loaded up for you."

Buckhorn tipped his head to indicate the single suitcase and worn old war bag he was carrying in his left hand, leaving his right free to access the Colt .45 riding openly on his hip. "Got everything right here."

"You travel mighty light," Lucien remarked.

"Well, these grips aren't exactly light. But they're all I got, nevertheless."

"Let me take 'em for you," Lucien said, holding out his hands.

"You sure? I wasn't kidding when I said they're kinda heavy."

"I can handle 'em. It's what Mr. Haydon sent me for."

"Very well. If you insist." Buckhorn set the two grips down and stood back so the boy had room to grab hold.

He got them up, tottering a bit, then turned and marched smartly to the carriage. Buckhorn followed along, grinning faintly at Lucien's determination.

The war bag went up into the carriage's storage bed without too much trouble. The suitcase was a bit more of a struggle and required the added lift of one knee before it got shoved in next to the war bag. Buckhorn held in check his urge to lend a hand because he understood Lucien wanted to prove he was up to the task.

When the grips were loaded, Lucien turned, puffing a little. "You sure that's everything?"

Jerking a thumb over his shoulder, Buckhorn said, "I got a horse and his gear, too, as soon as they start bringing the animals out of the cargo hold." He paused and then grinned. "But I don't reckon you'll have to lift him."

Lucien matched his grin. "That's good."

They didn't have to wait long before the livestock was

being offloaded and herded out. Sarge, Buckhorn's tall dappled gray stallion, was among the earlier animals to show. All saddled and bridled, he was led by a lanky fellow with straw-colored hair and a slight limp.

Buckhorn raised an arm and called out, "Scotty! Over here!"

Scotty didn't have any trouble spotting the source of the shout and veered in their direction, guiding the stallion gently through the throng of people scurrying impatiently in all different directions. Buckhorn and Lucien went to meet them halfway.

"What a great-looking horse," Lucien said as he reached up to rub Sarge's velvety snout.

"He's got the looks and everything else going for him," Scotty said. "He's one of the best animals I ever looked after. It was a pure pleasure to have him on our boat and for you to put him under my charge, Mr. Buckhorn."

"You looked after him real good, Scotty. I appreciate that. I see you got him all saddled for me and everything."

"I figured I'd save you the trouble."

"That was mighty thoughtful. Turns out I've got other transportation waiting for me"—Buckhorn jabbed a thumb at Lucien—"so I won't be making use of that saddle right away . . . but it was still thoughtful of you."

Scotty made a dismissive gesture. "Aw, think nothing of it. It gave me the chance to spend some extra time with Sarge. That was worth it all on its own."

Above the din of the various activity spread across the dock, a harsh voice suddenly shouted at the three admirers gathered around Sarge. "Hey, you lollygaggers!

Get the hell out of the way. That's nothing but a damn horse. Ain't you never seen one before?"

Buckhorn turned his head and looked at the individual doing the hollering, a sizable specimen, heavy-gutted and powerful looking with massive shoulders and thick arms. He was clad in a dirty homespun shirt and bib overalls. A slouch hat sat on a pumpkin-sized head complete with mean, piggy eyes and scruffy whiskers. He was leading a handsome team of sleek, reddish mules. On the opposite side of the team was a second man cut from almost identical cloth, except at about three-quarter scale to the one doing the bellowing.

Buckhorn squinted at the loud man. "You talking to me?"

"You're the jackass standing there smack in my path, ain't you? You and the cripple and the colored, taking up dock space better suited to just about anybody or anything else. Now move it. Make way for your betters—meaning me *and* my mules!"

"You're just gonna have to wait, mister," Buckhorn said through clenched teeth. "You can stand there until me and my friends have finished our talk. Or you can find room to go around."

The man's pallor, such as could be discerned through the dirt and whiskers that smudged his face, was the sickly pale color of sour milk. Suddenly it flushed flaming red with anger. "Like hell I will! The sun'll never rise on the day Oscar Turlick goes even one inch out of his way for the likes of you three and that vermin-ridden horse. Now you clear to one side—and be quick about it—or I'll do the clearing of you pieces of dock garbage!"

So saying, Turlick raised high one meaty arm and

took a step forward. Clutched in his fist, with a loop curling back around the wrist, was a braided leather quirt about two feet in length. "I'll start with that sorry piece of horseflesh that looks like he's been sadly lackin' the taste of leather up to this point, anyway!"

Turlick's forward motion stopped abruptly when, quicker than the blink of an eye, the Colt from the holster on Buckhorn's hip flashed into his hand and was extended at arm's length, muzzle centered on the point above the bridge of the beefy man's nose where his shaggy eyebrows came together.

"You lower that quirt one inch closer to my horse," Buckhorn said, his voice like two stones rubbing together, "I'll be looking at daylight through the holes I ventilate your head with."

Air whistled out of Turlick's flared nostrils as his piggy eyes glared directly into the Colt's muzzle. "You didn't have that gun, you wouldn't be so brave, would you, you dog-eatin' heathen redskin?"

"The point is, I *do* have the gun," Buckhorn told him. "And, even though I've only been in this neck of the woods for a short time, I'm already out of patience when it comes to dealing with wharf rats and bayou scum like you. Now, are you gonna try your luck with that quirt against my Colt? Or are you gonna find a path to slink around me and my friends and get the hell out of my sight?"

"Come on, Oscar," the smaller mule herder urged. "There's plenty of room to get around. Let's just go. Can't we? Please?"

Grudgingly, Turlick lowered his arm and began tugging his team wide around those he'd claimed to be in his way, but his glare stayed fixed on Buckhorn every step of the way. "Another day, dog-eater. We ever meet again, I'll be ready for you. I'll pluck out a section of your gut, just a short little string at first, and use it like a lead rope to take you back into the swamps." He gave Buckhorn a gap-toothed grin. "We'll have us a time."

CHAPTER 4

As it turned out, the message in the envelope Lucien had given him served to facilitate Buckhorn's intentions well. Inside the envelope was a handwritten note from Andrew Haydon.

Dear Mr. Buckhorn—,

As a first-time visitor to our heralded city, I can only imagine you must be anxious to experience some of what it has to offer before getting down to business. Toward that end, I have taken the liberty of booking you into one of the French Quarter's finest hotels, just off Jackson Park. You will find yourself in the center of much of the city's most colorful and charming diversions. Whatever you desire, use my name with any of the Laffite's front desk attendants and they will guide you. Enjoy. Tomorrow evening, I will send Lucien to pick you up. I request that you join me for dinner and a detailed discussion of the matter for which I seek to hire your services.

Sincerely,
Andrew Haydon

Buckhorn couldn't help thinking that Haydon was shaping up to be one of the most accommodating employers he'd ever worked for. *If* he ended up working for him, that was. But all signs seemed to be pointing toward that likelihood.

For the balance of that day and night and throughout most of the following day, Buckhorn did indeed have himself a time. It was something he'd been planning, of course, ever since agreeing to come to New Orleans for the meeting with his prospective employer.

Buckhorn used the time allotted him to full advantage. He cut a wide, busy swath through the French Quarter. He feasted on spicy Cajun food, drank a variety of excellent wines, listened to a fascinating blend of music, absorbed much in the way of local color and even some art, and inevitably dallied for a very memorable few hours with a breathtakingly lovely (and talented, in the way of such things) Creole belle named Lucretia.

When Lucien came tapping on the door to his hotel room late in the afternoon of the second day, Buckhorn welcomed him with what was closely akin to a sigh of weary relief. On the ride to Haydon's residence, the exhausted visitor leaned back in the well-cushioned seat of the carriage and actually dozed for a bit.

"We're here, Mr. Buckhorn."

He opened his eyes to find they'd arrived at a secluded home on the outskirts of the city. The house was at the end of a narrow, tree-lined lane with a circular turnaround area in front. In the middle of the circle, on a patch of neatly trimmed grass, was a somewhat weather-pitted statue of a stag.

The house was fashioned after a plantation-style

mansion, though scaled down in size. Still, it had tall pillars and a set of broad steps leading up to a rather ornate front door. In the rapidly dimming light of evening, brightly burning lanterns bracketing the door provided a wash of more than adequate illumination.

"Just go knock on the door, sir," Lucien said after bringing the rig to a halt. "Mr. Haydon is expectin' you and Sterbenz, his butler, will show you on in. I've got to tend the horse and carriage. Sterbenz will let me know when you're fixin' to head back. I'll be around front here when you're ready."

Buckhorn climbed down from the carriage. "Where do you take dinner?"

"I eat back in the kitchen with Sterbenz and my mama. She's the cook." Lucien grinned. "I don't know what she's makin' tonight, but whatever it is, I guarantee you're in for some good eats."

"You got me looking forward to it."

Buckhorn's use of the heavy brass knocker on the front door was promptly answered by a tall, painfully thin elderly man with wavy silver hair combed straight back and a blank expression that looked permanently stamped on his narrow face.

After he'd taken Buckhorn's coat and hat, the sight of the Colt riding prominently on the gunman's hip *almost* stirred a reaction on that stony countenance, but he held it in check and merely said, "Please come this way, sir."

The long dining room table where Buckhorn's host and potential employer sat waiting could have seated two dozen. From the silent, empty feeling of the big house, Buckhorn got the sense it seldom, if ever, saw anything near that many guests. In fact, his presence might be considered something of a crowd.

The man who'd been seated at the far end of the table rose up with some awkwardness and promptly tucked a dark, highly polished crutch under his right arm. As he came around the corner of the table, Buckhorn saw that he was missing his right leg below the knee, the empty bottom half of his trouser sleeve neatly folded up and pinned behind his thigh.

"Good evening, Mr. Buckhorn. I'm Andrew Haydon." He extended his right hand. "A pleasure to meet you in person at last."

Haydon's grip was firm, felt sincere. He was a couple inches above medium height, lean, and solid-looking. He appeared to be about fifty, the lines around his eyes suggesting that some of those years had not been without a share of hardship. He would be considered moderately handsome, with streaks of gray running through his otherwise brown hair and a neatly trimmed mustache given over completely to the grayness.

After they'd shaken hands, Haydon gestured Buckhorn into the only other chair with a place setting before it.

Buckhorn started to sit but then paused. Straightening up again, he unbuckled his gunbelt and said, "I guess I wasn't thinking. If I leave this hogleg on, I might scratch up some of your fine furniture."

Sterbenz stepped forward. "I can take that for you, sir."

Haydon held up a hand. "Perhaps it would be best if you didn't, Sterbenz. I suspect Mr. Buckhorn would prefer to keep his gunbelt close at hand, even if not actually on his person."

Buckhorn grinned sheepishly. "I don't suppose

trouble is likely to come blazing through the front door, but yeah. If you don't mind, I'll just lay it here on the carpet next to me."

"That will be fine."

Sterbenz withdrew a step and said to Haydon, "Shall I start bringing in your meal then, sir, or would you perhaps enjoy a drink before you dine?"

Haydon put it to Buckhorn. "Which would you prefer?"

"Whatever's going on back in your kitchen smells mighty good. If it's all the same to you, I'd just as soon go ahead and eat."

Haydon smiled wanly. "Excellent choice. Go ahead, Sterbenz. Start serving."

Once the butler had gone from the room, Haydon said to Buckhorn, "According to a reliable and highly impressed source, I understand you had occasion to use that Colt of yours almost immediately upon arriving here."

"I guess your source was Lucien," Buckhorn said with a smile. "He's right in that I had cause to take the gun out and wave it around some on the dock the other day. Didn't actually *use* it, though."

"Sounds as if it got the job done all the same. And, like I said, your actions were most impressive to our young Lucien."

Sterbenz reappeared pushing a cart loaded with an array of food, most of it covered with silver domes.

As he began dispensing the fare, Haydon said, "I made a guess that you probably sampled the French Quarter's more exotic dishes pretty thoroughly by now so I instructed my cook—her name is Melody and she's Lucien's mother—to prepare something more traditional. It appears she chose roasted pheasant, wild rice, and sweet potatoes. I hope the selection is to your liking."

"Not much chance otherwise," Buckhorn assured him. "You're looking at a fella who spends a lot of time on the open trail getting by on jerky and beans, or a jackrabbit I'm lucky enough to bag once in a while. I don't often see a spread like this before me, and only then usually in my dreams after I crawl into my bedroll."

"I can't say that your dining limitations sound particularly appealing," Haydon said, "but I have to say that other aspects of the open trail you mention— living wild and free under the wide sky and roaming the vast untamed country—stir a longing in me. A highly romanticized one, no doubt . . . but it's there, all the same." His face sobered suddenly. "If not for this blasted missing leg, it's even possibly a lifestyle I might have pursued after the war."

"You appear to have a lot of fine things about you the way it turned out," Buckhorn countered. "Life on the open trail versus this. Can't picture too many men who'd want to make that trade."

Haydon looked for a moment like he might want to argue the point, but then he gave a little laugh. "You're probably right. Like I said, I afford myself highly romanticized notions every now and again."

"Well, one thing's for sure," Buckhorn said, stabbing his fork first through a piece of sweet potato and then a cut of pheasant before popping the pairing into his mouth. "Your notion about what the cook oughta consider for this meal was a mighty good one."

Haydon chuckled around his own mouthful of food. "I'm glad you're enjoying it."

Buckhorn felt the need to prod his host along a bit. "Far as I'm concerned, it's plenty good enough to stand a little business talk mixed in with enjoying it. If you've a mind to, that is."

"Of course," Haydon agreed, nodding. "After all, that's the main point of the evening, isn't it?"

Before they could proceed, however, Sterbenz reappeared from the kitchen, followed by an elderly woman in an apron and head scarf. For once, his carefully neutral expression had a crack in it. He looked decidedly puzzled, maybe even a bit troubled as he said, "Begging your pardon, sir."

"Yes? What is it?" Haydon asked.

"We just had a caller at the back door, sir. He handed me this"—he held out an object he had been worrying in his hands—"and instructed me to show it to Mr. Buckhorn and also give him a message."

Buckhorn's eyes locked on the object Sterbenz was holding. It was little Lucien's bowler hat. "What message? What did he say to you?"

Sterbenz's voice was steady, but his expression was growing more anxious. "He said you should come out to the stable right away, unarmed. He said it was time to attend the party his friend Oscar had invited you to out in the swamp. He said if you didn't hurry, they would take the boy to the party in your place."

The woman moved up behind Sterbenz. She was quite thin and the deeply distraught expression pinched her blade of a face even tighter. "It's Lucien he's talkin' 'bout, ain't it?" she said in a trembling voice. "He's not come in yet from puttin' away the horse and carriage."

"What's going on! What is this all about?" Haydon wanted to know.

Buckhorn was already on his feet, buckling his gunbelt around his middle. "It sounds like that piece of bayou trash I tangled with on the dock the other day.

He said he'd be on the lookout for me, wanting to get even for backing him down the way I did. He must have spotted me and Lucien in the carriage on the way out here and followed us. The only thing to do is give him what he's asking for."

"But he said to come unarmed," Lucien's mother wailed.

"What he said, what he deserves, and what he's gonna get are all different things, ma'am," Buckhorn told her as he double-checked the loads in his Colt. "You'll have to trust me. I won't let anything happen to your boy."

"What do you want us to do?" Haydon said.

"Somebody go holler out the back door and tell 'em I'm coming, then the three of you stay away from any lighted windows. Better yet, come to an inside room like this one, turn the lights down, and just stay put. You'll likely hear some shooting. After you do, don't let anybody back in but me or Lucien."

CHAPTER 5

As he left the house and rounded its far end, heading toward the stable and other outbuildings he'd seen as he and Lucien had rolled into the turn-around circle out front, Buckhorn felt certain of one thing. Too much hesitation, any attempt at trying to reason or negotiate with Oscar and whoever he had with him, anything that might smack to them of scheming or trickery, would only heighten the risk to Lucien.

And Buckhorn handing himself over unarmed, meeting their demand, would basically amount to suicide and probably do nothing to save the boy, either.

The response that held the most hope, risky though it might seem to others, was to retaliate swiftly and unexpectedly. Do the last thing Oscar and his bunch would count on.

The descent of late evening darkness and the deep shadows thrown by the canopy of leaves high in the numerous trees surrounding the Haydon residence gave Buckhorn good cover. The only problem was the brightness of the boiled white shirt and colorful tie he was wearing. Crouching momentarily in some bushes, he quickly unbuttoned his vest and shirt and discarded them along with the tie. The smoothly muscled, dark copper skin of his torso blended almost invisibly with the other shadows.

As he edged along the back side of the house, he could hear voices not too far ahead.

"Tell that damn breed he better be quick about showing hisself or this little darky errand boy is gonna be the one to pay for it," the all-too-familiar voice of Oscar Turlick bellowed. "I want to see him with his hands held up empty and high and he'd better make it real sudden."

"He's comin', I tell you," Melody called from the back door to the kitchen. "Please, please don't do nuthin' to my little boy. He's all I got."

"That's up to the stinkin' breed you're hidin' in there! I'll give him to the count of five to show hisself before we start making this baby boy of yours do some squealin'!"

"No! Please!"

"One . . ."

Buckhorn had moved up to where he could see into the stable. One of its double doors was propped open. In a cone of weak light poured down by a lantern hanging from a nail on a post, Lucien was on his knees in front of the post.

A tall man stood directly behind him, one hand wrapped around both of the boy's suspender straps, holding them jerked tight between his bony shoulder blades. The man's other hand held the blade of a clasp knife to the side of Lucien's throat. The lantern's illumination angled across the tall man's chest, leaving his shoulders and face lost in shadows.

"Two . . ."

The man with the knife wasn't the one doing the talking. It was Oscar's voice, like Buckhorn had judged from the beginning, but it was coming from somewhere outside the lantern light. Buckhorn peered intently, trying to penetrate the deeper shadows. He thought he saw a murky trace of movement about four feet beyond where Lucien knelt.

That could be where Oscar was—*if* there were only two men involved. The elongated skunk by the post certainly wasn't the second, much shorter mule herder who'd been with Oscar the other day. Was he lurking somewhere in the stable, too, making it three men? Or was Oscar simply operating with another partner?

"Three . . ."

Buckhorn felt his vocal cords vibrate with a silent snarl deep in his throat. It was time to make his big gamble and play the surprise card he hoped would be an ace.

He drew his Colt, took careful aim just above the downward sloping edge of the cone of light where he calculated the center of the tall man's chest to be, and pulled the trigger. The Colt bucked in his fist and he heard a satisfying grunt as what he could see of the tall man's body jerked and fell back into the shadows, releasing his grip on the boy's suspenders. The knife in his other hand dropped from lifeless fingers.

A fraction of a second later, Buckhorn's next bullet screamed out and shattered the lantern, plunging everything into sudden blackness.

"Duck, Lucien! Run for cover!" he shouted. With no light to judge by, he could only hope the boy obeyed.

Buckhorn suddenly found himself occupied by return gunfire sizzling in his direction.

The muzzle flashes of whoever was shooting gave momentary bursts of illumination, but not exactly the welcome kind. Still, they *did* offer a target to pour more lead at, even though that meant continuing to mark his own position.

"Stay low, Lucien!" he hollered amid the fierce bullet exchange.

Triggering his last round ahead of having to reload, Buckhorn heard a gurgling yelp of pain that caused him to believe he'd scored a meaningful hit. Before he got too cocky or too quick to expose himself, he punched the spent shells from the Colt's cylinder. As he thumbed in fresh loads he became aware that the lantern he'd blasted apart had sprinkled enough sparks into its own spilled fuel for the mixture to reignite. Flames quickly spread into the loose straw scattered across the stable floor, fanning wide and crawling up the post from which the lantern had originally hung.

Snapping shut the loading gate of his Colt, Buckhorn moved forward, still with caution. An unplanned fire was always cause for concern but, in this case, for a brief time it also had the benefit of reintroducing some illumination to the inside of the stable.

In the flickering glow, the sprawled shapes of the two men Buckhorn had put down became visible. Both, he was relieved to see, lay motionless. The bulky form of the second one he'd shot, the one who'd begun firing back at him, was unmistakably that of Oscar Turlick.

But what of the boy?

The pulsing light thrown by the spreading flames

reached a little wider and Buckhorn made out a third sprawled form—a very slight one with feet encased in oversized shoes!

Buckhorn threw caution to the wind and ran forward. Holstering his gun, he skidded to his knees beside the boy and scooped one arm under his shoulder, lifting his upper body gently. "Lucien? Lucien!"

The only response he got was the crackle and heat as the flames crept closer. Startlingly, he became aware of another presence. Looking up in the eerie pulse of the firelight, he saw a man looming over him with a raised pitchfork, ready to strike.

In the instant of time he had before the gleaming tines thrust down, Buckhorn recognized the man as the other mule herder from the river dock. He also recognized that even as fast on the draw as he was, he had no chance of bringing his Colt into play before he was impaled.

Suddenly, a thunderous gunshot rang out. The man with the pitchfork hurtled backwards as a gaping red hole blossomed in the center of his forehead. The pitchfork clattered harmlessly to the ground.

Twisting around, Buckhorn saw Andrew Haydon and Sterbenz standing on the edge of the shadows at the corner of the house opposite the one he had come around. Sterbenz was planted tall and rigid with a long musket held at the ready. Slightly ahead of him, Haydon leaned slightly to his right, supported by his crutch, left arm still extended forward, Colt Navy revolver gripped in his fist, a worm of smoke curling up out of its muzzle.

Before anyone could say anything, the kitchen door slapped open wide and Melody burst out. "My boy," she said in a quaking voice. "Is he . . ."

Buckhorn stood up with Lucien in his arms and moved away from the spreading fire toward the anxious mother. "He's breathing good and strong," he reported. "He got knocked out, but I think he's gonna be okay."

Closer to the house, Buckhorn lay the boy down on the soft grass where his mother could fuss over him. Straightening up, he turned to face Haydon and Sterbenz as they came walking over. "Not that I'm complaining, mind you, but none of you take orders very good about staying clear of the fray, do you?"

Haydon pinned him with a steely gaze. "I'm a former officer in the Confederate Army, sir. I don't take orders, I give them. I never hid from a skirmish in my life and wasn't about to start tonight . . . especially not in the backyard of my very own home!"

CHAPTER 6

Once the threat posed by Oscar and his cronies had been dealt with, the fire naturally demanded everybody's attention. With Haydon frantically manning the pump handle of the nearby well, Buckhorn and Sterbenz flung bucket after bucket of the water he churned out. They managed to subdue the flames before the damage to the stable was too severe.

Even though the Haydon home was fairly outlying, the smoke boiled up high enough to draw the attention of some of his closer neighbors. By the time they arrived, however, the battle was pretty much won. Still, they were useful in helping with the cleanup. At Haydon's request, one of the young men who'd shown up rode off to summon the parish constable in order to advise him of the fire and the criminal activity that led up to it.

When the constable arrived to take statements and make his report, the official version he was given was that the three ruffians had tried to force their way into the back entrance with robbery on their minds. The added presence of Buckhorn, who was introduced as a visitor from out of town who'd served in the late war under Haydon, came as a surprise to the trio, his skill with a firearm even more so.

The result was that the robbery attempt was abandoned and a brief running gun battle ensued when the three men tried to escape, ending in the stable where an errant bullet broke the lantern that started the fire.

If anybody noticed any holes in this account, Haydon's high standing in the parish and the obvious low standing of the would-be robbers made it not worth mentioning. The case was wrapped up and closed on the spot.

It was close to midnight before the bodies were removed, the last spark declared cold and dead, and the constable and neighbors were all gone. Melody and Lucien, who seemed fine except for a slight bump on his head where he'd apparently run into the man with the pitchfork when he tried to flee in the dark, had retired to their quarters. Even Sterbenz was excused for the night.

Buckhorn and Haydon sat alone in the latter's den. Buckhorn had retrieved his shirt, vest, and tie and was once again wearing them. The two men were sunk deep in overstuffed leather armchairs, each puffing on a long, aromatic cigar and each with a bulbous glass of wine close at hand.

"I think," Haydon said, exhaling a plume of smoke, "it's about time we got around to discussing the details of the matter I want to hire your services for. Wouldn't you agree?"

"By all means," Buckhorn replied. "Whatever it is, don't see how it can be much more exciting than the leadup to it has already been."

"I don't know about that," Haydon said. "Besides, any excitement you've recently encountered has been attached to *you*. It hardly qualifies as any kind of lead-up to my proposal.

Buckhorn shrugged. "Well, yeah, if you want to be technical about it, I guess."

Haydon arched a brow. "I will say that tonight's events *did* provide a good demonstration of your qualifications for handling danger and, as you say, excitement. I fully expect you'll be facing more of each if you accept my job offer."

"Let's not forget, Mr. Haydon," Buckhorn said, "that in the course of me demonstrating my 'qualifications' earlier tonight"—he made air quotes with his fingers—"you ended up saving my bacon with that final pistol shot. That makes me plenty beholden to you. Short of you asking me to work for free from here on out, you can probably figure I'm gonna take on the job you need done."

"Good. That simplifies things greatly." Haydon took a sip of his wine then lowered the glass with a wry smile. "But of course, we won't reach terms that way . . . so let me lay it out the rest of the way for you. Ultimately, what I want is for you to kill a man named Thomas Wainwright."

Buckhorn leaned forward in his chair. "Whoa. We may have hit another showstopper about as big as me working for free. I don't know what you may have heard, but I don't do assassinations. I can't claim that killing don't often come with my line of work. You saw firsthand tonight that it does, and you saw I'm not shy about it when it's necessary. But I don't gun men down in cold blood. That's where I draw the line."

"I know that. I checked you out thoroughly before contacting you," Haydon told him. "Indications are that, in the past, you may have been somewhat less discriminating."

"This isn't the past. It's the here and now."

"I realize that. I also realize my choice of words in starting to describe the job I want done was a bit too blunt." Haydon's eyes narrowed markedly as he continued. "Make no mistake. I expect—and admit to even *hoping*—that you'll have to kill Wainwright before the job is done. But you won't have to do it in cold blood. If you go up against his corrupt operation on my behalf, you'll have to kill him in order to keep him from killing you."

CHAPTER 7

Haydon continued with his story. Wainwright had been a general for the Union Army in the late war. Haydon was a colonel for the Confederacy. They had clashed during that bloody conflict, though not in battle. Their meeting had come after Haydon was captured and incarcerated in a Union prison camp in southern Illinois . . . a camp run by Wainwright.

"Seems like all you ever hear about is how bad things were in the Confederate prison camp at Andersonville," Haydon related to Buckhorn. "But I'm here to tell you, firsthand, that life in a Union camp, especially one run by the likes of Wainwright, was no picnic, either. And he didn't have the excuse of massive overcrowding and severe supply shortages like they did in Georgia. By his nature, Wainwright was—is—just plain cruel and sadistic."

Waving a hand through the empty space where the bottom half of his leg should have been, Haydon went on. "I can thank Wainwright for *this*. I arrived in his prison with a relatively minor wound suffered in the battle that resulted in my capture. They had a competent medical staff on hand but, because I immediately spoke up against the deplorable conditions I saw elsewhere in the camp, Wainwright decided to make an example of me. He ordered me placed in a hot box with only minimal water and no medical attention to the leg for forty-eight hours. By the time they dragged me out, gangrene had set in. I guess I don't have to tell you the rest.

"The only time Wainwright left me alone was during the period the stump was healing. After that, I became his favorite little toy for regular bouts of humiliation and torturous punishment. He never broke me completely, though. I fooled the son of a bitch by staying alive, unlike some of the men. Too damn many . . . When the war ended and they opened up the prison camp, I lost track of Wainwright. But not in my mind. He was always there. For all these years, I've kept hating and wanting revenge on a ghost. Finally, a couple months ago I got word of him."

Another former Confederate soldier who'd spent time in Wainwright's prison camp had showed up in New Orleans and happened to hear Haydon's name mentioned. He'd come calling on the off chance it was the same Haydon who'd been his commanding officer in the war. It was from this man Haydon had learned where Wainwright was utilizing his all-too-familiar ruthless, ironfisted tactics.

Unlike many Southerners, Haydon had gone home from the war to find out he was not left penniless, thanks to his family's holdings in a handful of businesses in and around New Orleans. Taking over the operation of those businesses, he had kept them maintaining nice profits and actually flourishing in most instances. That had left him a modestly wealthy man with the wherewithal to check out the Wainwright story more thoroughly and to eventually send for Buckhorn.

"At first," Haydon explained, "my thoughts were to go confront the evil bastard myself. Another of my overly romanticized notions, I fear. But the limitations of my missing leg and the demands of my various businesses brought me back down to earth and made me realize it would be best for me to remain here.

"Besides, I expect he'd be too quick to recognize me. A stranger, someone with your experience, will be able to work your way in closer. I not only want Wainwright crushed, I want retribution meted out for far more than just what he did to me. He ruined the lives—*ended* lives, remember—of many a good man. He deserves a severe comeuppance and it would be ideal if he knew it was all toppling down around him and that I was the cause before he dies."

"Sounds like a tall order," Buckhorn said on the verge of accepting the job. "But the way you tell it, he sure as hell does sound like an hombre who deserves a comeuppance. Reckon I'm willing to be the one to take a crack at delivering it to him."

Two days later, in the first gray light ahead of the sun breaking above the horizon, Buckhorn rode out of New Orleans.

He'd had his visit to the famous city, gotten a good taste, and enjoyed it, except for the encounters with Oscar Turlick, of course. He told himself he might return to cut another swath someday but, for now, he was satisfied. He had a job to do for Andrew Haydon and on top of that he was ready to take a break from all the congestion and noise and general hurly-burly. It felt pretty good to get out on the open trail again.

It had better. A lot of open trail lay ahead of him—about twelve hundred miles, give or take. Three weeks of steady riding. With good luck, maybe a day or two less; with bad, some amount longer.

Wagon Wheel, Arizona, was his destination. A town and a territory, under the thumb of the ruthless man whose name Haydon spoke with such bitterness. Thomas Wainwright. It was there the man was swallowing up vast sections of good ranchland and driving off those trying to make a go of it on the smaller spreads he saw as being in his way. The fellow who'd reported it to Haydon had been one of the latter.

As he rode, Buckhorn remembered one other statement Haydon had said. *"I want as much of his ranching operation as possible ruined, too. If that sounds petty and small, I can't help it."*

Making it out of Louisiana took longer than anticipated due to the preponderance of small towns, meandering roads, farm fences, creeks, and swampy areas that had to be negotiated. It was nothing like the wide open spaces farther west where Buckhorn normally plied his trade.

Especially the damn swamps. He was used to keeping an eye peeled for rattlers and scorpions and other desert and plains critters that could do a body harm. The thought of all the slimy creepy-crawlies that lurked in the ooze and under the green-water scum of a swamp made his skin crawl. Why the hell anybody would choose to live around such places was more than he could figure. When he expressed these thoughts to Sarge, the big gray chuffed and swung his head in agreement.

By the second week, Buckhorn was well into Texas. The land was opening up, he was making better time, and was generally feeling better about things all the way around. Summer was wearing down, but it was still hot as blazes and the land was baked good and dry, thirsty for the moisture that winter would bring.

And for damn sure there wasn't a scummy green swamp anywhere in sight.

CHAPTER 8

On his twentieth night out of New Orleans, Buckhorn camped on a rocky slope just under some tall, partly collapsed spires within whose bases a small, stubborn pocket of stale water could still be found. He figured on arriving in Wagon Wheel the following day.

While that would mark only the beginning of the job he had to do there, it nevertheless also marked the end of a long trip. A step in the process that he fully intended to celebrate accomplishing with a bath, a hot meal, a cold beer or three, and a deep sleep in a soft bed.

For tonight, it was bacon, biscuits, and coffee cooked over a fire made of twigs and branches he'd scavenged from a stand of scrawny trees earlier in the afternoon. Buckhorn had provisioned himself well at the start of his journey and had done some replenishing along the way, but his supplies had again grown meager. Much as he didn't mind trail life, it would be good to lay up for a spell and enjoy some creature comforts like a bed and stove-cooked meals prepared by somebody other than himself for a change.

How long he'd be able to enjoy such creature

comforts would depend on how long it took before he got sideways with Thomas Wainwright once he started poking into the how and why of things around Wagon Wheel.

Buckhorn's way wasn't to put off facing up to something that needed doing, but in this case he sensed it might not be a bad idea to take it a little slow, try to get a decent feel for the situation, before barging too recklessly ahead.

He was still chewing on a bite of thick bacon and sopping up some of the pan grease with a piece of biscuit when he became aware of the riders approaching. From where he was picketed over in a clump of long grass, Sarge snorted a warning.

"Yeah, I hear 'em," Buckhorn muttered softly. He popped the grease-soaked chunk of biscuit into his mouth, washed it and the bacon down with an unhurried gulp of coffee. Then he sand-washed his hands to make sure they were free of any grease—wouldn't do for his hands to be slippery if he had to get the gun out in a hurry—and situated himself to a slightly different sitting position so that he had better access to his Colt.

Three riders came the rest of the way at a modest gallop. They reined up at the bottom of the slope, about a dozen yards down from where Buckhorn sat beside his fire.

One of them called up, "Hello the camp."

"Right back at ya," Buckhorn responded calmly. In the murky light of late evening, he could see the men all had the look of veteran cowpunchers. Dusty clothes, wide-brimmed hats above eyes perpetually squinted from too many hours in the blazing sun, spurs and chaps and kerchiefs to pull up over their faces when the wind whipped grains of sand so hard it could shred skin.

All three men wore handguns holstered around their waists but none had the look of a tested gunny. Their pistols were likely just protection against rattlers or the four-legged kind of varmints, but Buckhorn knew you could never tell for certain. He himself was an example of someone who was as fast as or faster than most men, yet there was nothing particularly showy about his Colt or the way he wore it.

The rider who'd called out the greeting appeared to be a shade younger than the other two and had an air about him that suggested he was the top dog—at least in his own mind—of this bunch.

One of the others was a stoop-shouldered Mexican with a spill of jet hair swept across his forehead and such a wide-brimmed sombrero it could have damn near doubled for a lady's parasol.

The third man was older, leaner, quieter-looking with washed-out blue eyes that might have harbored danger at some past point in his life but nowadays looked just plain wore out.

"Looks like you're tucked into a right nice setup there," said the young rider apparently in charge of doing the talking.

Buckhorn shrugged. "It's home, for tonight, anyway. Listen, my coffeepot's about drained. But I got the makings for another if you fellas are in want of a cup."

The offer was extended only for the sake of appearing neighborly, the gesture of a man with nothing to hide. Buckhorn had a pretty good hunch it wouldn't be accepted and was relieved to find out he was right.

The talker said, "Appreciate it, but we're running a little late as it is and got to keep a move on."

"Damn shame for a body to *ever* turn down a cup of coffee," the man with the tired eyes muttered.

"You'll live, Harlan," the talker told him. "Ain't much longer before we're back to the bunkhouse and then we all know you'll crawl into your nightly bottle without a whisker's thought of no damn coffee."

The Mexican snickered loudly.

"We rode over when we saw your fire," the talker went on, cutting his eyes back to Buckhorn. "Just wondering if you knew you were on Flying W range?"

Buckhorn shook his head. "No, can't say as I did. Decent looking rangeland, though, so I'll allow as to how I'm not surprised it belongs to somebody. But to me, it's just ground I'm riding over."

"Just like you said, it's only home for tonight. So all you're doing is passing through, that it?"

"That's all."

The talker nodded. "That's fine, then. General Wainwright don't hold nothing against passers-through, but just for something to keep in mind, he plumb hates squatters."

"I'll do that. Lock it right tight in mind."

"Hey, mister," the Mexican said, gesturing. "The way you are all duded up. The tie and hat and all. You look like maybe you are a drummer of some kind. Maybe whiskey? If so, maybe you have a bottle you can sell me for my amigo Harlan . . . in order to help him overcome his great sadness at not having time to stop for a cup of coffee."

"Keep it up, Chico, you damn greaser." The threat issued by the one called Harlan was weak as the faded blueness in his tired eyes.

Chico cackled with glee.

"Knock it off, the both of you," the talker said.

"Just for the record," Buckhorn said, holding up

one hand, palm out, "I'm no drummer. I got no trade or no wares to sell. Like I said, I'm just a drifter."

"That's real good. Tomorrow morning you do just that. Drift." The talker paused, scowling thoughtfully. "Chico does raise an interesting question, though. For a common drifter, you *do* dress awful dandified. What's with that, anyway?"

"I'm afraid that what you see is the luck of the draw," Buckhorn offered by way of explanation. "Beggars can't be choosers, like the saying goes, and a poor man given hand-me-downs can't be fussy about what he ends up wearing."

"I still think he's a whiskey drummer, Vance. Probably afraid to admit it on account of he thinks we might try to steal his product," insisted Chico. "Either that or he's a preacher of some kind. Hey, let's put him to a test. We can make him recite Bible verses to see if he knows—"

"How the hell are any of us gonna know if what he's spouting is garbage or accurate?" Vance cut him off. "We ain't got time to play silly games. Just forget it."

If Vance would have followed his own advice and they'd just ridden off then and there, everything would have been fine. But he took the time to hang one more thoughtful scowl on Buckhorn and then said, "Hey, wait a minute. You ain't just a duded-up drifter. You got the look of a stinkin' Injun, or at least a half-breed. That's what you are, ain't you?"

"By God, you're right," Harlan said, finally showing something more than weary indifference. "In the twilight it was hard to tell at first. But he's a breed! Everybody knows that the only thing worse than a full-blooded redskin is a sneakin' low-down breed!"

Buckhorn felt the old familiar heat of rage climb up his neck and rush over his face. He fought hard to hold it in check. "So what does that change?" he said in a barely controlled voice. "You've got places to go and I'll be away from here by morning. No harm'll be done."

"The hell there won't!" Vance roared. "Flying W land will have been contaminated by a stinking half breed. The only thing General Wainwright hates worse than squatters is Injuns. He'd hand us our heads if he found out we ran across you and just left you alone."

"Believe me. He—and you—will be a lot sorrier if you don't."

"What the hell is that supposed to mean?" Vance asked with a sneer.

Buckhorn stood up. "It means I lied before when I said I had no wares to sell, no trade. You see, the trade I practice, the product I have for sale, is this gun on my hip."

"That's ridiculous," Harlan said. "Who ever heard of a half-breed gunslinger?"

"Several did," Buckhorn told him. "Unfortunately for most of them, it was the last lesson they learned in their lives."

"What a crock!"

"I don't know, amigos," Chico said nervously. "I am looking at this hombre's eyes. They are black and soulless."

"Of course they're soulless," Harlan said. "He's a heathen Injun! They have no souls."

"All the same. I think he is not bluffing."

"He's got nothing else *but* a bluff, and a mighty lame one at that," Vance said. "In case nobody but me can count, it's our three guns against his one."

Buckhorn smiled icily. "Like I said before, it's the luck of the draw . . . and I'm real sorry you fellas turned up such lousy odds." He had a hunch it would be Harlan who'd go for his gun first. When he saw the spark of long-dormant danger flare again in those pale eyes, he knew he was right.

But not even the flash of that spark was quicker than Buckhorn's hand streaking for his own Colt.

CHAPTER 9

Following the shoot-out with the Flying W riders, Buckhorn struck his camp and took steps to remove himself and all traces of anything that might connect him to the three dead bodies left behind.

To confuse his back trail, he rode over the tracks the trio had left on their approach to his camp. When these eventually led him to a stretch of broken ground not friendly to taking on sign, he swerved away and reset his own course.

He swung down south for a spell and then angled north again, aiming for Wagon Wheel. His intent was to ride in from a direction quite different from that of anyone coming from the scene of the shoot-out. A couple hours before daybreak, he stopped to spread his bedroll and grab some shut-eye in a cold camp. He planned to arrive in town when it was full daylight and the direction he came from was sure to be noticed.

Tired and irritable, Buckhorn rode into Wagon Wheel midmorning. The town had the look of a typical Southwest border town. Since it was Whitestone

County, Arizona Territory, it was predominantly American in the style of its structures and the business names plastered on the buildings lining Front Street. On the south end, however, where the string of buildings extended and became a nameless, rather shabby village commonly referred to as Mexville, Spanish touches were more in evidence.

A fair amount of activity was taking place in the business district and, as he'd counted on, a number of faces turned to note his arrival.

Two businesses along the street advertising themselves to be hotels caught Buckhorn's attention. The first one he came to appeared to be simple and unpretentious, quiet-looking. TRAVELERS' REST HOTEL, its sign proclaimed. He reckoned it would do for his needs.

"I know it's a little early to be checking in," Buckhorn told the balding, bespectacled little man at the front desk, "but I've been traveling most of the night and I need a bath, a meal, and a bed to stretch out on for a good long snooze."

"The bath and the bed we sure got," the desk clerk said. "Unfortunately, we don't serve meals here except for having a pot of coffee available in the lobby most any hour. My missus puts out a tray of muffins in the morning and a tray of cookies in the evening. But that's about it. Just a couple doors up the street, there's a nice little restaurant that serves good food. The Good Eats Café, in fact, is what it's called. Nothing fancy, about like our place here, but it's good stick-to-your-ribs vittles at a fair price."

"Can't ask for more than that," Buckhorn said. "I probably oughta scrape some of this trail dust off and change duds, though, before I plop down to eat in public amongst other folks. How long before you could have a bath ready?" He watched the clerk's eyes, expecting there might be a hitch on account of him being a half-breed, but there wasn't even the slightest hesitation.

"We got a tub in the back room that the missus fills and heats up each morning," the clerk explained. "It's fresh and ready right now, not even been used yet today. If that suits you, you can hop in right away. If you're hankering for more privacy, though, and would rather bathe in your own room—"

"Hold it right there." Buckhorn held up a hand, stopping him. "The tub in the back room will suit me right down to the ground. Just tell me what I'll owe you for that and a night's stay—no, on second thought, might as well make it a couple nights. I'll need a place to stable my horse, too."

"We can take care of you all the way around, mister," the clerk assured him. "You came to the right place."

By the time Buckhorn made his way up the street to the Good Eats Café, after claiming his room at the hotel and then soaking, scrubbing, and donning fresh clothes, the noon hour was in full swing and the eatery was packed. It obviously was a popular place.

Since he didn't care for rubbing elbows with a bunch of strangers while taking his meals, ordinarily he would have waited, finding a way to kill some time until he could return when the place was less crowded. But on this occasion he had reason to alter his normal habit.

As a leadup to eventually locking horns with Thomas Wainwright, Buckhorn had decided it would be beneficial to first spend some time getting a feel for the lay of the land, gaining some sense of the mood of the townspeople. What better way to get a start on that than to have a leisurely lunch in the midst of this throng and listen to what was going on around him?

He allowed himself to be ushered to a place at one of the tables and ordered the lunch special of ham, mashed potatoes, peas, and a tall glass of cold buttermilk. His plate came heaped high and included a slab of cornbread.

Everything was delicious. Even the buttermilk was some of the best he'd ever tasted. It was no chore at all to take his time, savoring every bite, while inconspicuously watching and listening to those on all sides.

Much of the talk he picked up on centered around the scarcity of good water for the area. Seemed like it had been an especially hot, dry summer and if the coming winter didn't provide a good measure of moisture, things were going to be mighty tough on surrounding ranchers and farmers, even the town itself.

Buckhorn listened, barely able to hold back a wry smile. That complaint was common on most days. If he ever spent time in a ranching and farming community and *didn't* hear the residents lamenting about dry conditions, he didn't know what the hell he would do.

It was only when he heard somebody bitterly mutter something about "that damn Wainwright makes sure he's got plenty for himself, though, don't he?" that Buckhorn's ears perked up.

He identified the speaker as a beefy, jug-eared hombre in a sweat-stained blue work shirt sitting a couple tables over with a group of other men who all looked to be laborer types, though not of the cowpuncher mold. As soon as the fellow had uttered those words, he and a couple of the others looked around somewhat uneasily, as if concerned about who might have overheard the comment.

According to Haydon, in addition to sheer intimidation, Wainwright was taking over much of the land to acquire control of key water rights. Haydon had been a little slim on exact details, but he'd provided enough for Buckhorn to already have in mind that it was an aspect of the situation he needed to explore further once he'd arrived.

Catching the remark of the beefy man and then seeing the anxious way he and his friends had acted afterwards—not to mention all the other talk of the dry conditions and how much tension everybody seemed to be under as a result—only emphasized that it was something worth digging into a little deeper.

The beefy man and his friends were pushing back their chairs and shuffling toward the door just as the coffee and piece of apple pie Buckhorn had ordered for dessert arrived.

"Excuse me," he said to the stout German lady waiting on him. From what he'd gathered, she was one of two spinster sisters who owned and operated the restaurant. "That burly fellow there, the second to the last one going out the door"—he gestured—"looks mighty familiar to me, somebody I think I used to work with down in El Paso. I wasn't sure enough to go over and say anything, though. Do you happen to know if his name is Grable?"

"Oh, I am afraid it is mistaken you are, sir." The negative response came with a look of genuine regret. "That gentleman's name is Hampton."

"Whew," Buckhorn said, managing a sheepish expression. "I'm glad I didn't end up embarrassing myself then."

The pie and coffee were as good as everything that

had preceded them. Buckhorn took his time downing each, even accepting a refill on the coffee.

The lunch crowd had thinned considerably. He toyed with the notion of lingering long enough for the place to quiet down to the point where he might have a chance to strike up some small talk with one or both of its proprietors. But with just the two of them running the whole show, they stayed active, bustling about to clear and reset tables, do dishes, and start making preparations for the next round of meals.

In the end, Buckhorn decided they really weren't good prospects for what he had in mind. Number one, they were too busy; number two, neither of them seemed the overly chatty type. Toward that end, it occurred to him the talkative clerk back at his hotel had the makings of a far better candidate. Upon first encountering the bespectacled little man—Fletchler was how he'd gotten around to introducing himself—Buckhorn's priorities had been different. With that now changed, he'd have to make a point of looking up Mr. Fletchler again.

CHAPTER 10

Buckhorn stepped out on the street. The air was hotter and heavier and seemed to be carrying a tang of dust that hadn't been there before. Activity up and down the main drag appeared to have slowed somewhat, either as a result of things not yet having picked back up from the lunch break or the onset of the siesta period commonly practiced below the border.

His intent had been to return to his newly acquired hotel bed and partake of that very thing as soon as he'd bathed and had a meal. With the latter two items taken care of, however, he felt revitalized and no longer inclined toward losing time to a nap.

He could accomplish more by making the rounds of the local saloons and seeing what he could pick up in the way of small talk and gossip, but it was probably too early for that, especially during the afternoon lull. The best alternative seemed to be looking up Mr. Fletchler. Buckhorn wondered what he might learn if he could get the hotel proprietor's chin wagging loosely.

He had just started back toward the hotel when a lone wagon came rolling down the street. Nothing seemed remarkable about the wagon except perhaps the slowness with which it was moving. It was pulled by a thick-chested, big-rumped white horse and driven by an average-sized, middle-aged man with his face set in an intense expression.

The way the driver swayed and teetered in his seat made Buckhorn pause and watch as the wagon passed by. It looked like the fellow could hardly hold himself in an upright sitting position, as if he might be injured or very ill.

As Buckhorn watched, the wagon reached the first building on the corner of the next block. Its slow-plodding horse stopped directly in front of the business located there. It appeared that the animal knew its destination and had reached it.

A moment later, as if suddenly realizing where they were, the driver belatedly hauled back on the reins. He leaned into it so far as to nearly topple backwards off the seat and into the crowded wagon bed. When he straightened up and reached to set the wheel brake, he nearly toppled off that way.

It was then Buckhorn recognized the true condition of the wagon driver. The man was so drunk he could barely function.

Buckhorn's mouth twisted with disgust. He had no use for stinking drunks. His earliest memories were of one such stumbling, staggering, foul-tempered fool—his own father—and he was left with no charitable feelings toward anyone who tipped up a bottle with regularity. It sucked away all their dignity in a quest for the sorry substitution of mind-numbing inebriation.

Buckhorn once again turned toward his hotel, stopping when a woman emerged from the building in front of which the wagon and its drunken driver had halted. Even from three-quarters of a block away, it was plain to see she was one of Wagon Wheel's more fetching citizens.

Thirtyish, with a mane of thick chestnut hair and flashing eyes, she planted her fists on her hips. Her sassy mouth spewed epithets that could best any wrangler crew around as she threw a salty tirade against the drunk who'd pulled up before her establishment.

Bombarded by her words, the driver was attempting, with a good deal of fumbling awkwardness and inaccuracy, to climb down from the wagon seat. It was clear to Buckhorn that this stood little or no chance of ending well. It crossed his mind to assist in some way, but he was too far away and then suddenly it was too late.

The driver's foot thrust determinedly downward, found no purchase except for empty air, and he spilled out and down with a desperate squawk. Despite her caustic words, the woman nevertheless lunged to break the man's fall, which resulted in the two of them sprawling to the dusty boardwalk.

They were still trying to get untangled and make it back to their feet when Buckhorn reached them. Whatever injuries the woman may have suffered, it was quickly evident that the wind hadn't been knocked out of her nor was her voice box damaged.

"Stupid-assed, weak-willed damn fool. Of all the times to go on a bender . . . I should have known it was just a matter of time and when I'd count on you the most is when you'd piss away my trust and all the ground you had gained!"

"I'm sorry, Justy. You gotta believe I am sooo sorry," the drunk kept begging.

The worthless lament of every drunk in the world, Buckhorn thought as he leaned over and lifted this particular one off the chestnut-haired woman. "Take it easy, fella," he said as he stood the man more or less upright and leaned him against a post. "Just hang on tight and stay right there."

Next he reached for the woman, who had jack-knifed to a sitting position. She tipped her head back, gazing up at him for a moment before putting her hands in his and allowing him to pull her to her feet.

"You okay?" Buckhorn said. "You took quite a spill and got sorta buried there for a minute."

"I'm okay," the woman responded as she brushed dust from her arms and clothes. She was clad in baggy-legged trousers and a charcoal gray shirt tucked into a rather ornate belt. The trousers might be loose-fitting in the legs, but there was nothing baggy about the way they hugged the swell of her hips. Same for the way her shirt was strained in front by the swell of high, firm breasts. Add in a finely chiseled face and a pair of bright, intelligent blue eyes and Buckhorn certainly had no call to argue that she was *okay* and then some.

"The one you oughta be worried about," the woman went on, "is that jackass over there holding up the post. If he didn't already break something in the fall, I might just go ahead and do it for him!"

"I'll make it up to you, Justy. God, I'm sorry," the drunk moaned.

"Oh, you're sorry all right. That's for damn sure."

"Well, as long as everybody's okay . . ." Buckhorn said, edging back a step.

The girl turned to face him. She pinned him with those blue eyes, maybe the bluest he'd ever seen. "Wait a minute. I don't blame you for not wanting to stick around and get caught in the middle of this, but at least give me a chance to say thanks."

"That's not necessary. I saw the fall. Just wanted to make sure nobody got hurt, that's all."

"Well, it was decent of you. And I *am* grateful." She continued to regard him. "You're a stranger in town, aren't you?"

"Just got in this morning."

She thrust out an ink-stained hand. "I'm Justine York. I run the newspaper hereabouts. There's plenty of folks to be found who wouldn't spit on me if I was on fire because I print the truth. Not everybody is willing to face up to it."

Buckhorn took the offered hand. "My name's Joe. Joe Buckhorn." As they shook, he took a better look at the building they were standing in front of. The lettering on the glass of the big front window proclaimed THE SUN LEDGER and then in smaller print below that, THE TRUE VOICE OF SOUTHERN ARIZONA.

"For what it's worth, this jackass"—Justine jerked a thumb to indicate the drunk still hanging on the post—"is Carl Orndecker. Among other things, he works for me. If I had any brains, I'd bring that arrangement to a screeching halt right now."

"Your call to make. Keep the horse, though. He marched up and stopped right where he was supposed to."

"I'll be sure to keep that in mind." Her gaze shifted past Buckhorn and her eyes narrowed. "Oh, great. We go from horses right back to jackasses again."

Buckhorn turned to see what she was looking at. Diagonally across the street was a somewhat drab-looking saloon called the Watering Hole. Four men, lanky types, all with wide, toothy grins plastered across their whiskered mugs, had just emerged from the batwing doors and were sauntering toward where Buckhorn and the York woman stood talking.

"Well, well, well," drawled a member of the four-some who was stepping out a ways ahead of the others. "Looks like the bold, crusading newspaper gal has got herself in kind of a pickle."

Buckhorn glanced up and down the street. It was still nearly empty of other activity, but here and there a face was peeking furtively out a doorway or window.

"The only pickle you need to worry about, Conway," Justine replied, "is the kind you keep your insides fermented in. Why don't you and your three pals turn around and go on back to your elbow-bending so's none of that precious fermentation you already got stoked goes to waste. There's nothing going on here that you fellows need concern yourselves with."

"How can we be sure of that less'n we double-check to make sure there ain't some kind of trick being played? You see, we ain't the kind of hombres who just stand by and let a gal get hoo-hawed, no matter how brave and tough-talking she puts herself out to be."

"That didn't make a lick of sense. What the hell are you talking about?" Justine demanded.

"Consider it from our standpoint," Conway said, gesturing. "We look out the window of our saloon over yonder and what do we see? We see the brave employee and protector of our newspaper crusader lady pull up obviously bad hurt, hardly able to cling to his wagon seat. I mean, it's *got* to be that this poor man has been attacked and wounded in some low-down way, right? It *couldn't* be that he simply got snockered all to hell-and-gone like he has a hunnert times before, could it? 'Cause everybody knows he's swore off ever doing that kind of thing again.

"So, right when we're about to rush out and see

what we can do to help this dreadful turn of events, we see none other than the brave newspaper crusader lady hurry out her very own self to aid the wounded man. And, even though we see it right with our own eyes, we know it can't be. But yes, the wounded man did it. He fell *splat!* and landed right on the brave newspaper crusader lady. Left with no choice, we finally had to believe the horrible truth we had just witnessed—that *Carl Orndecker had fallen off the wagon yet again!*"

By the time he'd finished his elaborately taunting spiel, Conway had made his way across the street and was coming around the rear end of the wagon. His teeth were bared in a wide, lopsided sneer and the other three men walking in his wake were snickering and giggling like a pack of schoolboys at the show he was putting on.

Justine once again planted her fists on her hips and raked a fierce glare over the four idiots.

"All right. You've poked your fun. You've had your cheap laughs," she told them all. "Now get out of here and go mind your own business."

"But brave newspaper crusader lady," Conway said, "how can we abandon you to such dire circumstances? At a time when your staunch defender and protector, Orndecker, is so unfortunately incapacitated, what do we see but you being accosted by *this* heathen red devil!" With great flourish, he waved his arm in the direction of Buckhorn. "How can we *not* make such an outrageous threat our business?"

"All right. That's enough," Orndecker suddenly growled, pushing himself away from the post and turning to face Conway and the other three. He lurched unsteadily with the effort but managed to stay upright, feet planted wide, albeit teetering somewhat in his stance. "You four heard what the lady said. In case you didn't, now I'm telling you this ain't none of your concern, so beat it."

Conway laughed right in his face. "And what if we don't?" he challenged. "You gonna stagger over here and fall on all four of us?"

The men backing Conway thought this was hilarious and broke into a fresh round of howling laughter. Orndecker took another unsteady step toward them. At the same time, his right hand, curled clawlike, reached down and scraped at the side of his hip.

"Lookee there." One of Conway's buddies pointed as his shoulders shook with laughter. "The drunken ol' fool is reaching for the gun he ain't allowed to carry no more."

"It's a good thing for us they took it away from him," one of the others said, "or we'd really be in trouble."

Orndecker slowly raised his empty hand and then dropped his eyes to stare down at it, as if confused by the fact it held nothing. This fueled even more laughter.

Buckhorn squared his shoulders and turned to face the cackling hyenas, edging partly in front of Justine. "I'm having a hard time making up my mind," he said in a flat, commanding tone, "what annoys me the most about you boys. I can't decide if it's those girlielike little giggles you keep spitting out or if it's the plain fact that I have to look at so much butt ugliness crammed together right after I ate me a fine meal."

The laughter went abruptly silent and the faces of the four men gawked in stunned disbelief at what they'd just heard.

"*What* did you just say?" Conway asked in a strained voice, genuinely not believing his ears.

"Don't matter so much what I said just then. That was only to get your attention." Buckhorn's tone remained flat and calm as his eyes touched on each of the faces staring at him before returning to settle on Conway's. "What I'm about to say now is what you need to pay attention to. You've been advised twice to unstick your noses from where they don't belong and scamper on back to where you came from, without another peep. I'm not gonna advise you a third time. But if I have to, I'm damn sure ready to send you scampering."

Conway's eyes blazed. "Mister, you just—"

Before Conway could squeak out another word, Buckhorn's Colt was in his fist and extended at arm's length, the muzzle aimed unwaveringly.

"I know what I *just*," Buckhorn said through gritted teeth. "I made it plain I was sick of looking at your ugly faces and hearing what was coming out of your braying mouths. Now how damn dumb are you? Between the four of you, have you got enough brains to take a hint? To leave these people alone and get the hell out of my sight? Or do you insist on turning this into a real serious situation?"

The four men seemed to wilt as one. Shoulders sagged, eyes were averted, chins that had been shoved aggressively forward suddenly drooped.

In the tense quiet that clamped over the scene, Buckhorn became peripherally aware of a flurry of activity from farther up the street. The patter of running feet, the low, guttural bark of commands. He had a pretty good hunch what that signaled.

A second later, his hunch was confirmed by the crack of a gunshot that shattered the silence and condensed the tension all into one tight ball.

"Hold it! Everybody freeze right where you are!"

The four tormentors froze as ordered, but only

after flinching wildly at the sound of the gunshot. Buckhorn remained still, except for slowly turning his head to look in the direction of the voice shouting orders.

Three men were making their way down the street. One strode right down its center, the other two flanked him, their boots clomping on the narrow boardwalks. The man in the middle was tall, broad through the chest and gut, clad in high-top black boots, a flared-open black frock coat, brocade vest with a star pinned on it, and a flat-crowned, narrow-brimmed black Stetson. He had a square, ruddy face framed by gray-flecked muttonchop sideburns that made his head look too wide for the hat. In one gloved hand he held a long-barreled Remington revolver aimed skyward. A wisp of smoke from the warning shot curled out of the muzzle.

The two on the boardwalks were dressed similarly, except for plain black vests under their coats and cheeks shaved clean of sideburns. They were leaner and younger and each wielded a double-barreled scattergun like he knew how to use it.

The man in the street—obviously the sheriff and just as obviously the one in charge—slowed and shortened his stride but kept on coming. Barely moving his slash of a mouth, he said, "You with the hogleg. Drop it. Now."

Buckhorn held the sheriff's eyes for a moment and then, slowly, deliberately, lowered his Colt until it rested against his thigh. "I don't toss my iron to the dirt for nobody, especially when I haven't done a damn thing wrong. This'll have to do."

CHAPTER 11

"He's telling the truth, Sheriff," Justine was quick to speak up. "This man has done nothing wrong. He was only trying to help Carl and me when those obnoxious fools came over looking to make trouble."

"That's a lie!" Conway objected. "We was just poking some fun at ol' Carl on account of he fell off the wagon again. Literally, Sheriff. He *fell off his wagon!* If the drunken old bastard is gonna carry on in public that way, I say he deserves to get made fun of."

The sheriff came to a halt directly between Buckhorn and Conway. He looked from one to the other, poised with his right arm raised and bent at the elbow, still pointing the revolver skyward.

Over his shoulder, the sheriff spoke to the deputy on Buckhorn's side of the street. "Pomeroy, aim that street-sweeper of yours in the general direction of Mr. I-Don't-Toss-Down-My-Iron and, if he lifts that Colt so much as an inch, use it. Make sure Mrs. York is in the clear."

The deputy addressed as Pomeroy did as he'd been told. Buckhorn could feel the cold black eyes of the shotgun's muzzles staring hard at him.

The sheriff turned and stepped over in front of Conway, pressing his face to within inches of the loud-mouth's. He still held his Remington in that curious way, pointing skyward. "Did you just call Mrs. York a liar?" the lawman demanded.

Beads of sweat as big as cherries popped out on Conway's forehead as he stammered to find the right words. "No! W-what she said wasn't right . . . That is to say I don't agree with her . . . But I never meant to—"

The barrel of the Remington suddenly came down in a hard, slashing blow across the side of Conway's head. The stammering man was knocked sprawling, a bright red welt appearing instantly and then blood oozing from it in a matter of moments. The sheriff took another step to loom over the fallen man and Conway's pals backed away like he was a spreading fire.

The sheriff sneered down at a barely conscious Conway. "You get something straight. A single wisp of hair off Justine York's head is worth more than ten of you on the best day you ever had." The lawman lifted his eyes and raked them over the other three. "That goes for the lot of you! Because you ride for the Flying W, me and my boys might've cut you some slack a time or two when you've come to town. But that only goes in the saloons and whorehouses and even then it only goes so far. I catch any of you ever again bothering *decent* citizens of my town, I'll lock up your no-account hides and throw away the key. Understand? Now drag this piece of garbage out of the middle of the street and then the bunch of you get the hell out of my sight!"

The sheriff watched until the foursome had disappeared back through the batwing doors of the Watering Hole. Finally holstering his pistol, he then turned to face the others.

It was at that moment that Carl Orndecker, who had returned to leaning on the post in order to hold himself upright, suddenly doubled over and spewed a thick stream of vomit into the street underneath the wagon he'd driven up in.

"Oh, Carl!" Justine exclaimed, half in disgust and half in what sounded like pity.

The deputy who'd been holding his shotgun on Buckhorn looked ready to be sick himself at the sight. He had to turn away, in the process abandoning his duty when it came to keeping Buckhorn covered.

Out in the street, the sheriff, who'd begun walking over, stopped short and adopted his own expression of disgust. "For the love of Christ," he muttered.

"He can't help it," Justine said defensively. "When a body's sick, it's sick! No matter what anybody thinks, he doesn't like this any better than the rest of us."

"Well, can you at least get him out of sight or something?" urged the sheriff. "Don't he have a room in back of your shop?"

Orndecker appeared to be done throwing up. He remained doubled over, though, groaning weakly, using the back of his hand to wipe at his mouth and the strings of snot hanging from his nose. Justine pulled a handkerchief from her trouser pocket and went to him.

Something came over Buckhorn. Much as he loathed slobbering drunks, watching the caring woman go to the aid of the man who was making a fool of himself—and her, too, in a roundabout way—conjured images of himself as a young boy. All the times he'd helped his drunken father, hating it, hating him, yet feeling obligated because no one else would.

"Let me give you a hand," he said to Justine. Then

he paused, cutting a glance over to the sheriff. "If I'm allowed to move, that is, without getting shotgunned."

The sheriff tipped his head in a single faint nod. "Go ahead. Anything to get that disgrace off the street. But hear this. You come around to see me before the afternoon is out, so's we can have us a real thorough talk about obeying the law and obeying *me* while you're in these parts. Don't make me come looking for you."

As the sheriff had indicated, there was a small room in the back of the newspaper office. A cot, a chair and writing desk, and dresser with a mirror and washbasin on top identified it as somebody's living quarters, the somebody being Carl Orndecker. With Justine leading the way and one of Orndecker's arms slung over his shoulder, Buckhorn half-dragged, half-carried the man back.

"Let me put a towel down, in case he throws up some more, before you put him on the cot," Justine said.

Once she'd taken care of that, Buckhorn lowered Orndecker down. He stepped back as Justine fussed over their patient a minute more, getting him rolled onto his side so he wouldn't choke to death on his own vomit, taking the washbasin and placing it on the floor beside him in hopes he'd try to hit it if more came up. Each measure was one that Buckhorn recognized and remembered all too well from his childhood days.

When she'd finished, Justine straightened up and turned to Buckhorn, saying somewhat breathlessly, "The part I didn't mention outside is that, in addition to helping me with odd jobs around here, Carl is my brother. He wasn't always like this."

Buckhorn nodded grimly. "I think I understand. You can't pick your family, as the old saying goes. I had a father who let himself get owned by the bottle, too, right up until the day he died."

Justine regarded him. "I thought you were going through the motions like somebody who'd had some practice at it."

"Unfortunately."

"I can't tell you how grateful I am for—"

"Who's gonna unload the wagon?" Buckhorn interrupted her.

"What?"

"The wagon. The one your brother drove up in. Isn't there stuff in it to be unloaded?"

"Oh. Yes. Mostly bales of paper stock."

"From what I saw, they looked kinda heavy."

Justine nodded. "Yes. Heavy and awkward."

"I can give you a hand with them," Buckhorn offered. "Then what about the horse and wagon?"

"They go back to the local livery barn. I rent them whenever we need to haul anything. But I can handle that part, getting them back. If you could help me unload that paper stock, though, I'd surely—"

Buckhorn cut her short again by simply walking away and heading out to start unloading the wagon. Justine trailed after him.

When they got to the front door, they became quickly aware of a flurry of activity building out in the street. There was an excited buzz of voices and a number of folks were streaming down the boardwalks on either side.

Justine hailed one of the men hurrying past her

doorway. "Clyde! Clyde Andrews! What's going on? What's this hubbub all about?"

The man slowed his step but didn't halt. Over his shoulder he shouted back to Justine, "Didn't you hear? Two Flying W men just rode into town with three of their own shot dead and laying facedown across their saddles. They're reining up down by Sheriff Banning's office right now."

CHAPTER 12

Whether or not the sleepy feeling that had seemed to be settling over the town earlier that afternoon would have lasted for any duration became a moot point once the dead cowboys were brought in. The dead, curiously enough, had a revitalizing effect.

As far as Buckhorn could tell, about three quarters of those present in the downtown area drifted closer to the sheriff's office to at least have a gander at the bodies. About half hung around for a while, jabbering excitedly among themselves. The rest, having gotten their close-up look, returned to whatever it was they'd been doing before.

Buckhorn didn't wander down for a look. He'd already had his. In addition to not needing to see any more of the men he'd shot it out with the previous day, he had work to do—the job of unloading the paper bales he'd volunteered to handle for Justine York.

Since part of running the *Sun Ledger* meant she was also its lead reporter, Justine had legitimate reason for not only joining the throng that poured to the sheriff's office but for taking her place at its head in order to question the lawman and the men who'd brought the victims in, getting all the information she could about the identities of the deceased and the circumstances under which they'd been found.

Buckhorn had urged her to take care of that while he took care of the unloading and returning the horse and wagon to the local livery. They'd agreed to get in touch later, after things had simmered down.

Emerging from the livery, he saw there was still quite a gathering in front of the sheriff's office and that Justine was still part of it, wielding her pencil and notepad in the midst of the chatter. Given that, he ducked back into the livery barn to check on Sarge, whom Fletchler from the hotel had taken care of boarding there.

After the long trip from Louisiana, the big gray deserved some pampering and Buckhorn had given instructions for him to receive it. Assuring himself that was indeed the case, Buckhorn lingered for a few minutes to chat a bit with his trail partner and give him a good neck rub.

Quitting the stable once again, it occurred to Buckhorn that he, too, was still owed some additional pampering. Although diverted for a time, his initial intention had been to catch an afternoon nap up in his hotel room.

The appeal of that returned. Not that the chore of unloading Justine York's wagon had exhausted him to any degree, but the matter of last night's meager amount of sleep hadn't been settled. He also was reminded of his earlier plan to spend some time in the local saloons come evening, to see what else he could learn about things in general and the overall mood running through Wagon Wheel and surrounding Whitestone County. If that had been a worthwhile idea before, the discovery of the dead Flying W riders was bound to have tongues wagging even more so.

Buckhorn's nap lasted considerably longer than he'd anticipated. He woke to find the long shadows of evening reaching into his hotel room.

At the washbasin on the dresser, he splashed water on his face and slicked back his hair. He strapped on his gunbelt, shrugged back into his vest and coat, and straightened his string tie. Ever conscious of his humble beginnings and well aware of lacking anything close to handsome features, he nevertheless worked to keep his appearance as presentable as possible.

Early in his career as a hired gun, he'd done some bodyguard work for a wealthy, successful man who paid particular attention to his grooming and attire. That had left a lasting impression on Buckhorn—the lesson that a good start toward improving a body's status in life could be achieved by putting care into how you looked and showing the desire to improve.

Before quitting the hotel room, he took the time to enhance his wardrobe a bit more by dropping an over-under derringer into his right front coat pocket and slipping a spare revolver, a Colt Lightning, behind the waistband of his trousers at the small of his back.

Another lesson he had learned was that a man who made his living by the gun stood a better chance to keep on living if he didn't necessarily rely on just *one* gun. Considering how he was a stranger heading out to do some nosing around in the saloons of a town where he'd already managed to get crossways with some local rowdies earlier in the day, taking along extra firepower didn't seem like a bad idea at all.

In the hotel lobby, Buckhorn happened upon a plump, elderly lady wearing a ruffled, brightly flowered apron and, contrastingly, iron gray hair pulled into a severe bun. She was fussing over a medium-sized serving table positioned before the front window just off to one side of the double entrance. Taking a closer look, he saw she was arranging a tray of cookies, some cups, and a tall silver pot.

He remembered then how Fletchler, the clerk who'd checked him in, had mentioned that his missus made a habit of putting out a tray of muffins in the lobby each morning and a tray of cookies in the evening. About the same time, Buckhorn got a whiff of them, along with the aroma of fresh coffee from the pot, and it made a mighty tempting combination.

The plump lady turned with a smile as he walked over. "Good evening. You must be Mr. Buckhorn from room seven. The mister told me about you checking in this morning. I'm Mrs. Fletchler, by the way. I'm glad you chose our humble establishment. I hope you're finding everything to your liking."

"Everything is fine." Buckhorn nodded toward the display on the serving table. "And, by the smell of your coffee and cookies, it just got a little better."

Mrs. Fletchler emitted a pleased little laugh. "It's only a few simple sugar cookies. I like to put them out for the guests, even though we seem to have precious few of those these days. So, by all means, help yourself. Can I pour you some coffee?"

"Much obliged. Black is fine, no fixings necessary."

In a matter of moments, Mrs. Fletchler was handing him a cup of rich, dark coffee and a saucer containing three golden sugar cookies. The latter were still warm;

crispy on the outside, gooey in the middle, buttery sweet all the way through.

For a moment, he felt like a cookie-crazed little kid, though the truth of the matter was that there'd been damn few sweet treats like these during his childhood years. A swallow of strong, bitter coffee went down more like a dose of reality.

"If you're wondering about the mister," Mrs. Fletchler said as Buckhorn took his time, savoring each bite and sip, "he's wandered off down to the sheriff's office and jail again to catch up on the latest gossip regarding the tragedy from earlier today. You heard about that, didn't you?"

"The three men who were found shot, you mean?"

"Uh-huh. What with the Flying W gobbling up land the way it has been and more and more folks resenting it, something like this was bound to happen, I guess. Still a darn shame, though."

Buckhorn regarded her with new appreciation as he took another bite of cookie. Here might be a source for some information spiced with a bit of gossip—to use her own choice of words—that he hadn't figured on.

"I didn't pay a whole lot of attention, not being from around here and so not likely to know any of the unfortunates or anything," he said as he chewed. "But I did hear that name *Flying W* mentioned two or three times. I take it that's the brand the dead men rode for. Pretty big operation, is it?"

"The biggest, and getting bigger all the time," Mrs. Fletchler said with a nod. "The fellow behind it, Thomas Wainwright—he was a big hero, a general, in the late war—seems bent on owning the whole of Whitestone County all the way down to the border.

With everybody else's range drying up in this blasted drought while he's got Whitestone Lake right there in the heart of his property, he's sitting in the catbird seat to do it."

"His lake the only water source around?"

"The only steady one. The only one not showing signs of petering out if this drought continues much longer. Wainwright's lake is spring-fed, they claim. Will never dry out."

Buckhorn's mouth pulled into a thin, straight line. "Let me guess. While others around him are drying up, Wainwright's digging in his heels about sharing water from his lake."

"You got it. In the past it was a different story. There's a half dozen canals running off Whitestone and the water they carry has always served other ranges outside Flying W's own boundaries. Even though there was other groundwater to be accessed here and there, it was just easier for neighbors to tap into Whitestone. Everybody knew there was plenty there. I think those neighbors paid a little bit for the usage, but it didn't amount to much.

"That was the first sign of things changing and the start of hard feelings. Wainwright all of a sudden upped the amount he was charging for anybody using water out of those canals. Upped by a big jump."

"And that was after the drought was already in full swing?"

"Yes, it was. That's how Wainwright got his hands on some of the first land he bought. Those who were already on it didn't have enough water of their own and couldn't afford to pay the Flying W's new price to draw off from the lake. So they sold. From there, it's slowly gotten worse. The drought's worse, Wainwright is stingier about releasing any of the water from Whitestone Lake, and the resentment toward him and Mother Nature has built to a tension so tight it was bound to snap into violence."

"Now three men are dead," Buckhorn pointed out. "Any chance that'll ease the tension some? Maybe at least for a little while?"

Mrs. Fletchler shook her head. "I don't think so. More like it'll only add to it. Especially on the Flying W side. Whatever else Thomas Wainwright may or not be, he surely has been aware and prepared for the escalating hard feelings against him and his tactics. That's been clear by the kind of men he's hired lately to ride for his brand."

"Yeah, I know the type," Buckhorn muttered.

Mrs. Fletchler eyed him more sharply than before. "You're not one of them, are you?"

Buckhorn mentally cursed himself for letting the remark slip. He thought about steadfastly denying anything like the notion being suggested, but gazing back into Mrs. Fletchler's steady, penetrating eyes told him he didn't have a chance in hell of selling that much of a lie. So, instead, he aimed for something in between.

"Since you've got me spotted, I'll fess up to having spent a chunk of my life on the rough side of things. But am I here to sign on as one of Wainwright's crew? No, that's got nothing to do with what brought me here."

Mrs. Fletchler continued to regard him for a long moment before concluding, "You got the look. That means you're the type who, if you stick around for any amount of time, is likely to get involved regardless. I don't know what *did* bring you here, but it would probably be healthiest if you moved on as quick as you can."

"Healthiest for who?" Buckhorn wanted to know.

"That's the part I haven't quite decided yet."

He held up the last bite of his third cookie and flashed a lopsided grin before popping it into his mouth. "You want to hurry me down the trail, you'll have to quit tempting me with these. You can't have it both ways."

CHAPTER 13

Out on the street, the air had cooled considerably with the setting of the sun. Most of the businesses up and down the main drag of Wagon Wheel were closed, their doors locked, windows dark.

On the corner of the next block, however, Buckhorn could see light showing in the window of the newspaper office. Justine York undoubtedly was at work writing her first story on the shooting of the Flying W riders. He thought about going down and ducking in to talk with her for a minute, but decided against it. She had a job to do and needed to be left alone to do it. He'd catch up with her tomorrow.

Looking up the street in the other direction, he saw the sheriff's office and jail building aglow with light and the shifting shadows of several men milling inside. A single shape, most likely one of the deputies, stood outside smoking a cigarette.

Buckhorn had been given strict orders to check in with the sheriff by the end of the day, but he didn't think it would be a good time. Under the circumstances, he figured, that was something else that could wait until tomorrow.

Halfway between the sheriff's office and where Buckhorn stood on the boardwalk out front of the Traveler's Rest, on the opposite side of the street, was a saloon called the Silver Dollar. It was bigger, more gaudily painted, and—on that particular evening, at least—louder and busier than its competition, the Watering Hole. Normally the kind of place Buckhorn would shy away from if he had the choice.

But having already had a taste of what he might encounter in the Watering Hole and fully intending to pay a visit to both establishments before the night was over anyway, he decided he'd go ahead and give the Silver Dollar a try. Besides, it also happened to be the closest of the two.

He paused for a minute just outside the batwing doors, giving the place a good once-over before pushing the doors wide and going in. It wasn't quite as crowded as the racket spilling outside indicated, but it was plenty busy and those present were making up for any shortage in number by being extra loud and rowdy.

He found an empty space near one end of the bar, a spot that served double duty by tucking him sort of back and out of the way and providing a good vantage point for observing the goings-on spread across the rest of the room. He ordered a beer.

It came with too much of a head on it, but was cold and tasty once he'd gotten through the foam. Leaning back against the front edge of the bar, elbows propped high on either side, he settled in to watch and listen between leisurely sips of the brew.

The subjects on every tongue were the discovery of the dead men, the drought, and water rights issues. They were generally accepted as being related. Two camps seemed to hash over the matter. Gathered around tables in the center of the room was a large, loud contingent of men who either rode for or were otherwise associated with the Flying W brand. Along the bar and at a couple tables on the fringe was a lesser number—about half—who had interests apart from the big ranch. While no one was advocating the shooting of the cowboys, that bunch seemed not as interested in that aspect as they were in the divisive water rights issue that had been left simmering for too long.

Among the more vocal members of the smaller group, planted just a couple places down the bar from where Buckhorn had landed, was the beefy, jug-eared man he had overheard making a bitter comment about Wainwright earlier at the Good Eats Café. Hampton, the waitress had said his name was. He'd appeared reluctant to spout too much at the restaurant but in the saloon, fortified by liquor and surrounded by others who felt the same, he wasn't holding much back.

"Boil the pot too long and too hot," Hampton was saying, "the lid is bound to come off. Wainwright has seen this coming just as well as the rest of us. Why do you think he's hired so many gun wolves to fill out his crew? So now three men are dead and I say it's damn near as much his fault as the one who pulled the trigger!"

"You seem to know an awful lot about an awful lot. Leastways you think you do." One of the bunch from the middle of the room raised his voice a little to be heard. "How do you know there was just *one* trigger-puller who did for those boys? Them three fellas had more than a little bark on 'em. It would've took some doing for just one hombre to shade all three."

"Aw, it was just a manner of speech, that's all," said a man at the bar next to Hampton. "Hamp here's got no way of knowing how many it took to put down those three, do you, Hamp?"

"I can speak for myself," Hampton said through clenched teeth. "How many did the trigger-pullin' on those fellas ain't the point. The point is that it's been Wainwright and his stinginess and greed who's pushed this whole business to the breakin' point. Well, now it broke. It busted wide open and those three will be just the beginning if somebody don't do something to make Wainwright see the wrong and right of things."

"That almost sounded like a threat, Hampton," said another voice from the pack of cowboys.

"Call it what you want, but it's the truth," Hampton said stubbornly, "and you all know it."

"The truth I know," said a voice that sounded strangely familiar and caused Buckhorn's ears to perk up, "is that Wainwright did you a favor by buying your failing ranch from you. And now, since he's got cattle grazing just fine where you couldn't, you been doing nothing but bellyaching and making excuses until everybody's sick of hearing it."

Hampton straightened up at the bar. His whole body went rigid and his meaty hands balled into fists. "Who said that?" he demanded. "Step up here, whoever you are, and I'll call you a damn liar right to your face!"

Some men shuffled this way and that and a chair or two scraped on the floor from the middle of the crowd. When the bodies had parted a bit, Buckhorn got a clear look at the man Hampton was trading words with and it became evident why his voice had sounded familiar. The man was Conway, who'd been pulling some of the same taunting tactics earlier in the day out front of Justine's place.

There was no sign of the punchers who'd been with him then, but he appeared to have other allies in their place. Enough for him to feel confident in rising from his chair, body poised snakelike, mouth twisted in a sneer.

"You," Hampton said, like the acknowledgment left a bad taste in his mouth. "I should have figured as much, Conway. Everybody knows you're a born liar."

"Make up your mind," Conway replied. "Am I a born liar or a damn liar?"

"The meat of it is that you're a liar. You ain't worth fancying it up with any extra."

"Leastways I ain't some no-account whiner who spends his days looking up a mule's rear end and making accusations he can't back up."

"I can back up plenty when it comes to you, you weasel," Hampton said, raising his melon-sized fists a little higher. "But since you got half the Flying W crew backing *you*, is this a discussion between just the two of us? Or are you gonna flick a couple girlie punches from behind your pals and then hang back to let them carry the rest of the load?"

A man who'd been sitting at the table with Conway rose also. He was tall and lean, almost freakishly broad through the shoulders, and had unusually large hands encased in tight black leather gloves. Limp yellow hair fell to his shoulders from under a high-crowned hat, and a walrus mustache of the same color drooped around the corners of his mouth. He wore a matching pinstripe vest and trousers, the latter tucked into high black boots. A nickel-plated Colt with gleaming white grips was prominently displayed in a silver-studded cross-draw holster.

"What if the load turns heavy under the sudden weight of lead, mule skinner?" this man said to Hampton. "You and them fat ham hocks you call fists up to carrying it then?"

"Everybody knows I ain't no gunman. I ain't even heeled," Hampton said, not backing up but straining to hold his voice level.

"Fella starts calling other fellas names and goes blowing wind about how he's gonna do this and do that, it seems to me he oughta be ready to face the consequences of his words whatever shape they take," the blond man said. "Doing otherwise makes you look pretty damn stupid, wouldn't you say, mule skinner?"

"Just to make things clear," Conway said, squeezing the words in around a nasty chuckle, "I should make sure you know who my friend here is." He gestured to the blond man with a flourish. "This is Jack Draper. Dandy Jack Draper, as he's called. I do believe he would qualify as one of those Flying W *gun wolves* you referred to earlier, Hampton. Although I'm not entirely sure he's fond of the term."

"I know who he is," Hampton said tightly.

"I don't care if you do or don't, and I don't much sweat what mule skinners and other kinds of trash call me neither," Dandy Jack muttered.

An older man standing at the bar near Hampton said, "There's no call to be so offensive and turn this into—"

"Shut your piehole, you!" Dandy Jack cut him off. "Unless, that is, *you're* heeled and you're offering to step up and carry mule boy's load for him."

"Nobody has to shoulder my load for me," said Hampton.

Dandy Jack's cold eyes shifted and his gaze settled on Buckhorn. "Not even him?"

Heads turned and necks craned and all of a sudden everybody in the joint was taking notice of Buckhorn. He remained exactly as he was, unmoving, leaning back calmly, for a long count. Then, slowly, smoothly, he straightened up and let his arms slide off the bar and drift down to his sides.

"Hello, Jack. Been a while."

CHAPTER 14

"Every time I see you in your suit coat, matching vest, and string tie, I think you might be trying to outdo me in the dandy department." Dandy Jack paused, gave a faint wag of his head, then added, "But then I get to that god-awful derby hat and it all goes south. You ain't never gonna shade me when it comes to being a dandy, Buckhorn."

"Guess that must be why nobody ever took to calling me Dandy Joe."

"Wait a minute! You two know each other?" Expressions of surprise, confusion, and annoyance wrestled back and forth across Conway's face. Strictly addressing Dandy Jack, he added, "This is the hombre I was telling you about before, the one I tangled with earlier today."

"From the way you described him, I had a hunch who it might be. When I saw him walk in a minute ago, that sealed it."

"I never noticed him come in."

"That's because you work harder at running your mouth than you do at paying attention to things."

Conway let the remark slide. "You two ain't friends, are you?"

Dandy Jack's eyes stayed on Buckhorn as he said, "Fellas like us don't have friends. But in the case of me and Buckhorn here, our trails have crossed a time or three."

Hampton's expression grew conflicted. "So does that make you another gun wolf Wainwright has called in?" he asked Buckhorn.

"All I am," Buckhorn replied, "is a fella passing through who stopped to catch some rest in what looked like a nice, quiet little town. Just incidentally, though—much as I hate to agree with a gasbag like Conway about anything—you might want to tug back on the reins a trifle when it comes to tossing around that *gun wolf* stuff."

"Hey, bub," Conway piped up. "You'd best watch your own mouth when it comes to tossing out how *you* describe people."

"Hackles down, boy," Dandy Jack said easily. "If you want to worry about something, stick to what I was trying to get out of the mule skinner when I first called attention to Buckhorn. Since Hampton is the one who seems so hung up on the general hiring of gun wolves, makes me wonder if him and other bellyachers like him ain't put feelers out for a gunny of their own."

"I ain't ever felt the need to hire somebody else to do my fighting for me," Hampton responded.

"And if you're talking about me, Jack," Buckhorn said, "I just got done explaining how I only happen to be in the area on account of I'm passing through. If I pondered very long on you questioning that, it might cause me to wonder if you were calling me a liar. Was I to decide that, I gotta think it'd probably piss me off."

The men lining the bar nearest Buckhorn did some none-too-subtle shifting and shuffling to create a bit more distance between themselves and him. The Flying W bunch gathered around Dandy Jack did the same. Even Conway.

After also edging down from the line of fire, the bartender said, "C'mon, fellas, there ain't no call to commence shooting over this. We already had three shot-up fellas show up in town today. Ain't that enough? And if you *are* gonna go to shooting, can you at least take it outside?"

"You said your piece, mister. Now shove a sock in it," Dandy Jack told him. "If me and Buckhorn take a notion to shoot up this rathole of yours, then shot up is what it's gonna get and your blabbering ain't gonna change things a bit."

"Don't recall you being so prickly in the past, Jack. But for some reason you're awful quick to be proddy this evening," Buckhorn said. "First you go out of your way to get in the face of the mule skinner, then you 'bout bite the head off the bartender. You even did some crowding on me."

"What of it? You having any?"

"That's not especially what I came here for, but it could be arranged, I reckon."

Dandy Jack's lip curled nastily. "You always did rankle me, Buckhorn. Wearing those uppity duds the way you do, trying to copy me."

"Like you try to copy Bill Hickok, you mean?"

"Hickok's dead. I ain't."

"Not yet."

The tension that had been building throughout the room suddenly tightened all the more.

"Now *that* for damn sure sounded proddy," Dandy

Jack said. "You decide you're wanting some of it after all, breed?"

Buckhorn sighed. "All I really want is what I came in here for in the first place—to have a cold beer and be left to drink it in peace. I got one over here right now, as a matter of fact. Be my 'druthers to get back to it before it goes flat."

"You're welcome to do just that . . . as long as you do it somewhere else. If you're bent on finishing that particular beer, you'll have to take it with you. I'll even pay for the glass. So go on, pick it up and carry it on out."

Buckhorn's eyes went narrow and cold. "No. I don't believe I'll be doing that."

For a long, ragged moment, most of those watching couldn't really believe it was going to happen. That bullets were actually going to be traded over the mere handful of spoken words. And then, when it *did* happen, it went so fast it was like an eyeblink and it was all over.

Most agreed that Dandy Jack had gone for his gun first. And his hand streaked fast, blindingly fast.

But Buckhorn just stood there, amazingly relaxed, and seemed to do little more than shrug his right shoulder. That was enough. Just that simply and quickly his Colt was in his fist, gripped at waist level and extended only about a foot toward Jack. It roared once, planting a bullet alongside the bridge of Jack's nose, a quarter inch under his left eye.

Jack's head snapped back, his eyeball popping out to dangle by gooey wet fibers as his body toppled away. He got his own Colt drawn and also managed to get off a shot, but it didn't come until a second before his freakishly wide shoulders hit the floor, the slug doing nothing more than tearing a long gash in the saloon's wooden floor.

Buckhorn took a step back, leaning against the bar once more. He made sure no one was behind him and raked his eyes warningly back and forth over the crowd to make sure no one else looked ready to try him before he reholstered his gun.

After the Colt had returned to leather, he reached for his unfinished beer. He took a long swallow and, as he was lowering the glass, he heard the voices and boot heels clumping on the boardwalk outside the batwing doors, signaling the arrival of the sheriff and his men.

CHAPTER 15

"Since when do you throw a man behind bars for acting in self-defense?" Justine York demanded.

"You weren't there," Sheriff Banning barked right back at her. "How do you know what happened when he shot Jack Draper?"

"Because a whole saloonful of men are saying that's the way it was. Just because you're turning a deaf ear to their claims, I'm not! I can hear loud and clear what they're saying."

"You're conveniently choosing to listen to only *half* the saloonful of men who were there," the sheriff pointed out. "The other half saw it different. They're claiming Buckhorn here kept egging Jack on and then drew on him first."

"That's a lie!" Amos Hampton said. "I *was* there and saw how it happened. Wasn't nothing like you just repeated, Sheriff. It was Draper who did the egging on and who went for his gun first."

Conway jumped into the argument. "I was there, too. Dandy Jack did everything he could to avoid that shooting. And when he least expected it, this stranger—the same damn half-breed who pointed a gun at me for no good reason earlier today, if you remember, Sheriff—whipped out his Colt and plugged ol' Jack."

The spirited exchange was taking place inside the sheriff's office. In one of two adjoining cells built into the south wall of the room, Buckhorn looked on from behind the bars but held back from joining in. He had two pretty good champions in Justine and Hampton, he figured, so for the time being he was willing to let them do the talking on his behalf.

Other voices not showing so much restraint when it came to being heard, however, were making a steady rumble outside the squat adobe building that housed the sheriff's office and jail. It was a mix of Flying W riders taking the side of Dandy Jack faced off against others who'd been present in the Silver Dollar but leaned in favor of Buckhorn.

Banning's two deputies, Pomeroy and Gates, were stationed out there trying to maintain control of the crowd while the sheriff was trying to do the same with the three people he'd allowed inside. Justine was supposed to be there as an impartial member of the press but so far had done little to hide her personal feelings on the matter.

"Come on, Paul," Justine said, personalizing her plea to the sheriff. "You're surely aware of Dandy Jack's reputation. He killed nearly twenty men and was the first one to brag about it. He *craved* the notoriety. Does anything about that sound like a man who'd innocently, reluctantly allow himself to get pushed into a gunfight he wasn't itching to take part in?"

"He was itching all right," confirmed Hampton. "I was the one he started in on. I don't like to admit it, but I was doing some shaking in my boots at the

thought of having just my fists to go up against the likes
of Dandy Jack. Lucky for me this stranger—Buckhorn,
as I now know him—was willing to step in for my sake."

"Yeah, he was willing to step in. Like a dirty coward,"
Conway said. "While Jack was distracted by this blowhard mule skinner, that's when Buckhorn made his
play!"

That brought another burst of protests from Justine
and Hampton until Banning held up his hands, palms
out, and shouted, "Cut it! Jesus Christ, this is getting
us nowhere! We might as well go stand in the middle
of that crowd outside if all you're gonna do is holler
back and forth at each other."

"What *about* that crowd outside?" Justine wanted to
know. "There's the sound and smell to them of a lynch
mob. How far are you going to let this go, Sheriff?"

"Nobody's lynching any prisoner out of *my* jail, if
that's what you're driving at," Banning said. "Which is
exactly one of the reasons I hauled Buckhorn in here
in the first place. For his own protection. The Flying W
had already lost three men today, even before Dandy
Jack went down. Those first three were just common
wranglers, fellas a lot of those men out there had
worked and ridden with for months, maybe years.
Good pals to some of 'em."

"Dandy Jack didn't have a friend in the world,"
Justine said. "Unless it was some starry-eyed fool who
was impressed by his rep, or some floozie whose time
Jack was paying for."

"It's rotten to talk like that about the dead," Conway
said. "Not to mention unladylike."

"I save my ladylike talk for those who deserve it."
Justine's eyes blazed. "The point I was trying to make
is that whatever's got those men out there whipped up,

it's got nothing to do with feeling the loss of a friend, not when it comes to Jack Draper. He was a cold-eyed killer who would have thought no more about squeezing the trigger on any one of them than on a jackrabbit. The only thing anybody in that bunch had in common with Dandy Jack was being on Wainwright's payroll."

Sheriff Banning puffed out his cheeks and expelled a gust of air. "I never said those men's feelings of friendship were for Draper. I said it was for the three who'd been brought in before, and that partly explains what has them feeling so frustrated and edgy."

"Hell," said Conway, "for all we know, that quick-trigger breed might be the one responsible for gunnin' those poor cowboys, too."

Justine rolled her eyes. "Wonderful. Now let's get even more ridiculous."

"For Chrissakes don't be starting in with wild talk like that," Banning said. "Such a notion starts to spread, it could turn this whole thing into a powder keg."

"But you can't just ignore it as a possibility," Conway insisted. He jabbed a thumb toward Buckhorn. "This gunny shows up out of nowhere and all of a sudden Wainwright men start dropping right and left with cases of lead poisoning. I damn near was one myself."

"And that makes Buckhorn a *gunny*?" Justine asked.

"You were there. You saw how fast he pulled on me," Conway said. "And he beat Dandy Jack, didn't he? Even if he got the jump, that still proves he knows his way around a gun pretty damn good. And him and Jack *knew* each other from the past, from being in the same trade. They indicated as much before the guns came out. Even Hampton has to admit that."

When everyone swung to look at him, Amos

Hampton dropped his eyes and frowned. "Yeah, he's got it right. Buckhorn and Dandy Jack didn't leave much doubt they knew each other from being in the same line of work."

"See?" Conway practically crowed. "And that's from a man who's been grumbling and complaining all over the county about how General Wainwright has hired what they're calling gun wolves to protect his business interests. Starting to appear clear enough to me that some among the complainers decided to hire a gun wolf of their own. And you're looking at him, right over there behind those bars!"

Justine turned to Buckhorn. "Is that true, Joe? Are you a hired gun?"

Buckhorn, no longer able to stay out of it, met her eyes and held them as he said evenly, "Hired gun, gunslinger, gunfighter, shootist, a fella who does gun work . . . Yeah, I've been all of those things at one time or other in one place or other. But nobody around here has hired my gun. What happened between me and Dandy Jack happened because he pushed for it to happen. I'm not sure I understand why."

"You're the one who did the pushing, the prodding," Conway said. "And the reason why was because you had Hampton there splitting Jack's attention so's you could pull your sneak move on him."

Buckhorn gave Conway a cold stare and then slowly shifted his gaze to Banning. "I don't know how long you're gonna be able to keep me here, Sheriff, without somebody pressing official charges. But, when you do get around to letting me out, you might as well keep that cell key handy because there's a good chance I'll be giving you cause to lock me right back up again after I hunt down this little weasel and wring his scrawny damn neck."

"That was a threat! Everybody heard it, right?" Conway said excitedly. "He threatened me with serious bodily harm. He practically said he was gonna kill me!"

Before anybody could say anything more, the front door opened and Deputy Pomeroy stuck his head in. "I think you're gonna want to come out here for this, Sheriff. Thomas Wainwright is riding in with a handful of gun toughs."

CHAPTER 16

"What the hell is going on around here, Banning? Somebody's turning the county into a shooting gallery for my riders and you and your deputies are hanging around here instead of hauling your lazy asses out and doing something about it." Having reined his horse to a sharp halt in front of the sheriff's office, Wainwright remained in the saddle and began issuing his questions as soon as Sheriff Banning stepped out the door. Like most men, Wainwright presented a larger, taller, more imposing figure on horseback. He knew this, of course, and played to it whenever possible.

Even standing on the ground, however, although he was only of average height and stature, Wainwright still made an imposing impression. It was in his bearing, his attitude, the way he pinned other people with a direct, steady look from dark, almost black, eyes that shone like chips of wet coal from under a ledge of thick brows. His neatly trimmed beard and hair were almost as dark as his eyes and he spoke with a deep, assured voice that sounded custom made to give commands.

Paul Banning was one of the few men in Whitestone

County who showed signs of being able to hold his own with Wainwright and even stand toe-to-toe when the situation required it. Still, you didn't have to look too hard to find those who felt he nevertheless deferred a little too easily and often to the former general, leaving an opening for suspicions that he might even be taking payoffs to turn away on certain occasions when the long arm of the law should have reached a little farther and squeezed a little harder.

In response to Wainwright's current abrupt demands, Banning put on a good show to the once rumbling, grumbling crowd that had grown silent when the rancher spoke. Quickly demonstrating his authority and holding his ground, Banning said, "First thing in the morning, me and one of my deputies are gonna ride out to where your three men were found and give the scene a thorough investigation when we won't have to worry about darkness crowding in on us. That would've been the case today if we'd 've tried to make it out there after we questioned the riders who brought 'em in. As it was, it's a good thing we stuck around because now there's been another shooting involving one of the other men who worked for you."

"Worked for—past tense," said Wainwright. "That means he's dead, too. You're talking, of course, about Jack Draper."

Banning jerked a thumb over his shoulder. "I got the other fella who was involved in the shoot-out inside, and I'm interrogating him. I'm hearing conflicting reports about who prodded who and who drew first."

"I heard some of the details on my way in," Wainwright said. "A couple men rode out to meet us."

One of those who'd been taking Draper's side of the shooting spoke up. "Dandy Jack got snookered,

General. If not, that breed never woulda been able to outdraw him like he done."

"That flat ain't true," somebody from the other side countered. "It was a fair fight and Jack just plain got beat to the draw."

The rumble of opposing voices started in again, low at first but quickly picking up volume and intensity.

A new voice, not seeming to speak loud yet somehow possessing a tone that demanded to be heard, shut down the rumbling once more. "Dandy Jack Draper was an old fool. A blowhard and a has-been. It was past his time to die. If the breed hadn't taken care of it, somebody else would have—and soon."

The speaker was a clean-cut young man mounted directly to one side of Wainwright. Early twenties, trim though solid-looking, handsome features pinched slightly by a blade-narrow face. He wore black leather chaps, a black leather vest studded with silver conchos, and a flat-crowned black Stetson with more of the silver discs comprising its hatband. Around his waist was buckled a twin-holster gunbelt also of black leather, six-guns leathered butt-forward and angled slightly outward for a backhanded speed draw with either hand.

Despite the speaker's youth and blatant denigration of Dandy Jack, those in the crowd who'd been so strongly championing the fallen gunman only moments ago remained awkwardly quiet as far as making any objection to this new appraisal of the deceased.

"While Mr. Sweetwater's remarks might seem rather blunt," Wainwright said into the silence, "that doesn't make them inaccurate. From what I've heard of this evening's incident and what I know of Mr. Draper's temperament, I have no trouble believing that he played at least an equal part in bringing about the shooting at the Silver Dollar that resulted in his demise. I regret my poor decision to hire Draper's services in the first place and am relieved that no innocent by-standers were harmed in the exchange of gunfire. Given that, I'm satisfied to consider the matter closed."

Banning frowned. "You'll be pressing no charges then?"

"Regarding the incident with Draper? No, I don't see where anyone has any call for that." As he said these words, Wainwright's eyes swept over the faces of the men in the crowd—the same men who so recently had been shouting for revenge for Dandy Jack—his look clearly conveying that their thinking had best be in line with his. "Of course," he added, "if something new comes to light, that might change my appraisal.

"As far as the three riders who were found gunned down out on the range, that is an entirely different matter. I expect every effort put into hunting down their killer or killers and swift and sure justice being meted out. In the meantime, pending notification of any known kin who may have different wishes, I will have the bodies of the victims brought to my property and buried there with a full ceremony and religious services."

A ripple of approval went through the Flying W members of the crowd, offsetting the somewhat dis-concerted expressions many of them had still been wearing due to the previous dismissal of Dandy Jack's fate.

"Now," said Wainwright. "I know it's getting mighty late, but I reckon the slain bodies of my boys who were brought in earlier are at the undertaker, correct? I want to make a stop there, pay my respects, and set in motion the arrangements I just outlined. Then my men—*all* of my men—and I will be taking leave of your town for a respectable length of time, Sheriff. Nobody who works for me celebrates with whiskey and loose women in the hours after three of our own have met their fate."

"That's understandable enough," Banning said. "You can rest assured, first thing in the morning me and my deputies will launch an investigation into the gunning of your men. We'll run down the culprits behind it and see 'em swing."

Wainwright gave a crisp nod. "I'll hold you to that. And you're advised to know that I will be checking in regularly on your progress." He started to wheel away but then checked his horse and turned back to the sheriff. "One more thing."

"Yes?"

"This individual who shot Dandy Jack . . . I understand he's an Indian."

"A half-breed, actually. Name of Buckhorn."

"You know my history with Indians," Wainwright said stonily. "Even still, under the circumstances I am not going to make an issue about the misfortune of this man's heritage or skin color. But you also well know how bothersome those red devils can be. Full blood or any lesser percentage makes little difference. That has been my experience. If you allow this individual to remain in town after tonight, you're bound to have trouble on account of him. Heed my warning. There may even be those among my crew who have a more charitable feeling toward Jack than I've expressed. I just want the record clear that, should any further trouble occur because of this redskin's presence in these parts, I will have no association with it."

Banning's expression stayed blank. "Yes, sir. You've made yourself clear."

CHAPTER 17

"Well. You heard the man," Sheriff Banning said as he unlocked the door to Buckhorn's cell and swung it wide. "No charges. You're free to go."

Through the bars to his cell and the front door the sheriff had obligingly left open when he went out for his confab with Wainwright, Buckhorn as well as the others left inside had indeed heard the ensuing exchange.

"Free to go," Buckhorn echoed, one brow arched somewhat skeptically as he exited the cell with less enthusiasm than might be expected. "Just like that, eh?"

Banning frowned. "What more do you want? I had fifty-fifty testimony as to who prodded the shoot-out between you and Dandy Jack. Now, with nobody willing to press charges or push the matter any harder, I got even less than that. So why should *I* be the one to push it, especially when I've got three murder investigations squalling for my attention?"

"If you'd listen to me," Conway reminded him, "you'd stop and consider that this breed and those murders ain't necessarily two separate things."

"Dang, I almost forgot," Buckhorn muttered. "Keep

that cell key handy, Sheriff. You're gonna need it again. Won't take me but a minute for the neck wringing I aim to get out of the way."

He took a step toward Conway but the weasel slipped away and out the open door. "You keep away from me, you gun-happy redskin. I'll find somebody who'll listen to what I have to say. I ain't done with you!"

"Let him go. He's not worth the trouble," said Banning.

"What if he catches up with Wainwright and stirs him up? Gets him to change his mind about Buckhorn?" Justine said.

The sheriff shook his head. "Wainwright ain't the kind to change his mind. Especially not for the likes of Conway."

"And even more especially," Buckhorn added, "because Wainwright already figures I'm as good as taken care of."

Justine looked thoroughly confused. "What is that supposed to mean? Quit talking in damn riddles!"

"Not a matter of talking in riddles," Buckhorn told her. "It's a matter of reading between the lines. You heard Wainwright say he saw no reason for anybody to press charges over the shoot-out between Dandy Jack and me, right? Then he made it a point to right away tack on—in front of a whole passel of his men, mind you—that he couldn't be responsible in case there was somebody who felt a closer tie to Jack and decided to cause trouble for me on their own if I stuck around too long."

"In other words," Hampton said, "practically *encouraging* somebody to go after you as long as they did it in a way that left him out of it."

"Is that right, Paul? Is that how you took his meaning also?" Justine asked of the sheriff.

"I only know what he said. I can't read Wainwright's mind," Banning responded testily. "Besides, what would you have me do? Put Buckhorn back behind bars for his own protection?"

"I do a pretty good job of protecting myself, thanks," Buckhorn said. "Which reminds me, I'd like to have back the guns and bowie knife your deputies stripped me of when they locked me up earlier."

From a lockbox at the base of the office's gun rack, Banning withdrew the requested weapons and handed them to Buckhorn. "You won't be needing to use these anytime soon if you were to move on. Say tomorrow, the earlier the better. Since you said you were just passing through anyway, that shouldn't present a problem."

Buckhorn grinned as he buckled on his gunbelt. "You running me out of town, Sheriff?"

"No. I got no legal basis to do so. But if I had my 'druthers, seeing you hit the trail out of here would be pretty high on the list."

"Paul, that's a dreadful thing to say," Justine protested. "Whatever Buckhorn's past, the only trouble he's caused here in Wagon Wheel has been when others forced it on him."

"I won't argue that. But any trouble that comes the way of a fella like Buckhorn usually ends up in gunplay. If it was always between him and somebody like Dandy Jack, that'd be one thing. Wouldn't bother me a bit. But there are a lot of other folks in Wagon Wheel who ain't gun wolves, to use Hampton's term. Bullets start flying around on a regular basis, it's just a matter of time before some poor innocent catches a slug. The thought of that *does* bother me."

Justine suddenly looked uncertain.

Buckhorn seemed a little uneasy himself. "Look. Something like that is the last thing I'd want to see happen. I don't mind drifting on. It's mostly what I do. But the notion of being *hurried* on my way doesn't suit me worth a damn." He cut his gaze to the sheriff. "I got a hotel room booked for tonight and one more. Call it pure stubbornness, but I'm not inclined to break that arrangement. After that, I reckon I can find it in me to pick a direction out of here."

Banning didn't try to hide the fact he wasn't crazy about having Buckhorn around for that long. But all he said was, "Hope you pick a good one."

"Before I turn in tonight, though," Buckhorn said, "I got a couple more things I'm curious about."

"Such as?"

"I couldn't get a full look through the open door. My angle was partly cut off. But when Wainwright first rode up, there were a couple other fellas did some talking. One of 'em was kinda young-sounding and he spouted some unkind remarks about Dandy Jack. I believe Wainwright called him Mr. Sweetwater afterwards. What do you know about him?"

"Sweetwater's his name, just like Wainwright said. Leo Sweetwater." Banning's mouth tugged down at the corners, indicating he didn't think much of the subject. "And, yeah, he's a young one. Hardly into his twenties. Wears a two-gun rig and packs a snotty attitude that's always primed, just begging for somebody to say or do something out of line that'll give him an excuse to pull on 'em. Why? You know the whelp?"

"I've heard of him. Nothing good. I'd say you got him pegged. So he's Wainwright's top gun, is that it?"

"That's the way it shakes out."

"He come aboard before or after Dandy Jack?"

"After. He's only been on the scene about six months."

"So he replaced Jack at the head of the list?"

"That's the way he acts. The way Wainwright treats him." Banning made a face. "Hell, I can't say for sure the pecking order as far as who rates where on the Flying W crew."

Buckhorn nodded. "It fits. It'd explain why Jack was so proddy in the Silver Dollar. He was aware of his status slipping in the ranks of Wainwright's gunnies, saw going against me as a way to make a statement, bolster himself back up."

"Those who make their way with a gun have a lot of peculiarities."

Buckhorn's mouth twisted wryly. "Yeah, I reckon *peculiar* is one word for it." His expression turned thoughtful again. "Wainwright also made a comment about his history with Indians. That naturally caught my attention, too. I figure it might play another part in my chances of making it out of Whitestone County in one piece."

"I don't know about that," Banning said. "But the thing about Wainwright and Indians traces back to when he first settled in these parts after the war. He came with the start of a herd and a wife and baby son. There were still a fair amount of Indians around, mostly Apaches out of Mexico. Some say Wainwright hated 'em and fought 'em right from the start, others claim he tried to get along with 'em. Either way, there came the day when a small war party hit the house while he was away and wiped out his family.

"For a long time after that, he let his ranch go to hell and did nothing but hunt and kill Indians . . . until he'd driven every trace of a redskin from White-stone County for a hundred miles and wider. From there, he went back to building his ranch, concentrated on it just as fiercely as he'd concentrated on killing Indians, and built it up to what it is today."

"That's a sad and tragic tale," Justine said quietly. "It could even be an impressive one if Wainwright didn't also see fit to apply the same brand of ruthlessness to everything and everybody else he comes up against."

CHAPTER 18

Buckhorn's claim about his previously booked hotel room was partly a convenient excuse for not being rushed out of town and also partly a ruse. An old Texas Ranger he'd previously had some dealings with had taught him the wisdom of not being where you were expected to be upon first arriving in a strange town, especially when there was reason to suspect you might be in for trouble.

So, while another turn in the comfortable bed at the Traveler's Rest would have been most welcome, it wasn't to be.

After parting company with everyone at the sheriff's office, Buckhorn went straight to the hotel and up to his room. In case anyone was watching from the street below, he did a little fussing around with the lantern on to make it look like he was getting ready to turn in. Before blowing out the light, he even employed the old trick of lumping up his pillows under the blanket to give anyone entering the room a quick-glance impression there was a body snuggled there.

Then he waited.

After a quarter hour, he got up and relocated.

On stocking feet, carrying his boots and a spare blanket from the bottom drawer of the dresser, Buckhorn crept down the hallway, out the second floor's rear exit, onto a cramped landing and down the outside steps to the ground. He ducked in under the stairway and found a soft patch of weeds over which he spread his blanket.

Obscured by a crosshatch pattern of shadows thrown by the steps and an even denser shadow spilled by a tall rain barrel, Buckhorn hunkered in for the night. He pulled his boots back on and tugged a corner of the blanket over one shoulder and under his chin. The night air was chilly, but he'd endured far worse. He slowed his breathing, became part of the shadows, and slipped into the kind of vigilant sleep that managed to be restful and restorative yet kept him balanced on a razor's edge of alertness that could tip to full awake at the slightest wrong sound or disturbance.

Conway was angry and upset. He couldn't believe Wainwright had dismissed the shooting of Dandy Jack so casually. What was more, when Conway tried to suggest to the former general that Buckhorn might also have had something to do with gunning down the three other Flying W men, Wainwright had laughed in his face and called it a "ridiculous coincidence not worthy of another moment's thought." That got a big horselaugh from all the other men in earshot, none more so than that sneering, sarcastic young puke, Leo Sweetwater.

Sweetwater ranked as one of the biggest sources of Conway's agitation and not just because he'd laughed loudest and longest along with the others. Hell, he'd been doing that every chance he got since showing up and hiring out his gun to Wainwright. He snickered at everybody, but Conway, who wanted in the worst way to move from the Flying W's wrangler crew and join the growing force of gunmen being hired for the brand, was one of his favorite targets. Worse than any of that, though, was the way Sweetwater had treated Dandy Jack. His disgusting and disrespectful spiel against the deceased earlier in front of the jail was just the latest example.

Why Jack put up with it, Conway could never figure out. It wasn't like Jack was afraid of him. Dandy Jack was a damn legend! Sweetwater was just a punk kid.

Though Jack did say, without ever mentioning exactly how he knew, that the kid had lightning in both hands. What he also said, a time or two after the kid had treated him rudely, was that Wainwright had hired them to fight side by side, not against each other. Conway had always had the feeling that someday, when the time was right, Jack was going to decide enough was enough and by God, that would be the day he showed everybody by putting the snotty little so-and-so in his place—that place likely being six feet in the ground.

Before that could happen, the damn half-breed came along and ruined everything.

Jack was the one headed for a six-foot hole in the ground, and that damn Sweetwater was still strutting around like the cock of the roost, not to mention the stinking breed walking free to boot.

Maybe Dandy Jack *was* a has-been. Maybe he *was* afraid of Leo Sweetwater. And he had sure as hell proved he couldn't outdraw Buckhorn. But he was still the most important person who'd ever paid a lick of attention to Arliss Conway. Sure, it was mostly when

Conway was the one buying the drinks, but Jack was always ready to lend an ear. A drinking buddy and a confidant, that's what he was. He was a *somebody*, yet he found time for a common wrangler like Conway and had even promised to put in a good word with the general about Conway joining the gunmen's ranks.

Jack was dead and all those others were too ready to run him down and kick his name aside like it had never amounted to nothing. Conway couldn't let it go. Jack had to be avenged. At the very least, that would help keep his name alive, along with whoever did the avenging. Their names would be linked forever and the scoundrel who'd killed Jack would be blotted out.

Conway gave thought to what Wainwright had said. *"You know how bothersome those red devils can be. I just want the record clear that should any further trouble occur because of this redskin's presence in these parts, I will have no association with it."*

There it was. The words were plain as day to Conway. No matter how he acted on the outside or what he said or allowed Sweetwater to say, Wainwright wanted Jack avenged, too. And he wanted Buckhorn to pay. It was just that his high standing in the territory wouldn't allow him to say any of it right out.

Conway could see the truth, knew what was actually being solicited. The man who delivered . . . well, Wainwright would find a way to reward him. He could count on that.

Hiram Yost *wanted* to believe Conway knew what he was talking about, but he could never be sure about one of Conway's schemes. "Are you certain that's the way Wainwright wants it?" Hiram asked, his round face puckered tight with uncertainty around the bulbous whiskey-inflamed nose at its center.

"I heard it with my own ears," Conway assured him. "I just got done repeating it to you, word for word, for about the third time, didn't I?"

The two men were huddled in a dark corner of the Watering Hole Saloon. Despite what Wainwright had said about not wanting any of his men to liquor it up right after three comrades had been ambushed and especially after he'd been laughed at and ridiculed, Conway hadn't headed back to the ranch with the rest of the Flying W riders. He was convinced he had a mission in town.

Failing to convince any of the other men who rode for the brand that his interpretation of Wainwright's words was correct, however, he had resorted to seeking backup from some of the drinking buddies he'd established during his frequent bouts of elbow-bending whenever he came to town.

Hiram was large and powerful and displayed a seemingly endless supply of gullibility. Plus, Conway happened to know, he owned a big ol' double-barreled shotgun.

"I don't know." Hiram's expression remained painfully uncertain. "I listen to you repeating what Wainwright said, but I keep not hearing anything about him directly wanting somebody to go after the half-breed."

"I'm telling you it's there. You got to read between the lines."

"I never did understand when people say that. Besides, we ain't talking about reading. We're talking about what Wainwright said."

"We're talking about what he *meant*," Conway said with an exasperated sigh. "What's the real problem?

You too good to join in on blasting the pinfeathers off some uppity half-breed?"

"Hell, no. I love making it hot for redskins. Ain't hardly any of 'em left no more to have any fun with. Last I even heard of was that family Nestor Garth and his two sons run off the edge of Slippery Rock Cliff way back last spring. Boy, the rocks was sure slippery when they got done that day—slippery with Injun blood."

"Yeah, yeah. That's a real knee-slapper of a story . . . but the thing now is whether or not you're up for some fun of our own. I need a doggone answer!"

"Okay. Count me in," agreed Hiram. "How you figuring on going about it?"

"Good! That's what I wanted to hear. You see, I found out where that half-breed is staying. He got hisself a room at the Traveler's Rest Hotel. Can you believe that? They rented the heathen a room, big as you please. We oughta burn down the whole damn joint just for that."

Hiram shook his head. "Oh, no. I ain't up for—"

"Never mind. I didn't mean it. The thing is, I also know which room he's in. It's on the second floor. I figure we'll sneak up there, one from the back, one from the front, to make sure he don't catch wind of something suspicious and try to slip out. You bring that double-barreled shotgun of yours, right? Armed with that and you weighing about the same as a bull buffalo, I don't figure that flimsy hotel room door will slow us down much. We'll bust in together—you going high, me low—and we'll blast him right there in his bed until we've painted the mattress and wall with his blood. How does that sound?"

"Ought to get the job done," Hiram said with an eager nod. "Boy, coming up with such a swell plan, I can tell you been hanging around with that ex-general, Arliss."

"Don't let him hear you call him an ex-general." Conway downed the rest of the whiskey in the glass he held. "Thomas Wainwright is still in command." A wolfish grin stretched across Conway's face. "He's just got hisself a different army now."

At the first creak of someone starting up the outside stairway, Buckhorn came completely awake and alert. By the amount of star- and moonlight filtering into the alley between the hotel and the neighboring building, he judged about two hours had passed since he settled there, making it about three o'clock in the morning. Mighty late for another guest to be returning to their room, but not impossible.

Through the gap between steps, Buckhorn looked up and made out the shape of the person ascending the stairs. Large and bulky, almost certainly a male, stepping carefully and carrying something with one end sticking out in a straight, somewhat blurred line. A rifle barrel. Maybe a shotgun.

Buckhorn clenched his teeth. Every instinct he had honed on the cutting edge of surviving a danger-filled life told him that no, this was not some innocent fellow guest returning late from a night of carousing. Here was a man on the hunt. And, just as Buckhorn had anticipated, *he* was the intended quarry.

He stayed motionless for the better part of a minute, until he heard the door at the top of the landing open and close, indicating that the hunter was in the second-floor hallway and approaching Buckhorn's room.

Whatever happened next, the question that came

to mind was how would the hunter exit the building? Back out the way he'd gone in? Or out the front? It seemed likely he would use the rear, where it was darker and emptier, but Buckhorn couldn't be positive of it. He didn't intend to miss the opportunity he'd gone to all the trouble to set up by making the wrong guess.

Silently, he glided across the width of the alley, moving at an angle toward the front of the hotel building. When he reached a position where he had a vantage point on both the front and rear, he squatted in a convenient patch of shadows against the side of the neighboring building and once again waited. He held his drawn Colt pressed to his chest, feeling the steady, unhurried beat of his heart thump against the cold steel.

He didn't have to wait long.

First there was a loud, splintering crash followed by some guttural curses. Then came the unmistakable roar of a shotgun accompanied by the rapid-fire crack of a revolver. Then another shotgun blast.

Looking up, Buckhorn could see flickers of light in the otherwise darkened window that marked his room—the sputter of muzzle flashes from the guns being fired at the lump in his empty bed.

Ambushing yellow bastards.

As abruptly as it had started, the gunfire stopped, replaced immediately by the thumping, thudding sounds of heavily booted feet running down the hallway. The reports of a handgun as well as the shotgun carried by the bulky shape he'd seen going up the back stairs warned him he had two men to deal with, the other one having apparently gone in through the front. From the sound of it, though, both were planning on exiting at the rear.

Two questions remained. Had they spent all their rounds and taken time to immediately reload? Or would they be emerging with empty weapons? Either way, Buckhorn was waiting and didn't plan on letting them get very far.

The two ambushers, the bulky one and his taller, leaner partner, burst onto the landing and started down the stairs, practically tripping over one another in their haste.

Buckhorn let them get about a third of the way down before he stepped out of the shadows in the middle of the alley.. With his raised Colt, he commanded, "Freeze or die!"

A trace of hesitation on the part of the big one caused the lean one to bump roughly against him from behind and above. While they were momentarily tangled together, the lean one extended an arm and began firing a short-barreled pistol in Buckhorn's direction.

Buckhorn didn't hesitate. Unable to differentiate between the two tangled, shadowy forms, he simply emptied all six of the .45's chambers into the double mass, then smoothly shifted to the smaller Colt Lightning, pulling it from the small of his back. He used it to cover what spilled loosely to the bottom of the steps.

In the fall, the bulky one somehow ended up on top of the lean man with the handgun. Both bodies were twisted grotesquely. The big one was motionless, unmistakably dead.

Beneath him, the lean one flailed weakly and made bubbling, groaning sounds. "He's crushin' my . . . I can't . . . oh, God, it hurts."

Buckhorn walked closer and stood over them. He looked down into the pain-etched face of Arliss Conway and said, "Twice in the past twenty-four hours

I didn't kill you when I could have. I regret it's gonna come now . . . at a time that eases you of the pain you damn well deserve. But this time I don't intend to make the mistake of holding back."

The Colt Lightning barked once.

A black hole appeared in the center of Conway's forehead and all the agony relaxed from his face.

CHAPTER 19

News of the latest shooting in Wagon Wheel, once again involving a Flying W rider as one of the victims and once again with Buckhorn the half-breed being the perpetrator, reached Thomas Wainwright as he was in the middle of breakfast with his beautiful young Mexican wife Lusita. The report was delivered by one of Sheriff Banning's deputies.

Wainwright managed to hold his temper in check until after the deputy had departed. Only then, did he let loose a portion of his rage. "Blazing hell!" he roared, pounding a fist down onto the table so hard it caused plates and silverware to rattle and a steaming slosh of coffee to leap out of its cup. "The last thing I need is for word of this kind of notoriety to start spreading out of the territory at a time like this!"

"Try to stay calm, my husband," Lusita said softly. "You are always complaining how no one pays adequate attention to our little piece of Arizona. Who of any importance is likely to even notice, let alone care, when it comes to these recent incidents?"

Wainwright scowled fiercely. "I don't know. But I've been in enough skirmishes to have learned one thing.

You never get cocky, never let your guard down. Just when you think you've got the battle in your pocket and you relax even the slightest, that's when Fate will knock you back on your heels every time. Well, not this time, by God. I've got too much riding on this to risk letting myself get outflanked now . . . especially not due to that damn lunkheaded Conway or some quick-trigger stinking half-breed!"

Whatever he meant by *this*, Lusita did not know the details. She only knew it was some kind of big business transaction involving her own father, himself a wealthy rancher just across the border, and the seemingly insatiable acquisitions by both men of more and more land and cattle. The addition of hired guns—dark, dangerous men like Leo Sweetwater and the more colorful, recently deceased Dandy Jack Draper—was also a part of it.

The increasing intensity and moodiness she saw in her husband and father as a result of this escalating *thing*, nor the growing sense of danger she sensed from the presence of the cold-eyed gunmen, nor the vague reports of violence she was aware of in spite of attempts to shield her from it, were not the worst of it, though. Not for Lusita.

It was the sinking certainty deep in her heart that one of the initial steps in this big, all-consuming enterprise had been the union between her and Wainwright. She just couldn't actually *prove* it.

Her father had never actually demanded she marry Wainwright, the way some old-fashioned patriarchs were known to do, but he'd surely encouraged it. Lusita was so anxious to please her father, as sad and lonely as he was after the death of her beloved mother, that she had agreed.

Though quite a few years older than her, Thomas

Wainwright was still a dashing, relatively handsome man. She could learn to love him, she'd told herself, and live a life of attentiveness and comfort.

In a matter of months, she knew what a mistake she had made. Yes, she had plenty of comforts in her life and Thomas was reasonably attentive, but so much of his manner was cool and calculated. He wanted a child, an heir. It was soon evident that was the main purpose of their lovemaking, perhaps their whole marriage. When no pregnancy resulted, his coolness increased though he continued to treat her pleasantly and still saw to her material needs.

As time passed, the attempts at making a child waned and practically ceased completely, which was good, in one sense. But it left young, hot-blooded, unfulfilled Lusita all the more resentful of her circumstances. If Thomas would take the passion he was putting into the big business deal with her father or the angry outbursts such as he was displaying this morning and invest it in their lovemaking, Lusita thought longingly, somewhat bitterly, then maybe things would be different.

"I apologize for my outburst. That was uncalled for," Wainwright said to both Lusita and the maid Consuela, who appeared with a cloth to mop up the spilled coffee.

"You're under a great deal of stress. You needn't apologize," said Lusita.

"*Sí*, it was an accident," Consuela agreed. "I will clean this spill and then bring you a fresh, hot refill."

"That won't be necessary, I believe I've had sufficient coffee." Wainwright turned to his wife. "With your indulgence, my dear, I believe I shall take my leave from the table. I have some paperwork in my office I need to tend to, and then I mean to ride out to the spot where the bodies of our three riders were found yesterday. I expect the sheriff to be there, conducting his investigation into their shooting. I want to check his progress and also get more details on this most recent shooting incident last night in town."

"You won't be placing yourself in danger, will you?" Lusita asked. "All this shooting and violence . . ."

Wainwright smiled, appreciating the concern of his lovely wife but not wanting her to be upset. "Don't worry. I won't be at risk with any of that. If it makes you feel better, I'll be sure to have some men with me."

Lusita did not return his smile. "That is good. But when it comes to some of the men you've hired in recent months and weeks, I have to say some have about them a sense of danger that may be as bad as anything else out there."

"That is exactly the idea, my dear. To have those kind of men on *our* side." Wainwright rose. "On second thought, Consuela, I *will* have another cup of coffee. Bring it to my office, please, when you're finished here. And when you see Armando, have him find Mr. Sweetwater and send him to my office also."

Lusita looked up at him. "If you're going to do some work in your office and then ride out to the . . . murder scene, to meet with the sheriff there . . . do you expect to be back in time for lunch?"

After brief consideration, Wainwright said, "No, probably not. I'll try, but it would be best not to count on it. We definitely will dine together at dinner, though."

"Very well," said Lusita. "I shall plan accordingly."

Buckhorn sat in the lobby of the Traveler's Rest Hotel, drinking coffee and eating a freshly baked morning muffin from the tray that Isobel Fletchler had put out. It continued to amaze him that he was still welcome as one of the guests. After the events of last night and the resulting wreckage to the room he had briefly occupied, he expected the welcome mat would no longer be laid out for him.

That, however, was hardly the case. Not only did the Fletchlers harbor no blame against him for the attempted ambush, they'd moved his belongings to another room and insisted he complete the stay he had already paid for.

He thought back to their meeting.

Buckhorn agreed, but only with the proviso he also pay for some portion of the expense it would take to replace the bullet-blasted mattress and other damage. He had, after all, expected the ambush and allowed it to partly play out inside the hotel before closing the lid on it outside.

"You are an exceptionally fair-minded man or one completely without imagination. Maybe both," Mrs. Fletchler summed up in her outspoken manner. "You realize, of course, that once we have the damaged room again ready for occupancy it will probably become the most popular one in our establishment."

Her husband beamed at Buckhorn rather smugly. "She's right, you know. Think of it." He spread his arms and recited as if reading from a brochure. "Within these very walls is the gun smoked spot where two deadly assassins laid down a hellfire of blazing lead meant to end the life of a double-dangerous man who, in turn, ended theirs instead. . . . Why, heck, the room will probably never see an empty night for months, maybe years, to come."

"In that case," Buckhorn responded with a mock scowl, "I think I want to renegotiate. It sounds like instead of me

paying for a portion of the damage, you ought to be paying me a cut of all the extra money you're gonna be raking in on account of the ambush that nearly claimed my life in this bucket of blood joint you call a hotel."

"Now you got the idea. But I'm afraid it sunk in a little too late," Mrs. Fletchler said, wagging an admonishing finger. "A deal is a deal, Mr. Buckhorn, and you already made yours."

Buckhorn shook his head and smiled. When the friendly banter was finished, the Fletchlers had departed and gone on about their morning chores, leaving him alone with the coffee and muffins.

He appreciated the solitude after spending another long session with the sheriff and his deputies, going over the details of the attempted ambush, not to mention the scrutiny from another gaggle of nosy citizens willing to interrupt their night's sleep in order to gawk at the aftermath of the latest bloodshed.

It was exactly the kind of ghoulish curiosity the Fletchlers were reckoning would attract future guests to the room where the would-be assassins had struck. Buckhorn figured they were probably right.

For his part, he would have gladly crawled into the fresh bed of *any* room to catch up on some sleep. As it was, however, the sun was starting to come up before Banning was done with him and the crowd had mostly dispersed. By that point he was past wanting sleep, at least right away.

Left alone at last, his mind was churning with too many thoughts and questions, going in too many different directions with none of them holding any real promise. He'd gotten the lay of the land like he wanted.

Hell, he'd become part of it. A big ol' target, standing tall and inviting.

What good was that going to do him? Fighting to keep his own hide intact didn't make a very good tactic for trying to nail Wainwright's to the wall. What was more, he'd laid it on so thick with his "just passing through" spiel that it was going to be mighty awkward to come up with an excuse for staying. At the moment, it sure didn't feel like he was on the verge of wrapping things up in only another day.

As he was finishing his second muffin, a man came in off the street and entered the hotel lobby. He paused for a moment, looking around, then walked toward Buckhorn.

Tensing slightly, Buckhorn tried to read the man's face. Under the small round-topped table in front of him, his right hand slid a few inches closer to his holster. The newcomer was wearing no sidearm and did not appear to pose any kind of threat, but Buckhorn was always cautious.

"If you're looking for the Fletchlers," he said, "they're around somewhere. I'm not sure where. I think there's a little bell there on the—"

"Actually," the man interrupted, "it was you I was hoping to have a word with. If you can spare a minute."

It was only when he spoke that Buckhorn realized who the man was. Justine York's brother, Carl Orndecker. He looked so different, dressed in crisp, clean clothes, shaved, his hair combed, all in sharp contrast to the disheveled, staggering, vomiting mess he'd been when his wagon had rolled up in front of the newspaper office. Buckhorn hadn't recognized him at first.

Seeing the look on Buckhorn's face, Orndecker smiled a little sheepishly. "Guess I look some different from the last time you saw me. I wouldn't blame you if you told me to get lost. I can hardly deny I've got a drinking problem, but what you saw was about the worst of it. I seldom get as bad as yesterday. I'm working hard to get the demon wrestled to the ground, only some days my hold on him slips."

"Thankfully, I've never had to fight that particular demon, though I've got a pretty good idea how stubborn and strong he can be. If his hold on you is slipping more often than the other way around, I'd say that puts you ahead as long as you don't give up."

"No, I'm not about to do that." The sheepish smile came again. "For one thing, as long as Justine is in the picture, she darn sure won't let me."

"From everything I've seen, she's a good one to have in your corner."

"None better. She's also one of the reasons I came by to see you. She wanted me to remind you that you're scheduled to join her for lunch. She said to tell you that either she can prepare it or treat you at a restaurant."

Justine had been another of those present after the attempted ambush in Buckhorn's room. It hadn't been a matter of gawking but rather a case of once again doing her job as a reporter. After she'd gotten the necessary details, she had extended the lunch invitation as a way of thanking him for his help unloading Carl's wagon and returning the wagon and horse to the livery.

"Don't worry," Buckhorn replied to the reminder from her brother, "I'm not apt to forget a lunch date with your sister."

"No, I can't think of too many fellas who would," Carl said. "By rights, though, I'm really the one who ought to be offering you lunch or some sort of compensation for your help. After all, it was me who got stupidly drunk and couldn't finish the chores you ended up taking care of for me. At this stage of things, I suppose you'd rather leave it the way it is rather than me taking my rightful place instead of Justine."

"You'd be supposing very correctly." Buckhorn gestured toward the coffee and muffins. "You interested in a cup of coffee? Even though you're not an actual guest, I'm sure the Fletchlers wouldn't mind."

"I'm sure they wouldn't, either. The Fletchlers are the salt of the earth. But I've already had plenty of coffee this morning, thanks. I've got to get back and catch up on chores around the shop." Carl arched a brow. "With all the excitement you've stirred up since you hit town, not to mention the mysterious killing of those Flying W riders, Justine is going to crank out a special edition of the paper."

"Sorry to be part of making added work for her."

"You kidding? A slew of exciting events like this is what newspaper people live for."

"You say that like you don't necessarily consider yourself part of what you just called *newspaper people*."

"That's because I'm not. Justine's late husband was the real newshound. He had it in his blood and it rubbed off on her. Me? I'm just on hand to help her out while she helps me."

"Good for both of you."

"I guess. Better for me than her." Carl cleared his throat. "Well, I'd best be getting back over there. What else I wanted to say, though, was to thank you personally for helping out the way you did yesterday. For Justine's sake and mine, too. I know I must have been a pretty disgusting sight. Most folks would have turned away, never got involved. I'm grateful you did otherwise."

"No big deal," Buckhorn told him. "Think nothing of it."

Carl cleared his throat again. "Something more . . . you go to turn in tonight—or sooner, considering how you sure didn't get much shut-eye last night—I'd be obliged and honored if you let me stand guard so's you don't need to worry about another attempt to blast you in your sleep. It's a long story, but before the bottle, among other things, made me unfit, I used to wear a badge in these parts. I don't carry a gun on a regular basis no more, but I'm a pretty fair hand with one when need be. You'd have peace of mind and it'd give me a chance to pay some of the debt for helping me and my sister."

Buckhorn was a little taken aback. "That's a mighty generous offer, mister, and don't think I don't appreciate it. But it's also a kind of lopsided one. All I did for my part was to help Justine get you back to your room and then unload a few things out of a wagon. What you're offering might amount to putting yourself in the way of a bullet."

"Been there before," Carl said. "If somebody *does* take a notion to try for you again but sees you got some backup, there's a chance that would be enough to turn the yellow dogs away."

Buckhorn shook his head. "Like I said, I appreciate the offer, but I'm not ready to have somebody risking their neck for mine."

Carl looked like he wanted to argue the point further but decided against it. "You think about it," he finally said.

"I will, but I'm not likely to change my mind."

Carl started to leave, then paused and turned back. "About your lunch with Justine? My sister is a great gal and is really amazing at a wide range of things . . . but cooking's not one of them. Take my advice—and here I go *really* risking my neck if you repeat to her that I said this—but your best bet is to take your meal with her at the Good Eats. Should I go ahead and tell her that's what you want?"

Buckhorn grinned dubiously. "Sounds like the better part of valor. You've got me scared now to do it any different. Tell her about eleven-thirty, before the noon crowd starts to build, okay?"

CHAPTER 20

Thomas Wainwright lifted two sheets of paper off his desktop and held them out to Leo Sweetwater. "Bills of sale. For the Laudermilk and Wesslin properties. You know where to locate them, right?"

"I'll find 'em," Sweetwater said, taking the papers.

"Take some men with you, men who know the area," Wainwright instructed. He jabbed a finger at the papers he had just handed over. "Each of those has a two-hundred-dollar increase over my last offers for those same places. As is clearly stated, the offer is good only for twenty-four hours. If they're too stubborn and stupid to accept, they'll never see another offer anywhere close to the amounts given there. Make that very clear to them. Also make clear that, sooner or later, they *will* come to terms with me."

"How hard to you want me to drive home that point?"

Wainwright leaned back in his chair and sighed. "Not as hard as I would have suggested just a day or so ago. With the recent outburst of violence in Wagon Wheel, I'm afraid we need to be a little more subtle about driving home our points. At least for a while. I don't want to draw too much outside attention to our little piece of the country, especially not right at this time, due to exaggerated reports of violence."

"Sometimes," said Sweetwater, "just the *hint* of violence—as long as there's a basis for knowing it's more than only hot air—can be mighty persuasive by itself."

Wainwright smiled a thin, humorless smile. "It's uncanny how much you think like me. I wish to hell I had hired you in the beginning, rather than that has-been, to borrow your term about Dandy Jack."

"He's dead," Sweetwater said somewhat testily. "How about we quit wasting so much time talking about the old bastard?"

"Point well taken," agreed Wainwright. "As to your other point about using the hint of violence—or sudden misfortune, one might say—when talking to Laudermilk or Wesslin, here are a couple vulnerable spots you might consider working into your conversations with them. Laudermilk, it so happens, has a nice little pinto filly that he likes to race at festivals and other events around the county. Often as not, he wins or places very high with her. Enough to earn some extra money he badly needs to keep that place of his going. It would be a real shame, in more ways than one, if such a fine animal were to pull up mysteriously lame or, worse yet, be frightened out of her corral by, say, a cougar some night and break a leg fleeing across rough country in the dark. And the Wesslins have that brand-new addition they're building onto their house in anticipation of the twins Mrs. Wesslin is expected to give birth to in about three months. What a tragedy it would be if some of that fresh, exposed wood framing caught a spark somehow and the whole works went up in flames some night . . ."

Sweetwater's mouth curved in a mirror image of Wainwright's cold smile. "I see you've played this game before."

"You can't begin to imagine," Wainwright assured him, thinking back to the lessons he'd learned during his time running the prison for Rebel POWs—how to break a man physically with brutal, unimaginative torture . . . or how to crush their spirits more subtly by toying with their minds.

"When you speak with Wesslin and Laudermilk, be sure to give them my regards," the former general said, his attention snapping back to the business at hand. "Take however many men you'll need, report back to me as soon as you can."

"A couple men should be plenty."

"I'm riding out to the spot where our three riders were found gunned down yesterday. I expect to find the sheriff there and I'll get an update on where he stands with his investigation into the killings. I should be back here by the time you return."

"Sounds about right."

Wainwright pursed his lips thoughtfully and Sweetwater lingered in taking his leave. He sensed his boss had something more to say . . . which proved true enough.

"This half-breed who keeps popping into situations with our men . . . Buckhide or whatever his name is . . ."

"Buckhorn. His name is Buckhorn."

"Are you familiar with him at all? Ever hear of him before?"

Sweetwater nodded. "Heard the name, heard *of* him. Never crossed paths with him."

"What do you know about him?"

"From everything I ever heard, he's supposed to be pretty good. Tough, fast. Was a time he was considered especially ruthless. You don't hear his name mentioned quite so much the past couple years and there's some say he's tamed down a mite over that time."

"He's hardly acted tame since he showed up in these parts."

"No, he hasn't, has he?" Sweetwater's gaze was flat, calculating. "You want me to take care of him?"

Wainwright's mouth turned down at the corners. "Come on, Leo. I expect smarter thinking than that out of you. Would taking care of him in the way I presume you meant be in keeping with what we just discussed regarding Laudermilk and Wesslin? About temporarily keeping the violence low key when confronted with problems?"

"All you have to do is tell me what you want, General. I'll do it." Sweetwater didn't bother to hide his displeasure at being chastised nor at himself for making a bad assumption.

"What I want is your reaction to the possibility of me hiring Buckhorn to join our outfit."

Sweetwater blinked. "For starters, I'd have to ask why you think we need him."

Wainwright shrugged. "He's here in our area. He's available. If he's as good as you say he is, why not? Can we have too many good guns signed on for our cause?"

"Would I still be considered your top gun?" Sweetwater wanted to know.

"I'd make it clear to all parties concerned."

Sweetwater considered, didn't say anything more right away.

"While you're chewing on that, here's something else to take a bite of. Before we left town last night—and before he subsequently hung back to pursue his own ill-conceived plan—Conway babbled something about Buckhorn also being responsible for that ambush of our three riders. At the time, I shrugged it off as a nonsensical coincidence. But to be sure and give fair consideration wherever it might be warranted, what do you think of that notion? It *did* happen right around the same time Buckhorn showed up in the area. Any chance he might be responsible?"

Sweetwater shook his head. "Not likely. Not from what I know of the man. If he got tangled up with those three, it would have been a straight-ahead shoot-out, not an ambush."

"How about my earlier proposal, then? Think you could manage to get along with Buckhorn if he rode with us?"

"A body can stand most anything . . . for a while. You'd have to expect, though, that a pair like us in the same outfit would almost certainly reach the point of having to try each other, find out which one is best."

"As long as that sort of confrontation was delayed for a time, I think it could be tolerated."

Sweetwater considered for another long moment. "I suppose it could work for a while." His eyes narrowed. "Now, can I ask you a question?"

Wainwright gave a barely perceptible nod. "Go ahead."

"I've heard about your feelings and past dealings with Indians, even partial-bloods," Sweetwater said. "Can *you* stand having this breed around as part of our outfit?"

Answering with little or no hesitation, Wainwright said, "For what is at stake in the long run, yes. I'm convinced I can."

"I've got to tell you," Sweetwater said frankly, "this whole line of talk comes as a pretty big surprise."

"Let me try to explain. At a very low point in the late war, President Lincoln was casting about for a winning general to command our troops and first considered Grant. We've all heard the story of how several of his advisors brought up the subject of Grant's heavy drinking, to which Lincoln replied, 'Then find out what kind of whiskey he drinks, so I can have some of it sent to all of my other generals.'"

Sweetwater nodded agreeably, indicating he was familiar with the tale.

Wainwright went on. "But another discussion between Lincoln and his advisors took place that never got widely circulated because it was a bit too vulgar to be considered in good taste. Someone mentioned how Grant always stank of cigar smoke and horse piss and spending any time inside a tent with him was highly unpleasant, to which Abe replied, 'I don't care what he smells like. I can stand the stink of a little smoke and piss inside my tent if they're accompanied by the smell of victory.'"

Sweetwater managed a grin. "For us, so it is with Buckhorn."

"Exactly," Wainwright said. "If it will help keep things under control until the mechanisms of my greater overall plan start to turn, I can stand some Indian stink inside my tent."

CHAPTER 21

Buckhorn saw the stagecoach rolling into town as he was crossing the street, headed toward the livery stable after dropping off a bundle of soiled clothes at the house of a washerwoman recommended by Isobel Fletchler. He'd previously noticed the Chalmers & Obrey stage office located at equal angles across the street from the Traveler's Rest and the other, larger hotel in the next block, but it was the first sign he'd seen any activity around the place. He recalled hearing somebody say that the coach made a twice-weekly run from Farragut to the northeast.

"Look at 'em," said Nick Hebly, the stable proprietor, from where he stood to one side of the open barn door with a three-tined pitchfork over one shoulder. He was watching the handful of townsfolk milling around the general area of the stage office, hanging back a bit until the roiling clouds that had followed the coach in had a chance to settle down.

"Circling around like a bunch of hungry crows watching to see if any juicy-looking kernels of corn drop off the picking wagon as it rolls in out of the field. It's the same way two days out of every week, like the blame fools ain't ever seen a stagecoach before or like they expect somebody who really amounts to something is gonna climb out and step down."

"You have a bleak outlook on the human condition, my friend," Buckhorn told him. "All they're looking for is a break in the monotony of their lives, maybe a glimmer of something or somebody new and exciting."

Hebly was a long-necked, narrow-shouldered specimen with a bulbous potbelly pushing against the front of the bib overalls he wore over pink long underwear with the sleeves hacked off at the shoulders. His long, stringy-muscled arms were pale, almost sickly white above the elbows. In response to Buckhorn's remark, he said, "Huh. They wouldn't know excitement if it came along and bit them on the butt. Nobody paid any particular attention to you when you first showed up, did they? And then, lickety-split, you turned into the most excitement we've seen around here since . . . since . . ."

"You keep working on it, you'll think of something," Buckhorn said. "In the meantime, I'm gonna see my horse."

"Your horse is fine. I'm taking good care of him."

"I know you are. If I thought otherwise, he wouldn't be here. I'm just gonna talk to him a minute, let him know what's going on. He gets lonesome if he doesn't see me regular."

Nick reached up to scratch his head. "I never heard of a horse getting lonesome, not when there's other horses around. You say you're gonna talk things over with him?"

"That's right." Buckhorn started into the barn and

back toward Sarge's stall. "In this case, I figure I may have to tell him a joke or two."

"Jokes? You tell your horse jokes?"

"Not always," Buckhorn said over his shoulder, "but if I keep him penned up here around you and your sour disposition for very long, I may have to take drastic measures in order to keep him from coming down with a case of melancholy."

When he was finished at the stable, Buckhorn headed back to his room. He still had more than an hour until he was scheduled to meet with Justine. He figured he'd use the time to strip down and clean his guns. Any man who made his living in Buckhorn's line of work was a damn fool and destined for a short career and a short life if he didn't religiously take care of his weapons.

It was still cool in the room though the sunshine pouring into the street outside promised another scorcher of a day by the middle of the afternoon. Buckhorn spread out his gear atop the small writing desk, his well-practiced fingers going nimbly through the necessary motions as if they had minds and eyes all their own. He started with the derringer, his habit being to work with only one gun at a time, never having all of them broken down and unloaded at once.

The knock on the door caused his right hand to drop automatically and come to rest on the grips of his still-holstered Colt. He sat out of direct line of the doorway. "Yes? Who is it?"

A male voice answered. "I have a message for Mr. Joe Buckhorn."

"A message from who? I don't know anybody in this town."

"I brought it in on the stage. Be a lot easier if I just handed it to you. Let you read it for yourself."

Buckhorn rose to his feet and walked over to stand on what would be the back side of the door when it opened. Drawing the Colt and letting it rest down along his thigh, he said, "Door's unlocked. Come ahead in."

The door opened and the man behind the voice entered slowly but not hesitantly, sweeping one hand to close the door again behind him and then glancing over to look at Buckhorn as if expecting him to be exactly where he was.

The visitor was tall, thirtyish, thin almost to the point of looking like a stick figure clad in a light blue frock coat, darker blue trousers with a pinstripe pattern, and a wide-brimmed, pale yellow plantation hat. His sparse sideburns were a rusty brown in color, matched by brows of the same above washed-out blue eyes. In his right hand he carried a sealed envelope.

"Good morning, sir. Thank you for seeing me without prior arrangement." He shifted the envelope to his opposite hand and extended his right, adding, "My name is Martin Goodwin."

Buckhorn continued to hold the Colt down at his side and made no attempt to shake the offered hand. "You said something about a message."

"Yes. Of course. Right here." Goodwin held out the envelope.

Buckhorn took it, glanced down at it briefly, then lifted his eyes once again to meet Goodwin's expectant gaze. "If that's all, I thank you for your time and trouble."

An awkward pause followed during which Goodwin grew visibly a bit flustered. "I . . . er . . . I was expecting you would read the message before excusing me. I think that's what Mr. Haydon—the sender—expected, too. After you've seen what he has to say, I believe there'll be a good deal more details for you and I to discuss."

"Mr. Haydon, you say? Andrew Haydon?" Buckhorn glanced again at the envelope in his hand. "He sent you with this?"

"Yes. That is correct."

Buckhorn regarded Goodwin more closely, running his eyes up and down the considerable length of him. "You armed?"

Goodwin grinned sheepishly, holding his coat open wide. "No. It's not a habit I ever developed. Though I've become increasingly aware, the farther I travel west, what an oddity that seems to make me."

"Don't call it odd," Buckhorn said. "One of the best things about the West is that it gives a man the freedom to make his own choices. Not that I'm saying going around unheeled is a particularly smart one, mind you. But if that *is* your choice, stick to it and don't sound like you're apologizing for it."

"All right. I'll remember that," said Goodwin.

Buckhorn jabbed a thumb at the room. "I'm not set up real good for visitors, so you'll have to settle for the edge of the bed. Take a seat, give me a chance to have a look at what this has to say, then we can do our talking or whatever from there."

Resuming his own seat at the writing table, Buckhorn tore the envelope open and found Haydon's message to be a handwritten note.

Buckhorn,

Hope this finds you safely arrived in Wagon Wheel by now and engaged in the matter you were sent to deal with. In the meantime, my further investigations into the situation out there have revealed that the area's water shortage problem is something Wainwright is using for great advantage in whatever he is up to. Given that, I have sent along Mr. Goodwin, a renowned dowser who has had great luck finding underground water sources where none were previously known to be. It occurred to me that someone of his ilk showing up at this time might go a long way toward rattling Wainwright good and proper and thereby aiding you in knocking him off his perch. Use Goodwin as you see fit. If nothing else, to give the good folks out there some hope for relief in their water needs.

Sincerely,
Haydon

Buckhorn carefully read the message through twice, then lowered the piece of paper, smiling. He admired Haydon's craftiness as well as his determination to do whatever it took to bring down his hated former captor.

While no immediate plan on how to use Goodwin's skills leaped to Buckhorn's mind, he certainly could see how the revelation of them would be viewed as a threat by Wainwright. How *rattled* the former general would be was yet to be determined. But if it *did* cause a strong reaction, that was something Buckhorn had to be prepared to use to his advantage.

"You know what this says?" Buckhorn asked Goodwin, holding up the paper.

"I was there when Haydon wrote it."

"Then you understand he didn't send you down here to provide water for the lemonade stand at the Sunday school picnic."

"I understand fully the ramifications of what my being here might mean." Goodwin's jaw muscles bunched visibly and his washed-out blue eyes took on an intensity Buckhorn wouldn't have guessed possible. "The thing you need to understand, Mr. Buckhorn, is that my brother was in that same Northern prison as Haydon. He didn't make it out alive. My parents' demands on the Army for the details of his death came to the attention of Mr. Haydon. Unpleasant though the task was, he took the time to journey a long distance—displaying what he himself had lost in that hellhole—to fill them in on the brave struggle Virgil had fought before finally succumbing to the torturous conditions. It soothed them greatly."

"Knowing Haydon even just a little bit, I can see him doing that."

Goodwin's eyes held their intensity. "So when he asked me to come out here and see if my dowsing skills could be of any assistance to you and at the same time work to the disfavor of General Wainwright . . . well, any inconvenience or danger that might also be involved was not really an issue."

Buckhorn nodded. "Bravely spoken. At the same time, it sorta brings us back around to that other subject we touched on a minute ago. Namely, you not wearing a gun."

"For the record," Goodwin said, holding up a finger to make his point, "I said I don't make a habit of carrying a gun. That wasn't meant to imply I don't know anything about them or am in some way opposed to their use under necessary conditions. As a matter of fact, though I'm probably a little rusty, at one time I was quite proficient with a hunting rifle."

"That's a start, I guess," Buckhorn said, trying not to smile. "How about a handgun?"

Goodwin shook his head. "Never had call to use one . . . but I'd be willing to get one, acquire the feel for it if you believe it's necessary."

"I don't know. Carrying a gun and not knowing how to use it can be as bad or worse than not having one at all." Buckhorn frowned. "I've got to think on this some. When you do this dowsing thing of yours, how do you go about it?"

"I look over the land, study its contours," Goodwin explained. "When I decide on some places that look promising, I bring out my dowsing rod and use it to see if it can help me pick the best spot to sink an artesian well."

"Dowsing rod? Artesian well? To me you're practically speaking a foreign language."

Goodwin smiled tolerantly. "A dowsing rod, sometimes called a divining rod, is an instrument used for pinpointing an underground water source. There are those who also claim it can be used for locating rich ore or buried treasure, even buried bodies in criminal cases of searches for lost loved ones. But finding underground water is by far the most common practice. Some consider it a science, some plain bunk, some a Satanic device. In any event, it usually involves an instrument such as a Y-shaped hazel or witch hazel twig, like I use, that is held in a certain way and moved around above ground until it dips downward, indicating the presence of water below the surface. An artesian well is a nonpumping type of well where a hollow point is driven down until it hits the water source, which, because it's under great pressure, jets to the surface."

"No offense," Buckhorn said, arching a brow skeptically, "but fresh out of the gate, I'm afraid you'd have to put me in the category of thinking it sounds like bunk. You really believe there's a chance of finding water, no matter by what method, in this arid land?"

"I studied the contour of the terrain out the stagecoach window as we were coming in and, yes, I believe there's a chance. Some of the low-lying areas would naturally be the most likely. But you have to remember that the great High Plains Aquifer runs all the way down from Nebraska and the Dakotas and reaches into Texas and pieces of New Mexico off to the east. No reason to think that some outlying pockets of it couldn't be found over this way as well."

"Now you just spit out another foreign word. *Aquifer*?"

"It's an underground water table contained by layers of permeable rock. Pressure in this rock layer has been built up for tens of thousands of years. That's why, when it's tapped, the water is forced to the surface."

Buckhorn shook his head. "You make it all sound too simple, too easy. In that case, why is there ever a shortage of water for anybody anywhere?"

"Because it's *not* that simple or easy. For one thing, there aren't aquifers everywhere. Maybe there's not one here." Goodwin paused and his mouth curved into a faintly sly smile. "But even if there isn't, if I start going through the motions with my dowsing and it's enough to cause Wainwright to *believe* I have the chance of finding alternative water, won't that pretty much accomplish what Haydon sent me in hopes of doing?"

CHAPTER 22

The lunch with Justine York was pleasant, and no doubt would have been even more so if Buckhorn hadn't been somewhat distracted by thoughts of Martin Goodwin showing up and how his presence might best be used against Wainwright.

Luckily, Goodwin hadn't mentioned Buckhorn's name upon arriving in town nor had he made any inquiries as far as seeking him out. That was all taken care of when he opted to also take a room at the Traveler's Rest. As he was signing the register, there it was a couple lines above his—Buckhorn's own sign-in from earlier and the original room number scratched out and corrected to the current one. That was Goodwin's basis for knowing where to go when he'd paid his visit.

After talking, the two men had agreed that they would continue to avoid letting anyone know they had any association. They would meet covertly—the next time scheduled for after the patrons of the hotel had turned in—until they came up with a plan for utilizing Goodwin in the most effective way possible.

Ironically, while Buckhorn was attempting to keep

the lunchtime conversation with Justine focused on something lighter, it was she who dragged in the subject of Thomas Wainwright and his operation. "I think these recent displays of escalating violence are indicators of one of two things. Either Wainwright is getting ready to move on to the next phase of whatever his land-grabbing has been leading up to all along . . . or his plans aren't moving fast enough and he's trying to shake things up in order to get back on pace."

"Sudden violence has a way of moving things off dead center, that's for sure," Buckhorn said. "But I kinda figured—not that it's the way I wanted it, mind you—that a lot of folks around here would be looking to blame *me* for the gunplay that keeps popping up."

"Well, no denying you've been involved in more than your share. But it was always a matter of self-defense," Justine pointed out. "Nobody can blame you for that. Those three Flying W riders who were ambushed out on the range. Nobody knows *who* they ran up against, but that wasn't you."

"Yeah, the common thing in all cases is that it was Wainwright men who got dead. That might count as shaking things up, but to keep having your own cut down hardly seems like a good rallying tactic."

"The ones who fell to you weren't necessarily meant to be the ones cut down. You were. Had it gone that way, those who forced your hand would have been praised and anybody else riding for the Flying W brand would have been swept up in the momentum. Could even be that those first three victims were slackers who got gunned down as examples to help make the point."

Buckhorn said, "Anything's possible, I guess. For your sake, I just hope the stuff you put in that newspaper of yours—this special edition you're running, and otherwise—sticks to the facts and doesn't amount to stretching your neck out too far on speculation."

"I know all about running a newspaper. I learned from the best," Justine said coolly. "I know what to label as fact and when and how to speculate in an editorial. Wainwright damn well knows I know these things and the fact he's never retaliated against me, even though I've burned him in my pages more than once, proves he knows the power of the press."

"Was the same true when your husband was running the paper? Did he set himself against Wainwright, too?"

Justine frowned. "How do you know about my husband?"

Buckhorn shrugged. "Heard some things here and there. Carl said your husband was a real newshound, had newspapering in his blood. When you said a minute ago that you learned from the best, I took that to mean you were talking about him."

"I was. But I really don't feel comfortable talking about Gerald."

"Was he still alive when Wainwright started muscling in on more and more land?"

"Yes, he was. But I said I'd rather not talk about it."

"Sure. Whatever you say." Buckhorn leaned back in his chair, feeling bad for having leaned a little hard on the widow . . . but he still had things he wanted to know. "Let's go back to Wainwright then, and this big plan you think he's cooking up beyond just amassing land. Any idea what he's got in mind?"

Justine shook her head. "Don't I wish. Most people can't seem to see it at all. They see him gobbling the land and controlling the water and a lot of them don't like it, but that's as far as it goes. Those who've lost land or water rights to him bemoan only their own fates, and those who've gone untouched directly cling to the hope the drought won't last and they'll scrape by. They either *can't* or *don't want to* see that there's some bigger picture forming.

"Wainwright's claimed practically enough land for a small state and gathered enough hired guns for a small army. That's without mentioning the riders and wranglers he employs for his ranching operation. And since he's married Lusita, God knows how many in-laws he can also call on."

"How's that again?"

"About two years ago," Justine explained, "Wainwright married Lusita, an absolutely stunning creature, much younger than the general, and the daughter of Don Pedro Olomoso, a big rancher and mine owner just across the border. The marriage obviously formed a bond between the two powerful men. An offspring, which seemed obvious to everybody, was a big part of the union since Wainwright had no heirs—would have strengthened it even more. So far, no heir has entered the picture but that hasn't kept Wainwright and Don Pedro from growing chummier."

"You think this Mexican don is part of Wainwright's bigger plan?"

"Could be. I've thought of that, but can't really see the gain for either side. Whatever was added by a partnership would have to be split and shared by that same partnership. They have roughly equal amounts of land, though Wainwright's is better for raising beef. His herd is much larger and of better quality than the don's, from what I understand, and he has better established markets. What Don Pedro lacks in cattle-raising capacity he makes up for by silver-mining potential from the Barranaca Mountains that fall partly within his land—*if* he can keep the Indians who prowl there off the backs of his miners. From all reports, he seems to have finally killed or driven off most of them. After he's cleared the way, the Mexican government will be poised to move in and claim their share of any silver that comes out."

"Sounds like Wainwright, for sure, would come out on the short end of the stick by risking a fight with the Yaquis *and* the Mexican government if he threw in with the don."

"Except he likes fighting Indians, remember," Justine said. "And you can bet that any partnership between those two rascals would be geared toward dodging the Mexican government or anybody else who tried to trim their profits. Never forget that the lure of silver or gold has fogged the mind of many men, especially with somebody like Lusita adding some steam to the picture."

Buckhorn arched a brow. "You make her sound mighty bewitching."

Justine smiled crookedly. "She is. Or could be. I just don't know if she realizes it or not. She may be more an innocent victim than a temptress wielding influence. Either way, it unfortunately doesn't provide any answers as far as whatever it is I'm convinced Wainwright is planning—in cahoots with Don Pedro or alone."

They'd finished their main courses and were considering the question of dessert. Also, they were into the noon hour proper and the popular restaurant was rapidly starting to fill up.

"I think I'll pass on dessert," Justine decided, "but don't let me stop you. The Groelsch sisters make pies that are even better than their other dishes. You oughtn't deprive yourself of some."

"Naw, that's okay," Buckhorn said. "I might stop in

for a slice and a cup of coffee later on, but I'm plenty full for now."

"You could do both. You'll wish you had, once you try some. As for me, I need to get back to the shop. I still have plenty to do in order to get that special edition out. Let me take care of our bill so we can make room for somebody else."

"That's pretty awkward for me," Buckhorn protested. "Let me go ahead and take care of the bill."

"Nonsense. This is repayment for helping yesterday with that wagonload of paper stock and . . . well, with Carl, too. We're both extremely grateful."

"If you insist. You know, Carl stopped by earlier . . . to thank me in person."

"Yes, I was aware."

"That was mighty decent of him."

Justine smiled. "I'm glad you think so. Mainly, I'm glad you got to meet him when he was in a better condition."

"So am I."

Justine had just finished paying and they were starting to leave when gunshots exploded from the street outside. One . . . two . . . three.

The pacing of the shots was very measured and deliberate. Unhurried, somehow not particularly threatening. Nevertheless, Buckhorn shoved Justine behind him and stepped out, his Colt gliding smoothly to his fist. Up and down the dusty, sun-washed midday street, people were scrambling frantically, ducking into the nearest doorways.

All except one man who stood in the center of Front Street, facing the Silver Dollar Saloon. He was a young man, not much past twenty, hatless but otherwise decked out in standard range wear. The sun glistened brightly on his headful of unruly reddish hair. His left hand was closed around a small box of some sort.

 Hanging loosely in his right, pointed downward at the moment, was a converted Navy revolver with a wisp of smoke curling up from the end of the barrel.

CHAPTER 23

The young man lifted his face and shouted at the upper half of the Silver Dollar, "Hully Markham, you double-crossing, backstabbing son of a bitch, show your ugly stinking face! Right now!"

His words got no reaction.

The street was mostly empty, except for faces peeking around the corners of doorways and Buckhorn standing motionless on the boardwalk out front of the Good Eats Café.

The man in the middle of the street hollered again. "Hully! I know you're up there and you can hear me, you spineless coward. Don't make me come get you!"

Again there was no response to the demands from the man in the street. Not right away.

Then, accompanied by some muttering and cursing, some movement appeared on the second-floor balcony that ran across the face of the saloon building. As was common to establishments like the Silver Dollar, it served a row of rooms whose windows could be seen above the colorfully painted banister enclosing the balcony. The rooms were the cribs of the soiled doves who worked the Dollar and, on warm summer nights when cowboys were in town, the banister served as a showcase for the gals to advertise their wares in hopes of attracting customers.

What came on display, however, was something quite different. It involved a soiled dove, but only one—a pretty though somewhat plump little number who called herself Gladys. Her bright orange hair shone in the sun and spilled frothily down over her bare, freckled shoulders and got lost in the filmy folds of the gauzy robe she clutched closed at the front, scarcely containing a pair of oversized breasts.

Standing close beside and partly behind her was a very anxious-looking man in an unbuttoned white shirt and a pair of faded denim trousers. He looked roughly the same age as the one hollering down in the street, somewhat leaner, with a dimpled chin in need of a shave and a prominent Adam's apple that right at the moment was doing a lot of bobbing up and down.

"Oney-Bob," called down Gladys in a trembling voice, "what in the world are you causing such a ruckus for? You're making a dreadful and embarrassing scene is what you're doing!"

"Well, you'd better get used to it, Gladys, on account of I got a lot more to get to afore I'm finished," said the young man addressed as Oney-Bob. "You and that yellow dog Hully Markham have made a fool out of me and put me in a state fit to be tied. You, Gladys, I am through with, even though it breaks my heart. But I ain't through with that Hully, not by a bucket full! The only question is whether or not he's got the stones to face me like a man or I have to chase him down to take out of his hide what he deserves!"

"You need to simmer down, Oney-Bob, if you know what's good for you." Hully thrust his chin out defiantly as he said this, but all the time he kept his hands on Gladys's meaty shoulders and made sure he kept her pushed partly in front of him.

"What's good for me is what's gonna be bad for you, you snake in the dirt!" Oney-Bob snapped back.

Smiles were starting to appear on the faces of some of those peeking out of the doorways, and Buckhorn even heard a few titters of nervous laughter as the realization started to sink in that what they were witnessing was a pair of jealous cowboys vying for the favor of the same dove.

To Buckhorn's way of thinking, that smoking gun still in the grip of Oney-Bob wasn't quite so funny. He was relieved when he glanced up the street and saw Deputy Gates—the only lawman left in town, what with the sheriff and Deputy Pomeroy and some other men gone off to investigate the site of where those Flying W men had been found shot—walking measuredly toward where the surly exchange was taking place.

As he drew closer, the deputy spoke in an easy, soothing tone. "Hey there, Oney-Bob. What's all this hollering and carrying-on about?"

"Watch out, Deputy," called down Hully. "He's got a gun and he's been drinking. He can be wild mean when he gets like this."

Oney-Bob paid no attention to Gates. His blazing eyes just kept staring up at the Silver Dollar balcony. "You only *think* you've seen me wild mean," he said through clenched teeth. "You wait till I get my hands on you, Hully, then you'll feel it up close and personal."

"Come on now, that's no way to talk," said Deputy Gates. "You and Hully been pals for a long spell. Whatever's gone wrong between you can surely be worked out without threats like that, can't it?"

"No! How can I be pals with a skunk who'd do me

like he done? He promised me—both of 'em did—
that he'd stay away from her."

"That ain't true," Gladys wailed. "I never promised
such. How could I, a gal in my position?"

"There's sense to what she's saying," Gates pointed
out. "You can see that, can't you, Oney-Bob? After all,
Gladys is a . . . well, having fellas up to her room is
what she *does.*"

"You think I don't know that? How do you reckon I
met her?" Oney-Bob said, his face reddening. "Even
though I love her, I can understand how she has to do
her job, make her living. I don't like it, but I can tolerate it. Leastways until I'm ready to take her away from
that life."

"But then why . . ."

"A quick poke is one thing," Oney-Bob explained.
"Like I said, I can tolerate that. There's nothing personal in it, it's just a matter of doing some business and
getting things over with. But all night, now that's another matter. That's where things get, whatyacall . . .
intimate. That's how I come to fall in love with Gladys
in the first place, and her with me. I'm gonna take
her away from here and we're gonna get married just
as soon as I can scrape together enough taking-off
money."

"That's a dream, Oney-Bob. You lunkhead!" hollered
Gladys. "I got that same dream with a half dozen of my
other regular gentlemen callers. But we all know it
ain't true, ain't ever gonna really happen. Everybody
knows it except you, I guess. You silly damn fool."

"Yeah, everybody but me . . ." As he said it, Oney-
Bob made a motion with his left hand and cast onto
the dusty street the little box he'd been holding. As it
hit, the box popped open and a ring with a large

sparkly stone fell out. "And there's the engagement ring this silly damn fool was bringing you."

"Oh, Oney," said Gladys, her chin trembling.

"That's too bad, Oney-Bob. I'm sorry," Gates said, sounding genuinely sincere. "But that still don't mean you can go around shooting and threatening over it. Now, how about you put the gun down, too? Or, better yet, just hand it over to me."

Oney-Bob's whole body suddenly went rigid. "No!" His gun hand swung up and he turned toward the deputy, who'd taken a step closer and was holding out his hand. "Stay out of this, Gates, or you'll force me to hurt more than just that damn Hully. He's got to get his desserts, get what's coming to him. He knew how I felt about Gladys, even knew I was coming here today to give her that ring. And he for damn sure knew how I felt about her doing all-nighters, especially with the likes of him!"

"That's right. I knew all those things," Hully admitted. "And I know something else, too. I know she's nothing but a whore, Oney-Bob! That's what I wanted to try and get sunk into that thick skull of yours afore you went and made an even bigger fool of yourself. I *wanted* you to hear I was up here with her in order to get that point across. I just didn't figure you'd come gunning for me over it!"

"Well, then you figured exactly wrong, didn't you?" Oney-Bob twisted back to face Hully again, but the latter slid even farther in back of Gladys, giving Oney no clear target without the risk of hitting the gal he'd thought to be the love of his life.

"Here now!" Gates said, bringing his hand to rest on the grips of the hogleg holstered on his hip. "You're gonna fool around and get somebody hurt,

Oney-Bob. If you don't drop that gun, you're gonna force me to make it be you."

Oney's eyes whipped back and forth between Gates and Hully. His whole body was starting to tremble with rage and frustration. He couldn't shoot the man he wanted to—Hully—for fear of hitting Gladys, but he badly wanted to shoot somebody.

Buckhorn recognized the young man was working himself into the kind of blind fury where he was going to cut loose one way or another. Gates had better do more than just *rest* his hand on that hogleg, Buckhorn thought to himself, if he knows what's good for him.

In that same long, tense moment, Buckhorn spotted movement in one of the doorways across the street, behind and slightly off center from where Oney-Bob stood. The doorway was that of the *Sun Ledger* newspaper office. As Buckhorn watched, Carl Orndecker stepped out of the shadows and came to stand silently in his doorway, much like Buckhorn was doing in the doorway of the café, also with a revolver raised and ready.

Buckhorn heard Justine emit a soft gasp from in back of him.

"Damn it, Oney, enough is enough," Deputy Gates declared. "I want that gun, and I want it right now!" He took another step forward, his left hand reaching for Oney's gun, his right still resting on his own still-holstered sidearm.

The fury inside Oney-Bob broke wide open. "Stop meddlin', damn it!" he shouted, thrusting his pistol to arm's length and firing point-blank at Gates.

Oney got off a second shot as the deputy spun away and started to fall but, in the same instant, Carl Orndecker started shooting from the newspaper doorway. He punched two slugs through Oney-Bob's extended arm, causing the limb to flop uselessly and the Navy to fall from nerveless fingers.

Instead of also firing on the hapless Oney, some instinct told Buckhorn to concentrate on Hully. It paid off when, as soon as Oney was eliminated as a threat, the open-shirted man shoved aside the frantically wailing Gladys and raised a previously concealed pistol that he promptly aimed down at the pal whose love life he'd allegedly been out to assist.

Buckhorn's Colt spoke first. The .45 caliber slug smashed into Hully's shoulder and knocked him clean off his feet. The unfired hideaway gun dropped over the edge of the banister and onto the street below.

It was over that quick. An eerie silence settled briefly in its wake, broken only by the sobs and wails of Gladys, who lay in a heap on the floor of the balcony where Hully had shoved her.

CHAPTER 24

"Much as I hate to admit it," Paul Banning said, his scowl deepening as it shifted back and forth between Buckhorn and Orndecker, "I guess I owe you two a debt of gratitude. If you hadn't stepped in the way you did, there's no telling how much damage Oney-Bob would've done after he put down my man Gates. Hell, for that matter he might not have been done with Gates. He might have gone ahead and killed him and then gone on from there."

"So how is Gates?" Orndecker asked.

"Doc is still working on him, but he seems pretty sure he can pull him through okay." The sheriff's expression was somber. "One bullet tore through the outside of his rib cage, that one ain't so bad. The other went in more toward the middle of his stomach and ripped up his insides pretty bad. No telling how long that's gonna lay him up or what kind of shape it's gonna leave him in even after he heals as good as he's gonna get. I left Pomeroy there to wait it out until the doc had the final stitching done and could give us a more complete report."

"What about us?" Hully Markham called from his

cell. "They took Gates right to the doctor's office, where he's got everything for the most proper care and treatment. Me and Oney, the doc just took time to stop the bleeding and wrap our wounds, then said it was okay to lock us up until he could get to us and do more."

"So what's your point?" Banning asked testily.

"My point is we still ain't been proper took care of. I hurt like hell and some blood is leaking through my bandage. It looks like the same for Oney-Bob. He's laying passed out over there on his bunk."

"He's still breathing, I can hear him snore. Good enough, says I. It's better than either of you deserve, so consider yourselves lucky and shut up with your complaining."

Nearly three hours had passed since the shooting in the street out front of the Silver Dollar Saloon. With Deputy Gates seriously wounded and no other lawmen readily available, Buckhorn and Orndecker had taken charge of things. The town's only doctor was summoned. Like Hully had said, he temporarily treated the feuding cowboys right there in the street and then turned his full attention on Gates, having him moved to his office where he could work most effectively on the deputy's more serious injuries.

While that was going on, Buckhorn and Orndecker, relying largely on the latter's familiarity with the procedures and layout of things from his days of wearing a badge, had marched the wounded cowboys to the jail, where they'd locked them in separate cells and waited for Banning to show up.

"How about the ambush scene? Any luck out there?" Orndecker said after the sheriff had quieted the whining Hully.

Banning shook his head wearily. "None to speak of.

Couldn't even tell for sure how many did the shooting. Whoever did it went to a fair amount of work to hide their sign and made a good job of it. We couldn't tell which direction they came from or which direction they headed out, either one."

"Bad luck for all your trouble," said Orndecker. "And then more bad news when you made it back here."

"Could be worse," Banning said, his mouth twisting ruefully. "At least there ain't nobody dead this time. And neither of the two cowboys you shot are Flying W riders."

Buckhorn's mouth twisted. "I must be slipping. Last night only one of the two I killed was Flying W. Today, it not only wasn't a Wainwright man I shot, but I didn't even manage to kill him."

Banning gave him a look. "It's a good thing I know you're only joking. You *are*, right?"

Buckhorn didn't bother answering.

Heaving a sigh, Orndecker shoved himself up out of the straight-backed wooden chair he'd been occupying. "I'm not joking, either, when I say I'd better get back over to the newspaper office or Justine will be coming after my hide. She wanted to add another piece about this afternoon's incident into that special edition she's getting ready to run, which meant having to write it and then shifting the layout to make it fit. She's likely got that done by now, but there'll still be some things I can help with to get the press ready. So if you gentlemen will excuse me . . ."

As he started for the door, Buckhorn stood up, too. "Reckon I'm done here as well."

To which the sheriff quickly said, "If you can hold on another minute, Buckhorn, I'd like to have a word with you."

Caught a little by surprise, Buckhorn stayed where he was. Shrugging, he said, "All right."

Looking past him, Banning said to Orndecker, "Thanks again for stepping in and helping out today, Carl. I appreciate it. And I mean that."

Orndecker managed his own shrug. "Not a problem, Paul. It was the right thing to do, that's all. Plus, hell, it felt kinda good to get back into the harness again." He hesitated to jab a finger at the chair he'd been sitting in. "All except for that torture rack thing. Can't the county afford better chairs than that for visitors to your office? I'd wager you got more comfortable accommodations in the blasted cells."

"I'll keep that in mind and try to squeeze it into the next budget," Banning told him.

"You do that." Halfway out the door, Orndecker paused again and cut a glance over at Buckhorn. "Don't forget my offer from earlier."

When Orndecker was gone, Banning said, "I suppose whatever that was about is none of my business."

"You'd be right," Buckhorn said. "But I'll tell you anyway. Has to do with him offering to stand watch so I can get a good night's sleep tonight without having to worry about it turning permanent from another round of gun blasts."

Banning considered that a moment before saying, "Comes to that, you couldn't have much better than Carl Orndecker looking out for you . . . as long as he stays sober."

"He's sober today," Buckhorn said. "And he looked pretty darn good out there on the street earlier."

"Like I said, before the bottle started getting the better of him, there wasn't hardly a better lawman and not too many gunmen better than Carl." Banning gestured to the chair Buckhorn had only recently vacated.

"Don't know if those things are really as torturous as Carl let on but, if you sit back down, I'll tell you a few things you might find interesting."

Buckhorn returned to his chair.

"It was a woman who caused it. Caused Carl to crawl into the bottle, that is." Banning jerked a thumb toward the holding cells. "Ironically, the final straw came as the result of a situation not too different from the one those two fools brought on today. A pretty little saloon singer showed up in town. You probably know the kind. She liked to play both ends against the middle when it came to men. Lead a couple different ones on and watch 'em squirm in their efforts to be number one.

"Only trouble was, this little tease wasn't careful enough or smart enough not to choose men who were too dangerous to be toyed with. One was a gambler named Lloyd, the other was Carl. Came the night Lloyd demanded she quit playing her silly games and say what was what. She laughed in his face so he shot and killed her. Then Carl shot and killed him. After that, even though everybody else was willing to overlook the whole thing, Carl couldn't get over it. He didn't blame the saloon singer, like he should have. No, he blamed himself for letting her get shot . . . and for not killing Lloyd sooner."

"So he crawled into a bottle to blot it all out," Buckhorn summed up.

"About the size of it. When he realized he was drinking too much to do his job proper, he turned in his badge and went away. He came back after a while, after Justine's husband died, but he wasn't much better. He goes in spurts where he can stay sober for a spell. But then . . . well, you got a firsthand look yesterday how he can take a dive."

"Sounds like a hard-luck tale," Buckhorn said. "But most everybody's got one, in one form or other. They find different ways to deal with it. As far as the ones who turn into drunks, it comes down to only one person who does the elbow bending and the pouring of rotgut down their throats."

"Kind of a hard way of looking at it, wouldn't you say?"

"I got my reasons."

"I suppose you do."

Buckhorn shifted in his chair. "You didn't ask me to stick around so you could tell me the sad tale of Carl Orndecker and get my sour outlook on it. So what else was it you wanted to talk about?"

Banning started to say something but then stopped short. He cast a sideways glance over at the holding cells. Oney-Bob was still snoring loudly and Hully had rolled over onto one side, favoring his injured shoulder, to face the wall. Maybe asleep, maybe only feigning it.

"On second thought," the sheriff said, "let's step outside and talk in the fresh air. We'll have more privacy, plus it's kinda rank in here."

Outside, the heat of the day still hung in the air up and down the length of Front Street. Afternoon shadows from the building peaks along the west side were just beginning to lengthen. Within one such shadow under the narrow porch overhang out front of the sheriff's office, Buckhorn and Banning found moderate relief out of the direct sun.

Banning put both hands to the small of his back and stretched his torso straight back and then to either side. "Hate to admit it, but I've allowed myself to get so damned deskbound lately the ride back and forth to the ambush site stiffened me up something fierce."

"It'll happen," Buckhorn said.

Continuing to stretch, the sheriff said, "While we were there, Thomas Wainwright rode out to pay a visit. To check and see if we were going about our investigation properly, I reckon, since it was his men who got cut down and all. He didn't complain, so I guess what he saw suited him well enough. Before he left, though, he gave me a message. That's what I wanted to talk to you about."

Buckhorn waited.

"Before you ask," Banning went on, "I don't make a habit of serving as a messenger boy for Wainwright . . . though there's plenty around who'd be quick to doubt that. They think I'm pretty much at Wainwright's beck and call and that I hop whenever he commands. Maybe I do, at least to some degree, but so does just about everybody else around these parts."

"That's your business," Buckhorn said, getting impatient. "What's the message for me?"

Banning quit beating around the bush. "He wants to meet with you. He's invited you for dinner at his place this evening."

Buckhorn normally did a pretty good job of hiding his emotions, but his surprise at those words showed plainly on his face. "What the hell brought that on?"

"Beats me. Like I said, I'm just the messenger boy."

"Not much notice."

"Thomas Wainwright operates pretty much on his own schedule. Expects others to bend accordingly."

"And if I turn him down?"

"He really didn't give that as an option. Something else he don't expect is people turning him down." Banning cocked an eyebrow. "But if you was to make that choice, I'd advise you to plan on not wasting a lot of time riding wide of these parts."

"Is that a threat?"

"More like an interpretation. I could be wrong."

Buckhorn frowned. "Knowing the way he feels about Indians, what would make him extend an invitation like that to me?"

"Making a guess, I'd say he just might want to offer you a job as one of his hired guns. He's been bringing in top men from all over the West and here you turn up, right under his nose, showing yourself mighty handy with a shooting iron. Maybe he figures it just wouldn't be smart, Indian or no Indian, to let you slip away and ride off."

"I keep hearing about this army of hired guns Wainwright is putting together," Buckhorn said. "What is that all about, anyway?"

It was Banning's turn to form a frown. "Damned if I know. All I know is that I don't like it. I'm being kept strictly in the dark. So much for me being in tight with Wainwright, eh?" The shcriff's frown deepened. "I take that back. I do know something more, or at least feel it strongly enough so that it's like I *do* know it. Whatever Wainwright's brewing is something big. And it's going to bust wide open before very much longer."

CHAPTER 25

Buckhorn didn't have a lot of time, but he didn't need much to make up his mind. By the time he'd walked from the sheriff's office back to his hotel, he knew he would accept Thomas Wainwright's invitation to dinner. What was more, if the anticipated job offer was made, he would accept that, too.

What better way to get a closer look at the Flying W operation and maybe determine what this "something big" was that so many people seemed convinced Wainwright was up to? Also, Buckhorn reminded himself, becoming part of Wainwright's crew would surely put him in a better position for the ultimate confrontation that Haydon had hired him for.

His time in Wagon Wheel had hardly been uneventful. Suddenly, it felt like it was picking up more momentum. That's why he had to move fast.

In the second-floor hallway of the hotel, instead of going directly to his own room, Buckhorn paused before the door to room three. No one else was in the hall, so he tapped lightly on the door. Martin

Goodwin's slightly muffled voice said the door was unlocked, to come in.

When Buckhorn entered, the scene was an ironic mirror image of what had transpired in his own room only a few hours earlier. Goodwin was sitting at the writing desk with a revolver and an open box of cartridges before him.

He looked up, his mouth twisting wryly. "You should be glad to see that your advice for me to arm myself sank in. The shooting in the street that you were part of drove home the point even more. You fellas out here in the West don't mess around when it comes to settling your differences, do you?"

"You seem to be catching on," Buckhorn said. "Yet, you tell me to come on in while you sit right in the line of fire with an unloaded gun in front of you. If I'd been somebody with bad intentions in mind, what would you have done? Thrown the bullets at me, one by one? Remember what I said about the only thing worse than not having a gun is having one but not knowing how to use it?"

"Yeah, I recall you telling me that." Goodwin scowled. "I only just bought this thing a little while ago. I was hoping maybe I could get you to give me some pointers on using it. In the meantime, I was sitting here studying it and trying to get a feel for it on my own."

"Well, getting to know your weapon is never a bad idea," Buckhorn had to admit. "At least you had the sense to leave the bullets out of it while you were handling it and looking it over."

"So you'll give me some lessons, then?"

"I don't think I'll have much chance for that. But I know somebody who *could* serve that purpose, and he fits with the rest of why I ducked in to see you, anyway. You mentioned the shoot-out from a little while ago. He's the other fella who pitched in and helped take down those two troublemakers after the deputy got shot. Name's Carl Orndecker. He used to be a lawman himself, as a matter of fact."

Goodwin nodded. "Sounds like a pretty good substitute."

"I'll introduce you to Carl and also his sister. She runs the local newspaper."

Goodwin lifted his eyebrows. "I've seen her. Pretty gal. You can introduce me to pretty gals like her all you want."

"First things first," Buckhorn warned him. "Carl and Justine, to name just two around this county, have no love for Wainwright, either. Our meeting with them will be strictly business. Any *funny* business you might have in mind will have to wait until later, on your own time."

"Sure. Understood."

"How soon would you be ready to start your dowsing?" Buckhorn asked. "Have you got all the equipment you need?"

"Right there," said Goodwin, pointing to a suitcase tilted against the base of a coatrack. "I can start tomorrow. I'd want to scout the land a little more closely before picking my actual starting point is all."

"One more thing. When you do this for real—"

"I *am* doing it for real. The people around here are suffering. If I can find water, do something to ease their plight, I damn sure mean to do my best to accomplish that. Other motivations might have been involved in fetching me here but, now that I've arrived, I don't intend any fakery when it comes to my dowsing."

"That's real noble of you," Buckhorn said. "But what I was trying to get at was how it is you usually take on a dowsing job. I reckon you get paid, right? Hired by some town council or group of ranchers or the like? So what's your cover story for who hired you to come to Whitestone County?"

"I don't have one. Partly I didn't think of it, partly it would have been hard for me to come up with something on my own until I had a better sense of exactly what the situation was out here."

"That's all right. We can come up with something when we meet with Carl and Justine to go over the gun business and some other things that have come up."

"When is this meeting going to take place?" Goodwin wanted to know.

"Pretty quick. I haven't arranged anything with Carl or his sister yet, but I'm sure they'll make time for us."

"You're being rather mysterious."

"Just bear with me. I'll give you the rest of the details, at least as many as I know, in just a little while. Give me about fifteen minutes. Then I want you to go over to the newspaper office, walk in like you want to conduct some business. I'll be there by the time you arrive, but I'll have used the back way to make sure no one notices we're there at the same time. I'll fill you in, along with Carl and Justine, the rest of the way."

"Got it. It'll be good to get out and do something instead of waiting here and staring at these four walls. Fifteen minutes it is."

* * *

"Going out there amounts to almost certain suicide. You've got to be crazy to even consider it."

Buckhorn smiled wryly. "There are those who'd say that's already been established, many times over."

"Then all the more reason not to have to prove it yet again," Justine said.

"Stop and think a minute," her brother suggested. "It's far more likely Wainwright wants to hire him onto his crew of gunmen. If all he wanted was to kill Joe, he'd send hired killers to do the job *away* from his ranch."

"That's the way I see it," Buckhorn agreed. "Not to say he *eventually* won't want me dead, but for the time being I get the sense he wants to save face and take me out of the picture, only not do it with more violence. What better way to do that than to bring me into the fold where he can keep a close eye on me—maybe even get some use out of me and my gun—and then deal with me when it's a more suitable time."

"That seems awfully elaborate," Justine said stubbornly. "What would make one time more suitable than another if he intends to get around to killing you anyway?"

"Earlier, at lunch, you mentioned the recent surge in violence around here," Buckhorn reminded her. "You also said how it might signal Wainwright getting ready to spring the next phase of his big plan, whatever that is. Sheriff Banning said something similar just a little while ago about how Wainwright and the army of gunmen he's gathered feel like something big is ready to bust open. So more fringe violence, like the shooting this afternoon and the other stuff I've ended up in the thick of, could be the last thing Wainwright wants in order to keep folks from getting edgy and being on the lookout for signs of more trouble. Since I've managed to draw a fair amount of attention to myself already, him simply sending more killers after me would only attract added attention, sharpen the lookout of folks in exactly the way he wants to avoid."

The stubborn scowl on Justine's face appeared to lessen somewhat, but she still didn't look wholly convinced.

The discussion was taking place in the storeroom of the *Sun Ledger*, the rear area Buckhorn and Justine had passed through when they'd assisted a drunken Carl back to his room and then where Buckhorn had brought the bales of paper stock when he finished unloading the wagon. The four people present, including Martin Goodwin, who'd shown up as instructed, were perched on crates and bales of paper. Once the dowser had arrived and introductions had been made all around, Buckhorn had set the current exchange in motion by revealing his recent invitation to dine at the Flying W.

"So are you saying," Goodwin asked, "that if Wainwright *does* make you an offer to hire onto his crew of gunmen, you're going to accept?"

Buckhorn nodded. "That's the way I'm leaning, yeah."

"The crazy talk keeps piling up deeper and deeper," Justine said, shaking her head as if in disbelief.

"No, it may not be so crazy at all. Not if it's used as a means to infiltrate Wainwright's operation." Carl's eyes narrowed as he pinned a hard gaze on Buckhorn. "That *is* what you mean, right?"

"Exactly," Buckhorn said. "A lot of people seem convinced that Wainwright is on the verge of something big, but nobody knows what. From the inside, I'll have a better chance of not only finding out what it is but, when the time is right, maybe I'll also have a chance to foul it up at the source."

"I don't know about crazy," said Goodwin, "but it sure sounds awfully daring."

"All the same thing," Justine muttered.

"Since you've obviously got your mind made up," Carl said, "what's the rest of it? You didn't pull us all together just to tell us what you're going to do. Unless I miss my guess, you've got some parts for us to play, too."

"Your guess is right on target," Buckhorn told him. "For starters, you and Justine need to know that Goodwin and I are here to call Wainwright to account for past deeds totally separate from the land-grabbing and whatever else he's got going here in your area. We can't give you exact details on who sent us or why, and we'll be asking that you carry on like we don't know each other. What you get out of working with us is that we'd all be pulling together against Wainwright. And, just incidentally, Goodwin might also find your area a brand-new water source."

"You said he was a dowser. You really believe in that kind of witchery?" asked Justine.

"I do," Goodwin was quick to answer. "I don't consider it witchery nor can I guarantee positive results. But if there's underground water at some reachable point around here, I have a good chance of finding it. If you care to see, I have documented evidence from many cases where I've succeeded."

"It clearly would be great for the area if water can be found," Buckhorn said. "Initially, we figure the dowsing is sure to catch the attention of Wainwright. If he believes there's even a small chance Goodwin might succeed, no telling how he'll react."

"He'll blow his stack," Carl said. "If another water source emerges, it throws everything out of kilter for him. Never mind all the rangeland he already controls and however much more he has his sights set on, another season of drought would also put the town itself at his mercy. I don't know if that's part of his big plan or not, but he's sure not likely to sit back and watch that part of it get washed away."

"One way or another, he's bound to see a reputable dowser as a threat," Buckhorn said.

"So where does that leave Mr. Goodwin?" Justine asked. "If Wainwright *does* see him as a serious threat, you realize the danger that would put him in, don't you?"

Buckhorn nodded. "Yeah, I do. That's where I was hoping we could count on some help from you and Carl. For starters, I'm asking Carl to take his offer to stand guard over me and shift it to looking out for Goodwin when he commences his dowsing."

Carl didn't waste a lot of time pondering the idea. "Comes to tying a knot in Wainwright's tail or any troublemakers he sends around, I'd be happy to pitch in."

Justine was quick to show her own spunk. "What about me? What part would I play?"

"You can take the lead in spreading word about Goodwin and his dowsing. Print up and distribute some flyers. Word of mouth. Whatever you can think of."

"Right up my alley. I wish to heck you'd have told me about this sooner. I already revised my special edition once, to fit in coverage of that latest shoot-out. I'm not sure where I could have fit it. The layout's done now and we just finished running—"

"Don't worry about it. All you gotta do is mention of the dowsing in a few places and I'm betting it will take off from there like a prairie fire."

"Yeah, I guess you're right."

"One more thing. To make it look convincing, Goodwin ought to have some kind of group behind him, some kind of financing that hired him to come here and do his dowsing. Could be four or five ranchers still holding their land, or a handful of town businessmen, or even a mix of the two. They don't have to pay anything or do anything, just be agreeable to letting their names leak out if push comes to shove."

"That shouldn't be too hard," Carl said. "There are enough hard feelings against Wainwright by enough people to find plenty to fill that bill."

"I know ones I can get. I'm sure of it," Justine agreed.

"Not to throw too big a rock into the wagon spokes," said Goodwin, "but what if we're wrong with all of this speculation? What if Wainwright's invitation to Buckhorn doesn't include a job offer? What if it's just a trap aimed at trying to kill him after all?"

"It's not like I haven't dodged clear of more than one trap in my time," Buckhorn pointed out.

"But what if this time is the one where your luck doesn't hold?"

Buckhorn smiled wryly. "Well, in that case you'll have to forgive me for taking a little less interest in what happens next."

Carl said, "If Wainwright's dinner invitation turns out to be something different altogether, meaning Buckhorn ends up neither hired on to the Flying W nor shot full of holes . . . well, I guess we take a step back and decide what to do from there."

"Wouldn't have much choice." Buckhorn's expression hardened. "Be sure to keep in mind from this point on that anybody who sides against Wainwright in any way—us, a pack of phony dowsing backers, whoever—is going up against a dangerous, ruthless bastard. You folks know what he's done around here, me and Goodwin know about some additional nastiness from his past. He may have a small army of hired guns, but the most dangerous part of his outfit remains Thomas Wainwright himself."

CHAPTER 26

Buckhorn had gotten directions to the Flying W ranch headquarters from Sheriff Banning as well as from Justine and Carl. His destination lay a little over an hour out of town, so he made sure he got a good start.

Even after all the miles he'd covered on the way from New Orleans, Sarge seemed rested and eager to get clear of the confines of the livery corral. He acted downright frisky, wanting to kick up his heels and run some, but Buckhorn held him to a more moderate pace. He didn't want to show up late for the dinner invitation but neither did he want to get there too early and appear overly eager.

Also, he wanted to roll things over in his mind some more, reevaluate matters even though he'd already covered most of them more than once.

It occurred to him that the situation he found himself in would have been handled much easier back in the old days, when his temperament was harsher and he was far less discriminating about how he completed the jobs he took on. Basically, he would have isolated Wainwright and killed him.

Those days were gone. Buckhorn still killed—when he had to. That pretty much went hand in hand with doing gun work, the only trade he knew and was skilled at. Blatant assassinations or targeting somebody from ambush were tactics he no longer resorted to.

Painted in shades of gold and orange and pink by a beautifully shimmering sunset, he rode Sarge north and west. He could feel the heat gradually lift from the air and the land. Every now and then a faint breeze stirred.

In time, they topped a moderately sharp rise. Just off to the left was the curve of Whitestone Lake. The water—the blessed water—appeared as flat and motionless as the surface of a mirror. Farther to the north, and back to the east slightly, the main house and outbuildings of the Flying W ranch headquarters were visible.

Up to this point, Buckhorn had spotted only a few scattered head of cattle. From the crest of the rise to the ranch buildings, however, he could see several hundred longhorns spread over the grassy flat. Surrounding the cluster of buildings, to keep the cattle out on the otherwise open range, was a long, unbroken row of whitewashed wooden fencing.

Buckhorn nudged Sarge down the opposite side of the rise. They hadn't gone far after reaching the flatter ground before he took note of a single rider who seemed to be waiting for them in the shadow of a jagged-topped rock outcropping a short distance ahead.

When he got closer, Buckhorn saw the rider was Leo Sweetwater.

At least, based on present circumstances and past descriptions—young, lean, sharp-eyed, dressed predominantly in black, and wearing a two-holstered gunbelt—that's who he took him to be. He sat his saddle with casual indifference, right leg hooked up over the saddle horn. A cigarette hung from one corner of his mouth.

When Buckhorn reined up before him, the rider said, "You'd be Joe Buckhorn. That right?"

"It is."

"I've heard of you. Wainwright sent me out to make sure you found your way in okay."

Buckhorn cut his eyes toward the ranch house and buildings in the distance, then back. "Unless that's not the Flying W, looks like I made it okay."

"Fat chance any other cattle pusher in these parts has a home like that. My name's Sweetwater, by the way. Leo Sweetwater. Maybe you've heard of me, too?"

"Some," Buckhorn allowed.

"I'd offer to shake hands," Sweetwater said, a thin smile playing across his mouth, "but you know how they tell it in the dime novels. A couple blazing-fast pistoleros like us can't risk having our gun hand caught in the grip of somebody else's, right?"

"Yup. Nothing like those dime novels for hitting a thing accurate," Buckhorn said. "Although, in your case, since you pack two guns, I guess you'd still have a gun hand free."

"That's the general idea of packing two. I see you don't subscribe to that particular belief."

Buckhorn shrugged. "Always managed to get the job done with one. Besides, I can't hit a barn with my off hand."

"Most can't." Sweetwater smiled. "But I can. Equal. Maybe we'll find the chance for me to give you some pointers sometime."

"That'd be real interesting."

"First things first, though. We'd better get you on up to the house. The general plain don't like tardiness."

Sweetwater swung his right leg down and toed the stirrup as he leaned to mash out his cigarette against the rock outcrop, then the men set out at an easy gait for the ranch headquarters.

"You joining in on the dinner?" Buckhorn asked.

"Nope. I ain't invited. I've sat at the big table a time or two, but it ain't hardly common."

"Any idea why Wainwright extended an invitation to me?"

"Nope," Sweetwater said again. Then he grinned. "Maybe he wants to thank you."

"Thank me for what?"

"For culling out that old mossy-horn Dandy Jack."

Buckhorn frowned. "Reckon I must be missing something. Why would Wainwright want to thank me for taking out his top gun?"

"*I'm* Wainwright's top gun," Sweetwater said quickly. "Jack might have been for a while, when Wainwright first hired him on, but it didn't take long for the general to figure out all he got for his money was a has-been. When I came aboard the difference was even clearer. I figured it was just a matter of time before it'd be up to me to take the trash out, but you beat me to it. I maybe oughta be jealous, but it ain't no big thing. You can have the glory for cashing in the chips of that old has-been. I'm young. I still got plenty of time to make my rep."

Buckhorn cut him a sidelong glance. "You keep calling Jack a has-been. That's for sure now that he's dead, but I think there was more sand left in him there at the end than you give him credit for."

"Guess we see it a little different then," said Sweet-water with a shrug. "I remember hearing how you and Jack let on you knew each other from the past before you ended up slapping leather there in the Silver Dollar. I think maybe you're confusing what he *used* to be with where he'd gotten to at the end."

It was Buckhorn's turn to shrug. "Anything's possible, I guess. Doesn't make a hell of a lot of difference anymore. He's dead."

"Yup. Gone and soon to be forgot." Sweetwater's expression took on a sudden flintiness as he added, "Something best *not* forgotten is what I said about me being the top gun around here. You end up hanging around for any amount of time, be smart for you to keep that in mind."

"Oh, I will," Buckhorn assured him, his own expression flat, unreadable. "I surely will remember that."

CHAPTER 27

Sweetwater rode with Buckhorn up to the hitch rail in front of the Wainwright residence. There, with an abrupt "*adiós*," he turned and galloped off.

Buckhorn looked after him for a minute, then climbed down from his saddle and tied Sarge to the rail. "I figure I'll be a spell," he said to the big gray, "so I'm guessing they'll have somebody come and take care of you while I'm inside. If not, just stand easy while I'm gone. I'll be back out eventually."

Before leaving the side of the horse, Buckhorn reached to unstrap his saddlebag and from inside the pouch he withdrew a long-necked bottle of wine. One of the finest, he'd been assured, available in Wagon Wheel.

On a few different occasions, he had taken on bodyguard jobs for some very wealthy men. One of them in particular had impressed upon him the habits and mannerisms of proper social etiquette. While the rugged frontier seldom required the practice of such niceties, Buckhorn tried to demonstrate them when he got the chance. Showing up with a bottle of fine wine in response to a dinner invitation seemed appropriate.

As he carried the bottle toward the front door, he cast a glance back over his shoulder for another look at the barns, bunkhouses, corrals, and the long wooden fence he'd ridden by on the way in. All were tidy and maintained damn near to perfection, right down to nary a cracked board or smudged patch of whitewash on the fence.

Even if he didn't know about Wainwright's past as a high-ranking Army officer, he had a hunch the term *military precision* might have crossed his mind at the original sight of them.

If those features of the ranch headquarters were impressive, by comparison the ex-general's personal residence made them look almost shabby. Tall and expansive, buffed adobe, also whitewashed until it practically gleamed in the last glow of the setting sun, the structure seemed nothing short of imposing as Buckhorn paused before it. The ornate front door— made of some heavy, dark wood stained to a wine tint, carved with exquisite designs, and prominently displaying a dragon-headed brass knocker—was probably worth more than what a common ranch hand earned in a decade, Buckhorn reckoned.

Somewhat resentful of the inequity, he grabbed the snarling dragon's head and gave it an extra hard slam against the striker plate.

Moments later, the door opened and the most impressive feature yet of the Wainwright estate was revealed. Standing in a mixture of light thrown by the interior lanterns behind her and the final fingers of dusk reaching all the way from the horizon as if they'd lingered just to touch her, was one of the most stunning women Buckhorn had ever laid eyes on.

Jet hair tumbled to creamy smooth shoulders left intriguingly bare by the gown she wore. Smoldering dark eyes, lush lips, and a supple girl-woman form accentuated by the elegant sheath of cobalt blue completed the picture.

"You must be Mr. Buckhorn," the vision said.

"Yes. Yes, I am."

"I am Lusita Wainwright. Won't you please come in?" She took a step back, held the door open wider, and Buckhorn entered past her. The scent of her was as intoxicating as the rest.

Closing the door behind them, Lusita turned and said, "My husband extends his sincere apology for not being here to greet you himself. The unexpected arrival of an old friend and business partner has claimed his time and attention for the moment. He promises that he will be delayed only a short time. In the meantime, I will do my best to serve as a suitable hostess."

"I doubt you could be anything less," Buckhorn said. He presented the bottle of wine he had brought along.

"How very thoughtful," said Lusita, accepting it. "Would you like to have a drink now, while we await my husband? I can have this opened if you wish, or we have a wide variety of other wines and liquors to choose from. We even have some cold beer, a brand my husband highly recommends."

Buckhorn didn't drink much in the way of alcohol. Never whiskey, though he did enjoy a glass of wine now and then and a cold beer always stood a good chance of sounding inviting. That was what he opted for.

"Very good," said Lusita. "Since my husband is occupying the den, let us make ourselves comfortable in the sitting room. This way."

Buckhorn followed her from the front foyer into a sunken room containing a large fireplace at one end and a carefully arranged assortment of couches and overstuffed chairs. A set of longhorns hung over the mantle and some impressive racks of deer and elk antlers were suspended on the other walls. Animal hide rugs covered the floor. The room was decidedly masculine in tone yet Lusita's mere presence gave it all the feminine balance any space would ever need.

A chunky elderly woman wearing an apron appeared. Her seamed face was the color of rich cinnamon and her iron gray hair was pulled into a severe bun.

Handing her the wine Buckhorn had brought, Lusita said, "Please take this, Consuela, and place it with the rest of our stock. Then bring a tall glass of beer for our guest and a glass of white wine for me."

"Yes, señora. Will you be dining soon?"

"I hope so. As soon as my husband is finished with his business discussion."

"Shall I also set a place at the table for your father?"

A trace of annoyance touched Lusita's face. "I've not been advised about that. Wait for the time being."

Once Consuela had retreated, Lusita turned back to Buckhorn and made a gesture. "Please be seated wherever you wish. Consuela will be back shortly with our drinks."

Buckhorn sank into one of the chairs. His hostess seated herself opposite him. There were moments when he caught himself staring, her grace and beauty making it difficult not to.

"I guess I failed to mention," Lusita said, "that it is my father whom my husband is in such deep discussion with. My father, Don Pedro Olomoso, owns a large ranch directly across the border. Our lands butt against one another. The Flying W and the Rio-O have long been neighbors in this manner. Over the past year and more, the two patrons have become closer than ever, intently involved in some sort of joint business venture." She gave an exaggerated roll of her eyes. "When they put their heads together in order to grind out some stubborn detail, they can become frustratingly oblivious to all else."

"Maybe I should leave and return at another time," Buckhorn suggested.

Lusita shook her head. "Certainly not. I will put my foot down if their meeting threatens to drag on too long. You have ridden all the way out here and Consuela has gone to great lengths to make a nice meal on short notice. I will not allow their rudeness to prevail."

Consuela returned with their drinks and then disappeared again after serving them. Buckhorn tasted his beer and found it, not surprisingly, to be very good. As if any further proof than his wife was needed, Wainwright's tastes were excellent.

"I'm afraid I don't recall ever hearing your name mentioned prior to a few hours ago when Thomas said you would be joining us for dinner, Mr. Buckhorn," said Lusita. "Not really knowing anything about you, I'm afraid I must apologize and bluntly say that I will need your help in carrying on a conversation."

Buckhorn grinned. "We may both be in trouble, then. I've never been accused of being a brilliant conversationalist."

"Ah. The strong, silent type. Is that it?"

"I can do a little better than that. Let's aim for something somewhere in between." Buckhorn took another drink. "This beer is excellent, by the way."

"As I said, you'll have to thank my husband for that. He seems particularly fond of it. Myself, I never acquired much of a taste for beer."

"It seems not many ladies do."

"Speaking of taste, let me tell you what Consuela will be serving for our meal. Naturally, we eat a great deal of beef around here. Even though Consuela has mastered a wide variety of ways to fix it—and all quite delicious, I must say—it nevertheless becomes rather tedious. Tonight, it so happens, she planned something quite different. Roast sage hen on a bed of rice with sweet potatoes as a side. I do hope that sounds appealing."

"It sounds, and smells, mighty delicious."

Lusita scowled. "If my husband and father should threaten to ruin the fare by delaying it to the point of growing cold or becoming overcooked in an attempt to keep it warm, I shall be very displeased." She rose suddenly from her chair. "In fact, I refuse to let that happen. Please excuse me while I go check on the situation in the kitchen. If I have to, I will barge in on the rude men who are keeping everybody waiting. When I return, I will bring you a fresh beer."

"That's fine. Don't go to any special trouble on my account," Buckhorn told her.

"Make yourself at home, as you *Americanos* are fond of saying." Lusita paused long enough to point to a set of glass doors across the room. "Feel free to get some fresh air, if you like. The evening air should be taking on a welcome coolness by now, and you'll find the early flowers in the garden out there giving off a most pleasant scent."

Buckhorn remained seated after his hostess was gone. He drank some more of his beer. The spacious house was very quiet.

Whatever he'd expected in coming here, his treatment so far wasn't it. It was for certain that nowhere in his thoughts had he conjured up anything like Lusita

Wainwright. Having been in her presence, however, he told himself sourly it was equally certain she would be visiting there in the future.

Feeling abruptly restless, he shoved himself up and out of the chair and carried his beer over to the glass doors. Peering between the folds of filmy curtains, he could see a garden, just as Lusita had said. Neat rows of flowers and plants cast eerily shaped shadows from the glow of a pulsing lantern hung on a tall pole. He pushed one of the doors gently open and felt the cool air sigh in over him. The scents of the flowers were none he recognized, but they were sweet and pleasant all the same. He wandered out a ways, his feet following a flagstone path, then paused.

Off to his right, a wing of the house extended along the edge of the garden. Lights were on in a room as evidenced by two elongated windows. Seams of illumination showed through the horizontal slats of shutters on the nearest window. The shutters of the window farther down had been folded back. The odor and thin wisps of cigar smoke wafted out through the opening . . . also the sound of voices.

Two men talking.

Drawn by the voices, Buckhorn moved forward a couple more steps, edging off the flagstones and into a pool of shadows. By some quirk of acoustics, the voices of the men carried quite clearly to where he paused once again.

"One of the many quaint sayings you Americanos are so fond of is the caution against looking a gift horse in the mouth. Is it not so? I say the fates have aligned in a sequence that is like a gift. Therefore, we should not waste time looking down its mouth, so to speak, but should hasten to set into motion all of the plotting and planning we have worked on for so long."

The man spoke with a distinct Spanish accent. Buckhorn had little doubt it belonged to Don Pedro Olomoso.

The man paused, probably to move around a little, then went on. "For weeks now, my scouts have been assuring me that the last of the Yaquis have finally been driven from the Barranca canyon where I know there are rich silver veins. Their maddening ability to elude us yet strike and harass our ability to reach the sweetest spots has at last been overcome. And now, with the news that the rebel forces near Mexico City are ready to begin their overthrow at practically any moment— our time is most surely at hand!"

"Trusting in fate has never been a big thing for me, amigo," the second man said. "My experience has been that fate mostly comes through only after you've worked your tail off to set the stage for it. Still, there's no denying that you're right about things appearing to have fallen into place the way we've been waiting for."

When he was behind bars, Buckhorn had heard Wainwright speak from outside the jail. The second voice matched his recollection.

"A lot depends," Wainwright continued, "on the accuracy of your scouts and spies. We can be sure about the men and guns we each have at our disposal. The timing of the other elements—what is taking place down near Mexico City and in the Barrancas—is critical. A wrong note anywhere along the way puts the whole works at risk. If we tip our hand and fail, we won't get a second chance."

"You think I do not know this? I will have as much on the line, to use another of your phrases, as you. Maybe more. Forces of the Mexican government—

either old or new—are sure to take a harsh look at an independent endeavor such as we are planning. Especially one aimed at depriving it of riches like the silver to be mined from the Barrancas now that the Yaqui threat is eliminated."

Buckhorn heard the sound of a finger thumping paper loosely on a solid surface. A map spread out atop a desk, he surmised in accordance with the line of conversation.

"Clearing the savages from these hills will be welcomed by all . . . except the unfortunate Yaqui, of course. But for us to then claim the Barrancas and all their spoils as our own, for the sake of incorporating them into our independent country of Silverado . . . this would not be so widely welcomed."

Buckhorn's eyes widened a little. The plan he was eavesdropping on wasn't the most daring thing he had ever heard . . . but it came close.

"If the bigger revolution around the capital city keeps the standing government forces and the rebels busy long enough, no matter who wins, Silverado will be firmly established and less likely to be worth their attention and trouble while they're still licking their wounds after the fighting is over."

"*Sí.* That is, of course, our plan. Frankly, I am more concerned by how your country will react to the threat of losing a section of their Arizona Territory—the part you already almost completely control—as the other half of Silverado. They will not, as in my country, have another rebellion to distract them from what we are up to."

Wainwright emitted a short, gruff laugh. "Trust me, amigo, my soon to be ex-country is still plenty busy licking its own wounds from the much larger rebellion it went through a while back. Plus, what will become the northern portion of Silverado is nothing to them but a sun-scorched stretch of sand and cactus. They'll hardly think it worth the trouble. By the time they do—if they ever get around to it at all—the wealth from the Yaqui silver and my cattle operation will have financed us an army and established boundaries they'll pay a high price trying to break down."

"*Sí*," Olomoso agreed solemnly. "A price *too high* . . . if we have it figured correctly."

Reluctantly, Buckhorn backed away from the voices and out of the pool of shadows. He wanted badly to stay and keep listening, but outweighing the importance of hearing more was to not risk getting caught before he could pass on what he'd already learned.

He'd heard enough to have his head reeling as it was. Thomas Wainwright's big plan—and Don Pedro's too, as it turned out—was to break away bordering slices of northern Mexico and southern Arizona and forge them into a unified country separate from either of their current governing bodies.

Silverado.

It was wild. It was crazy. But was it so wild and crazy and just plain *audacious* that it might actually have a chance of working?

Wainwright had the existing wealth, not to mention the land and cattle to ensure more, plus the all-important power of an endless water source. Don Pedro also had land and cattle, though limited, but it sounded like—since the savage Yaquis had been dealt with—also wide-open access to increased silver riches.

Everybody knew that great wealth equaled great power, in and of itself. Add to that the combined force of hired guns amounting to a small army that the two driven men already had at their disposal—a force that could quickly be increased with the backing of more money—and they might very well have an entity powerful enough to carve out its own slice of two other wounded countries.

Buckhorn retreated to just within the glass doors that led off the sitting room. He left ajar the door he'd opened earlier and leaned against its frame, draining what was left of the beer he'd been holding. He immediately wished he had another. Where was Lusita? She'd promised to return with a fresh one.

The thought of his hostess triggered the looming prospect of the dinner yet to come. If Buckhorn had any reservations before about sitting through the meal he'd been invited to attend, they had become amplified.

How he would act around the former Yankee general he'd come to kill but who was extending his personal hospitality and probably a job offer suddenly turned into a minor concern. He also faced putting on his act in front of the coconspirator to a mad scheme for carving out their very own country.

Further reverie was interrupted by Lusita reentering the room. She was carrying the promised fresh beer. "We'll be ready to retire to the dining room in a matter of minutes," she announced. "It should work out to just about enough time for you to finish your drink."

Not if I chug it down the way I want to, Buckhorn thought to himself. He accepted the beer silently, smiled his thanks, and took only a restrained sip.

Not even the presence of Lusita was enough to tear his thoughts away from the talk he'd overheard coming from Wainwright's den. He wanted to focus on his lovely hostess, to savor the unexpectedly pleasant part of his visit to the Flying W, as he'd been doing before . . . but it wouldn't work. Not anymore. His thoughts kept straying.

Silverado.

What the hell had Andrew Haydon gotten him into?

CHAPTER 28

The much-anticipated dinner with Wainwright turned out to be of little consequence, in and of itself. The lovely Lusita was also present, as well as her father. The food was excellent. The conversation . . . cautious.

It was clear throughout that Wainwright and Don Pedro, exhilarated by the recent developments that seemed on the brink of propelling their plans into motion, wanted to get the meal over with as soon as possible in order to return to their plotting. Discourse was polite but rather terse. Whether she understood the reasons behind it or not, Lusita appeared to sense the hurried approach as much as Buckhorn and therefore kept her own participation in any discussion to an absolute minimum.

As far as the purpose behind Buckhorn's invitation, it had come down to a job offer for him and his gun. Wainwright claimed to have been impressed by the reports he'd gotten of Buckhorn's skill, totally glossing over the fact that skill had been largely demonstrated on Flying W men.

When it came to his purpose for putting together

the small army of gunmen he was asking Buckhorn to join, Wainwright merely explained that big changes were coming to Whitestone County and, to ensure his vast holdings were not threatened, he was making sure they were well protected. He didn't bother going into any further details on what the "big changes" might be, and Buckhorn didn't press it.

He did, however, accept the job offer, with the agreement that he would report for duty by noon of the following day.

When Buckhorn rode away from the Flying W after dinner was over and the terms of the job offer were settled, there was no sign of Sweetwater or anyone else to see him off. That was good. Because he had no intention of returning directly to town. Not quite yet.

He rode as far as the rock outcropping where he'd encountered Sweetwater earlier. There, he stopped and dismounted, ground-reined Sarge in a patch of good graze, and sat down with his back against the face of the rock. It still held some of the warmth of the day's sun that had sunk deep into it. Buckhorn waited and watched and churned things over in his mind.

The first thing he'd determined was that a patrol was in place to guard the perimeter of the ranch headquarters at night. Two mounted men, one riding clockwise, the other counterclockwise, made wide, slow circles around the fenced-in area.

It wasn't really a very effective setup. Stretches of approach to the buildings were left out of the sight of either rider for long periods. Plus the numerous longhorns milling outside the fencing made ideal cover for intruders to move in close. And the only irregularity to the timing of the riders' rounds was when they might stop and briefly converse once in a while as they passed one another.

Buckhorn could have moved dozens of men in past the so-called patrol, he told himself, and hit the heart of the headquarters without the riders knowing anybody was within fifty miles.

But he didn't want to move in dozens of men. Only one.

When the hour grew late enough for lights to begin blinking out in the various ranch buildings, Buckhorn got up and started walking. A whispered command to Sarge was sufficient to plant him where he was for hours.

The last of the lights to go out in the main house had been the lantern in Wainwright's den. By then, Buckhorn was crouched in the flower garden only a few yards from the window. Employing the patience instilled by his Indian blood, he waited another half hour without moving.

Then, using the blade of his bowie knife, he silently pried open the shutter and slid the window up to gain entry into the den. He smiled grimly at the ease with which he was able to do it. Wainwright's foolish arrogance allowed him to believe the sloppy patrol on his perimeter made everything inside it safe. The need for added caution was negligible.

Aided by a carefully shrouded lantern turned very low, Buckhorn spent another half hour poring over the papers and maps spread across the broad surface of Wainwright's desk. The same desk he'd heard Don Pedro thumping a finger on when he was eavesdropping.

By means of a commandeered pencil and sheet of blank paper, Buckhorn made notes and crude sketches from what he perused. With this paper folded and slipped inside his shirt, he quit the den, using great care to refasten the window and leave everything inside exactly as he'd found it.

Returning in the wee hours to the dark, empty, silent streets of Wagon Wheel, Buckhorn quickly but quietly rousted first Goodwin and then Carl Orndecker, telling them he had urgent new information to share. Wanting to also include Justine, Carl led them a back way to her house and got her to let them in.

In the kitchen of Justine's house, the four were once again gathered covertly. The blinds were drawn tight. The illumination from a single candle placed in the middle of the table cast the circle of faces in stark patterns of shadow and light.

The three listened to Buckhorn tell what he'd run across at the Flying W while they scanned his corresponding sketches and notes from the sheet of paper spread on Justine's kitchen table. The dully ticking wall clock hanging above a shelf of display china read three o'clock.

"Such a fantastic scheme!" exclaimed Justine York. "That's the only way to describe it."

"And that's exactly why they've been able to get so far along with it. You had all the pieces spotted. You were even talking about 'em over lunch," Buckhorn reminded her. "All the land Wainwright has taken control of, the small army he's put together, his chumminess with Don Pedro, and the marriage to Lusita to cement them even closer. You even mentioned the silver in the Barrancas Mountains and the Yaquis standing in the way of it. The reason you could never put it all together into the notion of Wainwright and

Don Pedro figuring on starting their own country is because it's too damn fantastic to conjure."

"It's more than just fantastic," Carl said. "It's . . . insane. Impossible . . ."

"We can go ahead and throw the whole alphabet at it if we want," Buckhorn said. "but it's gonna take a lot more than just words to stop those two."

"So what do we do? Notify the sheriff? Call in the army?" Martin Goodwin wanted to know.

His inquiry hung in the air with the weight of a fifth presence.

It was Buckhorn who responded. "For us to go to the authorities seems pretty pointless to me. Sheriff Banning may not be completely under Wainwright's thumb, but he's close to it. No matter, something like this would be too big for him to handle on his own. He might first turn it over to the U.S. Marshals but, even at that, it would end up in the lap of the Army. You oughta be able to reckon it from there. Who are they most likely to listen to? Me, with these wild accusations laid out on this paper here—or the word of a former Yankee general, now one of the wealthiest land and cattle barons in the territory?"

"They'd hand out the loudest horselaugh ever heard in these parts," Carl said bitterly. "And if Wainwright wanted to push it, they could probably find grounds for bringing charges against the lot of us."

"So what does that leave?" Goodwin asked. "We can't hold off and do nothing, just let them try and get away with it. Can we?"

Buckhorn thought of his original task. "I could ride back out there tomorrow and kill Wainwright. That's what I was sent here to do anyway, in a roundabout way," Buckhorn said. "Hell, if Don Pedro is still right there handy, I could go ahead and plant a couple slugs in him, too, while I was at it. That'd cut the heads off the two fattest snakes we know about."

He shook his head. "But what would it leave? Who else might be in on their scheme? Seems doubtful it all rests strictly on the two of them. For one thing, Don Pedro mentioned spies keeping him advised on the revolution getting ready to bust loose. If there's other snakes big enough in size—government officials, say, from either side of the border—all I'd do was give 'em warning so they could shift some things around and maybe still go ahead with a revised plan. And I'd 've made a target out of myself and maybe the rest of you for nothing."

"One way or another, we're in this with you," Carl said. "There's no backing out of it now."

Justine regarded Buckhorn intently. "If you believed it would end it all, could you really do that? Ride out and simply shoot Wainwright and Don Pedro?"

Buckhorn met her eyes with a hard, flat gaze. "That's how I used to do things. I said that so you'd know—all of you." He cut his gaze to Goodwin and Carl before coming back to Justine. "If I was the same as then, Wainwright would already be dead and I'd be long gone. If any of that makes a difference, say so now before we go any farther."

"I don't have the same background as Buckhorn," Goodwin said, "yet our mutual connection gives us the same outlook where Wainwright is concerned. I may not have the guts to do it myself, but knowing he was dead—by whatever method—would not trouble me in the least. He's long overdue. Now it's bigger than just killing him. We must also kill this crazy idea that, if carried out, will surely result in bloodshed and chaos on a scale nobody wants to imagine."

"Of course we must," Justine said, never taking her eyes off Buckhorn. "I never meant to suggest otherwise."

"Which brings us," Carl said, "right back to the little matter of how."

CHAPTER 29

"I've had a lot of time to think on that," Buckhorn said. "Way I see it, two things might give us a couple hammers to knock some pins out from under what's been put together. The first is right here, all around us." He tapped the rough sketch he'd made representing the area on both sides of the border earmarked to make up the country of Silverado. "Smack in the middle of all the rest of their land is the one thing neither Wainwright nor Don Pedro already own—the town of Wagon Wheel."

"Yeah, you're right about that," Carl agreed. "But I'm not sure I see—"

Buckhorn cut him off by turning to Justine. "You told me a lot of folks around town don't much like the way Wainwright has gobbled up so much land and brought in all his hired guns. Even in the short time I've been here, I've heard that kind of resentful talk in the Good Eats Café and again in the Silver Dollar Saloon. The ones behind those feelings aren't really doing anything about them, right?"

"That's the way it's been, yes."

"What *can* they do about it?" Carl said. "Nobody

likes Wainwright's heavy-handed tactics, but he hasn't broken any laws, for sure not in the eyes of Paul Banning. If the drought gets much worse, no matter how many people don't like the old general right now, they know damn well he might start to look a whole lot better if they have to rely on him for some of his water."

"I might have something to say about that," piped up Goodwin.

Buckhorn nodded at the dowser. "That's what I'm counting on, now more than ever." He turned to Justine and Carl. "If Goodwin here was to stir up a new water source, isn't it possible that would also stir up the townsfolk, maybe stiffen their backbones a little more? Given the way they already feel about Wainwright and then suddenly freed from having to worry about water, don't you reckon they'd make a more receptive audience for the tale I got to tell about what's coming around the corner?"

Carl frowned. "And then what? They might be more apt to listen to you, yeah, but do you really think a bunch of businessmen and shopkeepers and the like are going to rise up and stand against Wainwright and his gunslingers? What chance would they have?"

"Carl, what kind of talk is that?" Justine demanded. "You've lived and worked among these people. You used to look out for them. This is a tough country, even living in town, and these are tough, resilient people. They had to be to make it this far. Some townsmen have a few added years, but several of them are veterans of the war. You'd sell them short with just a shrug of your shoulders?"

"She's talking sense, Carl," Buckhorn said. "Going up against Wainwright's gunnies would take grit and sacrifice. Digging in and fighting for their town, for their homes and families . . . having reasons like that can make a mighty big difference to some men."

Carl's brow furrowed. He passed the back of one hand across his mouth. "Sure. Sure, you two are right. It wouldn't be pretty, but it might have a chance. It deserves at least that much consideration."

"It hinges, first and foremost, on finding a new water supply," Justine said, her eyes going to Goodwin.

The dowser smiled. "I haven't had any chance to mention it yet, but after we all met before, I *did* have a chance to take a stroll around the town and its out-skirts and actually spotted some ground up around the north end that I think looks promising. As soon as somebody gives me the word, I can take my rod and other paraphernalia up there and go to work. With a little luck, I might run across something in pretty short order."

"Go ahead and figure you've been given the word," Buckhorn told him. "Start doing what it is you do, the sooner the better. You parading around with that goofy-looking stick you showed me and Justine doing her part spreading awareness of what you're up to is bound to start drawing attention. Plenty of it. It won't take long, I'm betting, before a big chunk of that at-tention will come from Wainwright."

Goodwin made a face. "Can't say I'm looking for-ward to that part."

"Don't worry," Carl said. "I'll be there to protect you . . . 'less 'n I oversleep and don't get up in time." He grinned crookedly. "But hell, even then, Wain-wright's wild-eyed top gun, Sweetwater, wouldn't be crazy enough to shoot you down right in front of a bunch of onlookers . . . I don't think."

"That's not funny, Carl," his sister chided him. "You

know how rough Wainwright's wolf pack can play, even if shooting isn't a part of it."

Goodwin's mouth showed a grin, a lopsided, uncertain one. "If you're trying to make me feel better, Mrs. York, you're not."

"You just need to remember what your stake is in this thing," Buckhorn said. "You'll do fine. Besides, even though Wainwright is bound to take an interest in you and your dowsing, I'm hoping that at least by the time you sprout water, he'll have plenty else to worry about."

"What's that supposed to mean?" Goodwin asked.

"You remarked something about *two* hammers to knock the pins out from under Wainwright and Don Pedro," Justine said. "If your finding water and stirring up the townsfolk is the first one, Mr. Goodwin, what's the second?"

"Even though my dinner at the Flying W turned out to be a sort of hurried-up affair, it still gave me time to get a read on some added things about Wainwright and Don Pedro," Buckhorn explained. "Mainly, it wasn't hard to see that those two old pirates don't trust each other worth a damn."

"That's really not surprising," said Goodwin. "Men who are immersed in crime and double-dealing are prone to neither trust nor believe in the honesty of anyone else—not even a so-called partner."

Buckhorn nodded. "Well, that's sure as fire true with this pair."

"But how does knowing that really gain us anything?" Justine asked.

"Remember what I said before about how we'd have to come up with somebody or a group of somebodies to claim responsibility for hiring Goodwin and bringing him here?" Buckhorn scanned the faces around him. "What if we figured out a way to make Wainwright suspect that *somebody* was Don Pedro? Wainwright already has the simmering mistrust. Considering that the one thing that gives him most of his power over this whole region is his precious water, how big a double cross would he consider it if he believed none other than his own partner was trying to cut in and make Wainwright's water not so exclusive?"

"It would make him crazy," Carl said.

"Oh, great," Goodwin responded. "Just what I need, something to make him madder yet when it comes to me and my dowsing."

"No guarantees, but it actually might benefit you," Carl told him. "He'd be so enraged over what he believed Don Pedro was trying to pull, he might look right past you as just another hired hand."

"The more enraged and crazy we can make him, the better for us all the way around," Buckhorn summed up.

Carl nodded his agreement. "If we can trick those two old rascals into going to war against each other, the revolution and the breakaway new country and all the rest would fall by the wayside. Or at least be delayed—until one of them came out the winner."

"By then, we ought to have figured out a convincing way to expose the rest of what they're currently planning," Justine said. "What can we do to trigger such a rift between them?"

Carl said, "I might have an idea."

Buckhorn made a gesture. "Go ahead. Let's hear it."

Carl shifted a little in his chair. "Okay. The thing is, when I go on one of my benders, I often end up doing the brunt of my drinking at a little cantina down in Mexville. The tequila is cheaper and the atmosphere includes a couple *chiquitas* who I sort of favor. Truth to tell, I visit them now and then even when I'm not drinking heavy." He cut a sidelong glance over at Justine and gave a sheepish grin. "Sorry, Sis, but that's just the way it is."

Justine returned his glance coolly. "I think I had a pretty good idea you weren't living the life of a monk, Carl. Go on with telling us your idea."

"What I'm thinking is that me and Goodwin could take a little trip down that way tomorrow evening, after he's spent the day dowsing and has gotten everybody's attention. We could put on a show of hitting the sauce pretty heavy, like we're celebrating. Maybe do some cuddling with my chiquitas while we're at it. Somewhere in the process, once our tongues were oiled up good and loose, we could carelessly drop Don Pedro's name a time or three, making sure it was understood that he was the one financing Goodwin's water-finding expedition.

"I guarantee once we said it for the second time, word of the claim would have traveled *outside* the joint and would be on its way to reach Wainwright's ears before the night was over. It's that kind of place. The minute somebody overhears anything they think might be of interest—especially, of value—somewhere else, they're passing it on."

"I like it," Goodwin was quick to say.

"And hearing the claim in that manner," Carl added, "I think would be almost instantly convincing to Wainwright. Hell, what reason would a couple loudmouthed drunks lacking the sense to keep their lips buttoned have for lying? What could be their angle? What could they be looking to gain if it wasn't the truth?"

Buckhorn let the rhetorical questions hang in the air for a minute, then gave a nod of his head. "I like it, too. I think you're right about the impact it would make on Wainwright. He'll be quicker to believe it and quick to want to act on it. It stands a good chance of getting exactly the kind of reaction we want."

"I guess it's up to me to start my dowsing first thing in the morning and hope it serves as the catalyst for setting in motion all of these other things we're hoping for," said Goodwin.

"That's about the size of it," Carl said.

"There's just one other thing to touch on," Buckhorn said, "but it's one we have absolutely no control over and it could send everything in the wrong direction from what we want."

"What's that?" Justine wanted to know.

"The revolution that's brewing down in Mexico. Don Pedro won't be willing to start his part of the shindig until that kicks in and he can feel reasonably sure the current government forces are too busy down there to have time for what he and Wainwright are cooking up here. He's got spies keeping him up to date on how things stand." Buckhorn cut his gaze to Justine. "With all that revolutionary tension in the air, I'm guessing a gaggle of reporters from some of the big city papers must be keeping an eye on things down there, right?"

"There's bound to be," Justine said.

"Anybody you can make contact with?"

"Not directly. None that I know of. Tomorrow, I can send out some telegrams to people I do know, and through them set something up."

"If anything pops down there before the stuff we're trying to put in place up here, it obviously changes the whole picture. We need to know it as soon or shortly after Don Pedro does."

"I understand."

"I guess that's it then. Tomorrow shapes up as a mighty big day. Anybody got any final questions?" Once again Buckhorn scanned the faces before him. "If not . . . well, I guess the only thing left is to wait for all that we've planned to start kicking into motion."

CHAPTER 30

Buckhorn returned to his hotel room and caught about four hours of sleep. Before quitting the room, he took time to scoop some freshly poured water onto his face from the washbasin, repack his war bag, and check the loads in all of his guns.

On his way out of the lobby, he detoured long enough to snag three of Mrs. Fletchler's fresh-baked muffins. He ate two as he walked up the street to the livery stable and fed the third to Sarge once he got there.

After saddling up and squaring his bill with the liveryman, Buckhorn swung aboard the big gray and pointed him north out of town. Glancing over his shoulder, he was pleased to see Martin Goodwin exiting the hotel, carrying his case of dowsing tools, and starting across the street toward the newspaper office where Carl Orndecker stepped out to greet him.

A low-hanging sun above the eastern horizon bathed Buckhorn and Sarge in warming rays as they rode along over the rolling grassland. Just for the hell of it, and because he had plenty of time to make it to the Flying W ranch headquarters by noon, Buckhorn swung a ways farther to the west than the route he'd followed previously. He figured he'd come in at an angle that would give him a better look at White-stone Lake and then follow the curve of the water's edge around until he was again in sight of the ranch buildings.

The terrain that way was more broken than to the east. A handful of low buttes rose here and there, with other upthrusts of smaller, more ragged rock forma-tions in between. A few clumps of scraggly pine growth hugged the base of some of those rocks.

He reached a point where the overall lay of the land seemed to be on a gradual incline and he reckoned it shouldn't be long before the rise would crest and then slope back downward to where he'd come in view of the lake.

Before he got that far, he caught the stuttering noise of what sounded like distant gunfire. He reined Sarge to a walk and listened harder. It was gunfire, no mistake about that. And not all that distant—ahead and a bit more to the west.

Buckhorn brought Sarge to a full stop. His eyes narrowed and he scanned slowly over the rugged land-scape between where he was and where he thought the shooting was coming from. Numerous rocky out-crops dotted the space in between, most of them poking up in low, jagged spines, rising abruptly and then just as abruptly falling away. A wide, shallow dry wash wound its way in and out among several of them.

He continued to listen and the guns continued to bark, the sporadic reports sounding like an exchange between three shooters. One pistol, two rifles, he made it out to be. If the pistoleer was alone against the other two, he had a disadvantage in both number and firepower.

"Well, pal," Buckhorn muttered to Sarge, "since this is Flying W range and I'm supposed to be riding for that brand now, I reckon there ain't much for it but to ease up there and see if I need to take a hand in whatever the fuss is about." He heeled Sarge down into the wash and urged him steadily, carefully forward.

After they'd followed the serpentine course for several hundred yards, they found themselves at a spot where the ground just ahead rose up in a particularly high, sharp ridge topped by more jagged rocks. The rifle fire seemed to be coming from somewhere not very far over that crest.

Buckhorn dismounted, pulling his Winchester from its saddle scabbard. He ordered Sarge to stay put and began making his way up toward the peak of the ridge. He could hear voices hollering on the other side but couldn't make out the words.

Gaining the peak, he removed his hat and then eased his head slowly up into a notch between two rocks. From that vantage point, he surveyed the situation fully revealed to him.

The slope on the down side of the ridge was somewhat more gradual and strewn with almost nothing but rocky rubble, much of it in the form of large, odd-shaped boulders. At the bottom of the slope, a continuation of the dry wash wandered off into flatter, grassier ground. Two riflemen were concealed behind a pair of the bigger boulders.

The nearest was about twenty yards down from where Buckhorn crouched. Based on his lean, wiry build, Buckhorn judged the shooter to be a fairly young man.

Twenty yards farther down and jogged about half that distance to Buckhorn's right was a second rifleman. By his thickened upper body and a slice of bushy sideburn visible on the bulge of a heavy jowl, Buckhorn made him for considerably older, possibly the younger shooter's father.

Down on the floor of the wash, two horses lay shot dead. Beside one of them, a man sprawled motionless, arms and legs akimbo, obviously just as dead.

Beside the other horse, a second man was also on the ground, but he was far from motionless. He was jammed in tight against the carcass of his former mount, using it as cover as he returned pistol fire at the riflemen up in the rocks.

The pistol shooter was Leo Sweetwater.

It was plain enough what had happened. The men in the wash, Sweetwater and his companion, had been ambushed by the pair behind the boulders. Their horses were cut out from under them and the second rider was killed right away. Sweetwater had survived the opening volley and managed to scramble for cover tight to his fallen horse.

From there, the sandy bottom of the wash was too wide and too empty to provide him any chance of gaining a better position. He was making a fight of it so far, but he couldn't last. It was just a matter of time before he ran out of bullets or until one of the ambushers repositioned himself to where he could shoot down at an angle from which the horse carcass offered insufficient protection.

Leastways, that was how things had stood before Buckhorn showed up.

The quickest and probably surest way for him to turn the tide, Buckhorn told himself, would be to give the ambushers and horse killers a taste of their own medicine. He could put a bullet in the back of each man's head without them ever knowing what hit them.

If not for the evident youthfulness of the nearest rifleman—the son or nephew or younger brother under the influence of the older man—that's very likely how he would have done it.

Somehow, taking action that harsh against a young man, no matter what he was participating in, did not seem like a reasonable fit with the thin sliver of a chance for redemption that Buckhorn continued to strive for. He cursed under his breath. Instead of opening fire from the rocky notch, he slipped up and over it and began making his way carefully down behind the young rifleman.

From where he was pinned behind his fallen horse, Sweetwater quickly spotted what Buckhorn was up to. His face lifted momentarily, awareness and recognition spreading across it before he jerked it back down as more bullets instantly sizzled close but succeeded only in slamming horsehide and saddle leather.

In the midst of his predicament, Sweetwater saw how he might help his rescuer by diverting attention away from any noise Buckhorn might make picking his way down the rubble-strewn slope. He began hollering at his ambushers. "Laudermilk, you stupid son of a bitch! You've already lost your land, the bill of sale you signed is already in the hands of Wainwright's lawyer. All you've accomplished here this morning is to guarantee you're gonna end up buried in land that don't even belong to you anymore!"

"Not before I plant you in the ground first," called back the thick-bodied man. "I wish it was that cold-hearted bastard Wainwright down there in my sights, but you'll do second best, you bootlicking, horse-threatening little puke! I'll kill you, then me and mine will be miles before they even find your moldering remains."

"It won't matter. Wainwright will figure it out. When he does, he'll send men after you. Comes to that, you'd best go down fighting. If anybody takes you back to the old general alive, he'll introduce you to hell on earth while you're still breathing. He used to run a Yankee prison camp in the war, and the stories I've heard about some of the things he done to men in there will make your skin crawl."

"Shut up! I don't care what he's done in the past. What he's done since he came to these parts is enough to make my skin crawl. Too bad for you, you're all I'm able to get my hands on to make him pay."

Buckhorn had worked his way down to only a few feet behind the younger man. As he coiled to lunge the final distance, Sweetwater provided some more cover for any sound his attack might make.

"I ain't dead yet, you ambushing son of a bitch!" the brash gunman hollered as he raised up long enough to send three rapid-fire rounds pounding into Laudermilk's boulder.

In that same instant, Buckhorn hissed "Kid!" behind his about-to-be victim. When the young man wheeled part way around, Buckhorn chopped the flat of his Winchester butt hard across the side of his head and the youth was knocked cold.

As his body went limp and the rifle started to slip from slack fingers, Buckhorn grabbed the falling rifle before it clattered noisily in the rocks. He sank instantly into a low crouch behind the same boulder that had been shielding the young ambusher from Sweetwater, using it as cover from Laudermilk in case the thick-bodied man had somehow been alerted to what had just taken place.

The rancher was still totally focused on Sweetwater. "If you had all the bullets in the world, maybe you could keep shooting long enough to whittle away this boulder and get a clear shot at me," he crowed. "But that ain't hardly the case, is it, Mr. Hot Shot gunslinger?" In an attempt to drive home his perceived triumph all the more, Laudermilk raised his rifle and leaned out to fire another round or two at his pinned-down target.

He never got a shot off. From his new vantage point and with his Winchester braced across the top of the boulder, Buckhorn sent a .45 caliber slug sizzling just above the crook of Laudermilk's arm and smashing into the side of his rifle an inch ahead of the trigger guard. The impact tore the weapon from Laudermilk's grasp as he simultaneously issued a yelp of surprise and pain from the fierce stinging that shot through his hands and forearms.

As he rose to full view, Buckhorn triggered another round just for the hell of it, the bullet passing close enough to singe Laudermilk's left ear as the man twisted around to glare at where he'd expected only his fellow ambusher to be.

"Try anything funny," Buckhorn warned, "the next one goes straight into that stupid, slack-jawed expression you're wearing."

"Do it, Buckhorn!" Sweetwater urged from the bottom of the wash. "Shoot that bushwhacking son of a bitch or I will!"

"Just hold on," Buckhorn said as he began to advance on Laudermilk. "I got this under control."

"Who the hell are you?" Laudermilk said, rubbing

his stinging hands together. "What did you do to my boy Johnny?"

"Shut up!" Buckhorn ordered. "I'll ask the questions, and if I don't like your answers they may be the last thing to ever come out of your mouth."

"But my boy—"

"You brought him here to help in a low-down ambush," Buckhorn said through clenched teeth. "Kinda late to be worrying about him now, isn't it?"

Laudermilk's eyes widened.

Widened with heightened anger, Buckhorn thought at first. Almost too late, he realized those angry eyes were looking *past* him.

In the next instant, two things happened simultaneously. From below, Sweetwater bellowed "Look out!" Buckhorn heard the rattle of loosened rocks from behind. He wheeled around, eyes leaping to the spot where he'd left the coldcocked young Laudermilk.

Shockingly, the lad had already regained consciousness. He was on his feet, teetering slightly. Having picked up the rifle that had fallen from his grasp only minutes earlier, he started to raise it again.

Buckhorn wanted to shout out, to implore the kid to drop the rifle once more, beg him not to try anything stupid with it, but he could see in the dulled yet smoldering eyes that it was no use. No words on earth were going to stop the obedient son from doing his damnedest to try and kill him.

With only one way to prevent it, Buckhorn triggered the Winchester from his hip, levered in a fresh round with practiced speed, and fired again. The two shots tumbled nearly on top of each other and slammed less than an inch apart to the left of Johnny Laudermilk's sternum. He toppled back, flinging his arms wide and only then, inadvertently, in death, did he release the rifle as he went down.

"Noooo!" Laudermilk's anguished wail cut through the air like a knife.

Buckhorn could feel the father's pain in that mournful sound, but he couldn't afford to linger on even a twinge of compassion. A vision had streaked to his mind's eye—the sight of the handgun he had seen thrust in an old, cracked leather holster hanging from a belt around Laudermilk's middle.

Buckhorn dropped into a crouch and once again started to wheel about. He was barely into the turn before the sound of gun blasts pounded his ears. He completed his spin in time to see Laudermilk staggering backwards, two gouts of blood arcing from the middle of his chest. His right hand was gripping the handle of his pistol but he'd lifted it only a fraction of an inch out of its holster. As Buckhorn watched, the man spasmed and abruptly jerked forward. Bending at the waist, he pitched facedown across the end of the boulder and rolled several feet down the slope.

In the wash, Sweetwater was sitting upright behind his dead horse, both arms extended toward where Laudermilk had been, the fist at the end of each holding a smoking pistol. Sweetwater emitted a shrill whistle from between his teeth and then his lips spread in a wide smile. "Whooooe! Was that close or what?"

"Too damn close," Buckhorn said, straightening up and letting the Winchester hang loosely at his side.

"I didn't have a good angle on the kid when he clambered up and started getting ready to shoot you," Sweetwater explained. "You were right in my line of fire . . . but not so with the old man. Him, he was a clear target. When he locked all of his focus on you and forgot about me, that's what I made him—a target. I ventilated him just the way he'd been trying to do to me and was getting ready to do to you."

"Yeah, well, we ventilated hell out of both of 'em, didn't we?" Buckhorn said sourly.

Sweetwater squinted up at him. "You got a problem with that?"

"Reckon they didn't give us much choice."

"Damn right they didn't. But I can't help wondering—not that I ain't grateful for you leaving me a piece of the action, mind you—but why didn't you blast those two when you first came up behind 'em? That would've settled their hash right then and there."

Buckhorn's eyes turned flinty. "Let's say shooting in the back isn't something I hold in particularly high favor."

"Whatever floats your stick, I guess," Sweetwater said. "All's well that ends well, like they say. It ain't gonna be completely well for me until I get this damn horse off my leg. You in the mood to come the rest of the way down and give me a hand with that?"

CHAPTER 31

Until Sweetwater made mention of it, Buckhorn hadn't realized the man's leg was pinned under the fallen horse. He thought the young gunman was just hunkered there because he had no chance to gain better cover. Once Buckhorn had been made aware of the predicament, he got down on his knees beside Sweetwater and the two of them scooped away handfuls of the wash's sandy bottom from around the trapped leg until they created a kind of trough out of which they were able to pull the limb free.

Luckily, thanks again to the cushiony sand, the leg wasn't broken. It came out bruised and battered and quick to swell, causing Sweetwater to do some limping, but it could have been a lot worse.

On the ride to Flying W ranch headquarters, doubled up aboard Sarge, Sweetwater gave a more thorough explanation of how the ambush had come about. He told how he'd recently leaned on Laudermilk in order to get him to agree to sell his property to Wainwright.

Sweetwater and the other Flying W rider had been on their way over to the former Laudermilk spread that morning to make sure the ex-owners were packing up and getting ready to pull out. A humiliated, angry, embittered Laudermilk had apparently anticipated that and along with his oldest son had waited in ambush to exact some revenge before leaving.

"Reckon you know how it went from there," Sweetwater summed up. "Soon as we get to the Flying W, I'll send some fellas with a wagon to fetch the body of our man Parsons and to deliver those of Laudermilk and his son to the family. Let them see to their own damn planting."

At the ranch, Sweetwater's tale was met with anger, regret over the loss of Parsons, and concern for Sweetwater's injury, even though he insisted it wasn't all that bad.

Wainwright came down from the main house to hear the report and to quell the talk of administering a heated reprisal to the rest of the Laudermilk family. "No," he said firmly. "I think what's left of the family— a widow and three young children—have paid quite enough for the foolishness of their patriarch. Let them bury their dead and move on. I expect the times ahead will be punishing enough for them. They don't deserve for us to heap on any more."

He gave approval to Sweetwater's notion of sending some men back to the ambush site with a wagon to bring home the body of Parsons and to deliver the corpses of Laudermilk and his son to the widow.

Motioning Buckhorn aside, he said, "It's uncommon for a newly hired man to be so immediately put to the test of a violent confrontation. I must say, from the sound of it you handled yourself in a very satisfactory manner. Leo, I assure you, is not prone to being overly generous when it comes to handing out praise."

Buckhorn shrugged. "Just doing what was proper.

Couldn't hardly leave a fella who rides for my same brand in a tight spot."

"Well said. I just want you to know that it has been duly noted by myself, and how pleased and relieved I am to know I clearly made a good choice in soliciting your services."

We'll see how long that lasts, Buckhorn thought.

"I don't mean to pile too much on you all at once," Wainwright continued, "but I want you to accompany the men who are going back with a wagon. You can show them the most direct way to the ambush site. Further, since I read you as having a cool head and fair demeanor, I'm entrusting you to see to it that Laudermilk's widow and children suffer no coarse treatment from the others who'll be going with you. Can you handle that?"

"If that's the way you want it," Buckhorn told him.

Wainwright gave a crisp nod. "That's the way I want it."

The two men Buckhorn joined to go fetch the bodies were named Blevins and Poudry. They came out of Wainwright's fighting crew, not from among the working wranglers.

Big Bart Blevins was a brute of a man with spiky black whiskers, a mangled nose that looked like a scoop of oatmeal with purplish veins running through it, and suspicious dark eyes that seemed to be perpetually darting this way or that. His favored weapon was a double-barreled shotgun worn hanging from a sling down across the middle of his back. He also carried a short-barreled Smith & Wesson .38 in a shoulder rig on the left side.

Pepperjack Poudry was of medium height and build, sporting a shaggy headful of sandy hair that he adorned with glittery trinkets. He bragged a mixture of French and Mexican blood and possessed the worst traits of each. He had a particular fondness for bladed weapons and carried a wide variety of knives and daggers on his person at all times. He also carried a converted Navy Colt pistol, prominently displayed in a bright red sash worn around his waist.

They rolled out with Blevins and Poudry sharing the seat of a high-wheeled buckboard pulled by a team of chestnut mares. Buckhorn rode a few yards ahead on Sarge. Blevins worked the reins of the buckboard and clucked gruffly to the mares, obviously having done some teamstering in the past.

As Buckhorn led in the direction of the dry wash, the men on the wagon seat conversed steadily. They spoke in mutterings and mumblings, their words unintelligible to Buckhorn. Whether this was inadvertent or by design, Buckhorn did not know nor did he particularly care. He had plenty on his mind without worrying about the rambling of a couple low-rung hardcases.

He knew a little bit about Blevins, had heard Poudry's name mentioned a time or two, he couldn't remember where. It didn't matter. They were marked well enough. He knew their type as clear as if they had descriptions painted on their backs. They were mean and tough, that was about all you could say about them. Wainwright had been reaching pretty deep into the barrel when he scraped them up.

"This is the place," Buckhorn announced as they approached the bloating lumps of the horse carcasses on the floor of the wash. A couple buzzards were making lazy circles in the sky overhead and the buzzing drone from clouds of flies could be heard as they drew closer.

"Wonder what I did to piss off the old man so's he picked me for this meat detail," muttered Blevins. "I never liked Parsons all that much to begin with. I sure ain't got no give-a-damn about a couple ambushin' skunks. You think I'm gonna lug their no-account asses all the way down off that hill just to make a delivery of 'em? Not very likely, says I."

"We're gonna at least pick their bodies, though, ain't we?" Poudry asked.

"What the hell for? They was nothing but dirt-poor losers. What'd you figure they'd have of any value? Besides, don't forget the breed was already here once before. You put an Injun anywhere near a dead body laying around to be picked clean of any valuables, you can bet the redskin will have the job done quicker than a hiccup. Ain't that right, Buckhide?"

"The name's Buckhorn," came the correction in a flat, even tone.

"Whatever," grunted Blevins as he set the brake and started to climb down from the buckboard seat. He swatted at a swarm of flies. "Come on, let's wrap ol' Parsons in that tarp we brung along and then get the hell out of here."

"While you're seeing to him," Buckhorn said, "I'll go get the body up by that highest boulder and bring it down. Then you two can fetch the nearer one." He swung down from the saddle and started for the slope.

He'd gone only a couple steps when Blevins's booming voice rang out. "Hold it, breed!"

Buckhorn stopped and turned back to face the big man. He looked at him, not saying anything.

"Didn't you hear me say we ain't botherin' with them other two bodies?"

"I guess I wasn't paying attention. What I did hear, real plain, was General Wainwright saying as to how we were to take these bodies and return them to their family."

"And how's he gonna know the difference if nobody squawks?"

"Maybe we got us a little tattletale who tells every fart he hears," said Poudry.

Blevins guffawed. "A tattletale breed. If that wouldn't beat all."

Buckhorn had fully expected, sooner or later, that some of the Flying W hardcases would see fit to test his mettle. Sighing, he reckoned it was as good a time as any to get at least the first round of it over with.

Squaring his shoulders, planting his feet a little wider, he said in a voice that sounded like sandpaper brushing across stone, "Mister, you call me *breed* in that snotty tone one more time, the bed of that wagon is liable to get mighty crowded if we have to cram your fat ass in there along with the rest of what we came here to haul away."

Blevins's mouth gaped open so wide and so suddenly that a dribble of juice from the foul tobacco he was chewing ran out one corner. His darting eyes turned even busier than usual, snapping around like he was hearing voices inside his head or something. "W-what did you say to me?"

"You heard me plain enough. Or did some of that disgusting cud you're chewing leak up and clog your ears? I don't like being here in the flies and the stink with those buzzards circling overhead any more than you do, but I was sent to do a job, and that's what I intend to do—the full works, like it was laid out. The only question is, are you and Frenchie gonna do your share or are you just gonna add to what I've got to take care of?"

"By that, you mean takin' care of us, too?"

"Except for the loading you on the wagon part. I think I've changed my mind on that. Let somebody else come back and hoist your lard."

"You really think you're that good?"

"One way to find out."

"Amigo," Poudry said rather nervously, "I do not think this is such a good idea. If we shoot him, we will have to explain to Wainwright why it came to that. If he shoots us, that obviously is not a desirable thing. I do not see where it works out good for us either way."

"He's talking sense, Blevins," Buckhorn said. "We can leave it at each of us having done a little growling and just go ahead and do what we were sent here for. Maybe take our differences back up another time."

"Oh, we will definitely do that," Blevins promised.

Buckhorn grunted. "Yeah. I expect we will." He could see this was going nowhere, so he turned his back on the pair and started up the slope to where Johnny Laudermilk's body lay. Over his shoulder, he said, "If either of you think about shooting me in the back, stop and consider how hard it'll be to explain the bullet holes coming from that way."

No shots were forthcoming, but he'd gone several steps before the anxious tingling between his shoulder blades went away.

After the bodies were loaded, they headed for the ranch house formerly owned by the Laudermilks, where they expected to find the rest of the family packing and making final preparations to pull out. Since

Buckhorn had no idea where the ranch was located,
Blevins, at the reins of the buckboard, led the way.
After rolling away from the wash and in sharp contrast
to all the chatting they'd done on the way there, the
two wagon riders did very little talking.

Buckhorn trailed from off to one side and a few
yards to the rear. Although he'd determined his two
companions were neither desperate enough to shoot
him in the back nor brave enough to face him head-
on, he liked it a lot better being able to keep an eye on
them.

Over the last mile or so, however, they had started
up again. Once more it was low mutterings that Buckhorn couldn't make out. He had a hunch they were
cooking something up and it was probably a dish that
wouldn't be to his liking. Whatever it was, it appeared
they were going to try and serve him some.

Once their destination hove into sight, Blevins
hauled back on the reins and brought his rig to a halt.
"Now looky here, you," Blevins said as Buckhorn
pulled up even with the buckboard and reined Sarge
to a stop also. "Me and Pepperjack are needing to
know just how much of a Goody Two-shoes you are,
exactly."

Buckhorn almost laughed in his face. "Me? A Goody
Two-shoes? Mister, you'd better spit out that tobacco
you're chawing in a big hurry. I think you got a serious
batch of locoweed mixed in."

"So you're saying you're not?"

"Not by any measure I know of."

Blevins scowled. "Okay. Maybe that makes sense.
That other business back there, like you said, was laid
out as direct orders. I guess I shouldn't have thought
about shortcuttin' 'em."

"So what is it you're getting at?" Buckhorn wanted to know.

"Well, me and Pepperjack been talking. When we get up yonder"—he nodded his head to indicate the ranch buildings in the distance—"the only strict orders Wainwright gave was to deliver the bodies to the widow. Right? Beyond that, he didn't lay on any restrictions or give any exact instructions. That the way you remember it?"

"Go on."

"Well, you got no way to know this on account of you're new to the area, but it so happens that Mrs. Laudermilk—now *Widow* Laudermilk—she ain't a half-bad-looking woman. Not for these parts, she ain't. And that's for damn sure."

"It is true," agreed Poudry eagerly, his mouth spreading in a wide, lewd smile that displayed a shiny gold tooth. "What is more, she has a teenage daughter. Sixteen or seventeen, I think she is. Ah, but the woman has awakened in her, if you know what I mean. Every indication is that she will blossom to be as fine looking as her mother. Maybe even more so."

"So what me and Pepperjack was thinking," Blevins went on, "was that it would be downright shameful and rude to drop off these cold bodies and then just ride off and leave all that ripe womanhood untended. They're bound to need some comforting in their time of, er, grief. Especially the lonely widow, what with her husband gone and therefore the services a woman just naturally looks to from her man suddenly left empty."

"And the daughter," Pepperjack added. "Trying to come to grips with the loss of her beloved papa—think what solace it would be for her to discover feelings and pleasures to help her get beyond the suffering of such terrible sadness and emptiness."

Buckhorn remained silent and stone-faced throughout these disgusting spiels of self-serving hogwash.

Blevins, unable to tell if what they were pitching was sinking in or not, finally blurted, "Do you get what it is we're tryin' to say or don't you?"

"Oh, I get what you're saying real clear," Buckhorn responded. "What you're saying is that you two pigs, combined, aren't worth the price of the pair of slugs it would take to rid the world of your filth."

Quicker than an eyeblink, Buckhorn had his Colt drawn and leveled on a spot directly between Blevins and Poudry. With a slight twitch of the muzzle, one way or the other, he could plant a .45 caliber pill in either one. It wouldn't take more than a fraction of a second to blow both of them clean off the seat. "But since I'm pretty flush at the moment," he continued through clenched teeth, "I'd be more than willing to cover the cost."

"You wouldn't dare," Blevins said, sneering but clearly nervous again. "You'd have the same problem explaining to Wainwright that we would've had if we'd done you back down the way."

"One big difference. I'm not afraid of Wainwright. If he hires trash like you, I'm not so sure I want to work for him anyway."

"Big talk."

"Think what you want. Like before, there's one sure way to find out."

"So what are you going to do to us?" Poudry asked anxiously.

"I'm not sure. But I know I'm not gonna let you anywhere near that widow and her kids. We'll begin by you shucking your hardware. Slow and easy, one at a time. You first, Blevins. Start with the shotgun. Hand it to me. Then toss your sidearm and everything else back into the wagon bed."

When both men were disarmed, Buckhorn used the shotgun to motion them down off the buckboard seat. "Both of you on this side. When you light down, back away a half dozen steps and take your boots off. Throw 'em in the wagon bed along with—"

"To hell with you!" Blevins erupted. "I ain't taking my boots off for nobody, especially no goddamned redskin."

Aiming the man's own shotgun at him, Buckhorn said, "Your choice. You can leave 'em on if you want. You do, you'll be taking a ride in the wagon bed with 'em on and then from there you can wear 'em straight into Hell. I'll give you to the count of three to decide. One . . ."

"Do not be a fool, Blevins," Poudry pleaded as he began kicking off his own boots. "Look in that hombre's eyes. He means every word he says."

Blevins's restless eyes tried to stare down Buckhorn, but the flinty glare of the latter made it no contest. Mouth curling savagely, Blevins averted his hate-filled gaze and began removing his boots.

"All right. Here's the way we're gonna do this," Buckhorn said after both pairs of boots were in the wagon bed. He continued to talk as he dismounted and walked Sarge around to the back of the buckboard and tied him on. "You two are gonna wait right here while I take the rig on ahead and drop off the bodies of Laudermilk and his son. Stay right where you are, so I can keep clear sight of you."

He climbed up onto the seat of the rig and reached for the reins with one hand. All during this, he kept

Blevins's shotgun steadily trained on the two men now in stocking feet.

"I see you coming toward the house, I'll shoot and kill you. I see you trying to get away, I'll ride you down and kill you. You stay put and behave, I'll come back by, pick you up, and try to get you back to the Flying W alive. It's gonna be your call all the way. We got an understanding?"

Accepting their silence and baleful stares as sufficient answer, Buckhorn snapped the team's reins and set the buckboard rolling toward the former Laudermilk ranch buildings.

CHAPTER 32

"You send me out with these two ever again," Buckhorn said, reporting back to Wainwright and Leo Sweetwater after they'd returned to the Flying W, "either me or them won't be making it back alive."

Wainwright scowled. "I don't respond well to ultimatums, Mr. Buckhorn."

Buckhorn met his scowl with a stony, unyielding gaze. "Call it a suggestion then. Or a promise. In any case, you can count on me meaning what I say."

"He's a dirty damn liar, Mr. Wainwright!" protested Bart Blevins. "You know how humpbacked them redskin bucks get for white women. He was the one who wanted to violate the Widow Laudermilk and then take advantage of her poor innocent daughter, too. He was like a rutting boar hog! It was all me and Pepperjack could do to hold him back and keep him from—"

"Shut up!" Wainwright barked. "You sicken me. What's more, you make me ashamed of myself for ever having stooped so low as to hire you. I knew your reputations yet I was willing to overlook them because

I thought I could . . . Never mind what I thought. I hardly have to explain myself to the likes of you."

"No, you sure don't, sir." Blevins spoke again quickly in a mewling, condescending tone, trying desperately to get through the trouble without having it get any worse. "As a top officer of the blue and a wealthy landowner and successful businessman, you surely don't owe me or Pepperjack any explanation for—"

"Enough," Wainwright cut him short again, including a chopping motion with one hand. "I've heard all I can stand. I can ill afford to lose more men at a time like this, yet two of the traits I will least abide from men serving under me are whining and the vulgar abuse of innocent women."

"I tell you it wasn't us looking to debauch that woman," Blevins insisted. "You, the big Indian hater, would take the word of a damn low-down half-breed over white men like me and Poudry?"

"You and Poudry are vermin, not men—and lying ones to boot," said Wainwright. "And yes, I'm taking the word of Buckhorn over yours. What's more, the way I see it now, since I take the measure of him and his gun to be worth the both of you and more, by gaining him and shedding you I really won't be losing anything at all, will I?"

"What do you mean, shedding us?" Poudry asked. "I have not protested. I have said nothing."

"Then perhaps you should have. The pair of you are dismissed." Wainwright made a shooing-away gesture. "Get them out of my sight, Mr. Sweetwater. Take them to the bunkhouse and have them pack their things. Keep an eye on them. I will figure up their wages and have pay envelopes prepared by the time they're ready to go."

"You're making a big mistake, Wainwright," said Blevins.

"No, I am *correcting* one."

"What about our guns and boots from the wagon?"

"All of your personal belongings will be returned to you."

"Not this," Buckhorn said, patting the shotgun he held in the crook of his arm. "I've taken kind of a shine to it, plus I don't particularly care for the thought of having it aimed my way from behind some dark corner the first chance this skunk gets."

"I'm giving you a good deal of allowance, especially considering the brevity of our association, Mr. Buckhorn. But you'd be advised not to push your luck too far with me," Wainwright warned. "A man's belongings are rightfully his."

"He can have the scattergun back—both barrels first—any time he wants to come get it."

Wainwright heaved an exasperated sigh. "Mr. Sweetwater, you will escort the dismissed men as far as the lake. Make sure they keep going from there." He raked a hard gaze over Blevins and Poudry. "And you two would be advised to understand this. My property runs from here for more than a day's ride in any direction above the border. Be off of it by this time tomorrow. After that, anyone and everyone who works for me will have standing orders to shoot you on sight. Now get out of here and get your gear packed."

As Buckhorn entered the bunkhouse designated for the Flying W's gun crew, Blevins and Poudry were being noisily escorted out the door. Buckhorn held up the shotgun he had taken from Blevins and made a production of cracking it open and shucking its shells. Snapping it closed again, he handed it to Sweetwater and said, "Give it back to him when you're far enough out. I decided I don't want to keep it after all. Damn thing might be infested with vermin."

A separate building from the older adobe structure occupied by the crew of working wranglers, the gunnies' place was a converted wood frame horse barn, a bit roomier and also a bit draftier. Judging by the number of mismatched joints he spotted as he walked in, Buckhorn reckoned that whatever ranch hands had done the converting did not count carpenter work among their top skills.

Still, it was clean and relatively tidy with a bit of fresh-cut wood odor lingering in the air here and there. Buckhorn had for sure slept in worse places. A hell of a lot worse.

He counted more than two dozen bunks arranged in three rows. A few were empty, a condition at least partially accountable to him. He picked one out for himself, claiming an available one near the far back corner. It had good firmness to the rope mattress, a clean-smelling pillow, and a sturdy footlocker with a hasp for attaching a lock if he wished. In the storage space were two extra blankets. He tossed his war bag in on top of them and closed the lid.

As Buckhorn sat on the edge of the bed, elbows resting on knees, he absently studied a spot on the floor between his feet. Numerous things churned inside his head.

Sitting there on the bed, he could hear the three men riding out, Blevins and Poudry still bitching and moaning, Sweetwater silently doing his job to scoot them on their way.

Buckhorn wondered about giving back the shotgun. He wondered about a lot of things where Blevins and Poudry were concerned. Some of what he thought he didn't like very much. But then, there were a lot of things about the whole situation Andrew Haydon had sent him into the middle of that he didn't care for very much.

Before Buckhorn got lost too deep in reverie, a prune-faced old black man came over and said that Sweetwater had asked him to introduce the newcomer around, show him the general layout of things, and otherwise keep him company until Sweetwater returned.

"My name is Tyrone. Since I'm the cook for this outfit—the general's gun crew, I'm talkin' about—it might be that you end up keepin' *me* company if'n Leo takes too long getting back. In the kitchen, that is . . . on account I gotta start rustlin' up some grub for these curly wolves before too much longer."

Buckhorn shrugged. "No problem. I've peeled a potato or three in my day. Might as well start doing something around here to earn my keep."

"Now there's a rare outlook," Tyrone said. "When it comes to this lazy outfit, that is. Mostly they jes' sit around playin' cards or cleanin' their guns. Sometimes doing some target shootin' so's they can go back and clean their guns some more."

"Man who does gun work for a living has to take good care of the tool of his trade," Buckhorn pointed out.

"Yeah, and I keep my pots and pans clean, too," Tyrone snorted. "But sooner or later I also gotta cook with 'em!"

Tyrone did a thorough job of taking him around, showing him the washup facilities, the grub shack, and where he could target shoot. He pointed the way to the outhouses, told him the meal routines, and introduced him to the rest of the gun hands milling about.

Some were playing cards at the big round table near the front of the bunkhouse, some were reading tattered old magazines, a few were just lying or sitting around smoking cigarettes or drinking coffee to pass the time. Their introductions to Buckhorn were acknowledged by brief eye contact, simple grunts, and a few gruff "hullos." Nothing more elaborate or welcoming. He had crossed paths with a few men in the past, a couple others he knew by name. As a whole, they seemed to add up to a pack of reasonably seasoned veterans, though not exactly the cream of the crop.

As it turned out, he *was* in the grub shack kitchen with Tyrone by the time Sweetwater got back. Not peeling potatoes, just sitting off to one side making small talk.

"They seemed willing to tolerate me," Buckhorn summed up for the gunman, "but at the same time I don't get a warm feeling they're ready to nominate me to head up the Saturday-night singalong."

Sweetwater grinned. "Probably just as well. I got a feeling your singing voice is about as pleasant as a bullfrog's."

"My horse likes it fine," Buckhorn countered. "Leastways he don't buck me off when I take to singing out on the trail."

"Well, before you get the urge to bust into song around me, consider yourself bucked outta here," said Tyrone. "Move along, the both of you. I gotta have elbow room to work my cooking magic."

Buckhorn and Sweetwater retreated to the bunkhouse. The lengthening shadows of evening fell over them as they passed between buildings.

"In case you'd like to know, I gave your two pals a right proper send-off," Sweetwater said once they were inside and had moved on past the tableful of card players.

"Good riddance to bad garbage, is all I can say," replied Buckhorn.

When they reached the bunk he'd selected for himself, Buckhorn stopped short. Laying in the middle of it was Blevins's shotgun. Buckhorn cut his eyes over to Sweetwater.

"Seems to keep finding its way back to you," said the young gunman, answering the unasked question. "Reckon that means you're best suited for it."

"Next you're gonna tell me Blevins presented it to me as a gift."

Sweetwater shrugged. "Let's just say he's all through with it."

Buckhorn kept regarding him.

Changing subjects somewhat airily, Sweetwater said, "I stopped by the main house when I got back. Boy, is the old man in a tizzy now. Seems he got a report about some goings-on in town that really tied his tail in a knot. He wants me to take a couple men and ride in first thing in the morning to check up on what he heard. I told him I'd take you. That'd be enough."

"What kind of report did Wainwright get?" Buckhorn said.

Sweetwater rolled his eyes. "Crazy talk about some fella who's showed up with a magic stick or pointer of some kind who claims he can use it to locate underground water. Did you ever hear anything so loco? In spite of that, he's got a whole passel of the town folks all stirred up, half believing he knows what he's doing."

"I've heard of his kind. They show up wherever

there's drought and misery, trying to make money off the hopes of the desperate."

"You ever hear of any of 'em actually striking water?"

"Can't say as I have."

"Well, we'll see how far this one plans on taking his act. If it's farther than Wainwright wants to allow—and that wouldn't be none too far, I don't reckon—we'll have to see to it that he hits a dry hole."

"First thing in the morning you say?"

"Uh-huh. We'll have ourselves some supper here in a bit. After that, if you're a card player and worth beans at it, I'll tell you that sorry bunch over there is always good for some quick pocket jingle. Be a way to kill some time and make money doing it before it's time to turn in. We can head out tomorrow after a good night's sleep . . . since it won't get interrupted by you roaming out after Blevins and Poudry."

Buckhorn frowned. "What's that supposed to mean? Why the hell would I be roaming after that pair? I want 'em as far gone as possible with no desire to ever lay eyes on 'em again."

Sweetwater smiled slyly. "But what you got even less of a desire for is them to get anywhere near that widow lady and her daughter again. And you know damn well, just as sure as I did, that's where they would have beelined for as soon as I peeled off from 'em. That's why you had every intention of slipping outta here tonight, the first chance you got, and catching up to make sure they'd never be able to follow through with their low-down plans."

Buckhorn's eyes went again to the shotgun on his bunk. "So you took care of 'em for me."

"For you. For Widow Laudermilk. Hell, for the good

of mankind. Don't tell me the world's any worse off with those two scraped off of it."

"Wainwright know what you did?"

"Not by me telling him, but he's a pretty shrewd ol' rascal. Don't ever sell him short on that. I got a hunch that *he* had a pretty fair hunch what those curs might try and what you'd probably do about it. You heard what he said about the bad treatment of vulnerable women and such. He meant that. Me, I feel the same. As you obviously do." Sweetwater showed his teeth in a wide, crooked grin. "Hell, we're all just a bunch of shiny knights galloping around the countryside slaying evildoers and saving damsels in distress."

Buckhorn shook his head. "I think you must've taken a chaw of Blevins's locoweed-laced tobacco before you saw him off. In any case, I reckon I'm obliged to you. At the very least, you saved me some lost sleep."

"So you *was* gonna go after them rascals, wasn't you?"

"It was on my mind," Buckhorn admitted.

"I knew it. I saw it in your eyes when you handed me Blevins's shotgun." Sweetwater's expression turned somber. "But listen. You feeling obliged for what I done ain't necessary. I've never said a proper thanks to you for saving my bacon earlier today in that dry wash. I'd 've been a goner for sure, if you hadn't come along when you did."

"You already squared that," Buckhorn reminded him, "when you had to shoot the old man off my back because I failed to take care of his son proper in the first place."

Sweetwater shook his head. "No, I don't see it as being that clean. You were spinning on the old man and had a good chance of putting him down on your own. I just lent a hand, that's all. But the fix they had me in ahead of that—I had no chance. It was just a matter of time before they would've got me. I see it as me still being beholden to you."

"You're a stubborn cuss, aren't you?" Buckhorn arched a brow. "I guess the only thing for it now is to agree to disagree. Otherwise we'll end up arguing half the night away and all I'll accomplish is wasting the sleep you gained me."

CHAPTER 33

"The thing about drunks like me," Carl Orndecker was saying, "is that everybody says how we shouldn't drink at all because we aren't able to stop after just one or two social drinks. That's not really the problem. Speaking strictly for myself, I guess I should say, the problems usually start to arrive after I don't stop drinking after one or two *days*!" With that, he tossed back the shot of tequila he'd been holding in one hand and then let out a loud laugh as he lowered the emptied glass.

Next to Carl, leaning on the battered old bar of the nameless Mexville cantina just across the border from the south end of Wagon Wheel, Martin Goodwin listened and looked on with a guardedly dubious expression. Other voices and bursts of loud laughter filled the smoky, crowded cantina and drifted out into the dusty nighttime street. Off in one corner a mariachi band was playing poorly but loudly and with much energy. The mood throughout seemed lighthearted and happy.

Only Goodwin appeared a bit reserved, not quite caught up in the merry atmosphere although the plump, pretty brown-skinned young woman keeping herself plastered to his right arm certainly was doing her best to put him in a better mood. Her low-cut, off-the-shoulder blouse was showing a voluptuous amount of cleavage and the warmth of her large, cushiony breasts rubbing against his arm made it clear they were quite unrestrained under the thin fabric of the blouse.

"You look decidedly skeptical, Goodwin, about my well-researched discourse on the subject of drinking," Carl said. "Are you yourself such an expert on the subject that you can debate my observations? Or is it the opposite? Are you so ill exposed to the subject matter that you haven't the basis for a firm opinion one way or the other?"

Goodwin replied, "If you mean have I done my own share of drinking, the answer is yes. I'm hardly a teetotaler."

"You couldn't prove it by me. Not so far, at least," Carl said as he refilled his glass. "This will be my third, You haven't finished your first. Tequila not to your taste? You want to get warmed up with some wine? Maybe some beer?"

"The tequila's fine," Goodwin said. "It's just that I usually don't approach my drinking like a race to see how fast I can get smashed."

Carl laughed again. "Well, I do. And my tolerance to the damn devil's brew is so high I have the luxury—or curse, if you will—of being able to run for a very long time before I reach the point of getting, in your words, *smashed*. Isn't that right, darling?" He turned to the brown-skinned lovely on his left arm, a close twin to the girl with Goodwin and equally free with her display of cleavage, and planted a hungry wet kiss on her lushly accommodating lips.

When the kiss ended, the young woman threw her head back, tossing her long hair, and laughed gleefully. "No smashed for Mucho Carl—never for a long time!"

When the two men first entered the establishment, the two cantina girls had appeared immediately. Carl had introduced them as Conchita and Rosalita. Goodwin couldn't keep straight which was which, but it didn't really matter. Carl himself generally referred to them simply as his chiquitas most of the time.

When they gushed all over him, calling him Mucho Carl, he'd had to explain somewhat sheepishly that this pertained to how much he could drink and how often he elected to take one—or sometimes both—of his chiquitas to a private room.

Turning from the kiss back to his tequila, Carl promptly knocked back the glass he had just refilled. Goodwin joined in, then seized the bottle and began to refill both glasses.

Carl leaned closer and dropped his voice to a conspiratorial tone. "If we're going to make this work, damn it, you're going to have to do your part to sell it. Don't worry about me. I'm in control and I'll stay that way. But they're used to seeing me act in a certain manner and I've got to stick with that or the whole thing will fall flat. You're the water dowser who's been poking your stick all over town up north, and now you're down here to have some fun because you got plenty of Don Pedro's money to spend. Start acting like it!"

As soon as Goodwin had their glasses filled, he and Carl held them up and clicked them together.

"Viva Don Pedro!" Goodwin proclaimed before tossing his back.

Carl followed suit, hesitating slightly because he was caught off guard by the suddenness with which Goodwin had brought out the use of Don Pedro's name. On second thought, maybe it wasn't such a bad idea. Why waste time about it?

"You got that right, buddy," he said, grabbing the bottle to pour their next refill. "Since the old don is paying you so handsomely to work your water magic for him, you're damn right we'll raise a glass to him. Hell, he's footing the bill, right? Viva Don Pedro, indeed!"

Toward the middle of the room, two narrow-faced, dark-complexioned men sat over their own bottle of tequila and quickly caught the mention of Don Pedro's name. They exchanged thoughtful glances through the smoke that curled up from the dark cigarillos hanging from the corners of their mouths.

Over the course of the next two or three hours they heard the loud gringos speak the name of Don Pedro several more times . . . as did numerous others within the boisterous little cantina.

CHAPTER 34

"Yeah, I know the fella you're talking about," Sheriff Banning said. "The way he started drawing a crowd by yesterday afternoon, I couldn't hardly miss him."

"So what did you do about it?" Sweetwater wanted to know.

The sheriff frowned. "What do you mean, what did I do about it? What was I supposed to do about it? Wasn't like he was breaking any laws or anything."

"Wouldn't you call it disturbing the peace, stirring up a bunch of people that way?"

Banning's frown deepened. "Wasn't like he was stirring 'em up in a bad way, like a riot or anything. Basically, they were just flocked around, curiouslike, watching him parade around poking his stick this way and that."

"And the stick is the thing that's supposed to lead him to the water he's promising?"

"I don't know that he's 'promising' to find water. But, yeah, the stick is the thing that's supposed to lead him to it if there's any there."

Sweetwater leaned forward in his chair, eager, insistent. "There's the thing. Right there! Flimflamming folks like that—there's some kind of legal word for it, but I can't remember what it is. Ain't that something you can act on? He's getting their hopes all built up and then, when he's got 'em practically panting like a dog, he'll be asking for money to *finish* finding the water. The water that ain't there, as anybody with a lick of sense already knows. Once this trickster gets some money gathered up, he won't be there neither. He'll be gone like the last drop of rain. That's the flimflam!"

Banning arched a brow skeptically, leaning back in the chair behind his office's narrow, cluttered desk. Sweetwater, along with Buckhorn, was seated before the desk. The sheriff had poured coffee for everybody.

Just about the worst he'd ever tasted, Buckhorn judged.

The holding cells were empty. Outside, the main street of Wagon Wheel was coming alive in a wash of morning sun that was already hot and promising to grow steadily hotter as the day progressed.

"Well now," said the sheriff, "I appreciate you riding all the way into town to warn me about the ways of a flimflam artist, Mr. Sweetwater. But I've gotta say, I'm a little surprised by your deep concern." His eyes cut to Buckhorn. "And I'm even more surprised at the allegiances you seem to have taken up, mister."

"Never mind about his allegiances or my concern," Sweetwater snapped. "What *your* concern oughta be is knowing that General Wainwright don't like this nonsense about people getting all het up over a new water source."

"What the hell is that supposed to mean?"

"You figure it out."

"Look, just because Wainwright owns most of the land in every direction, he don't own the water that might be down in the earth and he don't own this town."

Sweetwater stood up. "Apparently you're forgetting what he *does* own around here. When we get back to the ranch, I'll have to remind him how forgetful you seem to 've gotten lately. In the meantime, me and Buckhorn are gonna take a stroll around town. Might be fun to see the show this dinker or dipper or whatever he calls himself puts on."

"Be careful about starting anything, Sweetwater. I've cut you plenty of slack in the past, but folks have been suffering and worrying about the drought for quite a spell now. The hope they've raised over this dowser maybe coming up with something is pretty high. They won't stand for anybody giving him a hard time."

Sweetwater paused in the doorway and shot a hard look back over his shoulder. "That sounds to me like the makings of a mob, Sheriff. If they rile up over me and my pal asking a few questions out of simple curiosity, I sure hope you or one of your deputies are around to save our hides. Elsewise, keeping in mind your advice not to *start* anything, if there's any trouble— strictly as a matter of self-defense, you understand—we might have to *end* it."

Martin Goodwin paused in the lobby of the Traveler's Rest Hotel as he contemplated the brilliant sunlight pouring into the street beyond the open front door. His face scrunched in a sour expression barely an improvement over the pale, haggard, bloodshot-eyed way it had looked a few minutes before. "Oh, God," he groaned. "My head already feels like it's going to explode. All that bright sunlight out there will set off the fuse for certain."

Standing beside the worse-for-wear dowser, Carl Orndecker, looking fresh and rested, urged, "Aw, go on. It's like taking the plunge into a pool of chilly water. Absorb the shock all at once and then the worst of it is over. Your eyes will water a little bit at first and then you'll be fine."

"I feel about a million miles from fine."

"You think you invented the hangover or something?" Carl said. "You had one night of moderately heavy drinking and got three or four hours of sleep. Hell, that's nothing. I've been on benders that lasted for weeks and came out of 'em alive. You'll be surprised how quick you snap back once you make up your mind to move on past it."

"I'm not sure there's any *snap back* in me."

"Oh, sure there is. There'd better be. If we didn't generate enough notice with our little act last night, we may have to go back tonight and do it all over again."

Goodwin gave him a sidelong glance with eyes as big around as silver dollars.

"Careful," Carl said, barely suppressing a chuckle. "You open those eyes too wide, you're liable to bleed to death out of 'em."

"That's not even funny."

"Just as well. You don't want to be laughing when you go through those doors. Your public is out there waiting for you and they'll expect you to look serious when you set about your business."

"What do you mean, my public?" Goodwin said.

"I mean the folks who've taken such a big interest in what you're doing. The ones who sort of collected around and began looking on yesterday . . . after they came to understand what it was you were up to. There's six or eight of 'em out there already, waiting to watch you go at it again today."

Goodwin groaned again. "You're just full of good news."

Looking out through the front window of the *Sun Ledger* building, Justine York was relieved to see her brother and Martin Goodwin emerging from the Traveler's Rest Hotel. Goodwin was carrying the leather case that contained his divining rod and other bits of paraphernalia.

Milling nearby was a small crowd of citizens who could only be waiting to see the dowser resume his attempts to find some indication of underground water. Justine was relieved to see this also.

All of these indicators meant the roughly assembled plan they had put together with Buckhorn seemed to be showing promising results. One of her biggest concerns had been that her brother could go on a pretend drinking spree with Goodwin and stop short of having it turn into the real thing.

She didn't know everything that had transpired in the nameless Mexville cantina last night, but the fact that both men were up and about this morning was a good sign . . . although Goodwin *did* look a little green around the gills, now that she watched him move into the sunlight.

The townsfolk showing interest and apparent belief in the possibility there just *might* be an alternative water source somewhere close by, fell right in line with how they hoped their plan would work.

Justine stepped out onto busy Front Street, leaving a note on the door of the newspaper office saying she would return in fifteen minutes. She was headed to the telegraph office to see if she'd gotten a reply to any of her inquiries as to the state of the latest revolution brewing in Mexico. If she succeeded in establishing communication with someone who had their finger on the pulse of the situation, they could consider that another piece of the plan in place.

She'd taken only a few steps when she saw Buckhorn and Leo Sweetwater leaving the sheriff's office and coming down the boardwalk on the opposite side of the street. She knew this was all part of the ruse, but seeing them like that—striding side by side, all friendly-looking—made a chill run through her.

God, they were banking so much on Buckhorn, the way he was the solid core to everything. If he decided to betray them in any way, perhaps get caught up by the wildly ambitious dream of Thomas Wainwright, it would be absolutely devastating.

She gave her head a little shake. No, Buckhorn would never do that. No matter how relaxed and natural he looked at the moment, walking alongside Sweetwater.

Buckhorn's whole purpose for being here was to crush Wainwright.

Nothing could ever swerve him from that . . . could it?

CHAPTER 35

Sweetwater stopped walking. "Well, looky there. Judging by the gaggle of folks who appear to be waiting for him and all, I'd say that stranger who just came out of the hotel with Carl Orndecker might be our dowser boy. What do you think?"

"Could be," Buckhorn said. "That stranger had just checked into the hotel before I checked out. I never caught his name or what his business was, though. You're right about there seeming to be a lot of interest in him, so I'd say it's likely he's the dowser."

"I wonder what Orndecker is doing with him."

Buckhorn made no comment.

Sweetwater looked at him. "You know Orndecker. Right?"

"Uh-huh. Sort of fell in with him and his sister on my first day here. Giving them a hand is what first put me crosswise of your man Conway, which led in a roundabout way to me having to kill Dandy Jack and then eventually Conway himself when he tried to ambush me in my hotel room."

"Boy, you hit town like a holy terror, didn't you?" said Sweetwater, grinning crookedly.

"Reckon so. Even if it was never my intent."

"Lucky for you all the Flying W men you shot were no-accounts. Conway wasn't part of our gun crew, just a wrangler, and not a very good one at that. Ol' Jack . . . well, you already know my feelings on him."

"Luck of the draw. That was just the way they came at me."

"And now you're working for the Flying W yourself. Kind of . . . what's the word? *Ironic,* that's it. Kind of ironic, wouldn't you say?"

"Not to mention surprising. Leastways to me."

"Imagine that's how it will seem to a few others, too. You already saw the sheriff's reaction. And, if I'm not mistaken," said Sweetwater, "you're getting more of the same from right there across the street."

Buckhorn had already been aware of Justine drawing nearer on the other side of the street. It bothered him not to be able to acknowledge her in any way, but that's the way it had to be. As for her, she was playing her part almost to perfection, looking his way with strong dislike and then hiking her nose in disapproval.

"That's Orndecker's sister, the newspaper lady, ain't it? You said you gave them a hand right after you got to town. And then, if I heard right, you even had lunch with the lady the other day. But unless I'm badly mistaken, as of right now you are getting a first-class cold shoulder." Sweetwater chuckled. "By that snooty look she just shot us, I highly suspect she don't approve of the company you're keeping."

"Reckon that'll have to be her problem," Buckhorn said.

"She's got a real dose of hard feelings toward Wainwright, you know. Just like her husband before her. It shows plain in that newspaper they put out . . . well, that *she* continues to put out now since she's a widow.

You know about how her husband died and how she blames Wainwright for it, don't you?"

"No, can't say I ever heard that part."

They started walking again in the direction of where Goodwin and Carl had struck out farther toward the town's north end, with the group of interested watchers following in their wake.

"This was back before I came aboard," Sweetwater went on, "but it seems York started walloping Wainwright pretty regular in the newspaper just as Wainwright was gaining land and cattle and wealth and was on his way to becoming the big he-wolf of the whole region. Wainwright didn't like it, naturally, but he couldn't get York to back off and York was sharp enough in what he printed to give no legal grounds for stopping him.

"Late one night, York rode out to some unnamed place to meet with an informant who supposedly had some real damning information on Wainwright. Somewhere along the way, something—a rattler, a coyote, or maybe a wolf, maybe even the two-legged kind, a lot of folks suspected that—spooked the newspaperman's horse and it threw him. Not all the way, though. One of his feet got caught in a stirrup and York was dragged to death. Horse showed up back in town with his battered body still trailing along behind."

"Real convenient accident for Wainwright," Buckhorn muttered, unable to hide some of the bitterness in his voice.

"Yeah, that's the way a lot of folks saw it at the time. But nobody could prove anything. York never told anybody where he was going or who it was he was supposed to meet." Sweetwater grinned. "Me, I figure that was probably the one worthwhile piece of business ol' Dandy Jack did during the time he was working for

Wainwright. Like I said, I wasn't here at the time so I was never made privy to the full story on what happened. The widow kept the newspaper going, as I guess you've seen, and she keeps using it to go after Wainwright. But she doesn't seem to get under his skin the way her husband used to. Was I her, though, I think I'd still avoid going for lonely horse rides late at night."

As Buckhorn listened to this, he cast another brief look at Justine and remembered something from the other night. When they were making their plans in Justine's kitchen and he'd made the sarcastic remark about riding back to the Flying W and simply shooting Wainwright and Don Pedro to end the whole problem, Justine had taken a sudden, sharp interest. She'd asked, "Could you really do that?"

At the time Buckhorn had taken it for a sign of disapproval from someone a bit startled another person could suggest something so cold-blooded. He wondered now if that interpretation was wrong and what he'd heard was the somewhat hopeful tone of a woman who wouldn't mind at all the prospect of her husband's likely killer meeting that same end.

He filed away further thought on that question for another time. For one thing, he had other more pressing matters to deal with.

For another, before this whole thing was over with, Thomas Wainwright was slated to be dead regardless of how Justine York felt about it.

For the next forty-five minutes or so, Buckhorn and Sweetwater mingled with the rest of the group following Goodwin around and watching him go about his dowsing rituals. Now and then, some members of the group would drift away and then new ones would show up. The size of the pack fluctuated a bit but stayed generally between twelve and fifteen.

As far as what Goodwin was doing in the way of his dowsing, there didn't seem to be much to it. He simply walked around holding his divining rod in a certain way, muttering to himself part of the time but always concentrating very hard on his task. Sometimes he would backtrack and go over the same piece of ground a second or third time. When he did this, a mild ripple of anticipation would pass through the crowd, but otherwise everybody stayed respectfully quiet.

Sweetwater decided it was time to stir things up a bit. "Okay," he announced in a loud voice, elbowing his way forward out of the pack. "This is about as exciting as watching buffalo chips dry on the prairie. You been poking that stick around in the air and mumbling to yourself for a day and a half now, Mr. Dowser. Ain't it about time you get to the meat of the show? Hate to break it to you, but your act is getting mighty boring, pal."

Goodwin gave him a look. "I beg your pardon? This is neither an act nor a show, sir. I am working here, trying to provide a desperately needed service to this community, indeed to this whole region."

The crowd grumbled its disapproval of Sweetwater's interruption, but he ignored them.

"Whoooee! You got that spiel down mighty fine," he said to Goodwin. "You're damn near good enough to convince me. Except I happen to have a brain just a little bigger 'n a mosquito's, unlike the rest of these suckers you're stringing along."

Carl edged forward to stand slightly in front of Goodwin. "What's your problem, Sweetwater? Nobody's bothering you."

"No, Carl, you're wrong. Stupidity bothers me. And liars and confidence artists. All of those things are on display right here in front of me, so I'm bothered. I hope you ain't planning to try and bother me, too."

"I don't intend to stand by and let you hoorah this fella, if that's what you mean."

Buckhorn decided it was time for him to step into it. Number one, because Sweetwater would expect it of him. Number two, because he didn't want a confrontation to spin too suddenly out of control. He was responsible for Carl siding Goodwin. He'd seen for himself that the former lawman could still handle a gun, but he didn't think Carl was a match for Sweetwater. He didn't want to get somebody killed, not if he could help it.

"I don't see nobody hoorahing anybody," Buckhorn said to Carl. "You're the one sticking your nose in and acting belligerent. My pal here was just expressing his concerns about these folks getting flimflammed."

"Your pal, eh?" smirked Carl. "Boy, you didn't waste no time switching the direction you ride to and from, did you, Buckhorn? You really had me fooled."

"And that's just what this smooth-talking hombre with his goofy-looking stick and oily promises is doing—fooling you. Fooling all of you," said Sweetwater. "Making fools out of you is more like it. You're desperate enough to just open your arms wide and let him do it. Is that it?"

"Yeah, and who is it that's made us feel desperate?" said an old man in the crowd. "We've seen your boss squeeze out the smaller ranchers all around him by starving them of water while he has the only lasting source. Who's to say he won't do that to our town, too, if this drought continues much longer?"

"You'd better be careful what you're implying, you old geezer," Sweetwater warned.

"I ain't implying a thing," the stubborn old fellow replied. "I'm saying it straight out."

"And you coming around with your threats at the first sign we might have hope for a new water source," a heavyset woman spoke up, thrusting her chin defiantly at Sweetwater, "is a perfect example of why we *do* feel desperate and concerned if things stay the way they are."

"Lady, I ain't threatened nobody," Sweetwater said, growing irritated, biting the words out through clenched teeth. "If and when I do, it will damn sure be clear enough."

"Well, whatever it is you're doing, or trying to do," Carl said, "all you're accomplishing is interfering with Mr. Goodwin doing his job. A job he has every right to do and one all these other people want to see him continue. Since you've had your say, how about just moving along? Ride back to Wainwright and tell him your scare tactics didn't work so easy. Not this time."

Buckhorn could see Sweetwater's body growing more rigid. He felt himself tensing, too.

"Who the hell do you think you are, Orndecker?" Sweetwater demanded. "You forgetting you're just an embarrassing drunk and has-been? You think you're still some kind of badge-wearing town tamer who can order people when to come and go?"

Buckhorn could see Carl also starting to tense up, old habits and reflexes kicking in. The fingers of his gun hand straightened, splaying wider.

"Leo," Buckhorn said in a low voice. "Don't you think we've pushed this far enough for the time being?"

"No, I don't," Sweetwater snapped. "You just keep quiet and be ready to back my play."

An uneasy ripple passed through the crowd and several of the onlookers moved back, sensing the exchange of words was suddenly on the brink of becoming something more.

At the same time, two men who'd been hanging back on the rear fringe of the gathering, staying largely unnoticed, shouldered their way forward. They were Mexicans cut from closely matching cloth. Thirtyish, whip lean, and coiled for danger, they had narrow faces and hard eyes under broad-brimmed hats. Fully loaded cartridge belts were cinched low around their trim waists and from each belt hung a tooled leather holster heavy with the weight of a shiny revolver. They might as well have had signs that read PISTOLERO dangling from around their necks.

"Amigo," one of them said to Sweetwater, "if you are concerned for the well-being of these people as you claim, why is it you are so determined to stop the chance for them to be presented with their own freshwater supply?"

Sweetwater eyed the speaker coldly. "First off, greaser, get it straight that I ain't your amigo. Second, why the hell are you up here worrying about Americano business anyway? Why ain't you back down in Mexville eating frijoles and sucking tequila and resting up so's you're ready for your siesta this afternoon?"

The pistolero smiled. "Because I decided I wanted to be up here instead. That is all the reason I need."

"Do you know who you're talking to?" Sweetwater wanted to know.

"*Sí.* You are the one they call Sweetwater. The name amuses me. Considering the work you do for Señor Wainwright and what you are trying to do here to these people, you should be called Mr. No-water." The pistolero smiled broadly and his companion followed suit.

Sweetwater's face flushed red with anger. "You think you're too damn cute for words, don't you? But what you really are is too damn cute for your own good."

Buckhorn was waiting and watching for Carl to glance his way. When he did, Buckhorn gave a quick, barely perceptible jerk of his head, motioning for him to step back and stay out of the way.

Carl seemed to hesitate reluctantly but finally complied.

"Maybe," the pistolero said in reply to Sweetwater, "it is you who do not know who I am."

"I know all I need to know," Sweetwater told him. "You're one of Don Pedro's pistoleros. Names don't matter. You're all second rate. You drifted down there and went to work for Don Pedro after Wainwright had hired all the best gunmen up here. You could say you sort of dribbled down there. You know, like piss dribbling down a coward's leg and ending up in a boot heel print in the mud."

Unlike the flush of anger that had flooded Sweetwater's face, the fury that gripped the pistolero manifested itself by all the color draining from his face. "You are an arrogant pig with an offensive mouth. You have convinced yourself that *you* are a pistolero by using your guns on slow, thick-fingered farmers and ranchers who stood no chance against you. You have fooled yourself into believing you are as fast as your reputation."

"I'm damn sure too fast for the likes of you, greaser," Sweetwater said, grating out the words. "The only reason I haven't already drilled you is because your boss Don Pedro and my boss General Wainwright are friends and business partners. That buys you one chance and one chance only to haul your asses out of here and go back to minding your own business on the other side of the border."

The pistolero sneered. "Don Pedro's business interests reach farther than you understand, Mr. Nowater . . . and it is our job to protect those interests wherever we find them."

Simultaneously, the pistoleros grabbed for their guns. They were fast, real fast . . . but not faster than the double-draw of Sweetwater—or that of Buckhorn.

Sweetwater's revolvers blurred into his fists and became twin muzzles extended at waist level. He triggered three rounds in a rolling clap of gun-thunder.

All three slugs hammered into the talkative pistolero's chest and sent him staggering back, turning slightly to his left, and then pitching onto one shoulder and the side of his head. The gun he managed to get unholstered was thrust down past his right hip and discharged a single shot into the dirt. His legs spasmed two or three times and then all of him went totally still.

Beating the draw of the second pistolero before the man even cleared leather, Buckhorn fanned two shots so fast they, too, sounded like a single report. The rounds punched into the base of his target's throat, just under his Adam's apple. Spouts of blood shot straight out and then arced upward as the man's head snapped back. His body stiffened and he toppled flat onto the dust.

CHAPTER 36

With blue powder smoke still curling in the air and his guns still held at the ready, Sweetwater wheeled to face the crowd of onlookers. His eyes raked the faces of those who had edged back several more steps from the outburst of shooting. "Any of the rest of you sons o' bitches want to try and stick your nose in my business or tell me some more what my business oughta be?" he demanded.

Buckhorn was aware of activity taking place back down the street, but he kept his eyes on Sweetwater.

The young gunman locked his focus on Carl once again. "How about you, you drunk old bastard? You had plenty to say a minute ago. You still wanting some of this?"

Carl met his gaze. Licking his lips, he said, "You know I can't beat you in a draw."

"Damn right you can't," Sweetwater said. "Nobody in this sorry town can. Seems to me a lot of you were on the brink of forgetting that before the two greasers stepped forward to try their luck."

"That don't mean you can go around outdrawing and killing everybody," Carl told him.

Sweetwater grinned. "No, but I can do it often enough to make sure you all keep it fresh in your minds. I'm thinking I must've let too much time pass here of late and that's what brought out the show of bravery from you bunch of losers this morning. I gotta remember not to let that happen again."

Sweetwater's focus switched to Goodwin. "In the meantime, what's your real story, water sniffer? What was it those Mexes were spouting about sticking their noses in on account of looking out for Don Pedro's interests? You got something to do with Don Pedro?"

"I don't think I care to answer that," Goodwin replied stiffly. "You've shown nothing but disrespect and ridicule for my work. What difference does it make who or what is behind it?"

Sweetwater took a step toward the dowser. "Maybe it would make a difference if I took that goofy-looking stick of yours and rammed it down your throat. How about that? Or maybe I just blast away your kneecaps so's you can't parade around waving your phony stick at all. You like that idea?"

At which point Buckhorn stepped up behind Sweetwater and swung his Colt in a short, chopping blow to the back of the young gunman's head, knocking him unconscious. He caught the lean body as its knees buckled and the pistols slipped from nerveless fingers, then eased it to the ground.

Carl came over and knelt beside Buckhorn. "Can I help?"

"Undo his gunbelt and strip it away," Buckhorn instructed. "His guns, too. Get 'em out of his reach for when he comes back around."

"What the hell's going on here?" demanded Sheriff Banning, arriving at the head of the spread-out string of townsfolk drawn by the shooting. Looking up and around, Buckhorn saw Deputy Pomeroy also approaching, shouldering his way through the other citizens. A little farther back, Justine was also hurrying in that direction, a look of deep concern on her face.

Buckhorn stood up. "What's going on here, Sheriff, is the beginning of cleaning up your town and freeing it from the grip of Thomas Wainwright. I don't know how much you're privy to what all that crazy ex-general has planned for this territory so, before I say more, you're gonna have to tell me if you're ready to pull yourself once and for all out from under his thumb and stand firm in your boots as this town's proper lawman . . . or if you want to throw that badge down in the dirt and slink off with Sweetwater here when I send him packing back to the Flying W."

From the back of his horse, Sweetwater glared down at Buckhorn. His wrists were handcuffed to the saddle horn in front of him. Hatless and stripped of his guns, he had just enough slack to work the reins. "You're gonna be sorry you didn't kill me," he said through gritted teeth. "You're gonna be sorry because I'm gonna kill you. And it ain't gonna be fast and clean, I can promise you that."

"You're a smart kid," Buckhorn told him, "but not as smart as you think you are. If you don't wise up in a hurry, you're gonna find out there's always somebody faster with a gun."

"You, I suppose you mean?"

"I don't know. I hope it doesn't come to that, but if you push it, I guess we'll have to find out."

"Oh, it's gonna come to that. I aim to make sure. You see me coming, you better start reaching for your hogleg. That's the only chance you'll have."

Buckhorn sighed. "If you have any brains at all, you'll ride away from here and keep going. Ride clear of Wainwright. He's heading for a fall and siding with him will only drag you down, too."

"Hell, you think I ever had plans on living a long life? It plain don't happen in this line of work. But I'll live long enough to take you down before I go. You can count on that."

There was a trace of sadness in Buckhorn's expression as he replied, "I've said all I got to say. I hope you change your mind. If you don't, I'll do my best to oblige you reaching that short life you seem so hellbent on."

"My guns?"

"They're in your saddlebags, emptied of cartridges. Same for your gunbelt. By the time you make it somewhere you can get those cuffs off and reload, maybe you'll have changed your mind."

"You go ahead and think that if it makes you feel better. One day, and it won't be long, you'll find out otherwise." With that, Sweetwater wheeled his horse and rode out of town in a cloud of dust.

Buckhorn stood watching him go. After a minute, he was aware that Carl had walked up and was standing at his shoulder. "You should have killed him. He'll make good on that promise to come after you."

"Yeah, I suppose he will. Be soon enough to kill him then, if I'm able."

Carl regarded him. "You got some strange ways about you, you know that?"

Buckhorn returned his gaze. "You just now figure that out?"

"No, not exactly. The part I really can't figure out is why me and so many others are willing to stick with you."

Buckhorn looked past Carl at the gathering of people about a dozen yards away. The bodies of the two slain pistoleros still lay on the ground a short distance to one side. Somebody had spread horse blankets over them. The group of townsfolk had increased in size considerably from before. In their midst, addressing them, were Justine and Sheriff Banning. Goodwin also stood close at hand, along with Deputy Pomeroy.

"How are things going over there?" Buckhorn said.

"Justine and Banning are doing a good job of laying it out. So far, I think they've managed to convince most everybody what Wainwright and Don Pedro have been setting up. The only thing folks are having a hard time believing is that none of them saw it taking shape sooner."

"They're willing to put their trust in Banning, even though he was cutting Wainwright more slack than he ever should've been?"

"Yeah. Could say they're following your lead. I'll put myself in the same category. I think folks are just glad to have a sheriff back who they can get behind, given the confrontation with Wainwright and his gunnies that looks to be on the horizon."

"It's gonna be more than just on the horizon. It's gonna be right in our laps before it's over."

"What about the Don Pedro angle we rigged for Wainwright to worry about? Judging by the way those two pistoleros stepped forward and what they had to say before they bit the dust, I'd say me and Goodwin sold our little show good enough last night to convince more than a few of the cantina patrons. If word of that has gotten to Wainwright and Sweetwater backs it up with what he saw and heard here this morning . . . well, I think it's a pretty safe bet that Wainwright will swallow the bait."

Buckhorn grunted. "Swallow it? Hell, he'll gobble it down like candy."

"That might make him inclined toward paying Don Pedro a little visit first. Give us more time to get the town ready for when it's our turn to receive a visit."

"Something to hope for, maybe. But not something we can count on. Either way, visitors are coming and we gotta figure they're gonna be coming hard." Buckhorn jerked a thumb toward the group of folks still being addressed by Justine and Banning. "That means it's about time to break up this gaggle from just talking about what's on the way and get 'em preparing for it."

CHAPTER 37

"Betrayal! Scurvy, black-hearted, low-down traitors! The very thing every commander fears and detests above all else!" As Thomas Wainwright paced agitatedly back and forth behind the desk in his den, his balled right fist was twisting, grinding steadily in the cupped palm of his left hand.

Leo Sweetwater sat in a wine-colored leather chair positioned in front of the desk. He was methodically pressing cartridges into the loops of the gunbelt spread over his lap. His already-loaded twin pistols were resting on a corner of the desk. The skin around his wrists, exposed by the way the cuffs of his shirtsleeves were shifted back, appeared reddened and faintly abraded.

"I felt the sheriff weakening steadily of late. I knew I'd lose his support completely and have to get rid of him when it was time to take the town," Wainwright went on. "And I certainly had no high hopes for Buckhorn. You can expect only so much from those heathen redskins. Short term, however, I did believe we could maintain control over him and maybe even get some use out of him if we brought him into the fold and kept him close."

"I'd like to think we did get *some* use out of him. Leastways, I did," Sweetwater muttered. "He saved my life once back in that wash, maybe even twice when he pitched in against those pistoleros earlier this morning."

"I think you sell yourself short. I think you could have managed both of those situations on your own," Wainwright said. "Either way, he spent whatever currency he'd earned when he turned on you and clubbed you from behind. Isn't that so?"

"Yeah, reckon I got a right to look at that as wiping the slate clean."

"Damn right you do. Same for me with Don Pedro. All these weeks and months of planning. All the money I personally poured in, plus the additional backing I was able to secure. You alone, Sweetwater, out of all the men in my employ, have I confided in about the dream of Silverado and everything Don Pedro and I have put in place to move it toward reality. Tell me, have I shirked at all in my share of the duties?"

Sweetwater shook his head. "No, sir. Way I've seen it, you've carried your share of the load and then some."

"Don Pedro's part all along has only been the *potential* for the silver he would be bringing out of the mountains to square things up. That and the daughter who was supposed to provide me issue to carry on my name and take over all that I am building." Wainwright made a disdainful snorting sound. "Well, the daughter has proven barren and, for all I know, the alleged silver mines will turn out to be more of the same. Maybe it's a good thing Don Pedro's duplicity has been revealed now, before I waste any more money or time or—"

"Attention to the breeding cow who has failed so miserably in her duties?" Lusita finished for him as she came bursting into the room.

"Lusita!" Wainwright exclaimed. "How long have you been standing out there? I thought I locked that door."

"I had a duplicate key made for that door months ago. You think I would spend so many hours alone in a house that is supposed to be my home and allow myself to be frozen out of a room within it? As for how long I've been standing out there, let's just say long enough to confirm what I've suspected for some time—that I was nothing but barter in this insane undertaking that you and my father have set in motion! Am I supposed to be honored that herding me into your bed for the sake of giving you an heir was the initial bargain that sealed your bold partnership?"

"Lusita, that's crazy talk," Wainwright said. "You are my wife. I love you."

"No, it is Silverado you love—or the mad dream that Silverado will ever amount to," Lusita insisted. She marched up to the desk and swept her arm, scattering several maps and corresponding papers that were spread over it. "*This* has consumed you. For months! Did you ever stop to think that if you hadn't poured all of your passion into these inanimate papers and maps of what will never exist, maybe you would have had enough left to produce the child you claim to so desperately want?"

"I *do* want a child. And I will have one. *Our* child, Lusita! I have not given up on that eventuality." Wainwright's nostrils flared and his eyes flashed with fierce determination. "I will not be deterred from that just as

I will not be deterred from my dream of Silverado, not even by the betrayal of your father."

"Why are you so willing to jump to the worst possible conclusions and condemn my father on such little evidence?" Lusita demanded. "The prattle of drunken cantina patrons. The bravado of a pair of pistoleros looking to make a name for themselves. These few bits of behavior are enough for you to suddenly cast aside all that you two have forged together? I'm not saying I either believe in or condone the concept of Silverado, but doesn't the integrity of my father such as you have known it up until now deserve at least talking to him about this matter of him allegedly seeking an alternative water source?"

Wainwright's face flushed with a new wave of anger. "If he had nothing to hide why didn't *he* talk to *me* about such designs? Why keep it a secret that he had gone and hired this . . . this water wizard or whatever the hell he is?"

"I have no answer for that," Lusita replied. "Yet I maintain that he at least deserves the chance to explain. What's more, I'm not sure I understand what is so bad about developing a secondary water supply, no matter who is behind it."

"Water is power!" Wainwright said forcefully. "Don't you see that? Don't you understand? Look what having control over the single great water source in this region has gained me. A new source—especially in town, the one place neither Don Pedro nor I have within our grasp—would tip the balance, drastically dilute this power I wield and have so carefully nurtured."

"So carefully and ruthlessly," Lusita said bitterly.

"One man's ruthlessness is merely another man's ambition. I didn't hear you complaining this past year and more, since becoming my wife and enjoying all the fineries my ruthlessness has provided you in that time."

A pained expression pinched Lusita's lovely face. "Perhaps you're right. Perhaps I am guilty of being as shallow and materialistic as every other whore throughout history who allowed—"

"Stop it! I won't listen to talk like that," said Wainwright.

Lusita leaned toward him over the desk. "Then listen to at least this much. I beg of you. Before you act too harshly on these negative conclusions you've reached in such haste about my father, please go and talk to him. Hear him out. Give him a chance to explain."

Wainwright smiled thinly. "Oh, I fully intend to talk to him. You can damn well bet on that. The sooner the better." He cut his gaze to Sweetwater. "The men should be about ready to ride by now, shouldn't they?"

"Should be for a fact," the young gunman confirmed, pushing out of the chair and rising smoothly to his feet. He swung the gunbelt around his waist, buckled it, and slammed the pistols into their holsters. "I'll go make sure. Whenever you're ready, you'll find thirty riders—that's the full gun crew and a couple wranglers to round things out—waiting to proceed under your command, sir."

"Thirty armed men on the way to confront and accuse my father at his own hacienda?" echoed Lusita. "That's your idea of a peaceful, constructive talk?"

"It's my idea of getting to the bottom of a thing without wasting a lot of time or allowing any room for crawfishing."

"You will only offend and embarrass him in front of his men. That will leave him just one way to react and it won't be with any attempt at a calm, rational explanation."

"That will be his decision, and no one can blame me for not trying."

CHAPTER 38

By late afternoon, a four-block section of downtown Wagon Wheel had been barricaded and reasonably secured against potential attack from either Wainwright or Don Pedro, even the remote possibility of both.

Each end of Front Street was blockaded by overturned wagons, heavy freight cases, stacks of adobe brick, and other pieces of building equipment. The alleys feeding in from either side were similarly blocked. The front windows of shops and businesses were boarded over.

All women and children were gathered into the roomy Baptist church, whose doors and windows were also securely sealed and guarded by a half dozen men specifically assigned to stand watch. They were mostly elderly, limited when it came to speed and mobility, but still sharp of eye and plenty skilled at planting lead in whatever they aimed at.

It wasn't anticipated that sparsely populated Mexville was under much threat, but word was sent down that anyone who cared to was welcome to come into the protected area, especially the women and children. Most of the latter accepted the offer and relocated to the church. About half of the town's men came, too, each readily volunteering his gun in defense of the pending threat. Those who elected to stay behind did so in the belief they would not be bothered.

As all of this fell into place with surprising smoothness, Buckhorn took the opportunity to grab a moment's rest in the company of Justine York and a cup of fresh-brewed coffee she provided. They sat together on the edge of the boardwalk in front of her newspaper shop.

"Just look at how everybody is pulling together," she fairly gushed. "I've never been more proud of our little town."

"Nothing like a common cause, especially facing up to a threat of some kind, to make folks get over petty differences," Buckhorn said.

"The two biggest surprises, I must say, are Sheriff Banning and my brother Carl. Do you think we can trust him?"

"Carl?"

She shook her head. "No. Banning. I can't help thinking that he jumped over to our side awfully quick."

"I figure he's been a man straddling the fence for quite a while. He got caught under the influence of Wainwright early on, I'm guessing, when he wasn't so sure of himself and Wainwright wasn't quite so bold and demanding. As Wainwright grew more powerful and took to throwing his weight around more and more, well, Banning didn't necessarily like the things he was seeing and hearing, but by then he was already trapped by what he'd allowed and by what everybody, including himself, expected out of him. It took something big, like what was revealed to him this morning, to finally yank him down off that fence. Lucky for us, he came down on our side and I think he can be counted on to stay there."

"You make a pretty convincing case. I hope you're right." Justine's expression took on an added earnestness. "That still leaves Carl. I don't mean I doubt his trustworthiness. Not as long as he's sober, that is. But that's just the thing. He's disappointed me so many times when I thought he'd finally beaten down the alcohol, only to have him crawl right back into the bottle again.

"Still, it's been a long time since I've seen him like he's been the last couple days—ever since he pitched in and helped save Deputy Gates from that shoot-out in the middle of the street. And then you asked him to look after Goodwin. He even had the idea of spreading false word about Don Pedro down in Mexville and it seems to have paid off. I *want* to believe that this time it's going to last but . . ."

"Then do it. Believe in him. Maybe that's what it'll take to help him keep the alcohol beat down for good." Buckhorn watched her tuck a corner of her bottom lip between her teeth and nibble at it as she pondered his advice. Forgetting a piece of advice he himself had recently received, Buckhorn lifted his cup and took a swallow of the coffee.

Too late, he remembered the warning from Justine's brother about what a bad cook she was. If her coffee was any indication, the term *bad* didn't begin to cover it. Her coffee was so terrible it made the recent awful brew he'd gotten at the sheriff's office seem almost tasty. Buckhorn managed to keep down the gulp he'd taken but then immediately began looking for an opening to jettison what was left in the cup without her noticing. If nothing else presented itself, he thought, he would even welcome the attack they were preparing for.

"Of course I'll keep believing in Carl," Justine said. "I really feel that this time he may have reached a place where he *can* keep the alcohol under control."

As if on cue, Carl and two other men came into sight on a path that would take them right past where Buckhorn and Justine were sitting. The three were carrying a bundle of hollow pipes, fifteen-foot lengths and about two inches in diameter, hoisted up on their shoulders. Carl was in the lead.

When they got close enough, Justine said, "Where are you going with those?"

"Up behind Clyburg's blacksmith barn," answered Carl. "Goodwin's found a spot that shows real strong indication of there being some water down in the ground there. Since everything is pretty well taken care of as far as barricading and posting men, we thought we'd go ahead and use whatever time we've got to sink some pipe and see if we hit sign of anything."

"Is it really the best time for that?" Justine asked.

"Why wait?" Carl said. "Like I said, most everything else is taken care of or in the process of being wrapped up. The next move is up to Wainwright, and there's still the chance he might go and confront Don Pedro before he gets around to us. Might as well put the waiting time to good use."

"Doesn't sound like a bad idea to me," Buckhorn said, using the exchange between Justine and her brother as a diversion to pour the rest of his coffee onto the ground beside his boot heel, then shift his foot to cover it up. All he had to worry about was the boot leather disintegrating from the contact and falling off his foot. "Maybe we can meet Wainwright and his boys with a flood when they show up."

Carl shifted the weight of the pipes on his shoulder and said, "Maybe. I'd love to stand here and talk some more about it but, if you don't mind, these pipes aren't exactly light. We need to get 'em unloaded so Goodwin can get started on what he calls his artesian well."

"I'll be along in a little bit," Buckhorn said. "I want to see this."

Carl and the other men trudged off under their load.

"I didn't mean for that to sound like I'm in a hurry to break up this conversation we're having," Buckhorn told Justine, abruptly realizing how it could have been taken that way.

She smiled. "I understand. I'd like to see how they go about it, too. It's my duty as a news reporter to observe. Especially if Goodwin succeeds in hitting water. That would be the biggest story I've ever run since . . . well, since I've taken over the *Sun Ledger*."

Noting how her tone and expression turned suddenly somber, Buckhorn said, "So let's tag along and have a look together."

"I'll come along in a little bit. I'd better take care of a couple other things first."

"Can't they wait?"

"One of them is to check and see if I've gotten any response from the telegram inquiries I sent out about the rebellion situation down in Mexico. I told the telegrapher to send word right away if anything came in, but with all this other excitement going on he might have forgot."

"The way we've lighted a fire under Wainwright—and maybe Don Pedro, too—I don't think whatever's going on with the rebellion is gonna be as important to them as it was before. Not until they've dealt with us and this whole business about a new water source."

Justine didn't say anything for a minute. Her gaze drifted once again over the stir of activity still taking place around them, as if drinking it in deeply, savoring every morsel of it. "God, I wish Gerald was here to see this, too," she said quietly. She gave a nervous, self-conscious little laugh. "Along with about a million other reasons I wish he was still here."

It was a touchy matter, but Buckhorn felt like he was expected to say something. "You miss your husband a lot, don't you?"

"Yes. Tremendously. He was the love of my life and the most fair and decent man I ever met. He had the talent to work for a bigger paper anywhere in the country, but he liked it here, liked the whole big, sprawling, raucous West, as he used to put it. He wanted to do more than just report the news and events. He wanted to tell the West's stories and he felt Wagon Wheel was an almost perfect place to start from."

Buckhorn cleared his throat. "The last time we were talking and got on the subject of your husband, you sorta clammed up. Didn't want talk about him at all."

"I usually don't. I'm not sure why I feel the need now." Justine turned her head and regarded Buckhorn intently. "No, that's not true. I know exactly why I want to tell you about Gerald. I want you to know the truth about how he died, Buckhorn. They killed him, that's how. I can't prove it, but I know with every fiber of my being that dirty bastard Wainwright was behind it."

"And you wanted me to know that because . . ."

"The other night when we all met in my kitchen after you'd learned about the plans for creating Silverado, you made a remark about simply killing Wainwright. You said that was how you used to do things and that, in a roundabout way, it was why you'd come here in the first place. Is all of that true?"

"I already answered that."

Justine continued to regard him, her gaze probing deep. Then, abruptly, she said, "Good. You see, I want very much for Thomas Wainwright not to come out of this alive. I realize that must sound awful and that's why, before I told you, I wanted you to understand my reasons. I know I have no right to ask and I can't afford to pay you anywhere near what you probably get for hiring out to do something like that. Plus you said you're out of the business, anyway. It's not like you haven't already done a lot of good in your short time here. For whatever it's worth and however you can rationalize it, I hope the thing you said you came here for remains among your priorities."

Buckhorn smiled thinly. "Considering how Wainwright and his top gun, Sweetwater, have their own reasons for wanting *me* dead, you can rest assured that I fully intend to make them that way first."

CHAPTER 39

As the last sliver of a boiling red sun was sinking behind the horizon, two things happened almost simultaneously in the town of Wagon Wheel. On the south end, coming up through Mexville, a rider arrived at a hard gallop. On the north end, in a weedy patch of ground out behind Clyburg's blacksmith barn, Martin Goodwin slammed his sledgehammer down on the third section of pipe he was driving into the ground and from out of the hollow iron sleeve came a gurgling, bubbling spray of muddy brown water.

For several seconds, the small crowd of onlookers who'd wandered over to watch Goodwin conduct his well drilling stood in dumbfounded silence, as if neither comprehending nor believing what their eyes were seeing.

When the truth of what they were witnessing finally sank in and the spell suddenly broke, a celebratory cheer burst forth like the water itself surging up out of the ground. The joyous sound spread and grew louder until others came scurrying to see what was going on.

All the while, water sprang forth like a geyser—

higher and higher, turning cold and clean and sweet to the taste. Before long, grown men were stomping around in the mud, scooping handfuls of the wonderful liquid to their mouths and splashing one another like a bunch of frolicking little kids.

It was this scene that the rider from the south, after gaining clearance to get past the guards posted at the barricades, came upon. He was one of the men who'd initially stayed behind in Mexville but it was obvious he had been riding hard for some time.

He paused to absorb the scene and a smile briefly touched his mouth then his expression turned serious again and his eyes returned to searching faces in the crowd. When his gaze locked on Buckhorn and Carl Orndecker standing together on the fringe of the splashing and carrying-on, he nudged his horse over to them.

"Tinto," Carl said, recognizing the man. "Too many times in the past I have visited your neighborhood in search of something to drink." Smiling, he spread his arms wide. "Now I welcome you to my part of town for a drink of something even better."

"*Sí, señor,*" said Tinto. "It is a most wonderful thing taking place here."

Over at the well, the sheriff and Goodwin were shouting for everybody to settle down, telling them to hurry up and bring any containers they wanted to fill before Goodwin capped the pipe for a while in order to rig a shutoff valve and spigot to gain better control over future discharge.

"But to the south, where I just came from," Tinto continued, "things are not so good. It is very bad. The gunfighter armies of Don Pedro and Señor Wainwright have broken into a bloody battle at the Olomoso hacienda. Many men have been killed or wounded."

"Is this battle still going on?" Buckhorn asked, suddenly oblivious to the frivolity taking place all around them.

"I did not get close enough to see with my own eyes," Tinto reported earnestly. "I met one of the servants from the hacienda who had fled. He told me. He said both sides suffered terrible losses and the hacienda was in flames, total ruin threatening. The last he saw, the Wainwright men were riding off but promising to return and finish what they had started."

Buckhorn and Carl exchanged looks.

Carl's eyebrows lifted. "Whoa. I'd say this night is turning out better and better. Goodwin's water has shown up but it sounds like Wainwright's gun wolves aren't going to. At least not any time soon. I'd say that's a mighty good trade."

"Sure sounds like it," Buckhorn agreed. Then he said to Tinto, "This fella you ran into, this servant from the hacienda—you have reason to trust him pretty good? You think he's telling it straight as far as what happened at Don Pedro's hacienda?"

Tinto responded quickly and firmly. "*Sí.* He is the cousin to my first wife's sister-in-law. He has long been in the service of Don Pedro and he was very frightened. I believe he was telling the truth."

Buckhorn nodded. "That's good. I'm curious, though. What made you decide to head down that way in the first place?"

"I heard the talk about Don Pedro hiring the man with the water stick. Like you, I got curious," Tinto explained. "I know some vaqueros who work for Don Pedro. We get together to play cards from time to time but have not done so for quite a while. I decided to try my luck at playing cards with them and I thought I could ask about the man with the water stick at the same time."

"That's reasonable enough, I guess," Buckhorn said. "I don't want you to take offense but this is mighty serious business so we have to treat it that way. That means I have to ask my friend Carl about you, just to make sure. You understand?"

"*Sí*, I think so," said Tinto, though he did not look as certain as his words.

Turning to Carl, Buckhorn said, "How about this fella? You know him well enough to trust what he's telling us?"

"I know him mostly from my drinking trips down to Mexville. I guess that's not the most solid basis for making judgment," Carl admitted. "But, still, I got no reason *not* to trust Tinto. I see no reason for him to be feeding us a falsehood as far as what happened between Wainwright and Don Pedro."

"No, neither do I. That makes you right about this night turning out better and better. That sets me to thinking on how we might be able to turn it even more to our favor."

"How's that?"

"Let's rope in the sheriff and Justine and Goodwin," answered Buckhorn, "and I'll explain what I have in mind."

Considering who he was talking to and all the wild schemes already in play, Sheriff Banning's tone was only mildly incredulous as he said, "So *we* turn into the invaders? Take a force of men and ride out to hit the

Flying W before Wainwright heads for Don Pedro's again . . . That's what you're suggesting?"

"It's a thought that crossed my mind," Buckhorn replied. "I'm tossing it out to see what the rest of you think, that's all."

"I think it's a damn good notion," Carl chimed in with ill-concealed eagerness. "It's bold and unexpected and it not only means hitting Wainwright when he's already bloodied and weakened, it would save the damage that the town would be certain to suffer—no matter how good we got it blocked off—if we continue to wait for the Flying W gunnies to hit us here."

Buckhorn, Banning, Carl, and Justine were huddled outside a far corner of the blacksmith barn, discussing the idea Buckhorn had put forth. Goodwin and Deputy Pomeroy remained over by the wellhead, maintaining some semblance of order as folks brought buckets and barrels to fill before Goodwin temporarily capped the water geyser.

"I think taking the fight to the Flying W would be a good idea, too," Justine declared. "Like Carl said, we've done a good job of fortifying the town for an attack here. Why risk it if we don't have to? We have enough able-bodied men to send a sufficient force out there and still leave an adequate number behind to guard the town in case of something unsuspected."

"I don't have an objection against hitting the Flying W, either," said the sheriff. "In fact, the more I hear, the more I like it. I'm just playing devil's advocate, that's all, to make sure we think everything through before we go ahead and act too rashly."

"I'm all for that," Buckhorn said. "We want to take advantage of the situation, not trade one set of problems for another."

"There's another advantage that could possibly be

seized by taking the Flying W ranch headquarters,"
Justine said. "Everybody's heard of the big safe Wainwright has in his office out there. Where he keeps not
only money, supposedly, but also all the deeds and related paperwork to the land he's gobbled up in the
past year or so. I don't know if it's true or who'd be
willing to admit it, but there's even been talk that he
holds markers on some of the businesses around town.

"My point is this—everybody knows damn well how
a lot of that land was taken by force. Now that we have
a sheriff again"—Justine's eyes cut meaningfully to
Banning—"and there's the added leverage of the town
possessing its own water supply, I bet we could get that
whole paperwork pile reviewed by territorial legal authorities who'd find a good portion of it not legally
binding. That would be one more blow to keeping
Wainwright's Silverado from ever coming about."

"It damn sure would," agreed her brother. "And it
would provide some good people another chance to
reclaim their land and move back in again."

"I'll do my part . . . meaning, what I should have
done in the first place." Banning met Justine's gaze,
though he spoke in a somewhat subdued voice. "I
know some strings to pull that'll bring in the right authorities. Once they show up and start digging, not
much doubt they'll turn up exactly the kind of things
in question."

"From my standpoint, that sorta ranks as frosting on
the cake," Buckhorn said. "First order of business is
still to ride out there and deal with whatever's left of
Wainwright's gunnies. We'll want to hit 'em just before
daybreak. I figure for sure you and me in the mix, Carl.
Beyond that, the rest of you know the right townsmen
to pick to go with us. You gonna be in on the raid,

Sheriff, or you figure it best for you to stay and keep watch over things here?"

"Try keeping me out of that raid," replied Banning, his voice coming back strong. "Pomeroy will stay and take charge of things here."

"I figure it's best for Goodwin to remain here, too," Buckhorn said. "He's better at spraying water than bullets."

Banning nodded. "Sounds right. I'll start selecting men and spreading word about the change in plans. Folks'll probably squall when they hear things may take a different turn, but they'll still have to stay bottled up with guards posted. That's the most sensible thing, don't you agree?"

"Absolutely. There's always the chance we're working on bad information. Playing it safe all the way around is the only smart move."

"There's one more thing everybody needs to consider," Banning said. His gaze touched each of the others and then he went on. "Not everybody in town was wholly in favor of making this stand against Wainwright. Once all the activity started, I can't swear for certain that somebody didn't slip away to warn him what we were setting up. By the same token, especially now that it's getting dark, I can't be any more certain that somebody won't slip off to warn him of this change in plans."

"Meaning he might be expecting us, be ready for us when we come knocking on his door," Carl said.

Banning nodded. "About the size of it."

Carl looked at Buckhorn. "That change anything?"

"Not as far as I'm concerned," replied Buckhorn. "Let 'em be ready. We will be, too."

A faint smile came and went on Banning's mouth. "I'll go start explaining to folks, then." He started away then paused and turned back to Justine. "Not to impose, but it will probably go smoother if you come with me. Not everybody is convinced yet I'm not still working more in Wainwright's interest than the town's."

Justine didn't hesitate. "Of course. Whatever I can do to help."

Watching them go, Carl said, "You think we're witnessing a romance starting to blossom?"

Buckhorn gave him a look. "Can't say I ever gave it much thought. If I did, the first thing that'd cross my mind was that your sister doesn't seem particularly fond of the sheriff."

"Oh, I think she's kinda drawn to him in a physical way. A lot of women around town are. I mean, you've got to admit Paul Banning is a handsome fella. I can tell pretty certain that he's been attracted to Justine for some time now." Carl sighed. "She's always been convinced—and I can't argue too hard against it—that Thomas Wainwright was behind the accident that killed her husband. As long as Banning appeared to be in lockstep with Wainwright, there was never any chance Justine could look at him without wondering if he wasn't in on what happened to Gerald, too. But things and people can always change, sometimes in mighty surprising ways."

Buckhorn regarded him some more. "You know what? I sure hope you're over being a drunk. If you turn out to be a drunk *and* a hopeless romantic, I don't know how much longer I'll be able to stand hanging around with you."

CHAPTER 40

Approaching the Flying W in the predawn darkness, they caught faint whiffs of the smoke before they could actually see anything. Only after the sky began to lighten were they able to spot the first smudged black curls rising up in the distance. Even then, it wasn't until they'd reined their horses and gazed down from the crest of the long, low slope overlooking the main house and outbuildings of the ranch headquarters that they begin to realize the full effect of what the smoke was part of.

The fire appeared to have been isolated to the main house. Its thick adobe frame had held up for the most part, but the roof was collapsed and all doors and windows were broken and outlined in thick smears of soot. A few flames still licked visibly through some of the openings. Apart from the fire, though no less devastating, were the dozens of slaughtered longhorn carcasses scattered over the grassy open area between the slope and the ranch buildings. In the corral area could be seen the motionless lumps of several horses apparently having met the same fate.

The scene held no sign of any living thing.

"Good God," Carl Orndecker muttered thickly at the sight.

"Kinda hate to think God had a hand in any of this," Paul Banning responded.

"Not God, not necessarily the Devil neither," Buckhorn said. "Seen too many times that mankind is capable of this kind of waste and butchery all on its own."

The three men sat their saddles in the midst of a roughly formed line of other horsemen, fifteen in all—the force Banning had assembled to confront what was left of Wainwright's army of gunfighters. At the moment, it didn't look like there was a whole lot left *to* confront.

"Mankind in the shape of who?" Banning asked.

Buckhorn rubbed a row of knuckles along his jawline. "My first thought would be maybe Don Pedro's men. Could be they weren't so tore up in that skirmish at their own hacienda as we were led to believe. Could be they decided not to wait for Wainwright's boys to return to them like he supposedly promised. Could be they decided, like us, to hit the Flying W while everybody was laid low and still licking their wounds, only they didn't wait for dawn to do it."

"All that fits up to a point, even the slaughter of the livestock," Carl said. "If you're gonna raid a place and inflict damage on your enemy, you might as well do it thorough. That would explain all the dead animals, but where are the bodies of Wainwright's men? The attackers sure as hell wouldn't have stuck around to give them a nice, tidy burial and I can't think of any logical reason to carry them off. So where are they?"

"That's a good question. On top of plenty of others," Buckhorn said. "I guess we all know there's only one way to find out."

"I was afraid somebody would get around to that," muttered one of the men farther down the line.

"But we don't go down throwing caution to the wind," Banning said in a loud enough voice for everybody to hear. "Just because it looks deserted and safe don't mean there can't be some trickery going on. Like a handful of ambushers in hiding maybe. You men on the right side swing out wide, keep a few yards' distance between you, and come in along behind that row of bunkhouses." Motioning to those on his left, he added, "You fellas over here do the same, go in along those sheds and holding pens and come in along that side of the house."

"I don't suppose you've got in mind for us to wait here and see what they flush out, do you?" Carl said dryly.

Banning gave him a look. "I figured the three of us would ride in right up the middle."

Carl heaved a sigh and then nudged his horse forward. "Yeah, I sorta figured that's what you'd figure."

"Now don't none of you rascals go gettin' itchy trigger fingers," spoke a disembodied voice once Buckhorn, Banning, and Carl had made it down to within the cluster of buildings. "Just hold your fire and stay calm, on account there ain't nobody left here lookin' for no trouble." Having thus spoken, the form of Tyrone, the wrinkled old cook who'd shown Buckhorn around on the first day of his brief turn as a

Flying W employee, eased out of the shadowy doorway of the grub shack.

"It's okay. I know him," Buckhorn was quick to say.

"They's a couple more in here with me," said Tyrone. "You might want to let those boys movin' around outside know, too."

"There are some people in here, but they're all friendly so far," the sheriff called out. "Keep a sharp lookout but don't be trigger happy."

"Thanks, Sheriff," Tyrone said. "But there ain't no *so far* to it. Like I said, we're all that's left and we ain't lookin' for no trouble."

"Why don't you have whoever else is in there come out," suggested Buckhorn.

Tyrone spoke over his shoulder and a moment later two more people emerged from the grub shack. It was Consuela and Armando, the married couple who served as maid and manservant to the Wainwrights. Consuela was sobbing almost uncontrollably and Armando looked badly shaken up, as well.

"Reckon I wasn't totally accurate," said Tyrone. "They's two more men in the near bunkhouse. They're bad wounded, maybe dead by now. They wasn't the last I checked, but close to it. Either way, they ain't gonna be no trouble to you."

"I'll check," Carl said, moving toward the bunkhouse.

Buckhorn pinned the old cook with a hard stare. "Where's everybody else, Tyrone? What happened here?"

Tyrone met his gaze and came back with straight answers, no embellishment. The events he related were direct and uncomplicated, though nothing along the lines of what had been expected.

Thomas Wainwright had tucked tail and run. Shortly after returning from the fight at the Olomoso hacienda—his forces badly shot up, many not returning at all and several of those who did arrived in sorry shape—the former general had gotten word from town about the water strike and also about a mob forming with plans to descend on the Flying W.

Believing that Don Pedro's pack of gunnies had not suffered as badly as his own in the hacienda skirmish and suspecting his ex-partner might already be mounting a retaliatory attack, Wainwright was hit hard by the report out of Wagon Wheel and especially the possibility of an additional threat on the way from there.

Already demoralized by betrayal and the heavy toll taken on his gunmen, the man with dreams of a personal empire had collapsed in defeat. Alternating between furious rants of rage and wailing lamentations about how the fates had conspired against him, Wainwright urged his wife and servants to pack up smaller household items of value that could be readily turned into cash while he cleaned out the money from his office safe.

This done, he'd soaked the interior of the main house with coal oil even as he ordered the slaughter of all livestock on the property and in the nearby fields, his purpose clearly being to leave behind as little as possible that would be of use or value to whomever occupied the place next.

Loading his wife and the items they'd selected to take along onto a sturdy wagon, Wainwright had thrown the first torch that turned his lavish home into an inferno, then pointed the team toward Mexico and whipped them to a hard pace. Accompanying the wagon on horseback were Leo Sweetwater and two other gunmen who'd returned from the hacienda skirmish unscathed.

The remaining handful of men, mostly wranglers, had been summarily dismissed and told they were welcome to anything that was left, including the out-lying cattle they could round up and sell for whatever price they could get. Tyrone and the two house ser-vants were not addressed at all except for tearful farewells from Lusita.

"What about her?" Buckhorn said. "Did she leave willingly with Wainwright?"

Tyrone gave a firm shake of his head. "No, sir. You could tell she didn't want to go with him at all, but she was too terrified of the way he was actin' to do anything but what he said."

Carl returned from the bunkhouse where he'd gone to check on the wounded men. He shook his slowly. "One's already gone. The other one's nearly bled out and don't have much longer. Not a damn thing we can do for him."

"How long has Wainwright been gone?" Banning said to Tyrone.

"Don't have a watch, but that wagon rolled out 'bout midnight I reckon."

"And the rest of the men? The wranglers?"

"Not long after. Less than an hour. Didn't sound to me like they was figurin' to go after no outlyin' cattle, neither. They was arguin' amongst themselves. Sounded like they'd put enough work into this outfit already and wanted to nothin' more to do with it."

The rest of the townsmen who'd circled out wide to the edges of the property were drifting back in closer.

Banning looked at Buckhorn and Carl. "Well, where

does that leave us? What we came here to do wasn't exactly legal to begin with, but if Wainwright has made tracks into Mexico, I for one sure have no basis for going after him."

"Seems like Don Pedro would make the best candidate for that little chore anyway," Carl said. "From a position of already being on that side of the border and from having a daughter caught in a situation it sounds like she don't want to be in."

Before Buckhorn could add anything, Tyrone took a step forward and held out a folded piece of paper. "Matter of fact, Wainwright scratched down a few things that might help you make up your minds. Told me to give this to whoever showed up first."

Buckhorn took the paper and shook it open. After first giving it a quick skim, he cleared his throat and then read it aloud. "Don Pedro—you might still be walking around, but you're a dead man, you treacherous dog. You won't know when or where, but I will return to make you that way.

"Buckhorn—same for you.

"Banning—you're not worth the trouble.

"To the dirt scratchers of Whitestone County who only ever had the guts to stand up against me after I was already betrayed and beaten down, to hell with you all. I hope your new well is poison and you all die.

"To anyone wondering about my dear wife, she claims she no longer loves me and does not want to remain at my side, but I say she will stay until or unless I decide otherwise. Meantime, should anyone attempt to come after her—or me—she will receive the first bullet at the first sign of trouble. Keep that in mind and keep in mind also that . . . Silverado will rise again!"

Buckhorn lifted his eyes and scanned the faces of those around him. To a man they looked a little stunned and more than a little concerned.

In a hoarse voice, Carl said, "If there was ever any doubt that Thomas Wainwright is stark raving mad, nobody needs look any farther than the words written there."

"And his madness," Buckhorn added, "only assures the grave danger that his wife, Lusita, is in."

CHAPTER 41

Leo Sweetwater was troubled and feeling increasingly more so by the hour.

The young gunfighter prided himself on always keeping a cool head, no matter the situation, and one of the ways he did this was to clearly see things as being black or white in accordance to his own values. Never any shades of gray.

The key, of course, was that Leo's values were pretty simple and straightforward, unencumbered by the boundaries of the law or religion or any other such influence. For Leo, it was as basic as hiring his gun out to somebody and then doing whatever it was that somebody directed him to do.

But all of a sudden, he'd run up against a situation with complications.

First off, he didn't like a quitter—somebody who'd cut and run at the first sign of serious resistance. That's surely what Thomas Wainwright had done. He'd gotten his ass burned in the conflict with Don Pedro and then, receiving the bad news from town on top of that, had folded and lit a shuck with only hollow words left behind as far as putting up any more of a fight.

Sweetwater didn't like being around anybody who showed that much yellow. It made him feel squirmy and uncomfortable inside, like he was afraid it might rub off on him.

Besides that, going on the run with Wainwright also meant running from the personal matter still left unsettled between him and Buckhorn. The man who'd emptied his guns, handcuffed him to his saddle horn, then shooed him on his way like a minor annoyance. Since it came at the direction of his employer, riding off without settling that score wasn't really the same as turning away on his own, Sweetwater told himself. It didn't mean showing his own streak of yellow . . . but it felt awful damned close.

There'd certainly been times when he'd terminated his employment from previous men who hired him. Sometimes the job was finished, sometimes it just got stale and came to a mutual parting of the ways. Sweetwater considered doing this with Wainwright, once the latter revealed his true color and announced his intent to run off for Mexico, but before he could speak up, Wainwright had specifically asked him to stay on. Practically pleaded. It was in that moment Sweetwater had seen the deeper torment in the man, something more than defeat and fear exposed.

Something had broken inside the old general. He'd become unhinged in the attempt to cope with the realization that his dream of Silverado was crushed and was never going to happen. There could be no mutual parting of the ways under those circumstances and, somehow, Sweetwater had not been able to force the break.

Finally, there was the woman. Lusita. Mrs. Wainwright. In his months at the Flying W, Sweetwater had certainly been aware of her. What red-blooded male could help but be?

He had drawn the line and held it firm right there. By his values, he didn't lust after another man's wife and for sure not the wife of the man he'd hired out to. He froze shut any such yearnings in himself and let it be known to those around him that the crude remarks and explicit fantasies they tended to regale one another with when he wasn't on hand were to be stifled when he was within earshot. He wasn't a prude, not by any means, but letting those kinds of thoughts go running in directions they didn't belong only clouded a body's brain and left a trail for potential trouble that plain wasn't worth it.

With the change in their circumstances, all of that had changed, too. It was clear Lusita didn't want to be part of any of it. Equally clear, she no longer wanted much to do with Wainwright, either.

His treatment of her wasn't doing anything to help Sweetwater keep to his values. The feelings a body could hold in check for the wife of a man who was kind and loving to her was one thing. A wife who was abused and taken for granted by her man was something else.

What was more, in addition to the way Lusita was being treated by her husband and the conflicted feelings it stirred in Sweetwater himself, the young gunman also had a keen awareness of how the other two men traveling with them looked at her. What else might be contained in the ill-concealed yearning that shone in their eyes, he could only guess. But it wasn't good.

The two men—Brazos Kent and Abe Tarvel by name—were two of the crudest, most foul-mouthed gunnies to have signed into the ranks of Wainwright's now defunct army. Their only saving graces were a shared propensity for ruthlessness and lightning speed with a gun. There'd been no indication back at the ranch of them being prior friends, but they were sure showing signs of getting chummy with one another and it was becoming more apparent with each passing mile.

Yeah, Sweetwater had good reason to feel troubled. It was because there was so much potential for trouble on all sides.

From what lay in back of them.

What lay ahead.

And what simmered from within.

CHAPTER 42

"What about the safety of my daughter?" the old man wanted to know.

"Naturally, I will take that into consideration as much as possible," Buckhorn answered. "By my reckoning, the best way to make your daughter safe is to make those who rode off with her dead."

The hint of a grim smile touched Don Pedro's mouth. "Yes, it is so."

The exchange between the two men was taking place on the edge of Wagon Wheel's main street, out front of the general store. A handful of townsfolk were gathered around Buckhorn. A half dozen of Don Pedro's gunmen, having just ridden into town and still on horseback, were strung out behind him. Overhead, the white-hot, blurred ball that was the sun had barely begun its descent in the afternoon sky.

The old don and his men had shown up only a short time ago, just as Buckhorn was preparing to take out after Wainwright and the small group who'd fled the Flying W. Buckhorn, Sheriff Banning, Carl, and half the townsmen who'd closed on the ranch ahead of dawn had returned to town with Tyrone and Wainwright's two house servants.

The remainder of the men had stayed behind to put things in some semblance of order and to be on hand in case anyone came nosing around. It had been decided among those making the return trip to town that Buckhorn, alone, would stock necessary provisions and then immediately head out after the fugitives.

That had been imparted to Don Pedro, who'd arrived already knowing about the Flying W being abandoned during the night but was left trying to come to grips with the status of his former partner and what it meant as far as the fate of his daughter. Once the note Wainwright had left was shown to him, the answers to those questions brought great dismay.

Slowly touching Buckhorn and the others before him with a gaze from weary, anxious eyes, the old don said, "I cannot atone, cannot even begin to explain the . . . madness I allowed myself to get caught up in with Wainwright. Nor will I try to lay it all on him. I was very willing, very eager . . . Suddenly, in the emptiness and bloody aftermath that was only a fraction of what would have transpired had we gone ahead with all that we were planning . . . I can but feel ashamed, remorseful.

"To ask forgiveness would be a pathetic insult, but for the sake of my daughter, who had no knowledge about any of what her husband and I intended and played only the part of a pawn—my greatest shame of all—I ask . . . compassion. My first instinct is to send out these loyal men behind me with instructions to hunt down and kill Wainwright in the most savage way possible. But upon reading the words on that piece of paper . . . more madness, bordering on evil, or perhaps the other way around . . . I see that cannot be the way. Perhaps it should never be the way, not the right one. In this instance, no doubt it would only lead to my daughter's certain death."

His gaze came back and settled on Buckhorn. "I cannot say why, but something . . . a cold certainty . . . tells me that, yes, you are the right man, the one with the best chance to succeed. To bring my beloved Lusita back alive. I don't know what that will entail, what else you will have to do . . . I don't care."

"I don't know what I'll have to do, either," Buckhorn said, "but, whatever it turns out to be, I'd best get at it. Too much time has passed already."

Don Pedro nodded. "Indeed. My arrival delayed you."

"That was only part of it."

The old don's gaze went to the sheriff. He gestured to the various citizens up and down Front Street who had paused in the acts of removing barricades and window boards put in place the previous evening. "My apologies if the sight of me and my heavily armed men coming down your street caused any disruption. We came in peace and we will leave the same . . . and we will remain that way in the necessary healing time that lies ahead."

"Sounds good to me," said Banning.

"I have heard about the wonder of a new water source that has blessed your town. Water that gushes cold and clean from deep within the earth." He gazed longingly up the street, toward where Goodwin's well was. "I had hoped to see this with my own eyes, but I realize that now is not the best time. My new hope is that I will be welcome to return again before too long and view it then."

"You would indeed be welcome," Banning told him.

"Only this morning," Don Pedro added, "I received word that the long-expected revolutionary action outside of Mexico City has dissolved without a shot being fired. Maybe the time for violence and strife is over for a while. Not forever. It never is. But maybe for a while."

Banning said, "That sounds good, too."

Don Pedro's gaze settled once more on Buckhorn. "*Vaya con Dios, amigo.* I will return to my hacienda and await good news from you." With that, he motioned his men to wheel about and they rode out the way they'd come in.

"Well, now we know where he stands," Carl said, watching the fading cloud of dust kicked up by the departing riders.

"And a relief it is, I'd say," added his sister, standing between him and Banning. Then she scowled. "What I'd really like to know is how the heck he gets his information from clear down in the heart of Mexico. I've been waiting for days for a telegram from somebody about what's going on down there and haven't heard a single click back yet."

"Maybe my pursuit of Wainwright will take me down that way and I can find out some answers for you. In my spare time," Buckhorn said.

"If you don't get started, you're not going to make it any farther than Mexville by sundown," said Banning with a wry grin.

"Well, if everybody'd quit crowding me, I'd be on my way," Buckhorn told him.

Carl frowned. "Seriously. You really think it's best for you to tackle going after that bunch alone?"

"It's the *only* way—one man dogging 'em, moving by night, closing in cautious. It's the best chance that gal has. You go after 'em with a posse—never mind the added risk of drawing the attention of the Rurales and the whole legal problem of being on the wrong side of the border—they'd spot a tail from miles away and the whole thing would be queered. If Wainwright means it about what he'd do to his wife, and there's no reason to think the crazy bastard doesn't, she'd be dead no matter what."

"We've been over it a dozen times," Banning pointed out.

"Yeah, yeah, I guess," Carl mumbled. "Damn it. What about just *one* more man? *I* could go with you."

Buckhorn put hand on his shoulder. "In a street shoot-out, Carl, there's nobody I'd rather have at my side. But that's the key—the street. You've been off the trail too much of the time in recent years. No offense, but town living has made you soft. And the bouts of alcohol haven't helped. I got no way of knowing how long it's gonna take to track down that bunch. A couple days on the trail over hard country in this heat . . ."

"Okay, okay. I get the picture," Carl said sullenly. "You're right. But I don't have to like it, damn it!"

"Not a matter of being wrong or right." Buckhorn cut his gaze over to Justine before adding, "I've got priorities. I need to stick to 'em."

CHAPTER 43

It felt good being out in the wide open again, not on a road or trail traveled regularly by others. Buckhorn could tell that Sarge sensed it, too, and liked it just as much as he did. All the riding they'd done over the past several days had merely been back and forth between the town and the Flying W ranch.

The first leg that afternoon had been the same. After provisioning in town, Buckhorn had ridden back to the ranch to pick up the trail of the fugitives headed into Mexico.

The ranch was behind them and they were on the track across grassy, gently rolling terrain that would soon start to turn more broken and rugged. The sun was high and hot in a cloudless sky, hammering down hard on man and animal, sapping them even though the going was relatively easy. Buckhorn held Sarge to a moderate but steady pace. At this time of day tomorrow, after the land had become much harsher, they would hole up and not travel during the punishing afternoon.

As it was their first day out and with the afternoon already partly gone, he meant to push through. Sunset would bring rapidly cooling air and as long as he could make out tracks to follow, he would stay on the move all night, stopping only once or twice to briefly rest and take on water.

The southwestern angle of the trail so far, pretty distinctly marked by the wagon tracks visible even through the higher grass, gave Buckhorn a good idea where his quarry was headed. Never having traveled that way before, Buckhorn had nevertheless familiarized himself with the region via maps.

If Wainwright's bunch stayed with the course they were headed on, they would be crossing the southern reaches of the Barranaca Mountains through a spot called Verdugo Pass and then on to the eastern coast of the Gulf of California. There, still roughly in line with the way they were starting out, was a waterfront hellhole called Trident City. Buckhorn had never been there, but he knew it by reputation.

Trident City made perfect sense as a destination for Wainwright. From there, either by land or sea, he could gain passage to wherever he planned to pick up the rest of his life.

Buckhorn was determined to see to it he never made it that far.

If old Tyrone was accurate in his estimate that the fugitives left the burning Flying W at midnight, that gave them about a fifteen-hour head start on Buckhorn. If they'd all been on horseback, that would have been substantial. It was still a considerable gap to make up, but the wagon would slow them down somewhat.

Buckhorn figured they would have kept moving all night and through this morning. If they were smart, they would be halted to wait out the pounding heat. That would allow him to close some of the gap, although he expected they'd be pushing on again when the sun went down.

As a lone rider, especially on a strong mount like Sarge, he should easily be able to catch up with them by day after tomorrow. Trouble was, as he drew nearer to them he would have to use caution not to be spotted.

Wainwright had Lusita as his hostage and the threat to kill her was his ace against anyone coming in pursuit. In conjunction with that, he surely would have Sweetwater or one of the other gunmen trailing behind to cover their back trail. It wouldn't do Lusita, nor himself, any good if Buckhorn was careless enough to ride into an ambush.

His goal was to catch up with the fugitives, but only guardedly. From there, the big trick would be snatching Lusita out in one piece and then killing the rest.

"I don't know what's worse," grumbled Brazos Kent, "sloggin' through the freezing damn night or layin' up like a biscuit on an oven shelf in the baking-hot damn day."

"I don't know, either," Abe Tarvel replied, "but listening to you bitch and bellyache the whole while don't help neither. Not a stinkin' bit, I can tell you that much."

"Aw, I'm just sayin', that's all. And you know you're thinkin' the same damn thing."

"So what if I am? All the more reason not to want to listen to you carry on about it."

Kent was a solidly built man not far into his thirties, an inch over six feet in height, with bristly straw-colored hair and a strong jawline perpetually stubbled with pale whiskers, never cleanly shaven, never grown into a full beard.

Tarvel was a handful of years older, equally as tall, but lean and rawboned. He had thinning brown hair and a weathered face, crinkled with what some people called laugh lines around a set of pale blue eyes, suggesting he might have had something to laugh about at some point in his life, although anybody who spent time around him these days seldom saw any remnants of a happy temperament.

The pair were sprawled in what amounted to just a sliver of shade up close against an upthrust of multi-layered rock that poked out of the gravelly ground at a forty-five-degree angle. A dozen yards from their spot sat Wainwright's wagon, its team of horses unharnessed and staked a few feet beyond in a sparse patch of dry, wiry grass.

Lusita Wainwright lay in the shade under the wagon, propped against the inside of one of the wheels. Her lovely face was clamped by the same look of despair it had worn since they left the Flying W. On the other side of the wagon, the feet and lower portion of Thomas Wainwright's legs were visible, tirelessly pacing back and forth the length of the wagon. Leo Sweetwater was nowhere to be seen.

Kent spoke again in a tone slightly lowered from what it had been a minute ago. "Hot, cold, or in between, it's for certain we have got one little item with us on this trip that could sweeten even the harshest conditions."

Leaning against the rock with his eyes closed, Tarvel didn't have to open them to know what Kent was looking at. But he did, anyway. A man would have to be a plumb fool not to use any chance that came along as an excuse to take a look at Mrs. Wainwright.

As the two men watched, lacking much in the way of subtlety, Lusita reached for the canteen resting against her hip, lifted it, and poured a trickle of water onto the handkerchief she held in the opposite hand. She used the wetted hanky to dab at her perspiration-beaded face and then tipped up her chin, exposing a long, elegant throat, and squeezed the excess water from the cloth to let it run down as two narrow rivulets that merged and disappeared into the open front of her shirt with the top buttons undone.

Kent groaned. "Good God, what I wouldn't give to be that hanky."

"Hanky, hell," Tarvel grunted. "I'll take being one of those drops of water sliding down over that creamy throat then down inside the shirt and down, down . . ."

"You just evaporated and are gone. Me, bein' the hanky, I'm still around. All I gotta do is wait for another splash of water and I'm back in business again."

"Yeah, you're in business all right. We both are." Tarvel issued a derisive snort. "The business of sitting around trading pathetic fantasies. And right here, right now, that's about as close as either one of us is ever likely to get."

"You think so, do you?" Kent's eyes lingered on Lusita and his mouth curved in a shark's smile. "Don't be so sure. It's still a long way to the coast. Just don't you be so damn sure."

Lusita was aware that the two men were looking at her. Leering at her. She could *feel* their dirty eyes moving up and down her body the way they often did during the course of a day. It disgusted her . . . but not as much as it had in the beginning.

She had grown so despondent, so hopeless in her outlook that no indignity heaped upon her made much difference anymore. Everything good and decent in her life—the material trappings about her as well as the hopes and dreams inside her head—had been torn down, crushed, and left in smoldering ruins.

Her husband and father had turned out to be madmen who'd bartered her as part of their deal with one another. The beautiful house she'd grown accustomed to and had come to consider *hers* was torched. Her meager handful of friends and family were left behind without notice, abandoned for she knew not what.

If the current horrid traveling conditions, conducted in the company of loathsome men and a husband who had become quite unhinged, were indicators of how she was going to live from now on . . . If they were headed toward a wretched coastal hellhole with a reputation for evil and debauchery, she'd just as soon—

"At last. Here comes Sweetwater now," Wainwright announced as he finally ceased his pacing back and forth beside the wagon.

Lusita leaned over and peered out from under the wagon, her eyes sweeping in the westerly direction her husband was looking. A cloud of dust with the figures of a man and horse within it was moving toward them.

Leo Sweetwater. The one person in what had become Lusita's drastically altered world who seemed tarnished to the least degree. Yes, she had heard stories of the sometimes brash young gunmen's skill with a firearm and the often lurid accounts of the violence that had resulted from his use of same. Truth be told, she had no cause to doubt those accounts.

Nevertheless, in her personal though limited interactions with the young man, she had noted right from the start the *gentleness*—there was no more suitable word she could think of—in his eyes, and the courtliness in his manner whenever he was around her. Those were rare traits, even back at the ranch. On the range, with the only other company being the coarse pigs Kent and Tarvel and the deranged thing her husband had become, they offered her the only glimmer of hope she had against the experience deteriorating to an even more wretched level.

"What have you to report, Mr. Sweetwater?" Wainwright asked as soon as the rider reined up and dismounted.

"Only what we had reason to expect," Sweetwater answered. He pulled a canteen from his saddle and tipped it high. As he gulped thirstily, Kent and Tarvel wandered over to hear the rest of what he had to say. "Nothing but miles and miles of flat emptiness," Sweetwater continued, lowering the canteen. "Expect it'll be more of the same until we catch sight of the Barranca Mountains. Figure that should be sometime tomorrow afternoon."

"That sounds promising," Wainwright said. "It seems our pace has been painfully slow but, if your calculations are correct, we are actually making good time."

"I think so," Sweetwater agreed. "The Barrancas this far south are mostly petered out to a few low peaks and smooth, sloping foothills. Verdugo Pass is the main route through where we're headed. I've heard there are markers for it all along the foothills so we shouldn't have much trouble finding it. We get through that, it should be only two, maybe three days to the coast."

"Now you're talking," said Kent enthusiastically. "The coast and Trident City. Boy, will we have ourselves a time there!"

"Don't forget we still have to make it there," Wainwright cautioned in a stern tone. "There's more than just time and distance involved in what Mr. Sweetwater describes so nonchalantly. I agree that until we get beyond the Barrancas we're not likely to run into much of anything. After that, the closer we get to Trident City, the greater the chance of running into road agents and scoundrels of every stripe."

"Just remember, any of those would be a run-in that cuts both ways," said Tarvel with narrowed eyes. He patted the six-gun holstered on his hip. "We run into them, also means they'll be running into us."

"It's good to be confident, just as long you can back it up when the time comes," Wainwright reminded him coldly.

Taking advantage of the word choice presented him, Sweetwater spoke up, saying, "And speaking of backing things up, starting tomorrow after daybreak, we're gonna dangle a man back on drag to keep an eye on our back trail."

Wainwright frowned. "You really think that's necessary, after the warning I left?"

"I think it's a worthwhile precaution," Sweetwater said. "No harm if it doesn't pay off. Plenty to be gained if it does."

Wainwright's frown turned into a nod. "You're right. It's a worthwhile precaution indeed. Go ahead and make that arrangement, then."

Listening from under the wagon, Lusita idly wondered what warning her husband had left.

CHAPTER 44

On his second afternoon tracking the fugitives, Buckhorn holed up from the worst of the battering sun in the shade of a flat wall notched into the side of a low hill. Before seeing to his own needs, he took care of Sarge, stripping the big gray of his saddle and blanket, watering him from his hat, and giving him some grain before ground-reining him to graze in a fringe of stubborn grass.

After that, aided by a folding shovel taken out of his war bag, which he'd retrieved on his return to the Flying W bunkhouse, Buckhorn increased the depth of the notch and made the wall slightly more slanted to add to the amount of shade it provided. When he spread his bedroll blanket and lay down on it, he found the freshly uncovered dirt underneath to have an added coolness. It only lasted for a little while, but it felt good while it did.

Lying there, propped on one elbow, he ate a hard-boiled egg and half a beef sandwich that he'd gotten from the German sisters' restaurant back in Wagon Wheel. He washed the fare down with plenty of water before stretching out flat to rest and hopefully catch a few winks of sleep.

The way he had it figured, he'd cut the time gap between him and Wainwright's bunch by about half. That meant he should be able to come within sight of them by tomorrow afternoon. If he wanted to, that was. Assuming they'd have somebody watching their back trail, he'd have to be careful to make sure that getting them in sight didn't also make him visible the other way around.

Given the flat, treeless terrain they were traveling across, it was going to be mighty tough to get very close without revealing himself. But the Barranca Mountains would be coming up before long. In those broken peaks and canyons, it would be a different story.

Confident in that thought and finding a surprising amount of comfort in his little notch, Buckhorn soon dozed off.

By late the following morning, judging from the freshness of the horse droppings and the sharp-edged, uncrumbled indentations of the wagon tracks and hoof prints, Buckhorn knew the fugitives were only a short ways ahead of him.

But a complication had arisen.

A new set of tracks, that of five horsemen coming up from the south, had appeared. They were equally as fresh as those of Wainwright's bunch, actually a bit more so. Buckhorn could tell where the five horsemen had halted to contemplate the development. He could see that they'd turned and followed the wagon and its outriders, deviating from their original northerly direction. That placed the five new riders *between* Buckhorn and his quarry.

Buckhorn reined up Sarge in the same spot and did some contemplating of his own. The new pack of horsemen likely meant one of two things—a patrol of Rurales or a gang of bandits. Either would take an interest in strangers passing through the barren, little-traveled region.

While their guise might be different, the result wouldn't be too dissimilar. Bandits would do what their type of brutal human scavengers always did— rob, rape, kill. Rurales, the notoriously corrupt rural police who patrolled the far-flung and sparsely populated reaches of Mexico's northern states, had a bad habit of acting pretty much the same.

While Buckhorn cared little about what happened to any of the men he was following, other than he'd rather it was him who settled their hash, he did care very much that Lusita didn't fall into the hands of those he feared were closing in on her.

Damn.

Not a good turn of events. Not good at all.

Without a clear idea how he was going to play the new cards that he'd been dealt, Buckhorn nevertheless knew an added confrontation lay before him— one on top of the one he'd figured all along to be having with Wainwright and his hired guns. As one who didn't believe in waiting for inevitable trouble to come to him, he nudged Sarge forward and rode straight toward it.

The nameless little village rose up off the desert floor as unexpectedly as the new tracks had revealed themselves. A smattering of mud-colored adobe huts clustered haphazardly at the base of a quirky volcanic deposit worn into a wind-rounded lump. Out of that, a spring-fed stream trickled and provided reason for the village's existence.

Not so unexpected was the fact that the tracks of the wagon and its outriders veered around the village, showing no inclination to stop, not even with the heat of the afternoon starting to build toward its punishing peak. It was clear that Wainwright wanted to avoid leaving any memory of him and his group passing that way.

The five riders coming up behind them showed no such reservation. Buckhorn spotted where the five had once again stopped to palaver briefly before veering away from the wagon tracks and heading into town.

The only question was, did that mean they were abandoning their pursuit of the Wainwright bunch altogether, or were they merely making a temporary stop in the village with the intent of picking up the easily discernible wagon tracks again a little later on?

Buckhorn had a pretty good hunch it was the latter, but the answer was too important to leave it riding on a hunch. He opted for a visit to the village himself, wanting a closer look at the five mystery riders in order to get a better idea what they might be up to.

Considering the meager population of the small cluster of buildings, there would never be a time when its streets were truly busy. The onset of siesta time and the buildup to the afternoon's peak heat for sure was not that time. The only activity Buckhorn saw outside any of the buildings was three little kids rolling a wobbly hoop down one of the side streets.

The only businesses Buckhorn could make out were a shabby-looking cantina and an even shabbier-looking building that appeared to be a store of some kind. At the far end of the street, near the lumpy mound from which the stream dribbled into a natural stone pool, stood a weary-looking church.

If the stream and pool were the reasons for the village's existence, Buckhorn wondered, was there a connection to the worship practiced in the church so close by? Religion or water . . . when it came right down to it, he wondered which was more precious to people in a baked-over region like this?

Not surprisingly, the horses of the five riders Buckhorn had followed in were tied at the hitch rail in front of the cantina. He doubted the nags spent much time hitched in front of a church of any kind.

After dismounting and throwing the ends of Sarge's reins around the sun-battered rail, Buckhorn paused for a minute with one hand resting on the big gray's shoulder. It was pretty apparent the mismatched saddles and overall ill-kempt look of the five horses didn't belong to a Rurales patrol, not even a sloppy, undisciplined one.

That meant the men they belonged to were almost certainly bandits. Banditos on the prowl for easy pickings, with no hesitation or remorse should violence be called for. The kind of men you could give no quarter to. It was the kind of treatment they deserved and the kind Buckhorn was willing to provide.

He pulled the saddlebags down from Sarge's back to carry them inside with him as if they held something valuable that he wanted to keep close at hand. To sell that impression even harder, he took the shotgun that was part of his arsenal—courtesy of Bart Blevins via Leo Sweetwater—and took it in also.

The inside of the cantina, contrasting with its shabby exterior, was clean and tidy, smelling strongly of soap and wood polish. Most of all, its thick adobe walls served as a welcome barrier to the punishing heat outside.

Going immediately into his act, Buckhorn swaggered up to the plank bar, exclaiming in a loud voice, "Whoooee! It's hotter 'n a branding iron's kiss out there! But, boy, is it nice in here." He plopped his saddlebags and shotgun on top of the bar, then addressed the barkeep, a short, round-faced man with shiny black hair parted in the middle and slicked back on either side. "Amigo, you ought to charge admission just for folks to come in here and breathe this nice cool air."

The barkeep smiled somewhat nervously. "That sounds very good to me, señor, but I'm afraid my customers would not like it so much. I cannot afford to lose too many customers."

Buckhorn shrugged. "Well, it was just a thought. Guess that's why I'm not a businessman, eh?"

The five riders were the only other patrons in the cantina. They were strung out down the length of the bar off to Buckhorn's right. A filthier crew you'd be hard-pressed to find anywhere. Ragged apparel, except for some obvious care taken to the guns and shell belts they were heavily adorned with, covered by a fresh layer of sweat and trail dust. Underneath, it was a safe bet, would be a not-so-fresh layer of old grime and dried sweat that gave the pack the overall stench of a garbage heap.

The pack member nearest to Buckhorn, somewhat surprisingly, was an American. He was a sawed-off, homely little mutt, potbellied and bandy-legged, wearing a sombrero whose crown was so high that, if the hat were placed on the ground beside him, it would have stood nearly as tall as he was. It wasn't bias on Buckhorn's part to consider the presence of the gringo a bit unusual. It was just that, upon running across a gang of banditos south of the border, it seemed natural to expect they'd be made up of Mexicans.

Perhaps because of what he lacked in height, the individual in question seemed to be carrying around a sizable chip on his shoulder, a trait not uncommon in small men. Hearing the exchange between Buckhorn and the bartender, though no way meant to include him, the weight of the chip caused the fellow to chime in with a snotty remark. "For damn sure you wouldn't last long in any business with ideas like that," he snorted.

Turning to his cohorts farther down the bar, he added sarcastically, "You buckos hear that? This hombre over here wearing a chamber pot for a hat is trying to convince Pepe that he keeps it so nice and cool in here he oughta charge admission just for the pleasure of coming in outta the heat."

Buckhorn gritted his teeth and reminded himself that kind of goading fit smoothly into the reaction he was aiming for when he swaggered in. Ignoring his loud-mouthed neighbor, he rested his elbows on the bar top and said to the round-faced hombre on the other side, "How about your beer? You do charge for that, don't you?"

"*Sí, señor.* Of course."

"And is it nice and cold, the way you've got it cool in the rest of your place?"

"*Sí, señor,*" the barkeep said again. He smiled broadly. "I have the coldest beer in all of northern Mexico. I chill bottles overnight in a special pocket of spring water down by the church, and then bring them here each morning and keep them in a bed of sawdust until I can serve them to thirsty customers like you."

"Oh, man. Now you're talking my language and you've got me pegged dead to rights," Buckhorn said. "I'm a thirsty customer sure enough, and for the coldest beer in Mexico my thirst just went up even more. Set me up a couple bottles of those rascals so I can get started. Don't keep me waiting no longer, pal."

At which point the Americano interjected himself again. "Whoa there, mister. Don't get yourself too worked up. You see, I'm afraid Pepé went and forgot all about how the rules change when me and my compadres are in town."

"Change how?" Buckhorn wanted to know.

The barkeep's face took on a bewildered expression as if he was wondering the same thing.

Grinning, the runt glanced over his shoulder, checking to make sure his companions were watching the show he was putting on. Cutting his gaze back to Buckhorn, he said, "It has to do with that cold beer you're so interested in. Happens that me and the boys like cold beer, too. A lot."

Buckhorn gestured to the shot glasses and tequila bottles scattered across the bar in front of the men. "Kinda funny that not a single one of you has a beer ordered up."

"We just ain't got around to it yet," the runt explained. "We like to warm up on tequila before switching over to beer. Then watch us go to town!"

The men behind the runt were peeking over and around him, chuckling and enjoying the way he was stringing along the stranger.

Yeah, they were teasing and chuckling, but their mood could change in the blink of an eye, Buckhorn knew, and they'd still be chuckling while they cut a victim's throat.

"Well, to each his own, I guess," Buckhorn said.

"Me, I like to go straight to the suds. If Pepe here will set me up a tall, foamy one, that's what I'll—"

"That's the problem. You don't understand." The runt's taunting smile widened. "You must be what people back home used to call *thickheaded.*"

Buckhorn narrowed his eyes. "Reckon I'm as quick on the uptake as the next fella, bub. If you'll quit stammering around the edges and get to the damn point, I'll try to keep up. *Then* maybe I can have me a beer in peace."

"That *is* the point. That's what I'm trying to explain." The runt made a gesture with both hands. "The rule when me and my compadres are in town is that nobody else gets served cold beer so as to avoid the risk of running out. You remember that now, don't you, Pepe?"

The barkeep continued to look bewildered and a trace of fear was added to his expression. He managed a weak nod of agreement.

Motioning for Buckhorn to lean a little closer, the runt added in a hushed tone, "You see, some of my friends get real annoyed and unpleasant when they run out of cold beer. Pity any poor unsuspecting fool who happens to drink the last cold one when my friends are still in the mood for another. That's why, for the sake of life and limb and not having Pepe's joint smashed to splinters over such a misunderstanding, we had to put the rule in place."

"The rule."

"Uh-huh."

"The one that says nobody else can have a cold beer while you fellas are in town?"

"That's right."

"What if"—Buckhorn smiled pleasantly—"I was to tell you that I think your rule stinks? And then, what if

I was to grab Pepe like this"—his left hand streaked out and his fist clamped the front of Pepe's shirt just under his chin, yanking it hard—"and threaten to shake him until his bones rattled apart or until he fetched me a *bottle of damned beer*!? What then?"

"In that case, you thickheaded fool," the runt snarled, all trace of a smile, even a taunting one, disappearing, "no amount of beer in all of Mexico would do you any good. Me and my friends would ventilate you so full of bullet holes that every ounce would run right back out!"

Buckhorn bared his teeth in a snarl that put the runt's to shame. "The choice is up to you, then. Change your stupid rule . . . or commence ventilating!"

The scene seemed frozen with ragged tension for a long minute. Then everyone burst into motion all at once.

The men behind the runt began to fan out in a sloppily executed maneuver, throwing back their serapes and clawing frantically for the revolvers holstered on their hips. Some of them got their feet tangled together in the process.

Buckhorn, in the meantime, released his hold on the barkeep and flung the round-faced little man away with his right hand, sending him staggering and then toppling to the floor. Buckhorn's left hand dropped immediately and closed over the shotgun lying atop the saddlebags on the bar.

When he first went inside, he had flopped them down with apparent haphazardness. In truth, he had placed them in a very purposeful way. The double barrels of the gut-shredder were pointed toward the center of the banditos lining the bar and angled slightly upward by the way they lay across the saddlebags.

Without needing to raise the weapon or take further

aim in such close quarters, he merely slipped his thumb through the trigger guard, squeezed, and discharged the twin twelve-gauge loads. The fact the blaster happened to be laying on its side made no difference at all to the release of destructive, life-taking hellfire.

Standing nearest, the runt took the first and worst of it. Half of his head disappeared in a scarlet mist of gore, skull fragments, and one wildly spinning eyeball. The diminutive body simply collapsed like a pile of empty clothes.

As the blast pattern carried down the length of the bar, it raked a spray of splinters and pulverized glass off the plank top. At a slightly higher level, it also slammed hard into two more banditos who hadn't managed to successfully shove away. One of them was driven straight back, taking a full hit to the chest and lower part of his face. The other took a more glancing blow and was sent whirling around and staggering toward the middle of the room.

While these bodies were still flailing and falling, Buckhorn took a step away from the bar, planted his feet wide, and brought his Colt out in a blur of speed. The remaining two men, who'd succeeded in spreading away from the bar, still didn't have their own guns drawn completely. Both weapons were on the rise but not yet clear of leather. Neither ever got any closer to being yanked free.

Buckhorn planted a pair of .45 caliber slugs into the heart of each man. They parted from one another like the opening petals of a flower, one falling one way, one toppling the other.

Only a single bandito was left alive—the one who'd been skimmed by the shotgun blast at the bar and staggered out to the middle of the room. He was on his knees, trembling, his face twisted by pain and rage.

Raising a bloody, shredded right arm, he thrust it forward unsteadily and triggered a shot from the converted Colt Navy he was fisting.

Unsteadily fired though it may have been, the bullet found a piece of its target.

Buckhorn felt fiery hot pain rip through the outside of his left thigh. The corresponding tug on his leg wasn't sufficient to throw off his own aim when he returned fire. The Colt roared again and a thumb-sized black hole, rimmed in bright red, appeared between the bandito's eyes. His head snapped back as if yanked by invisible wires and then his whole body toppled away, chasing the gush of blood that sprayed out the back of his skull.

CHAPTER 45

"Sorry to put you through this, pal," Buckhorn muttered to Sarge. "I'll make it up to you as soon as we land back in civilization, I promise. A week's worth of grain and the prettiest filly I can find to keep you company. How's that sound?"

Sarge chuffed, as if to say *You'd damn well better* and kept plugging along.

The *this* Buckhorn was putting the big gray through—as well as himself and the two horses he'd confiscated back in the nameless village—was to ride straight on through the blistering hot afternoon, without a halt during the worst of it. What was more, their route was no longer a direct one toward Verdugo Pass but rather a semicircle that looped wide to the south and then west again before converging once more on the pass. Somewhere in between was his quarry, probably motionless for the time being, waiting for the heat to subside.

For the first time since setting out in pursuit of the Wainwright party, Buckhorn had a concrete plan and a specific destination for implementing it. He'd forged it back in the bloodied cantina of the nameless little village, following the shoot-out with the banditos. A quick discussion with Pepe had confirmed some things he'd only suspected and from there the rest had fallen into place.

Pepe's wife, a plump, bosomy, pretty little thing who seemed quite indifferent to the carnage visited upon the barroom, had tended Buckhorn's wound. First a good dousing with tequila that burned like fire, then a gentle application of salve, then a fresh, clean bandage.

While she was treating him, Pepe had treated him with bottles of the much-discussed cold beer. True to the round-faced man's word, if it *wasn't* the coldest in all of Mexico, it had to be damn close.

By way of compensation for the care and the damage, Buckhorn offered a proposition. He would take two of the banditos' horses and three of their sombreros. That part drew decidedly curious looks from Pepe and his wife.

The rest—the remaining horses, saddles, guns, and whatever money the men had in their pockets—were Pepe's to sell off or utilize however he saw fit.

According to some of the things Pepe had told Buckhorn, the five scoundrels had been harassing the village and surrounding area for several months. Simply getting rid of them would have been a most welcome thing, but having them gone and gaining profit as well was a joyous proposition to Pepe and his wife.

As he rode his punishing, circuitous route away from the village, Buckhorn thought of the other things Pepe had told him about the banditos and the boastful talk they had been making before his arrival. About the small, single-wagon group they were stalking and how much they were looking forward to picking it clean after they'd easily caught up with it again following their restful and refreshing stopover at Pepe's.

One of the things that had them most excited was the anticipation of what the inclusion of a wagon possibly meant—females among the group of travelers. That led to much vulgar talk about what would take place if it indeed turned out to be the case.

Hearing Pepe relate this, even without going into detail on everything that was said, gave Buckhorn no small amount of satisfaction for having scraped the earth clean of such scum.

"I still don't see why we couldn't 've swung into that little village and took our afternoon break there," Abe Tarvel complained. "Everybody knows how those old adobe buildings block out the heat. Think how nice and cool it would've been to stretch out in one of them for a little while. What was the point? What'd we gain? A lousy three hours?"

"Three hours is three hours," Sweetwater said sullenly. "No use bellyaching about it now. It's spilled milk."

"Yeah, spilled milk that would've been nice and cold to drink. Or better yet, a shot of tequila or some beer. For sure, something better than this piss-warm slop." Kent brandished the canteen he'd just taken a drink from and slammed it disgustedly to the ground.

The three were sitting on the ground with their backs against a low, jagged-topped boulder. The rock was hot through their sweat-soaked shirts, even with a saddle blanket wedged up as a barrier. The steadily widening sliver of shade thrown by the boulder made it worth a little patience.

As had become routine with their afternoon rest stops, the wagon sat a short distance away, its team un-hitched and picketed with the saddle-stripped riding mounts. Lusita lay in the shade under the wagon bed. General Wainwright paced restlessly back and forth under the full hammering weight of the sun.

"The general is set in his ways, that's all I know to tell you," Sweetwater tried to explain. "He's made up his mind that he wants to avoid all contact with any-body who can say later on they remember us passing through."

"Long as we've already come and gone, what the hell difference does it make?" Tarvel said. "One minute he's telling you not to worry about scouting our back trail, the next he's fretting for no good reason about us seeking a little comfort in a no-nothing town in the middle of nowhere. Sometimes he don't make a whole lot of sense."

"Like the way he paces out there right smack in the baking hot sun," Kent said. "Every time we stop, all he does is pace. Almost makes you wonder if he didn't do too much pacing in the hot sun at some point in his life and baked part of his brain or something."

"Yeah," Tarvel said, "you especially got to wonder about that pacing business when you consider the better option he's got. I had something waiting for me like he's got waiting for him under that wagon, I sure as hell wouldn't be spending all that time and energy walking *away* from it."

"Don't even start with that kind of talk," Sweetwater growled. "What goes on—or don't go on—between a man and his woman ain't no concern of ours. Same for the pacing."

"You're mighty touchy and protective of the old goat, ain't you?"

"He's the boss." Sweetwater shrugged. "You sign on with a man and take his money, you owe him a certain amount of respect. Not to mention a certain *kind* of respect. Otherwise, why would you stick with him?"

"That's a good question," Kent said. "Why is it that *any of us* are sticking with him? He's obviously on the downhill slide. First he lost that skirmish with Don Pedro, which makes you wonder about that whole *general* thing and how good he ever was at it. Then he sets fire to his own damn house, and has a whole passel of his cattle shot and killed, which makes you wonder what's going on upstairs in his head. Now he's running—exactly to what or where I don't know. I ain't so sure he does, either."

"Let's face it," Tarvel said. "Money is what he dangled to pull us all into his private little army and that's why we're hanging on, even now. But I'm thinking Trident City is as far as I go, no matter what. And he'd damn well better have the payoff for me sticking that far."

"Oh, he's still got money. I can vouch for that much," said Sweetwater. "I saw him haul it out of the safe back at the house before he torched the place. I'm leaning the same way as you, Tarvel. I think Trident City is where me and the general will be parting ways."

Kent nodded. "Same goes for me. And there ain't no leaning about it. After we hit Trident City, the only way I'll be looking at General Wainwright is back over my shoulder."

They were quiet for a spell. The shadow edging out farther from the rock moved with agonizing slowness. It gave precious little comfort in the shade it cast, but it was something.

At length, Tarvel said, "You're sure he's got a bunch of money with him, though. That right, Sweetwater? Right there in the wagon?"

"Uh-huh. Helped load it in myself."

Another stretch of silence passed.

"Tarvel," said Sweetwater.

"Yeah?"

"Don't even think what you're thinking. Until I *ain't* working for the general no more, I *am*. You understand? That means my job, as I see it, is taking care of *him*. Wouldn't bother me a whole lot to kill *you*. I'd just as soon not have to."

CHAPTER 46

They reached Verdugo Pass well after dark. By then, their eyes had had plenty of time to adjust to the transition into night. The wash of light pouring down from the moon and stars, out of the cloudless sky, provided sufficient illumination even against the looming wall of the Barranaca Mountains

Plus the light from the glowing coals of a campfire directly ahead was guiding them like a muted signal beacon beckoning sailors to a safe shoreline.

"What do you make of it?" Wainwright called from the wagon seat, not slowing the team any as he raised the question. His question came out in puffs of whitish-gray vapor caused by the warmth of his breath against the chill night air that had settled over the stark land in such sharp contrast to the afternoon's blazing heat.

He was addressing Kent and Tarvel, who were riding about twenty yards ahead. Sweetwater was some distance to the rear, covering their back trail.

"Looks like somebody's pitched a night camp right

near the opening to the pass," Kent called back to the general. "No sign of anybody moving around, most likely all asleep."

"That wouldn't be unusual, of course, for most travelers," Wainwright said. "Go ahead, ride in closer and check it out. Use precaution, nevertheless."

Kent and Tarvel gigged their horses toward the mouth of the pass and the unexpected sign of occupants who'd apparently stopped there for the night. They fanned out over the short distance and then converged back together from opposite sides before reining to a halt.

"Hello, the camp!" Kent called.

No response except for a snort from one of the three horses picketed back in a stand of high, stringy grass. Closer to the fading fire, the shapes of three men lay wrapped in bedrolls. High-crowned sombreros covered heads and faces propped on saddles serving as pillows. Spurts of ragged snoring rose from the shapes.

That wasn't all that rose from the sleeping forms.

"Holy hell, do you smell that?" Tarvel exclaimed.

"I'd have to have my head cut off not to," replied Kent. "Jesus! These boys smell like they drank half the tequila in Mexico and are snorin' it back out."

Tarvel tried his luck at rousting the campers. "Pancho! Chico! Hey, you bean-eaters, wake the hell up, you're blocking the road."

All he got for his trouble was more snoring and more reek of secondhand tequila.

Wainwright rolled up in the wagon, announced by the creak of leather and plodding of the team's hooves as he pulled back on the reins. "What's the situation?"

Tarvel gestured. "Just like we figured, some travelers

decided to stop here for the night. Mexicans, from the look of it. Drunk as skunks, from the smell of it and the fact they ain't wantin' to be rousted."

"No never mind about them," Kent said. "They've built their doggone fire right in the middle of that mighty narrow mouth to the pass. There ain't enough room for your wagon to get around and the coals to that fire are still too hot for the horses to be willing to go through."

Wainwright frowned. "So what's your hesitation? They have the right to camp alongside the pass if they wish, but they're certainly not entitled to block the way for others. Quash that fire and scatter the coals. Clear the way as necessary."

"Consider it done," Kent said, swinging down from his saddle.

"Just be careful when you start kicking those coals around," Tarvel advised his partner as he, too, left his stirrups. "We don't want any to land too close to those snoring fools. A strong puff of raw tequila breath catches one wrong, we could all blow up or something."

Of the three lumpy shapes lying on the ground, Buckhorn was the one farthest removed from the campfire. The other two were not men at all but rather bedrolls tucked around some carefully arranged rocks and twigs and heaps of dirt, augmented by the saddles and sombreros commandeered from the dead banditos back at the nameless village. The tequila stink assailing the nostrils of Kent and Tarvel was courtesy of a good dousing Buckhorn had given the blankets and sombreros.

Lying in the thick of the stink and listening to the comments from Kent and Tarvel, Buckhorn wondered wryly if maybe he hadn't overdone it a bit with the dousing. That's all he needed was to make himself half-drunk from the fumes when the time for precision-timed action was at hand.

He remained still and listened closely. With the sombrero over his face he had limited vision. He could see the wheels of the wagon off to one side and could hear the two men brushing and scraping at what was left of the fire, but he couldn't see them. He'd heard no evidence at all of Sweetwater, which meant he was still lagging behind on their back trail. Buckhorn's plan was to make his move when the wagon was just entering the narrow opening to the pass, hoping Sweetwater wouldn't have caught up by then.

Abruptly, the sounds of Kent and Tarvel clearing the fire stopped.

"Hold it a minute," said Tarvel's voice. "Look at those horses on the picket line. Don't that big gray one look familiar?"

"Hell, I don't know," Kent grumbled. "I can't see over there that good. Besides, one gray horse is gonna look like another, especially at night like this."

"No, not the one I'm thinking of. But I can't quite . . . Wait a minute! Now I remember. I'm sure of it. That big stud belongs—"

"Freeze just like you are, boys." *Damn!* Clear what was coming next, Buckhorn couldn't afford to wait any longer. He'd flung back his blanket, knocked away the sombrero, and surged to his feet. His Colt was leveled on Kent and Tarvel. "Keep your hands away from your guns or those smoky coals you're kicking around are gonna seem like a puny taste of what's waiting for you if you make me blast you to hell."

The two men standing on the smoldering ground where the fire used to be did indeed freeze—eyes blazing, backs humped, hands curled over the hoglegs strapped to their sides. But the hands held, dropping no lower. Hating him with those blazing eyes, they were smart enough to accept that he had the drop on them, reinforced by a keen awareness of how deadly accurate he was with that big Colt.

On the driver's box of the wagon, Wainwright thrust to a standing position. "Buckhorn!" he roared. "Kill that son of a bitch!"

The force of the command, combined with Buckhorn's momentary glance in the direction of the mad ex-general, was too much for Kent and Tarvel to continue holding back. Simultaneously, their hands made desperate dives for their guns. In feeble attempts to try and throw off Buckhorn's accuracy, Kent dropped into a low crouch as he drew while Tarvel pitched himself to one side.

Neither effort gained any measure of success.

Buckhorn's first shot punched a slug square into Kent's throat, slamming his gore-wrapped Adam's apple out the back of his neck. Tarvel's dive-and-roll tactic caused Buckhorn to spend his next bullet on a grazing shoulder wound, but the next one punched a mortal hit to the center of Tarvel's chest as the gunman came out of the roll and tried to raise his own gun. He flopped onto his back and managed to shoot a hole in the sky with a spasm of dying fingers before his hand relaxed and the pistol slipped free.

Buckhorn wheeled around in time to see Thomas

Wainwright bringing a Winchester to his shoulder and taking aim with it.

There wasn't the slightest hesitation to Buckhorn's response as words filtered through his brain. *Priorities . . . The main job hired out to do . . . "You'll have to kill Wainwright in order to keep him from killing you" . . .*

He emptied the Colt's remaining three rounds into the former prison camp commander and blew him off the wagon box.

CHAPTER 47

"If you'll trust me, I'm here to help you."

Those were the words Buckhorn greeted Lusita Wainwright with when she poked her pretty head tentatively out from around the edge of the wagon canopy. He was advancing toward the wagon, replacing the Colt's spent cartridges as he went.

Lusita looked beyond him at the sprawled bodies of Kent and Tarvel. Then slowly turning her head, she looked down to where Wainwright had fallen on the other side of the wagon. Her eyes came back to Buckhorn. "Are they all dead?"

"That's the way they called it," he told her.

"There was another gunman," she said somewhat hesitantly.

"I know. Sweetwater."

"He may be the most dangerous of all. Except . . ."

"What?"

"Never mind. He's lagging somewhere behind, but not far."

"Uh-huh. He's bound to have heard the shooting, so he'll be showing up pretty quick. We need to get you to better cover over there in those rocks." Buckhorn holstered his gun, then raised his arms to help her down from the wagon.

As Lusita lighted, she said, "Did my father send you?"

"Among others."

"But only you? Only one man?"

"I was the right choice for moving fast enough to catch up and do what had to be done," Buckhorn explained. "Plus I had some unfinished business of my own where your husband was concerned."

Lusita looked ready to question him more about that, but they both heard the sound of approaching hoofbeats, coming fast.

"Get over there in the rocks!" Buckhorn ordered. "Stay down."

Lusita hurried over to some low, broken boulders and ducked down behind them. Buckhorn watched until he was satisfied she was safely in place, then turned back to the sound of the approaching rider.

Drawing his Colt again, he moved to the rear of the wagon and crouched behind one of its back wheels. The pounding hooves drew closer, slowed, and then stopped just inside the murkiness where the nighttime sky's illumination could not penetrate.

Everything was very quiet for a minute . . . until Sweetwater's voice called, "General? Kent? Tarvel?"

Buckhorn let the silence play out for several beats, then responded, "You're talking to ghosts, Leo. They gave me no choice . . . but I'm willing to give you one."

"I'll be damned. Is that you, Buckhorn?"

"None other."

"I should've known. I figured if we had a worry about anybody showing up to bite our heels it'd be you."

"Glad I didn't disappoint."

"What about the girl? Wainwright's wife."

"She's safe."

"I should've known that, too. Something else you can be counted on for."

"I can be counted on for keeping my word, too. Takes us back to that choice I said I'd give you. You ride off into the night and we can call this over and done with. You won't have to bite the same dust the rest of 'em did."

"That's real big of you. What if I ain't in the mood for riding off or dust biting, either one?"

"I don't recall giving a third choice."

"Then let's say I'm the one giving it. Goes something along the lines of *you* being the next dust biter."

"Don't be a fool. You don't owe Wainwright anything more."

"This ain't about Wainwright. It's what started taking shape the minute you showed up and gunned ol' Dandy Jack. It was building up between me and him first, but then you stepped in. I told you in no uncertain terms the first day we rode out together to the Flying W that I was top gun for the brand. We both knew right then and there that sooner or later we was gonna have to find out if I could back that up against you. It was just a matter of when."

"And you're saying this is *when*."

"I'm sorta demanding it."

"You're a bigger fool than I thought."

"Only if it turns out I ain't as good as I think I am."

"I hate to see it come to that. If you push it, I'll push back."

"I'm pushing. I figure to ride up there, slowlike, to where we can see each other plain. I'll get down and we'll walk it off. You'll have the chance to shoot me out of the saddle, if you're of a mind to, and make the outcome certain for yourself. I know that ain't your way . . . so here I come."

Once again the sound of a horse's hooves filled the silence. The clop of the hooves was slow, unhurried. Gradually, the forms of Sweetwater and his horse emerged from the murkiness and took on clearer, sharper definition as they grew closer. Buckhorn rose behind the wagon wheel, came around the end of the wagon, and began walking slowly toward the incoming rider. Sweetwater halted his horse, climbed down out of the saddle, and began walking, too.

"Whenever it feels right," Buckhorn said in a raspy voice, "go ahead and make your move for doing what you're so hell-bent on doing."

Seconds later, Sweetwater's hands dove for his guns. Both of them. And both came up with simultaneous blinding speed.

Buckhorn's Colt flashed from its holster within the same shaved heartbeat of time. Three shots split apart the still night. Two bullets ripped through flesh. Both men fell to the ground.

Buckhorn hit hard, dust puffing up into his nostrils, grit crunching between his teeth. Fiery pain raced up and down his right side, telling him he'd taken a fairly serious hit. But he wasn't dead. Not yet, by damn, and he meant to keep it that way.

He knew his shot had hit Sweetwater. He'd seen him go down. Uncertain the young gunman was down for good, Buckhorn gripped his .45, squirmed on the ground, half-rolled onto his left side, and tried to push himself to where he could determine how things stood.

He pushed and pushed for what seemed like a long time, not making any headway. Everything around him was pulsing in and out of blurriness and clarity and he couldn't seem to get all of the grit spat out of his mouth.

Suddenly, Lusita was kneeling beside him, her hands pressing gently but firmly against him. "Stay still. Lay back, quit struggling. You're hit in the side, through the ribs. I think you can make it if you hold still and let me stop the bleeding. You don't have to worry about Sweetwater. He's dead. Your shot was truer . . ."

CHAPTER 48

For the second time in only a handful of hours, Buckhorn found himself being ministered to for a gunshot wound. The damage was more serious and the young woman tending it less competent. Not that Lusita's shortcomings in the nurse department were due to any lack of intensity or well meaning; she simply didn't have the experience.

Sweetwater's bullet had passed between two of Buckhorn's ribs, meaning no lead stayed inside him. During its visit, the slug had torn up plenty of meat, cracked a couple bones, and left rather messily. Apart from the pain, stopping the blood flow at the exit hole proved to be the biggest challenge.

Finally, he sent Lusita to fetch a tobacco plug from Tarvel's body, took a big cut of it, and chewed it into a softened gob. Using that and a tight bandage they were able to stop the stubborn leakage.

That wasn't the end of it. Buckhorn knew enough about gunshot wounds to know that his blood loss and injuries—counting the leg wound from earlier—would take a toll on him pretty quickly, especially once they were on the move.

And move they must—for the sake of his injuries and for the sake of their overall safety. It might be days before any more travelers came this way and, when they did, it was a fifty-fifty chance they could be another gang of banditos or scavengers of some other sort who'd hesitate only slightly before slitting their throats and leaving them with the rest of the dead for the sake of their horses, saddles, guns, and the riches they would find in the wagon.

With luck, if Buckhorn's injuries didn't slow them too much, they could reach Wagon Wheel in two days. Neither Lusita nor Buckhorn knew of anywhere else in between; at least none where they were likely to find safe haven or the kind of medical attention he would increasingly need.

After quick discussion and agreement, they set about preparing their departure. Lusita assured him she was an accomplished horsewoman but had no experience at driving a wagon and team. With his wounds, Buckhorn figured he was better off sticking with Sarge rather than trying to wrestle the reins himself, so heading out on horseback was their choice.

They had no discussion of burying the dead. Given the matters of time and physical limitations, it was understood as something that simply could not be seen to.

Lusita selected Sweetwater's horse to ride and Buckhorn picked Kent's to serve as their packhorse, on which they loaded provisions, key among them being all the water they could gather and combine from various canteens and water skins. Additionally, Lusita added a small bag of her most prized personal possessions from the wagon.

She also took time to strip her husband's corpse of

the money belt he'd worn securely strapped around his waist.

"Money was never part of why I became Mrs. Thomas Wainwright," she announced fiercely and defensively to Buckhorn. "But given all that has happened and all I have recently learned, I am going after everything I can get out of being the only heir to what is left of Wainwright holdings. I started out as a bargaining chip between Thomas and my father. I'll be damned if I will settle for merely being that from here on out. Before I am through, my scheming, manipulative father will be called to account, also!"

"I believe you, lady," Buckhorn told her. "Damned if I don't."

They rode out before sunrise.

Buckhorn set Sarge to a steady, moderate pace. At first, he felt fairly comfortable in the saddle, rocking to the familiar gait of the big gray. Gradually, the pain in his side increased while at the same time he felt himself growing weaker.

The sun came up and the day's heat started to build. At the peak of the sizzling afternoon, they laid up for rest, but only for two or three hours during the worst of it. The horses were unsaddled, watered out of Buckhorn's hat, and then picketed in some scrub graze.

Lusita checked Buckhorn's wounds and found the one on his side to be leaking badly again. She methodically redressed it. Before applying the fresh bandage, she doused the tobacco cud with some brandy she'd brought along from the wagon. She tried to get Buckhorn to drink some of it, for the pain, but he refused.

He did drink lots of water, though, and encouraged

her to do the same. They had plenty so it was best to keep themselves as saturated as possible, rather than sip it sparingly. For nourishment, they ate jerky and split a jar of canned peaches.

In the middle of the night, when the deep chill of the sunless hours gripped the stark land in sharp contrast to the heat of the days, Buckhorn started to shiver. It didn't take long before his trembling became so violent that Lusita, looking on, feared it might cause him to spill from his saddle.

Against his protests, she finally called a halt in the heart of a shallow gully where they were protected from a low, cold wind that moaned across the land. She insisted he lie down against one side of the gully where she wrapped him in layers of bedroll blankets.

The blankets did nothing to diminish the shivering. Droplets of clammy sweat stood out on his face and ran down his neck.

Lusita was forced to leave him like that long enough to tend to the horses. Returning, she scraped together fuel and built a close fire for the heat and for the illumination to examine Buckhorn's wound. It was bleeding once more and his shivering continued.

She set a pot of coffee to cooking, and while it brewed, she redressed the wound. After that, she liberally laced a cup of coffee with brandy and forced him to drink it. Then another . . . but nothing diminished the chills or the shivering, or slowed the clammy sweat.

She heaped on more blankets.

Buckhorn maintained his senses throughout, though there were times he became a bit foggy and thick-tongued. "I'm tougher than this, damn it. I've got through worse than this. Just let me sweat this out and I'll be fit as a fiddle."

But he continued to sweat and shiver with no signs of improvement.

In the weakening light of the dying fire, Lusita checked his wound again and found no evidence of it bleeding. At least that was a good sign, she told herself.

She leaned wearily against the gully wall, beginning to feel her own exhaustion, not to mention a nagging hint of desperation. She, too, was getting cold even inside her heavy coat. The fire was fading fast and she'd already scrounged all of the fuel to be found anywhere close by.

It was then a thought struck her. A rather bold one, in more ways than one. She regarded Buckhorn, still trembling despite all the blankets she'd spread over him. She considered the chill of the night seeping deeper into her and the fact that sunrise was still two or three hours away, then longer still until the morning's heat would build appreciably.

She knew a way for her to endure those hours more comfortably but also to put forth another effort toward countering Buckhorn's suffering. Yes, it was bold. Shocking even. Anyone with proper morals would surely say so.

Yet all the while Lusita was telling herself these things, her hands were busy unfastening her clothing.

In the glow of early dawn, Buckhorn awakened. He was no longer chilled or shivering. And in his arms, snuggled close to him under a mound of blankets, was a nearly naked young woman. He recognized her, of course. *Lusita.* Achingly lovely, hauntingly beautiful Lusita. Under the blankets. Mostly naked. With him.

Buckhorn couldn't resist. He leaned to kiss her. Her eyes fluttered open, but she said or did nothing to resist. Their lips met and it was the first of many long, hungry kisses as their bodies pressed together with equal urgency.

CHAPTER 49

They reached Wagon Wheel early on the third morning after the shoot-out at Verdugo Pass. Their arrival spurred an instant flurry of interest and activity. At first they were bombarded by questions fired from all sides . . . until a cooler head in the form of Justine York quieted everybody down and reminded them that the returning pair had just gone through an ordeal that warranted an opportunity to get cleaned up, rested, and fed before being pawed at and too aggressively interrogated. Not to mention the medical attention Buckhorn clearly needed.

Lusita was whisked off to the Traveler's Rest, where she was provided a bath, fresh clothes, and a meal from the Good Eats Café. She was also offered a bed to rest in. Declining the latter, she asked that her father be sent for, and then requested to be reunited with Buckhorn as soon as the doctor was finished with him.

In the doctor's office, Buckhorn already had plenty of company. The sheriff, Carl Orndecker, and Martin Goodwin were present as the string bean of a medic went through a procedure of examining, cleaning, and treating the wounds. That involved the application of salves and a good deal of fresh bandaging along with a small bottle of pain medicine to be used as needed.

Whatever was in the bottle smelled god-awful and anybody strong enough to get past the stink and actually take a swallow ought to rate as healthy enough not to need it. It didn't smell so bad, however, that it ruined the taste of the plate of food sent over by the Good Eats or the two cold beers Goodwin fetched from the Watering Hole saloon.

The conversation that took place during Buckhorn's time in the doctor's office actually did a pretty good job of bringing everybody up to date on what had transpired while Buckhorn was away, both in Whiteside County and out on the trail. When Sheriff Banning heard about the shoot-out at Verdugo Pass, he promptly sent a party of volunteers to go retrieve the bodies and whatever else was left.

In Wagon Wheel, Goodwin's well had set in motion a surge of civic pride and entrepreneurial excitement like nobody could have imagined. Existing businesses were talking about expanding and a few telegrams had been received from others inquiring about relocating there. Plans were already underway to build a reservoir basin north of town, connected to the well by a feeder canal.

All of this was gone over once again in the presence of Lusita. When informed by the sheriff that the contents of her husband's safe, which had survived the fire, had been confiscated and was being held for a full legal review of the deeds and property claims it contained, Lusita understood completely and stated her willingness to cooperate in every way.

She further stated her intentions to rebuild and revive the Flying W, albeit under a new name. From whatever livestock could be salvaged, she planned to nurture it into her own land and cattle company. But only, she assured everyone, with property and holdings that had been acquired by fair and reasonable means.

When Lusita's father arrived, there was much rejoicing. Laughter and tears mixed freely. So much praise and gratitude was heaped on Lusita's rescuer by the old don that Buckhorn had to retreat to the edge of the crowd and make sure he stayed out of sight in order to keep from triggering more of the same.

Lusita responded with special warmth at the sight of Consuela and Armando, her former house servants, and even Tyrone, the old grub shack cook. All had been staying at Don Pedro's hacienda which, though damaged during the battle between hired guns, remained mostly still functional. The old Wagon Wheel was in the past.

Lusita also showed warmth toward the reunion with her father and he, most assuredly, in return. Looking on, however, Buckhorn couldn't help but note what appeared to be an icy glint in the corner of Lusita's shining eyes as she smiled and hugged Don Pedro.

He remembered vividly her words that night back on the trail. *"I started out as a bargaining chip between Thomas and my father—I'll be damned if I will settle for merely being that from here on out. Before I am through, my scheming, manipulative father will be called to account also!"*

Yes, Don Pedro was very glad to have his daughter back safe. But maybe, just maybe, Buckhorn thought, the old rascal would be well advised to keep a sharp lookout over his shoulder from here on out.

Before Lusita left to go back with her father and those who'd come with him, she and Buckhorn managed a moment alone together.

"I'll never forget you," she whispered as they stood close.

"Same here," Buckhorn assured her.

"And yet I know it is best for us to part this way. The special, wonderful moment we had that morning in the little canyon—"

"It was just that. A special, wonderful moment. One I hope we'll both treasure for the rest of our time. I know I will. We already talked about this on the trail. A moment is all it was, all it ever can be."

"But . . ."

"No buts. We're from two different worlds and there's no sense trying to fool ourselves otherwise."

Lusita gazed up at him. "My course is firm. I know what lies ahead for me. But what about you?"

Buckhorn smiled somewhat wistfully. "Oh, I reckon I'll hang around here for a while. Heal up a little more. Contact the man who sent me here and report that I've finished what he sent me to do. Then, before long, I'll drift on again. To the next job or whatever I find on the trail ahead of me."

"In many ways that sounds lonely and rather sad. And yet, for you, it somehow fits. For you, I cannot imagine anything else."

Buckhorn grinned. "Me neither. Leastways not yet. Maybe someday that *whatever* I find on the trail ahead will give me the answer."

"I hope so," Lusita said. She stepped into a lingering embrace and then, as they parted and she turned from him, she added a whispered, "*Vaya con Dios.*"

After she was gone, Buckhorn muttered under his breath, "I'm trying, lady. It ain't easy, but I'm trying."

**Keep reading for a special preview
of the first book in a new series
from WILLIAM W. JOHNSTONE
and J. A. JOHNSTONE**

THE JACKALS

*Alone, these justice fighters are dangerous enough.
Together they're a wild bunch known as the Jackals.
Now, national bestselling authors William W. and
J. A. Johnstone are turning them loose . . .*

Holed up in a West Texas way station after a savage
Indian massacre, ex–cavalry sergeant Sean Keegan,
bounty hunter Jed Breen, and ex–Texas Ranger
Matt McCulloch are determined to make good on
a promise to a dead man: deliver his blood-soaked
stash of $50,000 to his kin—especially when the
dying man promised them five grand.

The trio, soon to be known as the Jackals, aren't all
that honest, but they have one thing in common:
they keep their word, and they gave their word to
a dying man. It's rough enough backtracking over
warpath country. Worse—turns out the loot they're
hauling is the stolen property of the vengeful
Hawkin gang, and those prairie rats are merciless,
stone-cold killers. But McCulloch, Keegan,
and Breen aren't riding for their own lives.
They're protecting a prisoner in tow—
a hot-as-a-pistol female who can shoot with the
best of them. The Jackals are ready for a
showdown—and may not live to spend that $5,000.

**Look for THE JACKALS,
on sale now where ever books are sold.**

PROLOGUE

Front-page editorial from the Purgatory City, Texas, *Herald Leader*, Alvin J. Griffin IV, editor and publisher:

THE TIME HAS COME
FOR OUR CITIZENS TO STAND UP
TO THE JACKALS OF WEST TEXAS
AND MAKE A STATEMENT FOR LAW
AND ... ESPECIALLY ... ORDER!

The War Between the States is well behind us, the Mexicans have been behaving themselves of late, and the only thing that must be eradicated in the state of Texas—and our neighbors in the Southwest—are the menacing Apache marauders.

Yes, cowboys will be cowboys when they get paid, and most soldiers who risk their lives for our safety against these Apache butchers who torment our neighbors on the homesteads and ranches and small mines, or those lone travelers who make an "easy kill," yes, those soldiers get carried away much like cowboys when they have money to spend. Sure, we have gamblers who cheat and floozies who seek to soil our young men, and there is graft and dishonesty, even an occasional fistfight between friends.

All of this is part of progress, of sowing one's oats, of growing up. West Texas is seeing progress, and our towns and cities and communities are growing up. We have the telegraph. We have the railroad. We have stagecoaches. Our cities and towns have fine places to eat, comfortable beds that aren't ticky and are free of bedbugs. Our bankers are willing to make loans to reputable citizens at fine rates to build and build and build.

We must commend our fine city marshal, Rafe McMillian, and our county sheriff, Juan Garcia, for all they do. Likewise, we know MOST of the Texas Rangers under the command of Captain J.J.K. Hollister try to keep peace in our communities. Colonel John Caxton expertly commands the soldiers at Fort Spalding. Our district marshal for the federal courts, Kenneth Cook, and his valiant deputies are busy tracking down other offenders and lawbreakers.

The only thing we should have to worry about, other than the Apache menace, is the weather.

But, of course, the weather must be left to the Almighty's hand.

We should be free of worry.

We should be free of most crime.

We should, and we must, be free of jackals.

Yet, West Texas and the territories of New Mexico and Arizona, and even our neighbors below the Rio Grande, are not free of such beasts.

And as much as it sickens your editor of your

best and leading newspaper, I feel it is time to single out the worst offenders, the jackals who could prevent corporations from investing in our communities. Those who tarnish our good standing, who smear our good name, and who, if we are not diligent, may destroy all of our hard work.

Certainly, Jake Hawkin and his band of desperate bandits have been rampaging our towns, stagecoaches, banks, and our decent citizens for far too long, and have started to rival the James-Younger gang and other bushwhacking border trash up in Missouri and elsewhere. Where there is progress, where there is success, where you find money and people and beer and whiskey and wine and gambling halls, there will be a few rotten eggs. Jake Hawkin is a rotten egg. He and his cutthroats must be killed or captured and hanged by the neck until they are dead, dead, dead.

Marshal Cook assures your trusted editor this will happen, as his deputies are following leads and trails and believe that they have the outlaw butchers on the run.

But this paper—this editor—does not consider Jake Hawkin or his rogues to be *Jackals*.

A jackal, according to the dictionary on my desk, is "a wild animal of India and Persia, allied to the wolf."

Jake Hawkin is a coward. He wore neither blue nor gray during the late unpleasantness. He is too lazy to make the proverbial honest dollar. He is not wild. He has no allies, not even the men who ride with him, for all they want is that easy dollar. The men who ride with Hawkin, and Hawkin himself, have no calluses on their hands. Colt revolvers, Winchester repeating rifles, poker chips, and pastecards rarely cause calluses, and that's all these swine know.

In Thessalonians, it is written that we should reject every kind of evil.

We reject the Hawkin Gang, and they will be brought to justice. But we have not rejected all of our terrible jackals.

Alas, for the jackals in our midst, we must look closer to our homes.

At Fort Spalding, for instance.

Last week, Sergeant Sean Keegan all but destroyed The Killers & Thieves Saloon & Gambling Parlor on Acme Street. Oh, how we have asked saloon owner Ryan O'Doul to change the name of his establishment, but the fun-loving Irishman (meaning O'Doul, not Keegan, who speaks with not even the slightest brogue) says he wants people to have fun when they come into his place. According to O'Doul, "A man will remember The Killers and Thieves, no matter how much Who Hit John he drinks, and he will come back. Because, ladies and lasses, that name sticks out more than the Acme, the Place, and even The Alamo—saloons that line our streets on the other side of the railroad tracks." He went on by saying, "Folks, I try not to serve killers and thieves."

Yet he served Keegan and probably regrets it. The sergeant decided, after much too much Who Hit John, that he was being cheated at the roulette table. So he broke a bottle of rye whiskey over the operator's head, turned over the table, busted the wheel, drew his Remington revolver and began shooting out the lights that had been imported all the way from Saint Louis and were just installed a month ago to brighten the favored saloon in our great city.

Patrons ran out screaming in the street, as Keegan was the only man armed in the saloon, for bartender Saul Ferguson wisely left the sawed-off shotgun under the bar and helped Louie Roebuck, our lovable town drunk, out through the back entrance. Seeing he was alone, Sergeant Keegan walked to the bar and helped himself to more shots of whiskey. He then broke the mirror on the back bar with the whiskey bottle . . . that must have been empty. He kicked over the spittoons and as he walked out of the saloon, overturned tables and chairs—even busted three chairs—and tossed an entire table through the fine plate-glass window. He kicked open the batwing doors, ripping one off its hinges, and then holstered his still-smoking revolver, rolled a cigarette, and leaned against the hitching rail—which by this time was empty of all horses as the owners had wisely mounted up and moved at a fast lope for safer climes.

City Marshal McMillian and three deputies approached the drunken trooper, who finished his cigarette, offered his empty revolver, and was escorted to our new jail. Our fine constable said that the sergeant surrendered peaceably and has agreed to pay Mr. O'Doul for damages, by taking out a third of his monthly pay. Colonel Caxton insists that his officer in charge of payroll will make sure that this is, indeed, done. However, if you consider that a sergeant in our United States Army makes, perhaps, eighteen dollars a month, O'Doul might see those damages finally paid for in four and one-half years.

Sergeant Keegan, Colonel Caxton reminds us, was a decorated veteran for the Union Army during the war, riding for the Second Michigan

Volunteer Cavalry Regiment, rising from private to brevetted major from his initial enlistment at Detroit in October of 1861 until he and his fellow soldiers were mustered out in August of 1865. He was decorated for valor at the Battle of Island Number Ten, the Battle of Perryville, the Battle of Resaca, the slaughter and carnage at Franklin, Tennessee, and again at the Battle of Nashville. He has, likewise, Colonel Caxton said, shown his bravery time and again since enlisting in the regular army in 1867.

We do not argue with Sergeant Keegan's past bravery. But his actions last week were not the first time he has spent the rest of his leave in our jail.

Judge Preston Barnes says that, to the best of his memory, Keegan has been fined and jailed at least ten times over the past two years. Colonel Caxton said that the sergeant has spent several weeks in the guardhouse at Fort Spalding and has been demoted to private at least three times. Yet the sergeant's stripes keep being sewn again onto the sleeves of his blouse because, "Good sergeants," Caxton says, "are hard to come by, and the Apaches haven't all been turned into 'good injuns,' as we like to say."

The Army, we must say, needs to make a stand and weed out such jackals as Sergeant Sean Keegan.

> *"From their callous hearts comes iniquity;*
> *their evil imaginations have no limits."*
> —*Psalms 73:7*

But Sergeant Keegan is not the only mad wolf and demon that Texas needs to weed out.

Two months ago, Jed Breen brought in

another outlaw—dead. Breen does not live in one of our cities or towns. In fact, we doubt if Jed Breen has a home . . . or a mother or a father, for that matter, for he is, indeed, a jackal, a man kin to the wolf, and not any humans. Yes, Breen has rid our great state of vermin. It is said that he fights for justice, but, oh, what a sham that is. Justice?

Jed Breen wears no badge. He is neither sheriff, marshal, constable, Texas Ranger, nor Pinkerton agent. He has never been hired as a deputy. In fact, there are rumors that he is wanted for crimes in Kansas, Missouri, Louisiana, Alabama, Montana, and California. We have searched and made inquiries but have found no proof that Jed Breen is wanted for any crimes in any of those states, nor in our own glorious Texas. But who is to say Jed Breen is this vagabond's real name?

Breen, of course, is easy to recognize. He is lean, he is leathery, and although probably no older than his thirties, his hair is stark white, close-cropped. His eyes are a piercing blue. He has a unique countenance, and, indeed, many ladies have a tendency to swoon when he tips his hat in their direction.

Tipping his hat is about the only polite thing Jed Breen does, and I do not think that the man is recognized merely for his white hair.

You smell him before you see him. And the smell is that which reeks of death.

He brings in outlaws to various lawmen in towns from here to there. He collects the rewards posted for those men, but these wanted felons have not gotten their day in court. For they are dead upon arrival. Once, Jed Breen merely brought in the head of the criminal Fat Charles Wingo.

Dime novels are not noted for their veracity, but this quote from the author, Major Kiowa J. Smith (likely a pseudonym), rings true. It is from *The Last Days of Fat Charlie Wingo, Savage Outlaw and Comanchero; or Bloody Revenge on the Staked Plains of Texas.* "Why just the head? Well, Judge," the leathery killer said with a grin, "Fat Charlie runned his hoss to death in the middle of Comanch country, and the injuns weren't in no hospitable mood. Fat Charlie had to weigh nigh two hundred and fifty pounds, and that was before I put about a pound of lead into his body. My hoss was fairly winded his ownself, and iffen it come to a runnin' fight with dem red devils, well, my mustang wasn't likely to come out the victor in such a race. That'd mean I was either dead or wishin' I was dead after the Comanch took their pleasures on me. My Bowie knife was sharp, and Fat Charlie's grain sack was empty. It just seemed like the thing to do, Judge. 'Sides, the head's all you need to identify that scoundrel. Ever'body this side of the Pecos River knowed Charlie had a mouthful of gold teeth, and if you peel up that eyelid you'll see his marled eye, which he's also knowed fer. The rest of his body I left for the coyot's, Judge, on account that coyot's gots to eat, too."

The body of Jimmy Martin was intact, head and all, and, yes, Jimmy Martin was wanted dead or alive for the robbery of the Lordsburg stage. But Jimmy Martin was all of seventeen years old, just a misguided youth who was hurting after the Apaches killed his father and older brother on the malpais. Jimmy Martin was wrong, yes, indeed, he was wrong, and deserved to be punished. But he was no jackal. He could have been reformed.

And no kid deserves to be shot in the back.

"I called for the boy to surrender," Jed Breen told Judge Barnes (this comes from the fine jurist himself, and not from Breen, whose quotes to this newspaperman could not be printed in even the most gratuitous and salacious and scandalous publication). "He popped a cap at me, and I returned fire. He just happened to be turning around to make a run for his horse, when I touched that trigger."

Young Jimmy Martin is not the first corpse this awful bounty hunter has brought to our courts, our towns, and our dedicated peace officers. He has claimed to have brought in men alive, but we find no record that has ever happened. Your intrepid editor did question Jed Breen, and the response was one that, as it lacked vile and profane language, was something we could actually print.

Editor of the *Herald Leader*: "Why must you always bring in outlaws for their reward, and not for a sense of duty and justice?"

Jed Breen: "Ink slinger, I shoot a Sharps rifle. You ever tried pricing a box of .50-caliber Sharps cartridges in this country? A man's gotta eat, and an officer of the court has got to buy lead."

For the record, upon checking past issues of your *Herald Leader* and other newspapers in Texas and the Southwest, we have learned that Jed Breen does not use just a big and powerful Sharps rifle (although that long brass telescopic sight affixed to his murderous weapon likely gives him an advantage when it comes to facing his "deadly" adversaries). Breen has also brought in bodies riddled with buckshot from his Parker double-barreled twelve-gauge shotgun, which is even more brutal since the Damascus barrels have been sawed off. And at least twice, he has killed men with his 1877 double-action Colt Lightning revolver.

And, no, your honest and busy editor did not walk across town to Dillon's Gun Shop to find out the price of a box of double-ought buckshot for a twelve-gauge nor a box of .38-caliber cartridges for a Colt revolver.

In short, Jed Breen hunts outlaws for the prices on their heads. But who hunts this jackal?

> *"For it is from within, out of a person's heart, that evil thoughts come—sexual immorality, theft, murder, adultery, greed, malice, deceit, lewdness, envy, slander, arrogance and folly."*
> *—Mark 7:21–22*

Finally and most disappointing, there is another jackal in our midst—and perhaps he is the worst of the entire lot.

Matt McCulloch is a man of middle age, tall, lean, with a fine head of hair (yes, your balding editor is jealous of his black and gray mane). Once, he lived in our town, was respected, was honest, and the only time longtime residents recall him ever wearing a gun came when he went hunting for a deer or some rabbits to feed his family; or to rid West Texas of an unnecessary rattlesnake that had its fangs set to sink into the leg of one of the fine horses McCulloch and his sons raised and sold.

And then, some years back, Matt McCulloch returned home after driving six fine horses to sell to Texas Rangers Captain John Courtright—Courtright was killed in the line of duty four years ago, and ably replaced, but never forgotten, by our current Rangers leader, J.J.K. Hollister. McCulloch's home and barn were in ashes, his family butchered, and his horses stolen. The one daughter in the family was missing, kidnapped by those red-heathen butchers.

So McCulloch, after burying his beloved wife and sons, spent more than a year futilely searching for his daughter. Eventually, reluctantly giving the child up for dead like the rest of his family, he rode back to the Rangers headquarters and enlisted with Captain Courtright. He pinned on the *cinco pesos* star. He bought a long-barreled Colt revolver, and his Winchester carbine was replaced with a new, more current model, as his previous rifle had been consumed by the flames the murderous fiends had set to his home. The Texas Rangers in his battalion pitched in for the new carbine, I have been informed.

Of course, none of us at the *Herald Leader* can know how it must feel to lose one's entire family and home to such butchery. We do, on the other hand, feel Matt McCulloch's pain. And for a few years, Matt McCulloch wore his badge with honor and lived by the code of the Texas Rangers and by the law of the state of Texas.

Yet if you look at the stock of his Winchester rifle or the walnut butt of his revolver of .44-40 caliber, you will see the carvings that represent the men he has killed—as well as three Apache women, and one Mexican bandit woman—all reportedly as rough and wild as the brutes they rode with and all deservedly and justifiably killed. The brown stocks are now, literally, carved so much that the walnut is but a mass of ditches and scratches covered with grime, filth, and, yes, stained by blood.

"Sometimes," a former friend of the weary-eyed Ranger told me, "I get the feeling that Matt has to kill. He just doesn't know anything else after these years. He thinks every man he goes after, or every outlaw that comes after him, is responsible for the murders of his wife and children. And the truth of the matter is, it pains me to say, but we'll never know—not while we're living on this earth, I mean—who all committed that horrible crime. Those Apache vermin might be alive. Most likely, they're dead. And some think that maybe it was white renegades who made it look like the work of those red devils. And it just doesn't matter. McCulloch kills. He kills because he has to kill. He kills, I sometimes think, hoping that somebody will kill him."

It pains me to say this, too, but our state and our towns and our people and citizens and visitors and friends would be much better off if Matt McCulloch, the jackal with the Devil in his soul, would be killed.

> *"No one calls for justice; no one pleads a*
> *case with integrity. They rely on empty*
> *arguments, they utter lies; they conceive*
> *trouble and give birth to evil."*
> —*Isaiah 59:4.*

To these three jackals—Sergeant Keegan, the despicable Breen, and Ranger McCulloch—we quote from the Book of Kings: *"You have done more evil than all who lived before you."*

Yes, yes, yes, there are likely other jackals in our midst. And more will come. But for this town, this community, this county, this glorious state and the entire Southwest to grow, we need to get rid of—one way or another—this trio of jackals.

CHAPTER 1

"Begging the lieutenant's pardon, sir, but, if you were to ask me, sir, that's not a trail I'd be inclined to follow."

Sergeant Sean Keegan, Eighth United States Cavalry, stood beside his dun gelding, tightening the cinch of the McClellan saddle, and sprayed a pebble with tobacco juice. He knew the lieutenant, proud little peacock that he was, kept watching and waiting for Keegan to look up before he began ridiculing the sergeant in front of the men.

Keegan let him wait.

Eventually, though, Sean Keegan did look up, and even pushed up the brim of his slouch hat so Second Lieutenant Erastus Gibbons of Hartford, Connecticut, fresh out of West Point, could see exactly what Keegan thought of the fool.

"Did Captain Percival put you in charge of this patrol, Sergeant?"

"No," Keegan said, and wiped his mouth when he added, "Sir." He thought, *But he should have.*

"And Sergeant"—Lieutenant Gibbons seemed to

like this—"in what year were you graduated from the United States Military Academy?" It made him feel important. Made the kid with acne covering his face think that he was a real man. A soldier, even.

"Never went. Never even got to New York state." Keegan tugged on the butt of the Springfield rifle in the scabbard, just to make sure he would be able to pull it out cleanly and quickly. They'd have need of it in a few minutes if he couldn't talk some sense into the green pup.

"That's what I thought," the lieutenant said.

Keegan gathered the reins to his dun. "And when was it, sir, that you got your sheepskin from West Point?"

The eight troopers, all about as young and as inexperienced as the lieutenant, laughed, which made the lieutenant's face turn as bright as the scarlet neckerchief he wore around his fancy blue blouse.

"Quiet in the ranks!"

As Gibbons, who had been at Fort Spalding all of four months, took time to bark commands and insults at his enlisted men, Sergeant Keegan climbed into his saddle and lowered the brim of his hat.

The hat, he guessed, was likely older than Erastus Gibbons.

When he had talked himself into even a deeper red face, the kid sucked in a deep breath, and turned his wrath again on the sergeant. "Do you remember our orders, Sergeant?"

"Yes, sir."

"So do I, Sergeant. Captain Percival said if we were to come across tracks that we suspected belonged to hostile Apaches, we were to pursue—and engage—unless the tracks led to the international border. Is that your understanding of my, no *our*, orders, Sergeant?"

"Yes, sir."

"Have we crossed the Rio Grande, Sergeant?"

"No, sir."

"And what do you make of those tracks?" Gibbons pointed at the ground.

"Unshod ponies. Four. Heading into that canyon."

"Unshod. What does that lead you to believe, Sergeant?"

"Likely Apaches, Lieutenant."

"So why should not we, numbering *ten* men, pursue, as we have been *ordered*, four, *four* stinking, uncivilized, fool Apache bucks?"

If the Good Lord showed any mercy, Keegan thought, *He would let Erastus Gibbons drop dead of a stroke or heart failure right now.*

The way the kid's face beamed, there had to be a fair to middling chance that would happen, but the lieutenant caught his breath, uncorked his canteen, and drank greedily. His face began to lose its color, and Keegan began to think that nobody lives forever, and that he had lived a hell of a life, but getting eight kids killed alongside him wouldn't make him proud when he had to face St. Peter, or more than likely, Old Beelzebub or Satan himself. He didn't care one way or the other about Erastus Gibbons's fate. The punk had become tiresome, a boil Sean Keegan couldn't lance.

"Orders say *pursue*, Lieutenant," Keegan pointed out. "I'm all for pursuing. Just not following . . . into there." He nodded at the canyon's entrance.

"Sergeant, you disgust me."

Still, Keegan tried again. "Four Apaches can do a world of hurt, sir. Especially in that canyon."

The kid shook his head. "All right, Sergeant. What would you have in mind?"

Keegan pointed at the tracks. "Those Apaches didn't hide their trail. Tracks lead right into that canyon, and this canyon twists and turns about a mile and a quarter till it opens up. They could be hiding anywhere in those rocks, waiting to pick us off."

"Or they could be riding hard to Mexico."

Keegan shook his head. "If they wanted to be in Mexico in a hurry, they wouldn't ride through this death trap."

"You haven't told me what you have in mind, Sergeant."

Keegan pointed. "Leave Trooper Ulfsson here with the horses in the shade. He don't speak enough English, I don't speak no Swede, and his face is blistered already. Leaving him here might keep him from dying of sunstroke. The rest of us climb up to the top. I work my way ahead, and when I spot where those bucks are laying in wait, I fetch you boys. We ambush the ambushers."

The lieutenant shielded his eyes as he examined the mesa then swallowed while still looking at the top. "How long would it take us to climb up there, Sergeant?"

Fifteen minutes if I was alone, Keegan thought, but answered, "Us? Forty minutes."

"The other side isn't as high, Sergeant," Gibbons said. "Why not try that side?"

"Because the Apaches will be on this side. And they'll see us up yonder."

The young whippersnapper shook his head. "How do you know which side the Apaches are on, Sergeant? *If* they're even up there."

"Because you're shielding your eyes from the sun,

Lieutenant. And once we start throwing lead at those bucks, they'll be shielding their eyes to try to spot us."

The kid looked away, wet his lips, and stared hard at the tracks and the entrance to the canyon. "And what if we find no Apaches?"

Keegan shrugged. "Then we've rested our horses, gotten a good stretch of our legs, Ulfsson ain't dead, and you get to write me up in your report to Captain Percival that I'm a fool."

"And the Apaches?"

Keegan shrugged again. "We'll fight them another day." *If I prayed, would that change the punk's mind?*

No, no, that wouldn't do. If Sean Keegan prayed, God himself would drop dead of a heart attack—and that would be another black mark in the book on Sean Keegan.

The kid pulled down the chinstrap on his kepi, and Sean Keegan knew the boy had made up his mind.

"Sergeant, there's no glory to be found ambushing four Apache renegades. More important, I don't think those savages are waiting for us. We're going through that canyon, Sergeant. Follow those tracks, and catch the Apaches wherever they might be."

"You're in command, Lieutenant." Keegan pulled the trapdoor Springfield from the scabbard and braced the carbine's stock against his thigh.

"I gave no order to draw your long gun, Sergeant." The boy's face was brightening again. "Return that weapon, soldier!"

Keenan sprayed the ground with tobacco juice, then hawked up the quid, and spit it out, too. "I don't reckon I'll do that, bub." He was done showing respect to this know-it-all who was about to get killed some young boys who might've made decent soldiers.

The punk stuck his finger, hidden underneath that fine deerskin gauntlet, at Keegan. "You better put that Springfield away, Sergeant. Or when we reach Fort Spalding, I'll have you up on charges of disobeying a direct order."

"*If* we reach Fort Spalding, boy." Keegan looked behind him. "And I suggest you gents follow my advice and get your carbines at the ready. You'll have need of them soon enough."

A few Adam's apples bobbed, and some of the green pups even glanced down at their Army-issued .45-70 weapons. But none dared disobey the lieutenant. Not that Sean Keegan could blame them. He slightly recalled what it was like to be a young soldier after he had joined the Second Michigan in '61. Thinking that you had to do everything a fool officer told you to do. Not knowing any better. But Keegan had learned. Maybe some of these boys would live long enough to learn, too.

"You'll wind up a buck private, Keegan, and in the guardhouse for a month."

"I hope you're right, Gibbons. Means I won't be dead."

The kid turned around, angry, and raised his right hand. "Follow me! Follow me!" He rode, ramrod straight—Keegan would give the kid that much—into the canyon.

He let the other soldiers pass him, felt their stares, but he did not look them in the eye. Didn't want to remember what they looked like, for one reason. And he waited till the blond-headed, sunburned pup of a Swede, Trooper Ulfsson, passed by at the rear. Only then did Keegan nudge his dun.

"Hey," Keegan called out, dropping his reins over

the horse's neck, and holding out his right hand. "I'll take the lead rope to the pack mule, sonny."

The Swede stared at him blankly.

"The rope, boy. The rope." He gestured again, and finally, just grabbed hold of the lead rope and waited till the raw recruit understood. "You'll need both hands soon enough, Ulfsson," Keegan said.

The boy likely only understood his name.

The Swede rode ahead, pulled up even with another soldier whose name Keegan could not remember.

Column of twos. Riding to their deaths.

Keegan sighed and rode behind them, pulling the mule along. Yeah, Ulfsson would have need of two hands in a short while, but that's not why Keegan wanted to pull the mule. The mule carried the kegs of water. It also carried ammunition.

They'd have need of both shortly.

Connect with Us

Visit us online at
KensingtonBooks.com
to read more from your favorite authors, see books
by series, view reading group guides, and more.

Join us on social media

for sneak peeks, chances to win books and prize packs,
and to share your thoughts with other readers.

facebook.com/kensingtonpublishing
twitter.com/kensingtonbooks

Tell us what you think!

To share your thoughts, submit a review,
or sign up for our eNewsletters, please visit:
KensingtonBooks.com/TellUs.